Praise for *The Blackbird Season*

"Crime fiction adores girls in trouble. Moretti's latest nail-biter is no exception, but it is exceptional. . . . Though Moretti's emotionally astute tale can be heartrending, readers won't be able to look away. Moretti's tale of jealousy and obsession is nothing less than dark magic. Witchery indeed."

—*Kirkus Reviews* (starred review)

"*The Blackbird Season* explores the fine line between guilt and innocence, truth and perception, the moments that break people apart—and those that bring them together. Riveting and insightful, this is a book that lingers long after you turn the final page."

—Megan Miranda, *New York Times* bestselling author of *All the Missing Girls*

"A suspenseful mystery about small-town secrets and scandals."

—*PopSugar*

"The tale's suspenseful core should catch and hold most readers, especially *Gone Girl* fans."

—*Booklist*

"This cautionary tale keeps the reader guessing to the end."

—*Publishers Weekly*

"With her stunning new novel told through multiple perspectives, Moretti weaves a story that is equal parts suspenseful and chilling. . . . With the strangely haunting character of Lucia, steady pacing, and an intricately woven plot, Moretti's latest will leave its mark on readers."

—*RT Book Reviews*

"Kate Moretti's insightful, starkly human mystery about a girl they call 'witch' has that sit-down, gotta-cry eloquence readers long for. Mean-girl alliances and small-town loyalties collapse in unison on the day the blackbirds fall. This story will hold you tight to its pages well past your bedtime."

—Lisa Turner, author of the Edgar Award finalist *The Gone Dead Train* and *Devil Sent the Rain*

"*The Blackbird Season* pulls off a very difficult thing: it's nail-biting and thought-provoking all at once. It's rare that a book can make you turn pages like your life depends on it, but also give you food for thought because the characters are so perfectly drawn. A stunning achievement from an extremely talented writer."

—Gilly Macmillan, *New York Times* bestselling author of *What She Knew*

"A spellbinding tale of long-held secrets and small-town scandal, *The Blackbird Season* is one of those stories that sneaks up on you, each chapter building steadily to an ending that will haunt you long after you turn the last page."

—Kimberly Belle, bestselling author of *The Marriage Lie*

"The characters are authentically flawed and believable, and part of the mystery is the unfolding of their motivations . . . *The Blackbird Season* is about how people—teens and adults alike—get lost and disconnected. All that, plus a suspenseful mystery—what more can you ask for?"

—Holly Brown, author of *Don't Try to Find Me*

"Kate Moretti's trademark vivid characterizations, surprising storyline, and heart-stopping suspense kept me eagerly turning pages long into the night."

—Carla Buckley, author of *The Good Goodbye*

Praise for *The Vanishing Year*

"Great pacing and true surprises make this an exciting read. Fans of twisted thrillers featuring complex female characters will devour Moretti's latest."

—*Kirkus Reviews* (starred review)

ALSO BY KATE MORETTI

Thought I Knew You

Binds That Tie

While You Were Gone (A *Thought I Knew You* Novella)

The Vanishing Year

The Blackbird Season

IN
HER
BONES

A Novel

KATE MORETTI

ATRIA PAPERBACK

New York London Toronto Sydney New Delhi

ATRIA
PAPERBACK

An Imprint of Simon & Schuster, Inc.
1230 Avenue of the Americas
New York, NY 10020

First Atria Paperback edition September 2018

ATRIA PAPERBACK and colophon are trademarks of Simon & Schuster, Inc.

For information about special discounts for bulk purchases, please contact Simon & Schuster Special Sales at 1-866-506-1949 or business@simonandschuster.com.

The Simon & Schuster Speakers Bureau can bring authors to your live event. For more information or to book an event, contact the Simon & Schuster Speakers Bureau at 1-866-248-3049 or visit our website at www.simonspeakers.com.

Manufactured in the United States of America

10 9 8 7 6 5 4 3 2 1

Library of Congress Cataloging-in-Publication Data

Names: Moretti, Kate, author.
Title: In her bones : a novel / Kate Moretti.
Description: First Atria paperback edition. | New York : Atria Paperback, 2018. |
Identifiers: LCCN 2018010392 (print) | LCCN 2018015766 (ebook) |
  ISBN 9781501166488 (eBook) | ISBN 9781501166471 (paperback)
Subjects: | BISAC: FICTION / Suspense. | GSAFD: Suspense fiction.
Classification: LCC PS3613.O7185 (ebook) | LCC PS3613.O7185 I5 2018 (print) |
  DDC 813/.6--dc23
LC record available at https://lccn.loc.gov/2018010392

ISBN 978-1-5011-6647-1
ISBN 978-1-5011-6648-8 (ebook)

For Dad, who's read every book and liked most of them.
And because I can't dedicate this one to Mom.

IN HER BONES

Excerpt from The Serrated Edge: The Story of Lilith Wade, Serial Killer, *by E. Green, RedBarn Press, copyright June 2016*

Timeline of Murders (For reference)

FEBRUARY 1998: Renee Hoffman, stabbed nineteen times in her abdomen, chest, and face (the only victim with face lacerations); found in her car twenty-two hours after being reported missing. Spouse: Charles Hoffman, home, alibi confirmed (via phone call with mistress).

MAY 1998: Melinda Holmes, found stabbed eight times in her backyard. Fiancé: Matthew Melnick, at his residence. Father: Walden Holmes, asleep upstairs when murder occurred (alibi confirmed).

MARCH 1999: Penelope Cook, stabbed fourteen times in her living room. Spouse: Mitchell Cook, away on golf outing (deceased since 2010; alibi confirmed).

OCTOBER 1999: Colleen Lipsky, found behind her apartment Dumpster; stabbed three times. Spouse: Peter Lipsky, away on business (alibi confirmed).

NOVEMBER 2000: Annora Quinlan is stabbed seventeen times and her ring finger is removed, including her wedding ring, neither of which were ever found. This is the only victim to be missing this finger. Spouse: Quentin Kitterton, away on business (alibi confirmed).

JUNE 2001: Margaret Mayweather, stabbed twelve times in the abdomen and torso while in her bed. Spouse: Troy Mayweather, away on business (alibi confirmed).

JUNE 2001: Lilith Wade arrested for four counts of criminal homicide, murder in the first degree. She was thirty-four. She was eventually convicted of six counts of murder in the first degree in the city of Philadelphia and surrounding areas.

PROLOGUE

Eileen Dresden is blond, harried. Her wispy bangs brush along her brow line and she throws her head to get them out of her eyes. Her twin sons are seniors in high school, their arms ropey and thick, their laughs loud, their eyes dancing as they tease their mother. Eileen smooths back her daughter Rayann's hair with a flat palm and a kiss to the crown of her head. Rayann, awkward and quiet, watches her brothers roughhousing until one of them slaps down on the chicken ladle and sends it flying, chicken bits and gravy splattering on the white carpet (who has white carpet in a dining room?), and Eileen starts to cry. Kent barely looks up from his phone, oblivious to his wife's tears.

Kent is a motherfucker.

Kent is having an affair. He barely tries to cover it up. She comes over three times a week after Eileen leaves for her job as a teller at the bank. Kent is a software development engineer and works mostly from home.

Sometimes, he smiles at his wife, a quick blip of a smile, and her face relaxes and all the lines disappear and you can almost see how they used to love each other. Back when he was a pro-

grammer and she was working in marketing, making brochures for a software company, when software companies were all start-ups, when they held late-night meetings over Chinese food and dry-erase boards and had sex for the first time on the conference room table.

Everything is different now. See, in 2000, when the twins were barely toddlers, and Rayann was a bouncing newborn, Eileen was in the prime of her life. She was so happy then. She wasn't working, she was a mom. But the good kind, the kind who went to baby yoga classes and sang along to Barney. The kind who arranged toddler playdates with the moms in the neighborhood so the kids would all be best friends before they got to kindergarten. She hosted tea parties and sank into mother-hood the way other mothers sink into vodka. She hugged her children, freely and often, and smelled like Love's Baby Soft, which she has used since college.

But then in November of that year, everything changed. Ei-leen's sister, Annora, married a man named Quentin Kitterton. Not even a month later, Annora was found murdered in their townhouse in Philadelphia. They suspected Quentin for a long time. It didn't help that Quentin was black and Annora was white, so for months, maybe a year, they looked too long and too hard at Quentin before eventually moving on to his past. To all his women, and his philandering, and eventually, a smart, savvy young junior detective found a connection no one else did.

Lilith Wade.

Lilith worked at a bar called Drifter's. The kind with only a few blinking signs and even fewer patrons. Lilith was pretty, you know? A little overly made up, a little hardened around the edges, but she knew what to do and how to do it and didn't bring home any of the hassle, either that time or all the other times Quentin went back for her. She was a nice, easy, sure thing in a world with so many unknowns. That must have made a man feel good. Then he met Annora and moved on, as men tend to do.

Until Lilith snuck in through the bathroom window and stabbed Annora seventeen times while Quentin was away on business. Posthumously, Lilith removed her ring finger, including her wedding ring, neither of which were ever found.

With Annora gone, Eileen was never the same. All the life just eked out of her like she died the same day as her sister. Her children never knew the mother she could have been, how present, how attentive she used to be. They got used to the new Eileen. Harried. Distracted. Sad. Until it all just seemed like normal, regular life.

The most infuriating part for Eileen is that Lilith doesn't remember. There were six women in total, and she only remembers a few of them. Some of them she's even denied. How could anyone forget her sister, who was so full of life before Lilith stole it from her? It seems to Eileen to be the cruelest irony. Or at least that's what she rants about in the online forum, a gathering place for a handful of Lilith's victims' families and victims of other violent crimes. Healing Hope. Such a mawkish name for the graphic atrocities that are discussed there.

Eileen doesn't know that she and I are connected. We're both Remainders. We're what's left after Lilith, part of a small, exclusive, horrific club. Some of them know one another. None of them know me. It doesn't seem possible that one person can cut such a large swath of destruction through a city. If they knew who I was, they'd turn their rage—their helplessness, the never-ending hell of grief, the feeling that death row is not enough punishment— toward me. After all, we share the same blood: microscopic pieces of Lilith coursing through my veins, our molecules alike from the dark parts of the heart that no one can see, right down to our bones.

Lilith is my mother.

CHAPTER 1

Tuesday, August 2, 2016

Your life is more open than you think. You think you're safe. You have neighborhood watches and room-darkening drapes, password-protected computers, alarm systems, and garage codes that are absolutely not your firstborn's birthday. Even with all that, it's practically there for the taking. Anyone can find out anything about you, and sometimes, if they ask the right way, you'll just tell them.

People are too trusting. Naive. Even with the news blinking tragedy and fear in a nonstop cycle, we still trust. Well, you do.

I don't.

I'm a good person, although on paper, it might be difficult to convince anyone. I don't seem like a good person. I'll tell you that I only ever use what I uncover to help. Have I taken things too far? Sometimes. Am I sorry? Almost never. In the darkest parts of the night, when the truth is laid bare, I'd like to tell you that I have regrets. I have some, everyone does. But not about the watching. Alone with my thoughts, the only question I turn over and over is *Am I like her?*

I pull the hair off my neck, it's hot already and only 7:00 a.m., but that's Philadelphia in August. The air itself sweats.

I head north on York Street, where I'll pick up the El. I do feel a weird bubbling in my chest on Monday mornings. Not so much because I love my job, but because I love the stability of it. I enjoy being able to go somewhere, at a particular time each day, and be useful, industrious. I like sitting in my cube, tapping at my computer, hitting send or filing the latest report. I like answering emails, checking things off my list. I like being told I'm efficient. I am efficient, in every aspect of my life.

I am lucky to have a city job, a clerk, technically an "interviewer." It's a government job that I don't deserve, with good pay and decent benefits. I sit on the phone with criminals for hours at a stretch, obtaining bits and pieces of boring data that the police can't waste their time collecting: addresses, aliases, Social Security numbers, basic information for the public defenders. The other half of my day involves writing reports and processing court fees and parking fines.

Sometimes I see Brandt on my commute. Gil Brandt, the detective who arrested Lilith. The man who gave me a second, third, and fourth chance. It's complicated, but probably not in the way you think. Or maybe exactly in the way you'd think.

Today, there's no Brandt. Just the orange stacked seats of SEPTA, the blank, dreary faces on a Monday morning, the vaguely warm odor, like the inside of a public dryer: a little wet, a little musty. The man next to me huddles into the window, a paperback folded into his hands, his cracked lips moving to the words, even as his eyes dart up and out the window, down the metal floor, gummed with black. The seats are full, and the aisles are crowded but not packed, the faint fug of an armpit over my shoulder. I've taken the El every day for five years, early mornings, late nights, the train punctuating the days and giving me a structure and definition that keeps me forward-looking, which hasn't always been my strong suit.

Two rows above, a blonde turns, her hair falling into her eyes, her fingers scraping the metal pole by her seat, and her eyes resting on me, only for a second, but long enough to feel their zing. *Lindy Cook.* Couldn't have been more than twenty, her mother taken by Lilith's rage when she was a child, maybe even a toddler. Lindy, so small when she lost her mother, a toddling, swollen towhead with a red sucker and pink-ringed mouth in all the court pictures, was now a lithe, lanky dancer, an apprentice at the Pennsylvania Ballet. That was all I knew. I search my brain, my memory for something—any detail about her life—and come up blank.

And now she was here. Here! My train. Why? She'd never been on this train before, and I took the El every day. The brakes squeal at 13th Street, the forward momentum pushing me into the pole in front of me, sending the arm over my shoulder bumping against my head. I stand and Lindy stands, and across the train we make eye contact again, her face blank as a stone. My heart thunders, my ears so filled with it that I barely hear the loudspeaker garbling nonsense. We head for the same door and I hang back, watching her step onto the platform. She tosses her hair, and I catch the smell of damp jasmine. She keeps her head low, only to look back just once (was it nervously?) at me.

Up at street level, she heads north on 13th Street, my direction, and I wonder once, crazily, if she's coming to work with me. If she's looking for me, if she's found out about me, who I am and what I do, some kind of sideways revenge scheme for taking her mother, which is, of course, no more sideways than what I do to them. I follow her for two blocks, blocks I would be walking anyway, but I stay a good five people behind her, the bobbing heads of bankers and jurors, lawyers and judges, bopping headphoned dudes appearing in court to fight parking tickets, clerks at Macy's, and cubicle swampers from the Comcast building. Lindy's head isn't hard to follow, the blond shining like the sun against the gray.

She passes my building and I nearly jump out of my skin, thinking she's going to turn left onto Filbert and I'll be forced to follow behind her, wanded through by security. But she passes right by, picking up speed, her long legs moving her faster than I can keep up. She stops at an intersection, picks up a paper and a hot Styrofoam cup at a street vendor, offering him a smiling hello and a laugh. The kind of exchange that evolved organically, after an established routine. She darts across Broad Street, six lanes of traffic, and disappears inside the Pennsylvania Ballet studio building. Before pushing through the revolving door, she glances back at me once with a questioning look, her head cocked to the side. I stand on the street, frozen, watching her recognize me as the girl from the train, and now, oddly, the girl who followed her here to the place where she thought was she safe.

• • •

My desk is in the basement: a gunmetal gray and fabric nothingness that lends itself to both slog and productivity in equal measure. Unlike my coworkers, even Belinda who is relentlessly chipper, I don't mind the drear. The sides are tall enough to maintain privacy, and I tuck myself into the corner, compiling reports, processing parking and court fines with enough focused efficiency to please a myriad of bosses.

I hurl my bag onto my desk, knocking against Belinda's cube, and her black, bobbing head appears. Her face is flat in a pretty way, her mouth and nose pressed together like she's perpetually grinning. Her cheeks flushed with health. Belinda is simultaneously hard to like and dislike.

"Hi! You're late. You're never late." She says this without judgment or curiosity, just that it is a fact. She's right. I've never been late.

"I know. The train," I offer feebly with no real explanation, Lindy's face still fresh in my mind, her blue eyes widening with recognition, her glossed mouth parting, the faint scrutinizing dip in her eyebrows. I don't have the patience for Belinda's weekend recap: underground clubs with her singer boyfriend, the winding drama of her two closest friends.

"Weller is looking for you. There's a guy on line one, been in the tank since last night." She sucks a mint around her teeth, her tongue poking into her cheek to find it, and at the same time, takes a slug of coffee from a Starbucks paper cup. She means the interview lines, and she waves the contact forms in front of my face. *Name, address, aliases, birthday, age, arrest code.* Collecting information is something I'm particularly talented at. Criminals take a liking to me; I'm easy to talk to. The psychology of someone caught has always been interesting to me. Sometimes they open up, saying more than they should. Sometimes, they're new to the system, and they clam up, terrified, forgetting their addresses, their minds wiped. Sometimes they're high, or worse, coming down. Other times they're straight as a beam. The women are usually less trusting, but only at first. It's generally my favorite part of my job, talking to them.

"Can you do it? I think I'm coming down with something. My throat." But I motion to my head, some undefined sickness overcoming me, and she shrugs and wanders off, presumably to find Weller, my boss du jour. Management cycles through like the seasons around here; only the lower levels, the drones like us, persevere.

My computer chugs to life and before I open my emails, I navigate to Facebook and search for Lindy Cook, her wide smile filling my screen. Her profile is locked down; the only pictures available to me are those used for her profile. Her email and even her username are hidden. Damnit. Quickly, I navigate to her friends list and give a silent cheer when I find it's public. I download the profile picture of one of her lesser friends—toward the bottom of her list—and in a new tab, make a new Facebook profile. I use the same name, the same picture, and click on about twenty-five of their mutual friends and select Send Friend Request. Immediately, three of them accept. I wait five minutes, and Send Friend Request to Lindy. I push back my chair, walk purposefully to the kitchenette and make a cup of tea, dunking the bag, feeling the curl of steam against my face.

The Facebook trick was one I'd perfected on Rachel. She was so trusting. Truly darling.

I'd been sober, working at the courthouse for a year before it occurred to me to use the system to look up people I knew, before things fell apart. *Keep an eye on them.* Rachel was washed out and plain. Married to a man with a round belly and freckled nose, an infant tucked between them on the beach, his pale skin ruddy from the sun. It hadn't been difficult; she wasn't hiding. She worked as a teacher for a charter school, just like Redwood Academy. Her Instagram was heavily populated with filtered images: flowers, the sky, her baby girl; her posts captioned with long, poignant statements about love and life and motherhood and teaching. If I met her now, I'd forget her immediately: she was simple and emotionally displayed. I looked at every picture, dating back two years, and chewed on TUMS the whole time. I wonder if she ever thought about the girl from high school, the one with the murdering mother? You'd never think she knew such a person, not by looking at her.

But then, you can't tell anything about anyone by looking at them.

Mia had a Twitter account but no Facebook or Instagram.

She was a journalist with bylines in the *Inquirer* until a few years ago. Now she's an editor, practically invisible. She periodically tweeted out her articles, and other sociopolitical commentary. Zip on her personal life. I searched public records. No marriage. No kids. An order of protection against a man named Samuel Park, stemming from a controversial abortion story she'd written, dating back to 2012. It took some digging but I found her apartment, a condo unit in Radnor on the Main Line. Not horrifically expensive, but not cheap, either. One picture in her media files: a girl's night (#GNO!), sleek hair and little black dresses, high heels and red lipstick. Three women, all virtually interchangeable. I couldn't have told you which one was Mia.

Neither of them had a life I wanted.

Still. The hunt thrilled me. The flush of heat against my neck at each discovery, the way the keys flew under my fingertips, the information seemed summoned at will—almost effortless. The ease with which people gave up what felt to them like innocuous information: their first pet, their first car, their favorite teacher. Nothing about the internet felt real—to me or anyone else. I wasn't breaking any laws, doing anything immoral or unethical, none of it was tangible. It was all bits of data flying around in space; who cared about individual little bits of data? I enjoyed the manipulation, this gentle bend of virtual facts.

Mia and Rachel were boring. Then I realized that while Brandt knew me so well, I knew very little about him. I started with his ex-wife, now happily living in an Atlanta suburb with her new husband. I friended her on Facebook, my profile picture a stargazer lily, beseechingly raw, almost vaginal. *A pic from the garden!* I'd called myself Lily Beck, so stupid, so traceable to me—I was my own first lesson. People choose nothing at random. Not passwords, not usernames, not pet names, nothing. A few months later came a text:

Unfriend my ex-wife, Beckett. That was it. No explanation, no further instructions. I didn't ask how he figured it out. I didn't protest, although I'd wanted to. I hadn't done anything wrong. I just watched her life (Her name was Mabel. Mabel! Like a storybook heroine). Honestly, what else is social media good for? The pictures of her new husband, her gabled McMansion in a plush neighborhood, dinners at the country club, her mouth wide and laughing into the camera, her skin glowing and dewy from the southern humidity. Her skin looked dipped in gold, glittering and creamy.

Why? I know this is in me, this impulse to obsess, to stand on the outside with my hands pressed against the glass. Bored with Rachel and Mia, caught by Brandt, I had punched Mitchell Cook into the system at work on a whim. I guess that's how it started, but who's to say? Do you ever question how anyone starts a hobby? *When exactly and why did you take up knitting?*

I'd imagine that everyone on the precipice of thirty examines their life and finds it wanting in some way. But as an on-again, off-again alcoholic with no life, no boyfriend, and a job in the courthouse basement—which let's be honest, is as dank and dark as it comes—the gap between myself and everyone else my own age seemed interminable. Late one night, I saw an interview with Matthew Melnick, the fiancé of Melinda Holmes, during one of the docudramas. He had said some of them had found each other, found comfort together, in an online forum called Healing Hope. At first, I just watched them talk to one another.

Maybe I wanted to know: How did they move on?

I started to loosely keep track of them all. What had become of the people touched by Lilith? *Touched by Lilith.* Listen to me sanitize. What had become of the people whose loved ones were murdered by my mother?

I have more in common with the collateral damage of

Lilith's crimes than with anyone else. The only people I feel any affinity toward are people I've never met. Lilith Wade shelled me, scooped out my insides with her thin matchstick fingers, and derailed any meaningful life I might have had— and she'd done the same thing to them, too. I'd wondered how they moved on, grew up, became adults, had children. Did the rest of them move away, start over, remarry? Some did. Most stayed in the area, many within city limits: the Dresdens, the Hoffmans, the Mayweathers. Lindy Cook. Walden Holmes.

Peter Lipsky. Yes, I have favorites. Why? I don't know. He's the hardest, so there's that. I've always liked a challenge. I can hardly ever find anything interesting on him at all. It has to be there, though, it always is.

How quickly it became second nature, not something I did here and there, but rather something I now *do.* Repeatedly, if not daily. I find all their speeding tickets, their jury duty summonses, and once a public urination fine—Walden was a bit of a drunk—and simply erase them. Delete. Mark as PAID IN FULL. It's an easy reach and makes the rest of it seem fine. Justified, even. A few months ago, Walden got into a bar fight. I'd wanted to dismiss the arrest record, but I don't have access to that system. Yet.

Now it felt as routine as making coffee in the break room.

Back at my desk, Lindy accepts. I open her profile and scan through, looking for an email. Most people set their privacy to the default friends only and never think about it again.

LBaker62998. Lbaker. Lindy Cook. Cutesy.

In the Google search bar, I type in *LBaker62998.* A long list of results pops up, all the places she's been, the places she's logged on. Comments on Wordpress blogs, a Flickr page, a forum for dancers, and a long list of posts whining about the corps, being looked down upon as an apprentice, a question about back flexibility and bunion pain, and inexplicably, a forum for pregnancy, which I slot in the interesting-although-not-immediately-relevant column. Then I see it, a post, made six months ago on Healing Hope. I click on it, my hands shaking. *My mother was killed in a famous crime. I can't tell anyone. I think about it all the time now and I don't know why. I can't stop reading old newspaper articles. I was only a baby. Should I get counseling?* 722 responses.

"Beckett." Weller is hovering over my shoulder, a scrim of stubble along his jaw, his voice wet and garbled, a thin sweep of gray across his red, gleaming crown. He cranes to look around me, to my screen, and I angle in front of it and give him a smile. "Can you get the guy on line one? 5505, nothing major. He's drying out." 5505 is a drunk in public; these are most of my interviewees. These guys also like to fight, so sometimes I get the aggravated assaults, too. Which is fine, they all sound the same on the phone.

"Weller, I'm feeling kind of sick." I clear my throat, force my voice froggy. His eyebrows shoot up, I've never begged off a job in my life. "I think Belinda said she'd take it?" I hate the upward lilt in my voice, the question. It's unlike me and Weller knows it. He rubs his palm against his cheek and grumbles.

"Check your email. We've got a department meeting at one, okay?" He ambles away, stopping at a desk down the hall to pluck a Hershey's bite size out of an open candy jar. His pants hike up as he walks, exposing a thin, vulnerable strip of pink above his black socks and work shoes.

I swivel around, look back at my computer, and start skimming the responses. The first hundred are standard and repetitive.

Yes, you need to see a professional.

Please get help. Don't read the articles, you're fixating on it.

Have you tried hypnosis? Helped me tremendously!

Then, I see it. *Lindy, can you get in touch with me? PLipsky@ gmail.com.*

I knew I had seen Lindy's username before. She and Peter Lipsky talked sometimes, but I hadn't connected LBaker62998 to Lindy Cook. Why would I? Maybe I'm slipping. I feel the odd, unwelcome pang of jealousy, a thing I can barely justify, as I imagine Lindy and Peter, exchanging late-night texts, emails. I wonder if they'd talked on the phone, met in person? I imagine her long, gold-spun hair twisting around her finger as she listened to his doe-eyed talk about the grief that wakes him up at two in the morning, keeping him awake until his alarm goes off.

I imagine how taken he'd be with her, over a cup of coffee at Mickey's Diner, if he'd fumble with the sugar, trying to tear four packets at once, and if she'd cover his hand with hers, deftly opening them into his coffee for him. Peter is awkward, Lindy is young, charismatic. I click through to Peter's Facebook, only a handful of pictures. A narrow face, square jaw, blue eyes, hooded and sleepy. A thick roll of hair, scooped pockets of purple under his eyes. His cheeks flushed red against the fall backdrop of an outdoor biking trip. His smile thin, more like the memory of a smile, deep parentheses around his mouth.

•   •   •

Peter Lipsky is an insurance claims adjuster. He lives alone in a one-bedroom apartment on the first floor of a stone house in Chestnut Hill. His Facebook page is more public than it should be, but all I've been able to glean from it is that he's a Flyers fan. He posts a few updates during the games but now, in August, he's fairly quiet. Once a week, he checks his astrology and it automatically posts. I bet he has no idea. His smile is nice, if not vulnerable and almost wounded. In other words, he's nearly invisible. In a crowd, I'd never pay any attention to him.

He has an older photo: a church, a white, billowing dress and big blond hair, and himself, tall and thin, the tuxedo hanging limply from pointed shoulders. This picture I save to my desktop. I blow it up, try to look at her face, but it's too grainy. It's a photo of a photo, the original taken sometime in the nineties, before smartphones and social media. Before the internet really took off, so there's nothing about her online that doesn't come from Peter, which is fine, really, because I already know her name. Colleen.

Before she died, Colleen was a pediatric nurse. Lilith never talked about Peter. She's talked about the others: in interviews with police or psychologists or once a reporter. But if they bring up Peter she blinks wetly, confused and open mouthed. As far as I know there was no connection between them. No affair, no passionate love like Quentin. Colleen and Peter were married for nearly three years before Lilith came. Peter was at an insurance conference—who knew there was such a thing—and Colleen had taken the trash out to the Dumpster. They lived in a condo complex not far from where Peter lives now, and the Dumpster was on the dark side of the building. Lilith stabbed her three times in the chest and left her in the dark. Two of the three wounds were surface. Hesitation marks, they call them.

Another tenant found her eight hours later. They connected all Lilith's victims through psychological profiles, victim commonalities, and stab wounds. She used the same knife: a combination serrated and plain edge utility knife, a common tool for hunters because it cuts both wood and bone. Later she'd claim she'd gotten it from her daddy, a man I'd never known or even heard her speak of.

Colleen was somewhat of an outlier. Police, investigators, lawyers, even Lilith herself could not tell you why she was killed. This, as I learned through forum posts, drives Peter absolutely crazy. *Why Colleen? How do they know for sure, if*

Lilith Wade won't confess? He has nightmares about it, waking up at all hours, unable to fall back to sleep until he logs into Healing Hope. He talks to whoever is there. Sometimes that is Lindy, sometimes it is a handle called WinPA99. I had no idea who that was, a search of her name turned up nothing. I only knew she was female because Peter once asked another forum member where *she* was. I couldn't connect her to Lilith.

In Healing Hope, I spend my evenings watching the forum members' usernames blink in and out. I never post, only observe. WinPA99 has never posted, either, and she only speaks to Peter. She is grieving her sister, murdered almost twenty years before. Some of their posts and responses are public. Lindy comments all the time and talks to anyone who listens. Peter is only ever active in the middle of the night, like me.

He hasn't been online in a week. The longest I've ever seen him go.

The squeak of shoes brings me back to the present. Weller. I click out of the internet window and back to CrimeTrack, the city's system for logging dispatch calls and incidents. I fake a cough, hacking into the crook of my arm. He pauses behind my desk, shielded by the half wall, and thinks I can't hear him breathe: the hefty rasp of a man who likes his McDonald's and cheesesteaks. Then, he's gone.

I type Peter's name into the search bar, and I'm surprised to see a return. Logged two weeks ago: a suspected break-in.

Lipsky, Peter. 7/19/2016: Call received at 11:27 p.m. Suspected break-in. Nothing reported missing. Caller distraught. Claims apartment is disheveled. Officer on scene says apartment appears in order. See log #769982.

I'm irritated at myself for missing this. I'd been distracted by the others.

Maybe I'll leave early today.

CHAPTER 2

Gil Brandt, Philadelphia Police Department, Homicide Division, August 2016

When they got the radio call about the DOA in Chestnut Hill, Gil Brandt didn't think much of it. Another day, part of his job. Chestnut Hill was a bit unusual, not too many grisly scenes in those parts, but not so out of the norm that he'd given it much more than a passing thought. Called in by a down-the-hall neighbor; they meet every other morning at seven for a two-mile run. *He's never missed a day*, the neighbor stresses. He looked in the window and could just make him out on the bed. He watched him for two whole minutes, banging the side of his fist against the window, and he still never moved. Figured he had a heart attack and called 911. The squad had called homicide as soon as they arrived on scene.

He took his time, stopped for coffee. He wasn't the lead on the thing, he just had to show up. In Philly, they worked in teams; it wasn't like the movies. He didn't have a partner. The whole squad pitched in, whoever was available, and worked the case, top to bottom. Sometimes they solved it, sometimes not. Mostly, they solved it.

The guy in the apartment in Chestnut Hill had been shot. Two bullets to the chest—close range—while he slept. It didn't even look like he had time to sit up and fight back. He lived alone, a seemingly sterile apartment, but what did Gil know? Since his divorce eight years ago, on any given day, he had a three-day-old pizza box sitting on the counter. Brandt wasn't a slob, but he wasn't what you'd call tidy. This guy? Listen, there are two kinds of people: clean people and people who clean for company. You can tell if someone is a clean person by the hair in the shower drain and the inside of the microwave. This guy didn't just clean up for a guest, he lived this way. Brandt thought everyone should have better things to do.

They find the long, wavy hair in the drain. Turns out, the guy had a friend. They find the used condom in the basket next to the bed, wrapped thoroughly with toilet paper. They find the matching blond hair on the pillow next to him. He had a girl.

By luck or chance, Brandt gets assigned the task of finding the girl. The DOA's phone is PIN protected but the department's tech guys can crack it open in usually under an hour. A four-digit PIN yields ten thousand combinations, and it takes the code crack software only seven minutes to nail it down. After that, it's easy street. Sometimes Brandt thought technology was making cops dumber. His new guys could tell you in a second how to run a code and catalog someone's entire hard drive but sometimes they couldn't tell you the first thing about what to do with a DOA who didn't have a smartphone. You used to have to pound the pavement for clues, the gumshoe way. Now, between the contacts, photos, historical data, and GPS metadata, everything you need to know about anyone is sitting in their pocket.

The DOA was no different. Except no girlfriend that he could find. No pictures of them together on his phone, just a sad little collection of birds and panoramic views of Hawk Mountain in what looked to be fall. So, almost a year ago. His contact list was anemic—a handful of men's names. His texts were infrequent but the most recent was from a guy called Tom Pickering, mostly about work. Pay stubs in the kitchen told Brandt he worked at True Insurance.

The True office was subdued; just the appearance of a cop on the day their boss skipped work, the same guy who'd never even called out, not once in eleven years, sent hackles rising. Brandt asked for Tom Pickering.

"Jesus," was all Tom could say when Brandt told him. He hated telling people about their loved ones. But this guy didn't seem to have loved ones, just Tom, who kept running his hand through his hair, over and over. "Jesus, Jesus."

"When did you see him last?"

"Jesus," he said again, and Brandt had to wonder if he was a particularly religious man. "Last night. Everyone else went out for a retirement party. He took a girl home. I, uh, worked late and then my wife got mad, so I went home." And the weight of what he said and its implications hit him. His face paled and Brandt had to grab him a chair. He looked like he might pass out. "But it's all anyone's talked about. He took a girl home. Evie something. They said she was pretty! Shit, he never does that. Holy fuck, did she kill him?" Not religious, then.

"We don't know, Mr. Pickering. Thanks for your time, though. Who went to this party and where did they go?"

"Lockers. I guess they left together." Pickering shook his head. "Jesus."

"Who else can I talk to, Mr. Pickering?"

Tom Pickering gave Gil a list of names, rattling them off and motioning vaguely to the cubicles on the other side of the office door. Gil talked to all of them, the same story. *Eve or something. Left early. Pretty. They seemed to know each other. Together by the time we got there.*

The thing people don't get about murder is that it's a mostly stupid act committed by mostly stupid people in their most desperate moment. The other thing is that whoever you think did it in the first day of the investigation, nine times out of ten, actually did it.

Brandt just had to find the girl.

At Lockers, the bartender was leaning against the bar, watching a flat-screen in an empty room. It was barely noon.

"Yeah, I remember that guy," he said when Brandt showed him a picture. "Went home with a girl."

"Get a name?"

"Sure, she paid for drinks with a credit card." The bartender went to the computer and started clicking around.

See? Mostly stupid people.

The bartender printed out a transaction record and Brandt couldn't help but think that he was losing the excitement somewhere. Sure, technology let them be more effective, quicker. Ultimately, it was a good thing. The arrest rates were higher. The chief was happy. The mayor was happy. Still, some days it seemed to come too easy.

He took the paper and studied it. They had enough vodka tonics for two. Plus a few beers. He scanned to the bottom for the name and felt the blood drain from his face. He took out his phone and pulled up her picture, blew it up for the bartender to see. Just to be sure.

"Yeah, that was her," the bartender said, running a towel down the length of the wood.

He hadn't been surprised by the job in a long, long time.

CHAPTER 3

Wednesday, August 3, 2016

Tonight, I skip dinner, too tired to heat anything up, and instead lie in my bed on top of the blankets, picking a padlock. It's an odd little hobby, but a soothing one. I found a box of padlocks at a yard sale years ago, and have been working my way through them with a tension wrench and lock pick set. Something about the click and slide of those tumblers, like solving an illicit puzzle. It takes a fine touch, sometimes feather light, but it's predictable, too. I like knowing, a fraction of a second before it happens, that success is imminent, feeling the steel loop pop in my palm.

I listen to the television next door through the thin walls, a sweet plume of weed seeping under the door. The Georgian row home is old, the floorboards narrow and creaky, so I can hear every footstep. I can hear Tim, my neighbor, his voice low and deep, talking on his phone, and I imagine his hand pressed there, between our shared wall. I hold my breath, hoping he wouldn't suspect I lay merely feet away, and with the light off, would maybe assume I hadn't come home yet, had he ventured outside to look to the left at my bedroom window. I always come and go quietly, or loudly, depending on whether or not I'm in the mood for Tim. Tim's a good guy, in a teddy bear kind of way, with his well-groomed beard and big laugh and rumbling train of a voice. He's great-looking, that's part of the problem. Exceptionally good-looking men are all assholes. He's used to women who giggle at his jokes, corny dad jokes, jokes about how many people are dead in that cemetery (*all of them!*). I know deep down he just wants a wife: someone nice and sweet to settle down with, buy a big Colonial in Elkin's Park with a wrap-around porch, the kind with spinning ceiling fans on hazy August evenings.

He raps on our shared wall. "Beckett, you there?" I breathe shallowly, waiting until I hear him walk away, back through his apartment, away from our wall, and he's gone. It only takes a minute or two for the doorbell to ring.

Jesus Christ.

I get up, walk thirty steps, crack open the front door, and tell him he's a pain in my ass.

He laughs. "Let me in." He smiles, which is nice. He has straight white teeth and dimples that you can only vaguely outline through the scruff on his cheeks. He waggles a half-consumed bottle of wine at me.

"No." I'm 119 days sober. He has no idea.

"Come on, Beckett." He smiles again, all teeth, and I almost cave. It would be easy. He cranes his neck, looks past me into the hall, straight into my bedroom, where I'd left the door wide open, and I move to block his view. "Why are all the lights off?"

"Because I didn't want you to know I was home." I start to shut the door in his face and he slaps it open, his foot wedged between the door and the jamb. I roll my eyes and he again holds out the wine, a peace offering. I take it and give him a look. He backs up, holds his hands up, and laughs to himself as he walks away. I watch him retreat, the plank of his back, his long legs, and regret it, for a second, but only a second.

"Why do you put up with me?" I call to his back. He half-turns, I can't read his expression in the flickering hall light but his voice is teasing.

"You make me laugh," is what I think he says, but when I ask him to repeat it, I hear the click of his door.

In the kitchen, I pour the wine down the sink, holding my breath. I don't want to smell it, the tangy tannins making my mouth water. I might end up licking the stainless steel, just to feel the tart pop on my tongue.

I always get that same twinge around Tim, as though I'm pulling him along by a leash and he knows it. I can be this woman he wants, but only periodically, and we both know she's not real. He knows nothing about Lilith, or the booze, or my probation. He knows my brother exists but only because Dylan calls seven times a day. I'd think that normal women tell the man they're sleeping with these things. Maybe not?

The day he moved in, a year and change after me, he had a girl helping him. A tall, lanky blonde, the kind with low-slung jeans and high boots and a happy, burbling laugh that flitted through the walls, invading my living room. I thought she was moving in, not him. I had to leave, it got so bad, and all I kept thinking was, *Oh hell no.* If The Laugh was moving in, I was moving out. I escaped to the library and started browsing for a new place. When I came back later, as I tried to pad quietly past his apartment, the door flung open and there he was, a wall of a person. That smile, easy. And honest to god, my heart actually raced. Dark hair, dark eyes, but nice, you know? The kind of nice that would chase after a frazzled mom who dropped a five-dollar bill. You could just see him helping an elderly man on a bus.

You could see it all in an instant and that apparent kindness made me nervous.

The girl was gone. *I'm Tim*, he'd said, holding out his hand. The girl, I found out later, was a friend. Not a girlfriend. He'd told me this hopefully, a glint in his eye, with a smirk. Weeks later, I called her The Laugh and he'd hooted. I felt my cheeks grow warm, and that's when I knew I'd have to be careful.

The last guy I worked hard to make laugh was Brandt. I never have been cut out for this kind of thing: dating, relationships. Don't get me wrong, I like men. And I love sex. And neighbors, well, they're convenient. But the whole share-your-lives part? The pillow talk after? People whisper about their deepest-held beliefs, childhoods, parents, memories. All the building blocks that make a person. I couldn't navigate any of that.

Not to say Tim doesn't push me, he does. Last week, Wednesday, he tried to take me out to dinner, a real dinner, not this takeout Chinese thing we do on his living room floor, and I hid, the way I tried to do tonight, with the lights off, and listened to him knock on my door, call through the wall, *Beckett, I'm wearing a tie, for God's sake, I know you're in there*. I knew I was being an asshole. The day before, I fell asleep in his bed, something I rarely ever did. When I woke up, he was watching me, the edges of his face blurred like Vaseline over a camera lens, a tilt to his head, a hank of my hair twining between his fingertips, and I could just tell. People can tell when they're being loved. There was something duplicitous about it. How can you love someone you don't truly know? The answer, of course, is that he only thinks he does.

Then I think about how he's never been in my apartment, not once, and doesn't question me about it. I ask you, how is this normal? What must he think? Instead, he always laughs, chucks me on the chin, punches my arm, tugs my hair, a third-grade playground crush. He doesn't know what to do with a girl who is made of needles.

It all suits me just fine, because when I'm really gone, I can't feel guilty about him, too.

• • •

The last time I had a friend was high school. I was part of a crowd, maybe even the right crowd. Mia, pretty but mean, Rachel and I little shadows in her sun. Mia led, Rachel and I were happy little followers. Until I wasn't.

I remember the way Pop said it: *Your mom, Edie.* I thought she was dead and felt almost relief. A slipping into nothingness, the way you slide into a cold creek on a hot day. I swear I almost felt happy. Until he said, *She's been arrested.* I couldn't help it, I rolled my eyes. *For what?* It had happened before and I was certain it would happen again.

This is different, and I realized for the first time that my father was old. His skin was graying, his hair thinning, his lips cracked around the edges. In that moment, he looked a hundred. *She killed someone.*

When he said it, my mind went white, a faint whooshing in my ears like a TV tuned to a static channel. And we both felt it, the inevitability of finally colliding with the train rushing toward you. This day was always going to come, of course, and we had always known it. We could have ended it years ago, *should have ended it*, if only we'd known how.

I had asked who, and how, and Pop's voice had measured out the words, parsed into bits, which meant he didn't have all the details, but what she did was more horrible than he'd wanted me to know. He said she'd stabbed a woman, *but you know she's out of her head most of the time, right, Edie? It wasn't her; it's not* her *that did this thing.* Which is what he'd always said when she "went away." When she seemed to turn into a wholly different person, if someone can be a different person when, in fact, they're a different person all the time. I wanted to shake him and say *of course she did this thing, it's her, it's always her, you just never see it.* To see it, to fully see it, he'd have to act on it, which we did not do.

Which is why, despite what various psychologists have insisted, I realized at fifteen—*we all killed a woman.*

But I went to school that day. I guess I shouldn't have. I was late, skipped second period and instead sat in the library, at a computer terminal in the back, and read the news.

"Woman, 34, Arrested for Murder." It was short. Mentioned Lilith by name, the victim was nameless. Lilith stabbed her.

I remember the library was hot. It was June and the school didn't have air-conditioning.

I remember how the smell of the cafeteria hit me when I walked in: warm bread and hot onions and always the queasy undertone of bleach.

"Why are you here?" Mia asked, her voice cut with a razor, her upper lip curling.

"Why wouldn't I be?" No one moved over. I was still standing when I realized the cafeteria had gone silent. Even the teachers stared at me with bright, white horror. "It's not true." It felt good to say, like it *could* be true, but how do we know what really happened? People get accused of murder all the time and then get exonerated. I feel a sweeping, vertiginous relief. *Of course.* Why hadn't I thought of this earlier? It was a mistake. "We don't know the full story, my dad is going to find out today. I know the papers say she killed a woman, but—"

"Four," Mia said, her voice throaty and indistinct. "She killed four people, Edie." She almost laughed, halfway between a bark and a yelp, her red fingernails digging into the white bread of her turkey sandwich, still in her hand but wilted and forgotten. "Lilith Wade is a fucking serial killer."

Later, the number would increase to six. Later, it would be obvious there was no mistake. But in that moment, there was only the quiet and the word *killer* bumping up against my brain, sticking in my throat. Nothing would ever be the same: it was palpable. Every slumber party—those precursors to intimacy, where adolescents practice love—I'd skirted confessions about Lilith; like the time she picked me up at school, driving her car before she lost her license, in just a pair of jeans and a bra (*What? It's just like a bikini top.*), or the time in the woods with the gun when Dylan saved us. Any chance I had at someone else knowing these stories, knowing me, was gone.

I looked at my friends, at Mia's little, upturned nose, her blond, wavy hair, her bright blue eyes, and Rachel's dark, almost black hair, with the purple streaks I'd put in there myself the weekend before. I looked at their eyes and saw only fear.

• • •

In the dead of night, the phone rings and the display says *Dylan.* I answer it, garbled and bleary, and he says, *Edie-Bee, are you there? Were you sleeping?* Of course I was sleeping. I don't say this, but instead feel myself drifting off, the Restoril pulling me back into the black fog of unconsciousness. I hear him talking. My brother, plagued with our shared insomnia, which he's afraid to medicate but I am not, while he rambles the house, waking his wife and son, alternately exhausted and manic. *I had an idea*, he says, but I fall asleep before I hear what the idea is, only the soft drone of his voice, higher and softer than Tim's, coming through the phone, sounding both endlessly far away and close enough to touch.

• • •

In the morning, Tim is gone, off to work. He is a juvenile probation officer, a job for which he's perfectly suited, his bushy eyebrows menacing enough to scare even the hardest kids—and they were, he frequently reminded me, just kids. But he's not actually a prick. All the more reason why he can never know about the real me, and all the small ways in which

I bend the law. I pause at his door, the brass, peeling #2 above the peephole, and take a picture. Quickly, without thinking, I text it to him. *If I had a Post-it, I'd write sorry and stick it here.* He doesn't text back, but his days are busy.

Outside, it's misting. It feels good. I turn toward the train station, my face tilted up. It's supposed to be almost a hundred later.

I vaguely recall talking to Dylan the night before, but I can't remember a word of the conversation. I text him.

Did you call me last night?

I get an answer immediately. *Yes, you need to stop taking that crap. What if your building caught on fire?*

He has a point. Sometimes if you turn on the hall switch, the kitchen light flickers.

I'm fine. What did you want?

I'll call you later?

Before midnight this time?

He doesn't answer.

Excerpt from The Serrated Edge: The Story of Lilith Wade, Serial Killer, *by E. Green, RedBarn Press, copyright June 2016*

Some people will argue that Lilith Wade killed for love. More accurately, her killings were all rage-induced as a direct result of sleeping with married or soon-to-be-married men. She would not speak directly to us but has given various accounts of the sequence of events. The following transcript is taken from police and psychiatric interviews, all published and footnoted.

> *My mam always said the only thing that mattered was keeping a husband. Her whole life was lived for him, until they died together 'n left me alone, which if she had to pick is how she woulda picked anyhow. I ain't nothing but living competition to her. He was a snake, that one, my father, I guess, though I never called him that. Never called him much of 'nything to 'is face. [*Psy. Case Stu. 2004 Jul;19:310–12]*

Lilith Wade broke the serial killer mold on several fronts. She was female, of course; the majority of serial killers are men. She behaved more like a "mass murderer" who kills primarily to right a perceived wrong, except in her case, the wrong was personal, not societal. She did not kill for sexual gratification, like Ted Bundy or Dennis Rader. When asked why she killed six women, all wives or fiancées of men she'd seduced, she simply shrugged and said, "Because they de-served it." She was also one of the least prolific serial killers. Officials do not believe there are unaccounted-for murders.

"She'd laugh, you know? She said she didn't kill them all. I took that to mean she didn't kill all the wives of men she'd seduced. From what we've been able to gather, she was sexually active after her shift at the bar," says Dr. Phyllis Bond, a psychiatrist who has studied Lilith Wade exten-sively, referencing her case in her recently released case files nonfiction title, Serial Criminals, *New York: Pinkerton Press, 2014. "We do not understand why she 'picked' these women, specifically, to kill."*

Bond goes on to say, "No one has been able to get what happened in the house she grew up in out of Lilith definitively. She shows an incredible amount of rage toward her mother. She is very clear about her father. He raped her, regularly. I once asked her if she blamed her mother for all the hell her father put her through. If she was angry that her mother never protected her. She laughed. 'Protect me? That bitch would no sooner protect me than . . . well, let's just say she called me his little whore, that's all.' I'll never forget the way she laughed. You have to remember, she was ten when her parents died. What kind of person calls a nine-year-old a whore?"

Experts note that a key component in the characterization of a serial killer is repeated killings, spaced months or years apart, with a "return to normalcy" in the downtimes. Lilith Wade's normalcy was highlighted by bouts of mental illness, even once an institutionalization. Most serial killers have se-vere personality disorders but not necessarily a mental illness diagnosis. Lilith Wade had both.

Many psychiatrists have argued over Wade's various mental illness and personality disorder diagnoses. She has been labeled with borderline personality disorder, antisocial personality disorder, and narcissistic personality disorder, as well as bipolar disorder with delusions, obsessive-compulsive disorder, and severe depression. One prominent psychiatrist argued that Wade held no mental illness diagnoses at all, save for her personality disorders, because she was "devoid of emotion." This assessment has been largely discredited. Some of these diagnoses also conflict with one another, which makes a formal assessment difficult to obtain.

Serial killers, by nature, have learned to camouflage themselves. They are charming, well spoken, manipulative. Lilith Wade displayed all these traits when she worked at the bar, Drifter's. They can shape-shift into regular people on instinct.

Mitchell Cook, husband of victim Penelope Cook, gave one interview where he said this of Lilith:

> She could charm the pants off a snake. She looked at you like you were the only one in the room. Like you were interesting. She was just so goddamn interested in everything you had to say. In my whole life, no one has ever thought I was that funny, that smart. She made you feel like a hero, you know? She was damaged, too, you could tell. That combination, though? Beautiful, damaged, and intensely interested? It could lure anyone. People forget that, when they talk about her. That she was pretty.

This is not an uncommon description of Lilith Wade. Her coworkers and acquaintances describe someone who was always intensely interested in whomever she was talking to. She asked detailed, almost prying questions. She is described as having trouble with boundaries.

After an accident involving her neighbor's daughter, whom Wade's tweenaged daughter was tasked with babysitting, Linda Reston said that Wade brought her flowers.

"She'd always ask about Hazel. Was she doing okay? Was there anything they could do? She was so concerned," says Reston.

But Yolanda Fink, another neighbor in Faithful, Pennsylvania, only says this:

Lilith Wade was not a mother to those children. They ran feral from May to September. Half the time I fed them. They hung out on the steps with my boy, and Mrs. Wade paid them no mind until she wanted or needed something. Everyone said she looked at you like she cared, but I saw right through her. She didn't care about anyone but herself. She wasn't caring, she was calculating. Always wanted to know: What could you do for her?

CHAPTER 4

I look for Brandt on the train again, I can't deny it. I want to avoid him. Yet, sometimes I find myself seeking *him* out, calculating the time I'd seen him last (*was it 7:45 or 7:47?*) and timing my walk to get there at the same time. I hate my reaction, my fingertips gone numb, the slick of my palms. The knot of my stomach.

I'd be serving a prison sentence, or worse, if Brandt hadn't stepped in four years ago. I was a drunk. I drove. I got caught, my car blinking and crashed against the streetlamp, the lights flicking against the blackest part of the night, right before dawn. All I think now, every day, is *thank God*. Not in some actual praying way, because despite being (mostly) on the wagon, I never found my higher power. I don't mock those that do, I just haven't found mine yet. It all feels too hokey and crazy, throwing some wish up into the clouds and hoping they do the real, hard work while you're down here, sweating your ass off, trying not to lick the bottom of a stainless steel sink for that last swirl of red.

But I do thank my fleeting good luck that Brandt saw

my name pop on the blotter that night and showed up to the drunk tank, rattling cages literally and figuratively. I got probation before I ever killed anyone (this is the part I really thank God about), and part of the deal was that I stay sober, join AA, and get a job. Brandt said if I took the civil service test and did passably well, he could pull some strings and get me in as a county clerk. The hours could be questionable, the overnights sucked—after all, most misdemeanors happened at two in the morning: bar fights and drunk in publics. But the pay was above minimum wage, and it came with the added bonus of Brandt being able to keep an eye on me.

He pops up now and again, on SEPTA, in line behind me at Starbucks, hanging outside the 13th Street station, his cruiser doing a slow crawl past my apartment. I always give him the eyebrows and a nod and we move along. It all seems too frequent to be coincidence, but not frequent enough that I could question him about it if I dared.

When the PPD came crashing into Lilith's house and found her curled up in the bathtub wielding a large electric carving knife (not plugged in) drunkenly in front of her like a bushwhacker, Brandt was just a rookie on the team. Now, fifteen years later, he's a middle-aged, seasoned detective, his chin sliding slowly into his neck, his hair slipping backward toward the crown of his head. Still, despite his obvious aging, he's held on to his Italian good looks. His eyes almost black, his eyebrows unkempt, his jawline still carved up along his ear. His smile could melt the makeup off the night girls. I'd seen it happen.

The weirdest part is this. More than anyone else, more than Dylan, certainly more than Tim, more than Belinda, the other clerk who sometimes asks me to coffee, where I play along, pretending to be a regular, normal girl who cares about Belinda's new shoes (*DSW! Only $150, can you believe it? They're Miu Miu.*), Brandt knows me. The only one outside of Dylan and Pop, before he died, to know my entire life story: Lilith, Dylan, Faithful. So deeply unsettling was this, that when I turned and caught his eye as we waited in line at the Filbert Street station, ready to get wanded and badged through, I sometimes felt this jolt. Not a romantic kind of thing, more the zap you get from being recognized, the feeling of a slipping invisibility, that comforting mask that kept people at bay. He always gave me a distinct Brandt face, somewhere between friendly and smirking, but mostly just a normal hello (*Detective Brandt, Beckett*), and sent my mind into a swirling panic.

So brief were our regular exchanges that I wondered if I registered as a blip on his radar at all. How timed were they, really, how incidental? We hadn't had a real conversation in about two years.

Except he was watching me and he made sure I knew it.

● ● ●

The day passes. Weller breathes. Belinda talks. I take a detour on the way home, a quick stop to True Insurance. When Peter leaves, he grabs a taxi instead of taking the train. So many new additions to his routine. I can't chase him. I watch the yellow cab pull away, helpless. Oh well, maybe tomorrow.

I go straight home and I'm at my building by five, which feels new, almost decadent. I pass Tim's door quietly but I'm restless. Jittery.

I haven't been keeping up.

On my desk sits a stack of new computation notebooks. They're large, meant for engineering majors, with green quad paper. I found them shrink-wrapped on the curb. In May the Penn students graduate, leaving piles of garbage bags, overflowing Dumpsters, and plastic laundry baskets filled with whatever didn't fit in their late-model hybrids or their parents' BMWs. Half my apartment is outfitted from what locals call "Penn Christmas." Last year I dragged Tim with me and he pretended to be appalled by the number of people ripping open trash bags—many with actual trash, banana peels and half-eaten paper bowls of macaroni and cheese. I only touch the non-bagged stuff: the furniture, the electronics (an iHome, a set of computer speakers, a digital wireless mouse with a gel ergonomic mouse pad: cheap, utilitarian electronics). The alleys behind boxy off-campus apartment buildings are stuffed with leather sofas, beanbag chairs, glass end tables, IKEA bookshelves. A ceramic crackled-porcelain vase, bursting with red silk peonies the size of grapefruits, was my favorite take. When I grabbed the piles of notebooks and threw them in Tim's trunk, he asked, *What are you going to do with twenty graphing notebooks?* I never answered him.

Journaling has always come naturally to me. I kept them as a child: recording my days. Making order out of chaos. Telling stories. Some invented, some truth, some entries an amalgam, although now, fifteen years later, I couldn't tell you which was which. It seemed natural to carry the hobby to adulthood, even if now I don't journal about my own life but the lives of others.

I pull the most recent from the stack and record the latest: the lag from Healing Hope, the reported break-in. I run Peter's name through Google again, which returns very little. A new entry: the public police blotter, almost verbatim from CrimeTrack. I still monitor Healing Hope for a while, but no sign of Peter. Lindy Cook blips in and out, as does Eileen Dresden. Sometimes they talk to each other, but not all the time. Lindy and Peter were the ones who gravitated together. Eileen prefers another woman; she avoids the men.

When there's nothing else to record, I settle back onto the bed. I work on the padlock: a shrouded shackle Stanley I stole from the file cabinet at work. It's a six-pin core with counter milling and security driver pins. Difficult, but not impossible, I've read. Still, it eludes me.

I'll return it when the lock pops. I heard Weller grumbling about it yesterday. *People will steal anything that isn't nailed down around here.*

I wonder if Peter has friends. A girlfriend. A neighbor he had sex with, just to feel a warm hand against his skin.

There is a soft knock on the wall, right above my head. *Tim.* The clock reads 9:13 p.m. The night stretches before me, empty. I may or may not sleep. I do most of my internet research between bouts of insomnia, generally falling back to sleep between three and four, only to have my alarm sound at six. It's an exhausting way to live, but it's all I know.

The knock comes again, and against my better judgment, I knock back. I hear his laugh through the wall, it's that thin. Next to me my phone vibrates against my thigh, signaling an incoming text, and I know what it says without looking. My head is full of the stupid Stanley and of course, Peter, his nothingness, his invisibility. I need the distraction, a restless buzzing in my arms and legs. I'll never sleep like this. I throw on a robe, a fluffy white thing I bought on a whim at a thrift shop on South Street last week. It's unlike me; it's soft, feminine, pretty. For some reason, I look in the mirror, run my fingers through my hair. I've never preened for Tim.

Across the hall, I knock, just once, just barely, and he's there, the door flung open.

"Beckett." In his mouth, my last name sounds like the sweetest endearment. "I don't get you." Which might be one of the sweetest things he's ever said to me.

"Lucky for you, you don't have to," I say back. He's shirtless in gym shorts, his arms the size of my legs. When I step forward and kiss him he smiles against my mouth, which makes me swat his arm. "If you're going to mock me, I'll leave," I say, but it's a lie. He backs me against the wall, his hand hitching under my thigh.

"Liar," he whispers back, his fingertips swirling against

my skin driving me crazy. He stills for a moment, and leans against me, so heavy I can hardly breathe. He smells like soap and mint. "Will you stay tonight? Or will you sneak out as soon as I fall asleep?"

I don't sleep over. It panics me, the initial waking up, not knowing where I am. I hesitate. Finally, "I'll stay." We both know I won't.

I drop the robe and follow him to his bedroom.

• • •

At four, I slide out from under Tim's arm. He grumbles and rolls over but doesn't wake up. In my apartment, I stow my laptop into my messenger bag and dress quickly, without showering. I like the smell of Tim on me, that mint and musk in my hair, on my skin. Out on the street, the lights are dimmed, the city is silent. It's my favorite time of day, right before dawn, when I presume even the murderers are sleeping. Philly has generally been considered a violent city, although the crime rate has fallen dramatically in the past five years. I've rarely felt unsafe, even now with the black alleys, the empty streets. If anything, I've felt a weird sort of ownership over the city when it's like this. If I'm the only one awake, then everything I can see, touch, is mine. I amble loosely toward the CJC; I'd usually take the El, but today, I walk. It's only three miles, mostly on Front and Spring Garden Streets, both four lanes normally teeming with cars but this early, almost nothing. A horn blares as I cross the 95 underpass, its bleating echoing off the concrete, but that's the only acknowledgment that I exist at all. My thoughts are jumpy and bleary, my inner thighs still tender and sore from Tim's bulk. I like the pull in my muscle as I walk, a reminder that I actually have a life, someone soft and warm in the bed.

At 5:30, I call Dylan back again, his voice clicking a low, heavy "'lo," and I can tell he didn't check the caller ID.

"Dyl?" I say. "It's me. You're always up by now."

"Rough night. I'm up. I'm up." I can hear a rustle, then a whisper as he gets out of bed. Camille, his wife, left behind, a soft, rumpled toddler folded in her arms. I hear the padding of his feet into the living room of their small house. My brother works from home. He's in technical support for a gaming company. *Freelancing*, he calls it. *Waiting for management opportunities*, I've heard him say. Camille smiles and nods, a blank bobbling of her head. I can't know if she ever wonders what sort of management opportunities will befall my brother while he hunches over a computer in his underwear at two in the afternoon. Camille, instead, works as a loan auditor at a bank, a regular nine-to-fiver. She wears heels and rides the train. I can't figure out what she sees in him, or if she even actually *sees* him.

They met at a bar, an unexciting story. Camille, on the cusp of thirty-five, her ovaries pulsing to the technobeat. My brother, barely thirty, had said the magic words, *I've always wanted kids*. He may have said it on the first or fifth date, I don't know. It's not a lie, God knows he practically raised me. They've always seemed mismatched, although my brother is nice to look at. Big, sturdy, the outward appearance of reliability. When he really tries, he's charming, erudite. He keeps up on current events and politics. On the surface, he's a catch. He has a nice smile, straight teeth, clean nails. By the time you realize he's a bullshitter, you're eyeball deep in it.

Still, she saw a man-child in need of saving with the added bonus of also being a sperm donor. Just my assessment; I could be wrong.

They have a fourteen-month-old baby, whom she calls Baby Matty (never Matthew or Matt or even just Matty, but *Baby Matty*), and who spends the days at Camille's sister's house. I've been to dinner at Dylan's only once, when Matty was maybe six months old, and Camille spent the entire time touching the baby: smoothing his hair, kissing his temple, patting his behind in search of a wet diaper. She paid very little attention to me, her voice listless and wandering when I asked her questions, her eyes skipping around at the answer, sometimes squinting as though she barely remembered who I was. She paid even less attention to Dylan. He just exists in the same room, as though he's a particularly ugly floral sofa. Before Matty, she'd tended to him. Preening, and waiting on him. They had a habit of talking to each other in baby voices. I'd only seen it once and it was enough.

I've never held Baby Matty. I haven't held a baby since I was eleven and almost killed one. I wonder what Camille knows about Hazel.

"Are you okay?" he asks. He always asks this, ever since my car accident four years ago, like it wasn't just a simple crash into a blinking streetlight, but instead something wholly tragic and divisive. His voice is urgent, cut through with panic. "When I don't hear from you for days, I worry, Edie-Bee. I almost called Brandt."

"For God's sake, Dyl, don't ever call Brandt. I'm fine. I'm a person with a job. A life." I almost say *a boyfriend* just to get him off my back, but that'll invite more questions. Dylan doesn't come to my apartment; Camille doesn't like my neighborhood. She thinks our attachment is unnatural; that I'm weird and if Dylan spends time with me, he, too, acts weird. If she had her way, she'd excise our mother from his life, and lop me out for good measure.

There exists one photo of us all together. It was from a family reunion when I was nine or ten, years before Lilith was arrested. I have no memory of the actual event. In the original photo, Dylan, Lilith, and I are standing in front of a stone outdoor fireplace underneath a picnic pavilion. I am holding a white-and-blue casserole dish, Dylan is holding a baseball bat, and Lilith is laughing. She is beautiful, her hair wisping in the wind. She is taking her medication. Her eyes look focused, although her lipstick is smeared above her top lip. No one would notice that but me. I have a copy of the photo; it's the only one I have of the three of us. On Dylan's nightstand, the photo has been cut in half and only Dylan remains, his arm flung around some ghost shoulder, his body off center, the baseball bat in his hand becoming the central image. Camille did that. I'm quite certain that she hates us, Lilith and I. The kind of hate that manifests itself as indifference. We are a reminder of Dylan's life before her: messy, perverse, twisted, sick.

"Where have you been?" he whines. "Not just yesterday. You're working too much. We hardly see each other. Camille misses you." A lie.

Dylan knows nothing of my hobby. I sense, but can't be certain, that I've been more absent than usual.

It occurs to me that I haven't hacked Peter's email. I could, it's not hard. There's a phone/PIN trick I could use.

"Dyl," I begin, and hesitate. "Remember Peter Lipsky? His wife was killed?" We never say Lilith killed her, we say *was killed*, as though it was a passive death, almost accidental, a tub fall, a pedestrian hit-and-run, a heart attack. "Odd thing, Lilith never knew him. Isn't that weird?"

"Well, you don't know that." This time he pauses, I hear the running of the tap, a gulp of water. "I can ask her." Dylan visits Lilith every few months. I never have.

"Maybe," I say.

"She'll never remember, you know." He's right. Lilith's mind is gone, eroded by years of intermittently treated bipolar disorder, paranoia, and mostly the solitary emptiness that is death row. The women's correctional institution in Muncy, Pennsylvania, houses fewer than two hundred inmates in its maximum-security wing. Only three of them have death sentences. Lilith is one of them. She spends twenty-two hours a day in her cell, even eating meals there. Nothing about that is comforting to me. They'll never put her to death; Pennsylvania rarely executes. He changes tack. "Do you want to meet up for dinner tonight?"

He must be desperate to ask Camille for a spur-of-the-moment dinner out. He doesn't reveal much about their relationship, preferring to paint them with the same placid brush she does. When he hints at trouble between them, it's always because she is overwhelmed, anxious, *the baby.* He says it condescendingly, like I could never understand.

"No. I have plans." I give him the out. I make a final right on Filbert Street. I can see the CJC a block and a half away, and it's only six. I am an hour early for work. I don't give him a chance to ask what my plans are. "I'll talk to you later, okay, Dyl?"

"Be careful today."

I stand on the empty sidewalk, in front of my office building, and look up. The sky is just beginning to pink with dawn.

My phone buzzes, indicating an incoming text. Tim has woken up.

I knew you'd leave.

Excerpt from The Serrated Edge: The Story of Lilith Wade, Serial Killer, *by E. Green, RedBarn Press, copyright June 2016*

"That girl was never right in the head."

This is what the neighbor of Lilith Wade's childhood home says. Betty Putnak has lived in Faithful for her whole life. For nearly a decade, she was neighbors with the Wade family. Calvin and Wendy Wade had a ten-year-old little girl when they died in a car accident in 1977; the car was run off the road by a drunken driver who fled the scene. Lilith was home alone and didn't answer the door when the police came. Eventually, authorities chained the doorframe to the tow hitch of a truck and pulled the door right off the hinges. They found the girl, screaming, underneath her parents' bed.

The Putnaks felt bad for the child and took Lilith in.

Betty Putnak: She hardly had a thing with her. A few tank tops, some hippie skirts, a nighty of her mama's—hardly appropriate for a child, all silky and lacy, and she wore it every night. Wouldn't even let me wash it. Not a toy. Not a book. A cigar box filled with weird stuff: a lighter. A knife.

Interviewer: A knife? She was ten.

BP: Yep. A hunting knife. Half serrated, half plain edge, white-bone handle. I still remember it because it was such a fine knife.

Interviewer: Was she ever threatening with it?

BP: Oh Lordy no. The girl hardly spoke a word, 'cept to say please and thank you. She stayed on here about three years before she ran away. No more trouble than a common house cat. We tried, Bill and me, at first. To get to know her, like her, love her, even. Tried to play board games. Did her room up.

Interviewer: Did you know the Wades well?

BP: I knew the wife. She'd say hello or good-bye to me. When Bill had the heart attack, she brought us an Entenmann's. Always with her head down. Never saw a stitch of makeup on her. Never. Just these dresses. Long and thin fabric.

Interviewer: Did she work?

BP: Not that I ever saw. I only saw her drive one time, and that was to take the girl to the hospital. She had measles, I think. Almost died. She was too skinny—both of them.

Interviewer: What about Mr. Wade?

BP: I never met him.

Interviewer: You lived next door to them for almost ten years and you never met him?

BP: They moved in on a rainy day, with a little infant who couldn't have been more than a few weeks old. I went over to say hello and Mrs. Wade answered the door and stood outside on the porch talking to me. Never invited me in. It was April. Cold, maybe fifty degrees. She didn't even have shoes on. Spoke so softly I had to lean in to hear her. I came home that day and told Bill, "These people are oddballs." He didn't believe me. But ten years in, we still never met the husband. Little girl came over and played in my yard, though.

Interviewer: Why your yard?

BP: You wouldn't know it to look at it now, but the whole thing was filled with weeds. So tall you could barely see the front porch. Bill complained, you know? Snakes, voles, ticks galore. If I wanted to live in the woods, I'd live in the woods. Looked terrible. Not that the houses around here are worth a shitting nickel, but we keep 'em clean. Nice enough. The girl got tired of playing in the weeds. I'd find her over here, talking softly to herself. No friends, ever, to speak of. Never saw her talk to another child. I fed her cookies and milk. She ate them like she was starving, always said thank you, and left.

Interviewer: Did she go to school?

BP: Her mama said she was homeschooled. This was in the 1970s. People didn't do that then, although it's in fashion now, I suppose. I think it was illegal. But no one questioned the mother as far as I can tell.

Interviewer: Why did you think she was so strange? What did she do?

BP: More about what she didn't do, really. She wasn't a normal child, that's all. There was this one time . . . [pauses for a long time] No one came to take care of the house and the weeds just got taller and taller. We started getting mice, I hated them. I'd scream, you know? That's not weird. People don't like mice. One day, I found her and she'd caught about five of them. One big one and a few little ones. She'd set a trap and I hadn't even known it. But it was what she did with them . . .

Interviewer: With the mice?

BP: Yeah. She'd cut off their heads, with that knife. When I found her, she was talking to them.

Interviewer: The headless mice?

BP: Oh, she kept the heads. She lined them all up, you wouldn't even know they were dead. That image still sticks with me: that seventy-pound girl, that washed-out hair, in her mother's filthy nightgown, talking to all those decapitated mice. Cooing at them, like they were babies or something.

Nicer than she'd ever talked to Bill or me, that's for sure.

CHAPTER 5

Thursday, August 4, 2016

Belinda is out sick. Her computer sits dark, and within seconds, Weller is standing over me, his hot coffee breath on my neck.

"I can cover her, no problem," I say without turning around. I hear his snuffling, the phlegmy gurgle in the back of his throat, a noise of impatience. He hates when I don't look at him. He says it's what's wrong with our generation; we don't give respect to our elders, commanded by years alone.

I wave my hand behind my head. "Just leave the contact forms on my desk." I'm docking my computer and swearing at it, pretending that it gives me more trouble than it does, the curtain of my long hair falling in front of my face. Through the strands, over my shoulder, I can see him, shifting his weight, picking at his thumbnail, waiting for me. Finally, I stand up and he takes a step back, startled. "What?" I say.

"We've gotten some complaints, Beckett," he says, regretfully. "You and Belinda, taking some longer lunches. Mistakes on the intakes, that kind of thing." He chews the side of his cheek before continuing on, "I'm just saying, people are paying attention. So, watch it, okay?"

Poor Weller. He wants to be a good boss. He wants to look out for us, for me more than Belinda, who he seems to barely tolerate, wincing at every screech of her voice. I think of Brandt then. Losing this job would be it for me, he wouldn't help me find another one. "Okay, thanks for the heads-up, Weller."

I don't tell him that Belinda likes to shop on her lunch break and that Macy's is a block away. She comes back with bags: lingerie and makeup, small club clutches and strappy heels, all purchased with a glossy plastic Macy's card. I have no idea how she pays the balance. Her level of abandon is so foreign to me. I like to imagine doing the same, tossing slinky black dresses over the top of the dressing room door and choosing one for how it hugged a curve rather than whether the price tag was black or slashed red, nipped from the clearance rack for the appearance of a wonky hemline. I tagged along once and she chided me, *Just buy one thing*. I got to the counter, a red lace bra in one hand, thoughts of Tim, but stashed it on the return rack before Belinda even saw it.

At my computer, Weller safely down the hall, I sip coffee and check email. I schedule three inmate calls, starting at eleven. I submit a report I'd been working on for a week. With enough ticked off my list, I navigate to Facebook. I log in as Lindy Cook's friend and friend request Peter, doubting my plan. I haven't clone friended any of the others, either. Too many Facebook accounts to keep track of. I also tend to focus on research on people in bursts. The Dresdens, with their excessive dysfunction, have been keeping me occupied.

Middle-aged men are more suspicious of the internet than twenty-year-old women, but we have Lindy Cook as a mutual friend. I can imagine him thinking about it, blowing up the picture, trying to ferret out how they know each other, had they met? The pretty smile will win him over. Men can be easy.

He accepts a few moments later, faster than I thought he would. I'm able to see his friends list (112 friends), his wall (scant more than was public), thirteen photos (mostly mountains and lakes; he's a hiker), and his email address. Barely more than I had ten minutes ago.

I open Google and create a new account, LindyCook55 @gmail.com, and send Peter an email. *Peter, it's Lindy. New email and phone. I got hacked! Lost all my contacts. Can you send me your phone # again? Lindy.*

I don't know the nature of their relationship, the level of familiarity.

It's called *phishing*, and most hackers or wannabe hackers do this for sport. Or to obtain credit card information. I'm not doing that. But still, the thrill is there, my heart is a jackhammer. His email comes back, quick but succinct. *Hey Lindy, sure. 610-555-8821.*

Now the tricky part. In Google, I navigate to the login page and type in *PLipsky@gmail.com.* I click the forgot password link, and the send to SMS option. Google will send a text message to Peter with a verification code. The next part must be done quickly, and I activate my phone before I can second-guess myself. I open an app called FreeText that allows me to send anonymous text messages. I type in Peter's number and select an outgoing phone number from the app's list. I type: *Google has detected unusual activity on your account. Please respond with the code sent to your mobile device to stop unauthorized activity.*

Within seconds, Peter responds: 305067. I'm almost disappointed in him, I thought he was smarter. I know I have seconds to work before Peter tries to log in. I type in the verification code, and change his password to gprt*4971, just a collection of random numbers and letters. In his settings, I add one of my many dummy email accounts as a forwarding address. I then send the contents of his inbox to my dummy account and delete the sent folder. I note with some satisfaction that his inbox has less than fifty emails in it. I don't understand how some people live with thousands of unread emails. Some are work related, a few seem personal, but there is nothing exciting at first glance. I then log out, and send a text to Peter: *Thanks for your patience. The issue has been resolved. Your new password is gprt*4971. Please change your password immediately for security purposes.*

I delete all the FreeText messages and change the phone number. When I log into my dummy account, Peter's inbox is waiting for me. There has to be something valuable in there. *Has to.*

• • •

The answer comes at three in the afternoon. I've talked, at length, to two inmates. The first one was drying out, his voice drifting and sleepy. The second one, Trent Porter, was manic. These guys don't have good lawyers to shut them up, put the fear of God in them, so they ramble. Trent keeps me on the phone for a full twenty minutes, tripping over his *t*'s and *s*'s. The stutter is going to kill him inside, but I don't say that. *T-T-T-T-twenty-three s-s-s-s-ixty-s-s-s-six North F-F-F-Fourth SSSSSStreet.* I look at his intake: possession and armed robbery. The guy isn't new here, he's not scared. I want to say *good luck*, but I don't. While Trent talks, my Gmail dings. A forward from Peter's email:

To: Plipsky@gmail.com
From: Rt4699@gmail.com

Pete! Rooney says you were talking about bailing on tonight. It's his retirement, r u kidding? I better see you there. Buy you a beer? Lockers, ok? Everyone's going at 4, I'll be there around 5, have a meeting. —Tom

Trent is still talking, but I've lost my focus. Lockers, a loud, crowded sports bar, all wood paneling and blinking TVs, is two buildings away from the CJC. Peter will be there in—I check the time—a half hour. My throat is suddenly dry, scratchy.

I imagine Peter, surrounded by friends, watching whatever game happened to be on television, shouting and pointing at the screen. I imagine pitchers of foamy beer and pert waitresses and the casual, oblique sexism of a sports bar. Despite my hot and cold with Tim, I love men. I love watching them all together, trying to figure them out. Men should be easier for me, it was my mother who was always the mystery. My father, my brother, they've been there my whole life, a steady drumbeat of maleness: boxers on bathroom floors, hair in the shower drain, a pervading mustiness to the upstairs. And yet, something about men still drew me: the secretiveness of all their thoughts, coiled and guarded, drowned out by the volume of their voices as they shouted about a game, a girl, money, the sheen of competitiveness slick on their lips, their tongues frosted with beer. I imagine Peter among them, seeming so mild-mannered.

I text Belinda, figure she's faking. I'm just going to watch. And besides, she likes a good Thirsty Thursday happy hour. She texts back, *Actually sick! Bad clams. Unbelievable, I know.*

I'd stay an hour, nurse a club soda at the bar. What could it hurt?

• • •

I clock out early. I remember Weller's words: *people are paying attention*, but shake them off. As I leave the air-conditioned building, the hot city air hits me like a wall, smelling of sweet fried food and something cloying, garbage and sweat. Dylan is waiting outside, his hands pushed into his pockets. His dark hair falls into his face, about four weeks past needing a haircut.

"Hi!" I give him a quick hug. "What do I owe the surprise?"

"I can't stay." He steers my elbow to a bench at the corner, a narrow alley stretched behind us. "I just wanted to talk to you."

We sit and he leans forward, his elbows on his knees. He's lost weight—he was never obese, just big. Bones and muscles and tendons and nerves all cut out for a giant. Built like Pop but taller, wider. His forehead hangs low, an awning over his eyes, his eyebrows always pushed down in concentration. He stares at me intensely, because Dylan does everything with *intensity.*

"I'm worried about you," he says finally, his hand pulling at mine.

"Why? I'm fine." I laugh and glance beyond his shoulder, toward Lockers. When Dylan gets like this, sometimes there's no talking him down. It could take hours. I don't have hours, I have—I check my phone—fifteen minutes at best.

"You take those pills. I know you still drink sometimes. We had dinner plans last night. You blew me off. I think you should see my therapist." He folds his other hand over mine so now I'm trapped. I don't remember making dinner plans.

"Which one?" The laugh escapes before I can stop it. Camille insists that Dylan see a therapist, but he collects them like other people collect coins or stamps. He tells his story over and over, he gets a thrill out of dissecting his childhood, piece by twisted piece. Especially the summers.

Lilith lived, for a few years, in a town called Faithful, north of the city. The town had two stoplights, a pizza parlor, a gas station, and a library stocked with sweat-stained textbooks from the sixties and Judy Blume paperbacks that all smelled like old ham. Ironically, there was no church. The town was only twenty-five square miles, and the SuperMart was two towns over if you had a car, which sometimes Lilith did, depending on the year. After school would end and other kids would go to camp, or bike around the city, or hang near the pool, Dylan and I would be sent to a half-empty trailer park in Faithful, Pennsylvania, where I would spend hot, dusty afternoons in a lawn chair outside of Lilith's trailer reading Danielle Steel novels, enraptured by the idea of sex.

I can measure the four summers we stayed there, from the time I was eight until I was twelve—when Lilith had her "break" and Pop moved her back to the city—by her mental health alone. Was she on medication or not? Did she come out of her room or not? Did we have electricity or not?

In the early years, it was just me and Dylan, running feral through the neighborhood, to the creek bed down behind the park, looking for crayfish and salamanders, their red tongues flicking as Dylan snapped their little tails off and left them to die.

He likes to recount the worst of it with bland nonchalance. He likes to shock his doctors until they insist upon something—a diagnosis, a therapy—that Dylan disagrees with, resulting in fiery blowouts or cold cancellations. He argues about courses of treatment, about which he's never specific, and instead prefers to tell me of only in the vaguest of terms, all couched in double-speak: *They were completely unqualified. That one was a charlatan. A scammer.*

"I'm being serious, Edie. I'm seeing someone now, her name is Dr. Tremond." He fishes around in his pocket and produces a wrinkled, slightly damp piece of card stock with her name and phone number. It looks homemade. "I think she's the best I've ever had."

"You say this every time." I smile at him and flatten the card against my thigh. "And then you change your mind." I look up at him apologetically. "I have to go, though. I have an appointment."

I stand up to leave him there. I bend down and kiss his

cheek. He stinks. "Dylan," I say, making a face. "Take a shower. You reek, brother." I realize then that his sweatshirt is dirty; a worn patch in the sleeve is working its way into a full-blown hole. His jeans are frayed. I stop, just for a moment. "Are *you* okay?" I ask.

"Me?" He laughs, shakes his head. He doesn't stand up. "I'm fine. I'm great." He snaps his fingers. "I got a promotion at work."

"Are you Senior Gamer Dude now?" I mock him and he waves me away.

"Actually, yes, thank you very much." Dylan has never had patience for sarcasm, especially mine. "8A Games," he says, with pride. "A good company." Something Pop used to say. *Get a job for a good company.* To him that meant a union, a pension. *Remember Ben Martin? He works for a good company now.*

I stand for a beat, unsure of what to do, then ruffle his hair. "Congratulations," I tell him. I have to leave him there, on the bench. I wait for him to stand, but he doesn't. He watches me go, and before I turn the corner, I give him a last little wave. I can't read his face, but I think maybe he looks sad. I almost turn around, *Let's go out to dinner; I've changed my mind.* But then I see the Lockers sign ahead and feel the rush of something. Maybe excitement, it's hard to say.

• • •

I'd wanted to be there early, before anyone else. But I still see him before he sees me; he's at a table in the corner, a round high-top. The waitress stops and he gives her a polite smile, no teeth. She writes something on her pad and walks away. Her shorts are short and tight and his eyes don't follow her. He's on his phone, a thinning patch of hair in the back of his head slightly shining, his glasses blinking in the light of the television.

I didn't expect him to be alone. I sit at the bar where I can watch him discreetly over the rim of my glass of club soda. He alternates between scanning the bar and checking his phone, glancing at the door. He looks like a guy waiting for a date. It's oddly thrilling that I know the truth and he has no idea.

When I'm caught staring, his eyes settling on mine in the light of the front windows, I am jolted. I feel my face redden; I look away, toward the bar, toward the bartender drying glasses, whistling with the music. When I glance back, he's still looking at me. He smiles, and without thinking I smile back. His face is nice in person, a long, straight nose, smart glasses, a squared jaw with a faint line of dark stubble. I can feel my heart banging in my ears.

Without question, coming here was a bad idea. The back of my mouth tingles with wanting a real drink. God, I'm so stupid, *I came to a fucking bar.* My sobriety always feels like a vague joke. I can be sober for months, even a year. Sometimes the break isn't even tripped up by anything in particular. Six months ago, I found an old bottle of vodka stashed behind the cookie trays and muffin tins in a cabinet in my kitchen. How I forgot it was there, I'll never know. It had been a shitty day with Weller. At first I mixed it with Crystal Light, just to taste it. I knew once I put my lips on the bottle that there was no going back. I woke up in Tim's bed with no recollection of the night. He'd loved it, said I'd never been so free with him. He said he felt like I finally opened up a little. He didn't know I was an alcoholic.

I stand up and down my drink, pretend it's fire down my throat, think about how much I'd love that burning, just for one second to forget. When I slam the glass down on the table, with dramatic flair for my own amusement, my hand catches on my purse strap and sends it to the liquor-stained floor. Chapsticks, receipts, a wallet, a notebook, about thirty pens, all scatter. Goddamn it. I'm crouched, squatting, when I see him stand up and cross the room. *Fuck, fuck, fuck, fuckity fuck.*

"So this is weird, and not at all a pick-up line, but do we know each other?" His voice is quiet, smooth, not overly deep. I sweep all my errant pennies and Chapsticks into my bag and stand, unsteady, too close to him. He laughs.

"I don't think so, why?" I feign innocence, scanning the room like I'm waiting for someone.

"You look familiar?" His head is turned, his eyes studying me, and for a second I can't breathe. Does he think I look like her? Is that why I'm familiar? I feel inches from being exposed. I don't resemble her, not exactly. Our noses are similar, our hair is wiry and wavy. Her eyes were more close-set; mine are my father's, wide and round. I'm told they're my best feature, brown flecked with gold.

Peter's eyes behind his glasses are green. I resist the temptation to reach up, take them off his face.

A waitress appears, white smile and red lips and pad in hand. "Do you want a drink?" she asks me, handing Peter his beer that he'd ordered from across the room before.

Without taking my eyes off Peter's face, I murmur, "A vodka tonic, please," and at the same time Peter says, "You can put it on my tab."

• • •

Three drinks in and my vision is bleary. It should take more; I'm a fairly pathetic alcoholic. I'm skinny, that's the problem. I'm also 122 days without a drink, which can toy with your tolerance whether you're a drunk or not. The guy they call Rooney shows up with a few other guys from Peter's office. We move to a table and they crowd around, peppering me with questions.

They didn't know Peter had it in him, to pick up a pretty girl at a bar. Rooney, in his mid-sixties, leans close when he says that, his mustache feathering my ear. He smells like nicotine and whiskey. I like their camaraderie. They like that Pete found someone. I can tell by the way they rib him that it's not an everyday event. Rooney is an old perv and he keeps touching me—innocuously, a hot hand on my back, my arm, his belly brushing against my ass. Peter runs interference and distracts him, *Rooney, did you see that game? Extra innings, the Phils might go all the way this year.* I chime in, my voice warbling, *It's only August, boys*, and they laugh, tell Pete to keep me around. They all think my name is Evie and I don't correct them.

Pete keeps my glass full, until my ears ring and the edges of the room blur. I'm laughing at something; in a second it's gone and I don't even know what it was, and I stand up to leave and the room is all waves and colors and summer songs turned up loud. And then, just as quickly, I'm disgusted. The smell of the bar, Peter, the way Rooney keeps watching my breasts. I have to leave, start over again tomorrow at day zero. What am I doing here? God, I'm so sick of starting over. I think I say good-bye, but I can't remember. I know this feeling, so close to blackout. Oblivion. I think of Dylan. Only mere hours ago, telling me I need help. He's right, I do.

I pay Peter's tab, a silent apology for not being who he thinks I am. At the door, Pete catches up to me. There's a little alcove before the exit and he pulls me to him, just so I can hear him. "Let me walk you home. It's almost midnight."

It's unfathomable. It was just five o'clock. I have to work tomorrow. I shake my head. "I'll get an Uber," I say.

"Come home with me," he says impulsively. Even through the liquor, I can tell he's nervous to say it. He runs a hand up my side, tentatively, his voice thick. His fingers catch on my shirt, brushing against my skin, lighting it on fire. There is something attractive about his hesitation.

I close my eyes, the heat of him so close. Outside, the temperature hasn't dropped at all; the steam off the pavement wafts in when the door opens. The windows are fogged from the air-conditioning. He touches my cheek, his breath on my neck. To him, I'm just a girl at a bar. To me, he's a taboo, a secret.

My mind flits to Tim, home, rapping on the wall, waiting for the knock back. I feel a darting pang of guilt. I don't expect that he doesn't have other women. I've never seen them, but that means nothing. I could walk away from Peter now, except that of course, I can't. Excitement and danger are an aphrodisiac; his panting against my cheek illicit. And most attractive of all: temporary. Secretive. Hidden. Desire has darkened his eyes, made them black with want. I think he says *please*, but I can't be sure and I lean against him. Close my eyes. The room spins but then rights itself and I laugh, my head tips back.

In all my watching, my invasions of their lives, I never considered this could happen. But I used to fantasize about befriending Eileen, sending her anonymous notes about her shithead husband. Finding her crying quietly into her bagel at the cafe around the corner from her house. Buying her coffee, feigning ignorance, asking her if she wanted to talk about it.

I hadn't fantasized about Peter, not *yet*. Now, before I could realize I'd wanted this, he was here, his throat a rapid, irregular pulse against my fingertips, the short buzz of hair at the back of his neck tickling my palm, a shock of erection against my thigh.

I feel his breath hitch. I close my eyes. It's all fine, he never has to know.

"Okay," I say.

CHAPTER 6

Friday, August 5, 2016

Peter's apartment is uptown in Chestnut Hill, a twenty-minute Uber ride. I hadn't figured out his address yet, and now I was seeing it up close and personal. Peter lived in a converted stone Victorian, in the lower-right apartment. He opens the bright red front door with a key and leads me inside. In the darkened hallway, he kisses me and our teeth clink together, my purse hanging off my arm clumsily, the sound of our breath amplified in the small space.

"I never do this," he whispers, his mouth finding the sensitive scoop of flesh between my neck and my shoulder bone.

I can't help but laugh. "That's what everyone says," I say, and I realize it sounds like I, in fact, do this all the time. Which is patently untrue, but I don't clarify. Once again, my mind skips to Tim, guilty. This is so one-sided: Peter is off-limits because of who he is and who I am. There's a raw power in that: I know everything, he knows nothing, and yet, we're indelibly connected.

Peter leads me down the hall and into his bedroom, the original, thin wood floor creaking under our quiet footsteps.

In the dim bedside lamplight, I see his face more clearly than I've seen it all night. The deep lines from his eyes, the up-close curve of his mouth, a faint scar above his upper lip, the way his eyebrows grow wild, uncombed.

The room is hot, stifling, and he tracks kisses down my neck, my breasts, my abdomen, his mouth warm. Our bodies bump together, the awkward dance of discovery, of not knowing each other's hills and valleys. Later, I'd try to remember the sex and only be able to recall snippets through the haze of a fever dream: his thoughtfulness, the way his hands touched me everywhere, parts that had never felt sensual: the back of my knee, the inside curve of my ankle, the bow under my ribs, the arch of a hipbone. Like he never wanted it to end, like maybe he didn't know when he'd make love again, which was, of course, pure conjecture. I know that I never wanted it to end. In my memory, we touched and kissed for hours, my mouth raw from it. I had no sense of time.

Much later, when I was in a weird sort of mourning, it would strike me the most how kind he was and how he deserved so much more than whatever I would be capable of giving him.

• • •

In the morning, I wake with a dull pulse behind my eyes and no other hangover symptoms. The blessing and curse of alcoholism: my periodic binges now come with little consequence, or else my tolerance for them has increased. The clock on the nightstand blinks 6:32. Peter sleeps on his belly, head buried beneath a pillow. I slide out from under the sheet, and slip into his bathroom for a shower. I run the water down my back, the steam works on the headache, the water a hot pulse against my skin that turns it pink. It's a fast shower. I dry off and slip into my jeans. I imagine Weller, huffing and pacing outside my cubicle, checking his Timex and clucking about it.

Peter's kitchen is neat. I run the tap and fill a rocks glass that I find in one of the cabinets, knock it back in one gulp. There are no dishes in the sink, no coffee mug gathering muck on the countertop. His refrigerator front is clear except for a single photo held with a magnet: an older woman, her features mirroring Peter's, with her arm around a much younger version of him. I scan the room for anything interesting.

I have to leave now if I don't want to talk to Peter. I can't imagine him waking up, the awkward small talk in the kitchen. Would he want my phone number? I have no intention of giving it to him. No. Best to be the one-night stand that slipped away, under the cloak of early-morning darkness. A sexy, perpetual mystery.

On my way to the front door, through the living room, I spy a Moleskine notebook on the end table. When I carefully lift the front cover, I can see that it's about half full of small, tight handwriting. In the dim light of early morning, I can't read any of it. I tuck it into my purse. He'll miss it, I know. If I have guilt later, I could certainly return it in any number of ways.

In his entryway, I slide into my flats. I wonder if Weller will notice that I'm wearing the same clothes. With my computer bag and my purse, I pause in the small front hall one more time. I consider going back, leaving a note. Instead, I slip out the door and onto the street, beginning my day much as I had the day before.

• • •

Belinda is out sick again, which Weller tells me with a resigned sigh. I tell him I can cover her and he shakes his head, doubtful. I conduct back-to-back phone interviews from ten to three, grateful for the busy day. I find myself running my fingertips over my lips, thinking of Peter. My stomach rumbles for food, but the very idea turns my insides. I feel hollow. I have senseless guilt about Tim, and a dull ache when I think of Peter, like a heartbroken teenager. Relationships never have been and never will be my forte, but somehow I've entangled myself anyway. I think of Belinda, juggling guys as quickly as she changes her shoes, and briefly wish she wasn't sick.

On my lunch break, I get a text from Dylan. *What time did you get home last night?* I hesitate. My brother doesn't need to know the details of my life, particularly not my love life, but I have no real reason not to let him in, even just a little. *Late, met a guy. Tell you some other time (not on text). Dinner this week?*

Tonight? he texts back.

I ignore him, and go back to work, my mind still racing around Peter. My brain hands me images, unbidden. Peter's teasing smile, his surprise when I removed his glasses. I check Peter's email; there's only one, from Tom: *Can't believe you took a girl home. Literally never thought I'd see the day.* Between interviews, I pull out the Moleskine, flip through it.

August 3

Call T
Set up eye dr appt
Check on Mrs. Charron
Milk, butter, parm cheese

I don't know what I thought I'd find—a diary of sorts? Some illicit spilling of his internal thoughts, the way a thirteen-year-old does into a pink locked journal? Peter is in insurance, for hell's sake. I wonder who Mrs. Charron is: an elderly neighbor? Is Peter so charitable?

My phone rings only once, and embarrassingly, my heart races. I'll admit, my initial irrational thought was Peter, but I hadn't given him my number.

The display reads *Brandt*, and I almost answer it. He

hasn't called me in a long time, maybe years. I look at the Moleskine, the remaining fifty pages or so, thick with Peter's neat print.

I hit decline. I can call him back after work. As I walk to meet Dylan, maybe.

I don't want to be distracted by Brandt. He'll be asking me for something, to find someone, a next of kin. He knows I'm good at finding people, particularly talented in digging up a distant cousin of a seemingly untethered victim. He's never just called to say hello, no matter how friendly we'd been in the past. It isn't his style.

Before my father died, he and Brandt had formed an un-likely friendship. I was never sure when they saw each other or how they kept in touch, but I remember the day I dropped out of school. Finally said *fuck it*, it was too hard, after Lilith. They had already let Dylan slide. It had been June after all. He stopped showing up for classes, opting to take finals vir-tually. We could have gotten away with anything.

One night, I found Pop on the sagging, rotting porch of our duplex, looking out onto the street, swirling a rocks glass with two fingers of whiskey, his plaid shirt pulled tight over his belly. He hadn't known I was there. I thought he was asleep, his feet pushing back against the wood of the porch, back and forth and back and forth, his chin tipped into his chest. Only when he gulped once, noisily, did I realize he was weeping.

At sixteen, I witnessed what it looks like when, as an adult, your life doesn't come to pass the way you expected. When you'd stood on the county courthouse steps as a hope-ful twenty-two-year-old, knowing your wife was wild, and maybe a little unpredictable, never expecting an exhaustive devolution into madness before your thirties. When you still love someone who has it within them to inflict terror. When you love someone you don't even know anymore, mostly just love the person they used to be, and hold on to the hope that they still are. I hoped I'd never push onto another person what Lilith had saddled Pop with.

But Brandt and Pop kept something up. A friendship, perhaps? I didn't know. I know that at some point he promised Pop he'd watch out for me. Despite what I did to him.

• • •

The basement office can be deserted on a regular day, but a Friday in August? Just the dust, and me. Weller seems to have vanished. I hear footsteps but see no people; the air is filled with sporadic noises, random clinks, and the squeaks of mice, caught in government-issued traps. Twice, the motion sensor lights flick off and I wave my hand wildly behind my head until they buzz back on. I focus on the backlog of reports and file them, one after the other, until the hours stack up and it's four o'clock.

I wonder if this is the last of it, if this is how my obsession will end. I've slept with him and he has no idea who I am. I imagine him finding out, seeing a late-night rerun of one of the many docudramas and true crime shows. Or flipping through *The Serrated Edge*, the book that names me as Lilith's daughter, though it thankfully doesn't include my picture. How would that feel? Shocking. Violating.

I'm causing him, possibly, some level of pain, regardless of how small. If he wants to see me again, he cannot. If he wants to find me, he cannot. Neither he nor his friends know my real name. All the cards are in my hands.

A text from Dylan: *Dinner at China Wok @ 5:30 tonight?*

I am so close to saying no. Unnerved from our conversation yesterday, his unexpected appearance in front of my building. A headache has come back, thrumming behind my eyes, the lingering hangover.

Sure, I text back. *Let me stop home and change first.*

Even the train feels subdued, jockeying back and forth

with less enthusiasm than usual. I have a seat and I slink down, tapping my phone. I check Peter's email to see if he'd responded to Tom. A newsletter from an indoor rock climbing gym and a coupon to a big box electronics store.

The train dumps me off a fifteen-minute walk to my apartment and I hike up Amber Street toward York. The street is narrow, almost an alley, and I palm a can of pepper spray, the safety flicked off. The sun is a bright, hot August ball hanging low in the sky. I turn right onto York and the street opens up. It's wider and cleaner, the metal fences are at least still standing and the small patches of lawn are mostly green, not dusty dirt. Ahead, I see a twirl of red and blue. Police. My building is a tall and skinny box. It stands alone, row homes on either side. As I get closer, I realize there are several cop cars, not just one. My building has been cordoned off with yellow crime scene tape. Tim. Has something happened? All those troubled kids, he always defended them. But I've seen troubled kids, I guess I used to be one. And I've seen what they turn into as adults. I deal with them daily. I imagine one of them angry at Tim's gentle, quiet insistence on following all the rules.

Across the street, a huddle of people is barely visible under the shade of a large pear tree. I can see Tim's shape among them, taller and broader than anyone, and I'm flooded with relief.

I take a step forward, to go to him, ask him what's up, but I stop. Call it intuition, call it whatever you want. My gut is rarely wrong. I pull out my phone, check the display. Brandt has called, twice more, while my phone was on vibrate in my purse. I never felt it. That's three phone calls in one day.

Between the row homes west of my building is a small alleyway. I duck into it and call him back. He picks up on half a ring.

"Beckett, are you there?" His voice is urgent, pushy.

"Brandt, what's going on?"

A shiver goes up my spine. Brandt is calling and the police are at my apartment. There is no such thing as coincidence.

"Beckett, come home, okay? We need to talk to you."

"We?" I asked.

"There's been an incident. Where are you?"

"I'm at work," I lie. He can't trace the call if he's at my apartment, at least not quickly.

"Still?" He sounds unconvinced.

"I'm a hard worker. What's going on? You've called me fifty times today." I keep my voice light, airy. Like I don't know he's got the place swarmed.

He sighs deeply. "I'd rather do this in person, Beckett. Can I come to you?"

"So help me God, Brandt. Is it Dylan? Is he okay?"

"Dylan is fine, as far as I know. There's just some crazy shit, Beckett. I'll come to you, okay? Sit tight, wait for me."

"No way. You tell me what's going on." My vision starts to swim and I can feel my breath hitching. "Brandt, I mean it, why is my apartment filled with cops?"

"Jesus, Edie. Where are you? You said you were at work—"

"Goddamnit, Brandt. What's going on?" I practically yell into the phone. It has to be Lilith. She's escaped and she's killed one of my neighbors.

I almost laugh at myself. I hear Lilith can barely feed herself these days.

There is rustling across the line, like he's leaving the room. It gets silent on his end, and I almost say *Hello?* thinking he'd hung up. Finally, unexpectedly, he says, "Did you know Peter Lipsky?"

Did?

A million thoughts race at once. Brandt will know the connection to Peter, through Lilith. If they're in my apartment, they've seen my logbooks. They're all stacked neatly on my desk. I never even tried to hide them. I have pictures, addresses, emails, Facebook usernames, parking tickets paid in full, jury summonses, all stuck into the notebooks like a travel journal. Instead of headings like *Rome!* and *Paris!* I have dates and ages, lists of friends and activities (*The Dresden twins both played football! Halfback and wide receiver, neither of them quarterbacks, to the disappointment of Kent, who is a motherfucker.*). A detailed outline of Kent's affair. Rayann's friends, and girls at school who gave her trouble. A list of her swim times, posted to the school website. A girl on the team had begun giving her shit for her slow 100 fly. I started, at one point, writing down their comparative times and getting unreasonably happy when Rayann won. It was easy enough to get online.

I look unhinged.

I look like Lilith, or worse. Lilith, at least, was mentally ill: bipolar and delusional, with a healthy dose of narcissistic personality disorder. I look meticulous and sociopathic.

Did you know Peter Lipsky?

"Brandt," I cough out. My throat won't clear. "Is Peter . . . ?" I let the question hang, waiting for Brandt to fill in what I know to be true.

"He's dead, Edie." He's silent for a long breath. "What happened? Just tell me, okay? Just meet me and tell me, we'll talk, friend to friend."

Brandt is still talking, trying to cajole me, when I press my finger to the red button on the screen. Peter is dead. Peter is dead and they will think I killed him, if they don't already.

I have nowhere to go, but I can't stay here.

• • •

I head north.

I open my phone, and in settings, I click clear to factory settings. I run through every delete cycle and wipe cycle I can find. I shut down my GPS, my internet, my network, and finally, I turn the whole thing off. I tuck it into the bottom of my messenger bag.

How did Brandt get a warrant so fast? They must have more on me than I thought. They surely have me at Lockers, leaving with Peter. My scrawl on the receipt at the bar. DNA at his apartment. Seems anemic. But then, oh yes, they have the Lilith connection. How quickly would they leap from reasonable average person engaged in a one-night stand to psychopathic serial killer's daughter sleeping with a victim's family member? How that little fact must reframe what would look like a chance meeting into an engineered setup. Their speed told me two things: 1. They were sure I was guilty, and 2. They thought I was dangerous.

It would become interesting to me, later, how quickly I moved. How easily I slipped from hunter into hunted. How natural it felt to slide underground. In the moment, I hardly thought about it. It seemed simple, almost too easy, to decide to become invisible. As though all the years of working in the system had been subconsciously preparing me to circumvent it.

I slip through the grid of Philadelphia, between buildings, along alleyways, even through backyards. I move quickly, but don't run. I look up, calm, but don't make eye contact with anyone. How do I know to do this?

I remember: the summer I was ten. Before Lilith was arrested, before Pop sent me to charter school. Lilith hadn't come out of her room for days and I was hot. Bored. The air in the trailer was growing dank and unclean. I'm not sure how I'd gotten the money; I'd stolen it to be sure. Lilith kept tips in the kitchen drawer. I took the bus from Faithful back to the city, to Pop's plant; I was curious what my father did when Dylan and I were away. When we'd asked him any other time, he always grunted, *Work.* It was more than curiosity, it was a pitted longing. The idea that he could exist so easily without us felt gutting when we both felt his absence so intensely. I couldn't have articulated any of that at the time, I just needed to know: What was so important to him that he'd always sent us back?

I skirted the guard shack, the small inroad for employees, and entered through the shipping and receiving dock. I remember skulking around, even then, instinctively clinging to the shadows, hugging the brick walls. I saw him, finally, hanging around outside a trailer, digging the toe of his work boot into the ground to stub out a cigarette. I'd never seen him smoke. He stood with three other guys, all men that looked like him, broad-shouldered and ruddy-faced, their teeth yellowed and skin graying. He laughed then, my father. Bent over at the waist, laughing until he coughed and the guy next to him slapped him on the back. I'd never seen anything like that, his face going purple with the effort.

I had run home then, to Pop's house. Let myself in with my key and stayed in my room. I heard the door bang open around nine that night, the clumsy bumbling of a drunk. I listened through the door as he groused at something. I imagined him banging a shin against the couch and cursing. Then, I fell asleep on top of my bed and was awakened by the doorbell and a voice. Female. Pop's low rumble in reply. A high, tinkling laugh, the vibration of Pop's underneath it, smaller than it was earlier. Not the doubled-over coughing like with his friends. Footsteps in the hall outside my bedroom and the open-and-shut creak of Pop's door.

The next morning, after I heard the floorboards under Pop's heavy footfalls, the running of the shower, the slamming of the front door, I took the bus back to Faithful, back to Lilith's. Paid for the ticket with cash I found in Pop's bedroom. In the trailer, Lilith hadn't come out of her room. I could tell by the toast on the plate that I'd left on the table the day before. I stood in the silence of her living room and realized that for twenty-four hours, I'd been invisible. I'd found out things: my pop smoked. He laughed with his friends. He had a woman over. He'd taken her to bed. He was a person I hadn't known. I recorded everything about it in my journal: frenetic, frenzied, the handwriting bobbing one way, then the other. At the time, I'd felt dizzy with it: all this secret knowledge about the adults in my life. The idea that I could learn more about my family by secretly watching them became a high, an addiction I'd return to. It was the same high I felt in the Dresdens' front yard. Following Lindy on the train. Tracing Peter's emails. Now a silly, fleeting thought: it has all been preparation.

I double back and grab a bus from Butler to Susquehanna Street. The best place to hide is in a crowd. On the bus, a red UPenn hat sits on a seat, its bill folded under the Velcro adjuster strap, and when I open it, a long blond hair drifts down onto my lap. The hat smells like TRESemmé. I look around and then unfold the cap and put it on my head, pulling my own hair through the loop. It'll work, but not for long.

I've spent a lot of time listening to criminals endlessly ramble about their crimes. Some of them love to talk; they want you to know they're clever. Years of information have been dumped into a part of my brain I haven't accessed. I can feel it activating, chugging to life like an old diesel engine in winter.

I book it across Butler and into the Walmart Supercenter. There are cameras on the bus, in the parking lots, at the registers, I know this. I have precious little time before Brandt mobilizes. On the way into the Walmart, I see a Dollar Tree. I duck inside and pay cash for three pairs of fake glasses: one wire-rimmed, one chunky plastic hipster, and one nerdy tortoiseshell.

Inside the Walmart I buy a prepaid smartphone and a regular flip phone, a handful of activation cards, a pair of scissors, a bright red backpack, and a yellow poncho.

"How much cash back can you give me?" I ask the clerk. Her mouth is bright pink and her teeth are stained yellow.

"How much is in your account?" she asks, as a joke, and then she sees my face and sighs. "A hundred bucks, hon."

"Can I do two transactions and get $200?"

She wrinkles her brow and thinks. "Sure. Don't ask for three, though, okay?" As she bags my phones, she says softly, "Who are you running from?"

I must pale, because she stops bagging and looks at me. "Don't let him hurt ya, okay?"

I nod without speaking. If she thinks I'm battered, she might not call the police. But I need to be careful: I was trying to blend in, be unmemorable.

In the parking lot, I see the bank. The ATM faces the street, which is a risk, but I take off the cap and the fake glasses and toss them out of the view of the exterior camera. I withdraw eight hundred dollars, staring up at the blinking red light, right above the keypad, willing the camera to record my face. I can see Brandt viewing it later, or maybe even instantaneously. He wouldn't be dumb about it, he would know what I was doing. Any disguise I'd don later wouldn't be worn while they could connect my new identity to a card, and therefore a location.

My daily max is a thousand dollars but I'll need more. I can't think past the week, haven't worked out where I'll stay yet. Likely a hotel, but where? As soon as the police publish my picture, any hotel desk clerk will call them in a heartbeat, bartering down a misdemeanor.

First, I need to be firmly lost in this city of a million and a half people. I'm not even close yet. With some basic detective work, Brandt could find me in a second.

I break up the cash and tuck some in each jeans pocket and a thick fold of twenties in my messenger bag.

I turn and face Butler Street, and it feels like I'm seeing

it for the first time. I'm used to whipping out my phone, checking directions on a train schedule. This is what this will be like, losing the pieces of me that make me who I am, shedding them and tossing them into Dumpsters around the city. Across Butler, there is a ShopRite. With my baseball cap and glasses back on, I jog to the store and purchase brown hair dye with cash. Something mousy and utterly forgettable.

Now for the risk. The big risk. I cross Butler and follow Glenwood Avenue, darting between buildings and alleys to stay out of sight. It's easy to figure out where security cameras might be mounted and dodge doorways as necessary. The alleys are the safest, but also the most dangerous for a myriad of other reasons. I keep on my hat and my glasses, my makeshift disguise, and walk for almost five miles to the Wayne Junction station, for the train I'd take to Hatboro. At the station, I let my hair loose and tuck my glasses into my bag. The sides of my canvas bag are bulging from the growing heft of various disguises.

I find the camera and stare into it, as though surprised and then contemplating it. I board the train; the SEPTA agent takes my monthly pass and scans it. I find a seat near the gangway and reapply my disguise of hat and glasses, folding my messenger bag into the bright red backpack and pulling the yellow poncho over my head before ducking out the door and back onto the platform right before the doors close. This time, I keep my head bent away from the camera, and hustle past it.

Wayne Junction has a bathroom with two stalls and two sinks; the drain is rusty brown. I lock the main door and pull the scissors out of my backpack. In the stall, I hack across the bottom of my hair and then shear up the sides and across my forehead in a blunt and shaggy page-boy cut before I flush it in stages down the toilet. I mix the hair dye with the activator and shake the bottle. I run the applicator tip up and down my head in stripes until it feels like a soggy, eye-watering shampoo. There are mud-brown drips all over the sink and floor—it looks like a grisly murder. I wipe them up. No need to give anyone a heart attack. The words no sooner flit through my brain than I am overcome with a lurching sort of sickness. I have ten minutes to kill as I wait for the dye to set, and for the first time in what feels like days (has it only been two hours?), I can sit and think about what's happening. What I have to do. What I've done. What Brandt thinks I've done.

Almost unwillingly, I think of Peter. I think of his fingertips on my skin, the glint of those green eyes rimmed with brown, the weight of him on top of me, the curve of his neck into his shoulder blade. How did he die? Was he shot? Stabbed? I'll find out, it will be in the paper.

There are no coincidences. Lilith said this, mostly in the throes of paranoia when she believed the FBI was monitoring her telephone lines. It can be disarming how many of my major life moments are internally narrated by my mother.

Where will I go? Any real ideas elude me. I can't go to Tim's or Dylan's. I can't call Brandt. Belinda? Weller? I have almost no friends; I've never minded it before.

I'm rinsing my head upside down in the world's smallest sink when I think of it.

T-t-t-t-wenty-three s-s-s-s-ixty-s-s-s-six North F-F-F-Fourth SSSSSStreet. The stutterer in my last interview before Lockers.

Roommate? I had asked, bored and disinterested, just wanting to check the yes or no box. I had been scrolling through Peter's emails.

Nobody but me, place is barely a shoebox.

I squeeze the remaining water and dye out of my hair and use a paper towel to dry it. I stare at myself in the mirror, so different from what I'm used to seeing. I've never seen myself with anything other than medium-length blond hair. I put on the hipster glasses and realize with some relief that I look like a completely different person.

Back out on the platform, I look around. It's mostly empty. The clock above the defunct ticket window blinks 6:17 p.m.

I've stood Dylan up. *China Wok @ 5:30 tonight?* I can't call him, I can't text. I imagine him hunkered in the red booth, watching the minute hand, nervous sweat popping on his upper lip. He'll think I've been killed, hit by a car, attacked by a criminal, left to die in an alley. This is the way his brain works: half-asleep to blind panic in thirty seconds. When my phone goes to voice mail, he'll call the police. Then what? It hardly matters, he'll find out soon enough what has happened to me. What they think I'm capable of.

I've done it: I'm effectively hidden for the moment. Cameras will see me get on the train; the system will have logged my ticket. My current appearance is different enough from my real self that any image taken with a grainy security camera will not be a threat. He'll send some guys up there and it will take some time for him to realize that I've duped him.

My biggest issue will be running out of money. I can get more at an ATM, but not without tripping an alert, and the accompanying camera would catch my new appearance. I have more to figure out, but for now I've been given the gift of time.

Which is convenient because I need to think.

Peter is dead. I was the last person—correction, second-to-last person—to see him alive. Someone killed him after I left his apartment. Peter, whose wife was killed by my mother. *There are no coincidences.* Whoever killed Peter had intended to kill us both, with me as the primary target. But why? And why now, fifteen years after Lilith's arrest? It made no sense.

Also possible: I wasn't the target, I was the scapegoat. The fall guy. The schmuck. Peter was dead and I would be inextricably linked, undoubtedly blamed. It couldn't be coincidental. Which meant the murderer knew who I was, who my mother was, and more important, what I had been doing with her victims.

Except, as far as I know, no one knows. Not Dylan, not Brandt.

Unless.

We went to a bar, drank, came home, and had what I think was probably great sex. It occurs to me that I don't remember much about the night. I remember being let into his apartment. I remember leaving in the morning. The rest is a fever dream. Snatches and pieces of scintillating film: a hand, a tongue, the skim of expensive sheets against my back, the sliding of my hair against a luxurious pillowcase. At one point, we both laughed. I don't remember falling asleep. I don't remember the orgasm.

Instead, I study my fingers. They're long like Lilith's, but squared at the tip, with wide, flat nail beds like Pop's. I've never held a knife in anger, the handle clutched into my fist, white-knuckled. I wonder what kind of strength it takes to sink a blade into a person, to break the skin, tear tissue and muscle and bone. I'd imagine a lot.

I wonder briefly, crazily, if I'd remember doing it. My shower this morning, had there been blood? It seems silly to question it now, hours later. I vaguely remember a grumbled sigh as I slid out from underneath the covers. Or did I imagine that, just now? He'd been alive.

Hadn't he?

CHAPTER 7

Day 1: Friday, August 5, 2016

2366 North 4th Street is an absolute shithole. The good thing is, people don't care about shitholes. Landlords don't care who's in them. Neighbors don't care who comes and goes. And owners don't care enough to lock them. The second good thing about this place is that it's far from where I both live and work, and while the connection is there, it exists only in paperwork. The report on my desk sits unfiled and practically anonymous. It would be a reach for any detective, even one as slick as Brandt, to connect this crummy apartment to me. It would likely take them a day or two to even get to my desk. I can see Weller now, smoothing his hair over his forehead, sweating. *Murder? My Edie?*

The building is a light blue box, the paint peeling off the concrete sides in chunks. There is a front door that opens with only a slight jimmy of the handle, the lock barely functioning. The hallway smells like smoke and weed and something sickly sweet and chemical. There are only four doors. I wrack my brain trying to come up with a letter, something the stutterer might have said. Nothing. The mailboxes line up in the hallway, their labels peeling. I look for Trent Porter's name, but no dice. Fuck it.

I knock on the first door and it opens so fast, I jump back. "Hi, uh, I'm looking for Trent Porter?" I shift uncomfortably and jimmy my leg. The guy in front of me is shirtless, the expanse of his chest broad and hairless. His face is wide and pasty, his nose acne-scarred and the skin around his lips flaking. He nods, barely grunts once across the hall. "B," is all he says, and then he shuts the door on me. I take my gum out of my mouth and thumb it over the peephole, just in case.

The brass "B" hangs by just one nail, listed to the right. The door is firmly locked but not deadbolted. I fish around in my bag for my lock pick kit. With the tension wrench inserted in the bottom, I jimmy the pick up and down until I feel the tumblers lift. People have no idea how easy it is. If they did, they'd surely invest in security systems. Nobody tells you how easily even a deadbolt could be picked. We'd never sleep again, would we? If we knew that nothing stands between a mildly determined criminal and our sleeping children but a paper clip and a tension wrench?

The door handle moves under my palm and the door easily pushes open. The apartment is dark, the shades drawn tight against the outside, and I fumble for a light switch. The air inside is thick, a fug of smoke and something greasy. The light switch clicks but the room remains dark. Awesome. I pull out my flashlight. Years ago, when I'd gotten out of rehab, before Brandt got me the clerk job, he sent me an LED tactical flashlight. Something to help me on the late-night walks to the train after work. He'd also gotten me a can of mace. The flashlight is small, but blinding. Only five inches or so, but man, would that thing burn the shit out of your retinas if you looked right at it. I've carried it around on my keychain ever since.

In the kitchen the light flickers when I click the switch, but it comes on, illuminating the garbage and piles of trash, food, and flies. I almost gag, the smell is so bad. The lower cabinets, the wood stripped, list toward the back of the kitchen. The floor is sloped. The sink is filled, overflowing onto the countertops. There are bags of trash on the floor, more McDonald's cups than I can count. I back out slowly and survey the small living room. There is a single couch, sunken almost to the floor, the cushions blackened and burned in spots.

What did I expect, the Ritz? Such a Pop thing to think. I almost laugh.

I don't need luxurious. I don't even need clean. I just need walls.

I find a light bulb under the sink in the kitchen, and it fits the lamp in the living room. There is a single large braided rug on the floor and I sit, crossing my legs, and retrieve my laptop. It boots up and looks for a Wi-Fi signal. Nothing. I curse. I didn't want to tether to a phone this soon. Police need your IP to track you: a unique combination of your device ID and your network ID. I can make my burner smartphone a hot spot but it's an opening: every session becomes a chance for exposure. My best shot is to limit my sessions. If Brandt ever contacts me either by email or phone and gets either of those two IDs, I'm found. It won't take long for Brandt to figure out I've ditched my real phone. I've got the smartest guy I've ever known tracking me.

I go right to Peter's emails. There are a bunch from Tom at work: *Buddy, are you ok? I just heard a crazy rumor.* I check his Facebook. Nothing public. I remember the Moleskine.

I flip to the back and voilà, there it is: a full page of passwords. Like a true skeptic, his IDs and passcodes aren't identified by site, just listed out. It's easy enough to figure out, which username and password combinations go with which sites. I'm in: Facebook and Healing Hope. I'm almost manic with the rush of it, opening new windows, typing in new passwords with shaky fingers. I am certain of these facts: someone killed him, and there will be clues online. There have to be, it's all I have. I have no doubt I'll beat Brandt to the punch because I have no doubt Brandt is very busy looking too closely at me.

An hour passes, maybe more. It is now decidedly dark outside, which means it's dark in the shithole. I've found nothing. Absolutely fucking nothing. This apartment is a sauna. A stinking, garbage-filled, hot wasteland. I can't go out. I don't dare open a window. Outside I hear yelling, the pulse of a subwoofer, the crash of broken glass, a beer bottle or a window, it all sounds the same. I miss my quiet street. Tim.

I explore the rest of the apartment. The toilet is shit-stained. The bedroom smells like piss, the hardwood floors are sticky; my flats make a smacking sound when I walk. It's still better than jail.

The rug in the living room is fine. I'll be fine. In the living room, my computer is blinking, a message on the Healing Hope board. I left it logged in, such a stupid mistake. If Brandt ever sees Peter's name active, he'll know it's me.

Peter's inbox is blinking. I expect Brandt.

WinPA99: Hello, Edie.

I gasp out loud. *PLipsky: Who is this??* I type furiously.

WinPA99: An old friend.

PLipsky: I don't have any friends.

WinPA99: Not of yours. Of Peter's. And Colleen's.

Colleen, Peter's wife, killed by Lilith over fifteen years ago. I type five replies and delete them all. My heart and mind race. Before I can figure out how to reply, a message comes through: *No internet service.* When I finally log back on, WinPA99 is gone. I wait for her to log back on for hours, but she never shows.

. . .

In the category of irony, I sleep like a baby. Someday I'll analyze that but for today, I need a uniform. Specifically, something a private investigator would wear—a blazer and a pair of clean slacks, maybe a pair of jeans. I can't get away with impersonating a cop, all it would take is one nervous person, one suspicion and a tip to the police. When all this is over, I don't need to be caught up in the hassle of *actually* breaking the law.

And since I'm going to have to live here, in this hovel, I can't be constantly distracted by the sounds of skittering rats in the kitchen or the blink of a retreating cockroach. I'm going to need supplies.

With my new dark shag and my plastic hipster glasses, I should be unrecognizable, at least temporarily. The CCTVs on the buses and trains are low resolution, grainy and muted. If anything, I'm worried about becoming too comfortable. I try to imagine myself two weeks, a month, from now. Still camped out in Porter's greasy apartment, trying to solve Peter's murder. No job. No Tim. No Dylan.

At the thought of Tim, my stomach knots. I can't risk a call or a text to him; he's such a rule follower. An old church lady stuck inside that hulking body. What could he think? Does he believe I'm a murderer? Have the police questioned him? Asked him what he knows about me, really? I try to envision the conversation, what would he say? *She likes to break into my apartment sometimes, but other than that she's law-abiding.* I try to imagine their questioning: friends, family? Aside from Dylan, he wouldn't know the answers.

Dylan.

Dylan must be going crazy. I imagine Brandt, calm, reassuring, trying to question Dylan. Has he seen me? Have I called? Emailed? What did he know about what I'd been doing? My notebooks? I envision him calling my cell phone over and over, the phone off, going straight to voice mail. And hanging up. I can see Dylan pacing his apartment. He'll lose his mind. He's always been so protective, his own happiness blurred with mine, dependent on me. Sometimes suffocating, mostly sweet.

I remember a middle-of-the-night phone call, maybe two years ago. After he'd married Camille, his voice hoarse and cloying into the phone: *I saved you that day, in the woods, right? I did, didn't I?*

I open my burner phone, the smart one. I send him a text from one of my anonymous email accounts: *Hey bro. I'm fine. I'm off the grid for now. Need to solve a problem. I'll be in touch. Love you, E.*

I have no idea if I'm in the news. Last night, after WinPA99 logged off, I shut everything down. Sat on that sticky rug and tried to focus. In the back of Peter's Moleskine I began to write down what I knew: Peter was dead. His wife was dead. The police must think I killed him. Someone came to his apartment after I left at six thirty but before he would have gone to work around eight and they killed him.

Someone must have seen me leave. How did he die? I could trawl the internet newspapers, but the faster option is to visit the PPD site. It keeps a running ticker of all city crime. I click on the 14th district, where Peter's apartment resides, and there it is: *At 7:05 a.m., a man named Peter Lipsky was found shot dead in his Chestnut Hill apartment from two gunshot wounds. Neighbor called 911. Medic #9B responded and pronounced the victim dead at 8 a.m., on the scene. The investigation is ongoing with the Homicide Unit. PPD are seeking person of interest Edie Beckett, 30, in relation to the crime.* A small picture of me, taken from my city employee ID, a little grainy but with definitive long, dirty blond hair, is centered under the brief article.

He was shot? Who found him? Why didn't his neighbors hear the gun? I don't even own a gun. Did Peter?

I was a person of interest. Did that mean a suspect, or a witness?

• • •

When I was nineteen, Brandt took me out for coffee. I hadn't been to rehab yet, but I was trying to dry out and failing. Pop was still alive, although bumbling around our row home a bit lost. Both Dylan and I still slept in our bedrooms upstairs, Dylan flitting out with his friends, but coming home at night. Watching old movies and TV reruns, eating peanut butter out of the jar. And always, always drinking. The years before rehab but after Lilith are hazy, smudged together like a drab watercolor. I know the liquor did that. I was grateful for it.

Brandt twirled the mug in his hands, the coffee a light tan, overburdened with half-and-half poured from a half-dozen plastic cups. He asked me what I wanted to do. I'd completed three semesters at community college by this point, did I want to finish? I'd recently dropped out because of low grades and general disinterest. I had only shrugged, a nonanswer.

"I saw Lilith today." He'd said it slowly, a softly spoken confession, and I remember feeling like all the air had been sucked right out of the dirty front window of that dingy diner. This was before Dylan had started visiting her, before I knew that anyone had seen her. The idea of Lilith in prison existed to me only in theory, suspended in some metaphysical time and place. I didn't know where Muncy, Pennsylvania, was. I'd never even heard of it. Death row was a concept I'd only seen in movies: black and soulless. She'd only just gone up there two years before; it had taken over two years to convict and sentence her to death. It felt like a blink.

"And?" I remember laughing, the notion so absurd. Lilith hardly felt real to me anymore. My mother, the murderess. All the memories of my childhood tainted: When she left Dylan and me alone for two days in her small apartment in the Tucker Homes housing project in Grays Ferry, the walls thin and rattly as sheet metal, where did she go? That had been after Pop had her committed, and after she'd been released, he'd moved her back to the city so he could keep an eye on her. We would spend years trying to line our memories up with Lilith's murder timeline. The news stories had died down, but the four-year anniversary had just passed, reviving a rash of articles. I thought the fifth year would be the worst. I expected that.

I hadn't expected the book at the fifteenth.

The thing is, Lilith made Brandt's career. Because of her, he was a homicide detective, maybe years before he would have been promoted. He was young, less than thirty when it happened. It came with a substantial pay raise. The idea that he could be a career detective, not just a beat cop. Lilith, inadvertently, gave Brandt an identity. In the endless dissection of facts and blurring with fiction, Gil Brandt became famous.

When I laughed, Brandt had looked at me as though I was maybe like her: crazy, evil-prone. It wasn't a terrible assumption. So much about me was like her: not just our looks, but the way we spoke, slowly and deliberately, the way we both bit our lower lip when we were thinking. Neither of us could whistle or snap our fingers. How many other shared genetic deficiencies were threaded through our blood?

Later, he walked me home. Pop was gone and Brandt was off duty, so he lingered. We sat on Pop's front step, the wood sagging underneath us, and talked. I'd run into the bathroom and nipped off a vodka bottle to settle my jangling nerves, so most of the conversation is lost to me. But I remember asking him how he liked homicide now that the fame was fading, now that he was a million news cycles away from the trial and he was no longer inextricably tied to the name Lilith Wade. I remember Brandt telling me, *Whoever seems to be the guiltiest that first day, nine times out of ten is guilty.* I remember telling him it seemed like an easy job, then. His laugh when I said that charmed me. It was the first time he'd seemed like a person to me, real flesh and blood, his skin warm.

I'll blame the confusion, my age, the vodka.

When I think of it now, and I hardly ever do, I have to keep my eyes closed. I was young. It was ten years ago.

"How was she?" I had asked, my breath catching, my lungs aching.

"Lilith?" He had reached over and plucked a yellow leaf from the shoulder of my sweater, twirled it by the stem in his fingers. "She's . . . she's not there. She didn't know who I was. I asked her questions, about you, about Dylan. Just to gauge her mental state. Nothing she said made sense." He paused, watching me. "She'll only get worse. Prison does that. There are studies that show what isolation does to people with bi-polar disorder."

"Did she remember us?" There was no hope in my voice, my feelings for Lilith had deadened. Brandt hesitated before I said, "I really don't care either way."

His hand was still on my shoulder and the knuckle of his thumb touched my cheek. I turned my face into it.

"Edie," Brandt had started to say, but never finished be-cause I leaned forward and kissed him. His lips were cool and dry under mine, but he kissed me back, if only for a second. He stood quickly, clasping my hand in his, and gave me a regretful smile.

At the time, I hadn't been embarrassed. I'd been, more than anything, determined to change his mind. I was twenty, damaged, semi-infamous, flush with self-importance, and half drunk. He left quickly after that, but sent me a text: *I'm sorry.*

He'd gone home to his wife.

By the time he wasn't married anymore, I didn't want him. Not that he ever made it known to me that he was available. In fact, I went years without seeing him or hearing a peep. The only thing we had between us was an overarching sense of wrongness about our friendship.

Then Pop had his stroke. After the funeral, the course of our relationship flipped upside-down, and I'd never been able to right it.

I'd drunk more than I could handle—I was getting used to that feeling, my feet clumsy and my legs wobbly, the idle buzzing in my head, my vision hazy and sleepy from the alcohol. Lilith had been arrested almost a decade earlier, and I had been anticipating the ten-year anniversary specials. But Pop's death made barely a ripple in the news cycle, and I'd been surprised and relieved. When Brandt showed up at Pop's house, the catering cold and slimy on the kitchen table, Dylan and Camille with locked hands on the sofa, I'd been grateful for someone to talk to. Pop's buddies from the plant seemed content to laugh and reminisce for hours, and I felt invisible, porous, in the hot kitchen, the greasy smell of fried chicken turning my stomach. But suddenly, Brandt was there, his presence both out of place and urgently appreciated. I remember taking his hand, Dylan shooting us a sharp look as I led him outside. I remember asking him to drive me home. I'd moved into my own apartment by then, a shoebox, really, just two rooms: a living room/kitchenette and one bedroom.

The seduction was more of a feeling than an idea, something pressing down on me, weighty and breathless. I'd felt Brandt's hand tap my arm, as his car sped through the darkened streets, the transfer of electricity between us, like a movie, the streetlamps flashing like a strobe—illicit and secretive. I remember licking my lips, holding his hand against my thigh as he drove, my palm pressing down on his wrist, feeling the nervous flex of his tendons. I remember the flush feeling of power—at twenty-five, I'd never seduced anyone before. Sex, sure, mostly drunken. There was something different about the pursuit of someone, the conscious decision to beguile another person. This man, nearly fifteen years my senior, seemed a good place to start. Our shared history. The fact that he cared so much for me.

In my apartment, I remember pouring him a drink. The two fingers of bourbon Pop liked to drink, over ice. I didn't ask, I just did it, thinking that made me more adult. Isn't this what men who were forty did? The idea of forty was foreign, light-years away. I don't remember what we talked about, probably Pop. I played Nina Simone, swaying my hips to the music while I mixed drinks at my dry bar and feeling his eyes on me, even from behind. I told Brandt about when I had scarlet fever and Lilith, for a few nights, was my mother. He tried to talk to me about her, to tell me about the last time he'd seen her, and I remember kissing him to shut him up, my mouth pressing against his, clumsy and rough, our teeth clinking. I remember wondering if his wife had done it better. If he had a girlfriend. I remember him protesting, softly, a bit too weakly to be effective, even while his hand stayed trained on my waist, his chest rising and falling with hitching breaths.

I remember stripping, right there in the living room, the flash of a television on mute, playing a rerun of *M*A*S*H*.

I remember the feeling of his bare shoulders under my fingertips, his thighs between mine as I straddled him on my sofa. The gentle skim of his palm up my side, like a feather. I remember he stayed in my apartment, rubbed my back when I vomited up the vodka. He was never unkind.

I remember when he said it was a mistake and I closed my eyes when I agreed with him. *Yes, absolutely. Inappropriate.*

And then, "Edie, we could never have a real relationship. Because of who we are." He said this reasonably, like of course I should know this and what he'd meant was because of who I was. Who Lilith was. It was a ripple effect.

I remember smiling brightly as I said good-bye, a coy turn of my chin, to cover the hurt at his leaving. He'd paused in the doorway, rubbing his hand along his jaw as he asked if I'd be okay. I had laughed. I was always okay, I told him, leaning up to kiss his cheek, pressing myself against him, a last-ditch effort to get him to stay. He'd pulled me against him, holding me there, like a desperate, drowning hug.

I never waited for him to call. I knew he wouldn't.

A year later, my car smashed against a tree. He saved me, got me a job, gave me a flashlight and a can of Mace. I'd accepted his kindness and his favor, both humiliated and grateful, eyes averted, trying not to think of the taste of his mouth, the stipple of his skin beneath my fingertips.

And now here we were, thrown together again. Maybe I would go my whole life with Brandt hovering around the fringes. He'd become part of my landscape.

If anyone could find me, Brandt could.

CHAPTER 8

Gil Brandt, Philadelphia Police Department, Homicide Division,
August 2016

Edie Beckett.

Her name had haunted him more in his life than any other. It's a cliché, right? The cop with the one case he can't shake? Usually, it's a victim that gets to them. A picture. Sometimes a child. Sometimes a beautiful woman, her lips parted in death, that makes the heart ache. The idea that she could have had so much more. Maybe that's sexist. Hell, it's probably sexist. Still, cops don't get moony over a man. Sexist or not, facts are facts.

Not that he was moony. Without getting all poetic about it, something about her plucked the right string inside him. Yes, he'd gotten her a job. Yes, he'd made her pledge her sobriety. Yes, admittedly, he sometimes accidentally on purpose ended up on her train, at her coffee shop, her sandwich cart. He even relied on her, occasionally, to find someone for him. She always came through—a seemingly untethered victim, no next of kin, no connections to anyone. She was smart as a whip, that girl. An hour on the internet and she'd present him with not just a name, but also an address, sometimes a phone number, a place of employment. *A second cousin, once removed,* she'd say with a smirk. He'd buy her coffee as a thank-you, just to watch her talk.

Sometimes while she talked, her hands moving, he'd think of them on his chest. The night when the moonlight lit her skin on fire, her hair on his face.

He wasn't in love with her. Call him curious. Even fascinated. Whatever you called it, it was inappropriate, any idiot knew that. She was fifteen years younger than him. He made a name for himself off her mother's back. Still, he could never quite shake her off. He'd go weeks, months, without thinking about her and then her name would pop up: on paperwork, in the system, or like that one night, on the radio. He'd snapped up the call so fast, driven to the tree, the car crumpled like a Coke can against the trunk at 2:00 a.m. There'd been a passenger in the car, a guy. Walked away without a scratch—both did. He told the guy to bug off. The guy had protested, wanted to make sure Edie was okay. He had lipstick smeared on the corner of his mouth.

That's how it was with them. Which was fine with Brandt. Until he saw her name, that loopy cursive scrawl on the bottom of the receipt from Lockers, and it had felt like a sucker shot right to the kidney.

"I want in on this one," Brandt had told Merket. Lincoln Merket, the closest thing he had to a partner, gave him a look.

"Is this the lady killer's daughter?" He was chewing a beef jerky. Merket was trying to quit smoking. He chewed beef jerky when he wanted a smoke. His blood pressure had to be sky high by now, with all that salt. The lip-smacking set Brandt's teeth on edge and their whole cubicle area smelled like smoked meat.

"Yeah." Brandt avoided eye contact and booted up his computer. "Hey, remember that horrible car fire a few years back? Two people died?"

"Yeah, when half of Bella Vista smelled like a barbecue?" Merket loved that story. When he told it, people recoiled at that line. He waited for the punch line, *Hey, meat is meat.* He said the neighbors came outside, thought it was block party day. Brandt knew Merket made that part up.

"That's what this whole office smells like," Brandt said, but Merket only grinned.

Brandt went along when they banged through her apartment door. When the techs and the officers and two other detectives had pulled open her drawers, emptied her closets. Her undergarments had littered the bed, the lacy bras, and Brandt briefly wondered which one he'd seen before. Perhaps touched.

When her desk had been dismantled, they found everything: her notebooks, detailed drawings of their houses, long lists of comings and goings of victims' families, and he'd felt sick. All this time, he'd felt like he knew her: that by seeing her on the subway every two months, or buying her coffee, or dropping by her desk with a file, he'd known the scope of her life. He'd assumed it had been small. Invisible, even. Work. Home. Her brother. That she'd shrunk herself down because of her mother; blended in gray with the city and the sky and the buildings and the CJC, the grayest, dreariest place to work. But now here he was, evidence of the depth of her malfunction splayed out in her own bedroom. Indefensible, really. That's the part that made him angry. The conversations around him among the techs, littered with chatter and innuendo and the assumption of guilt. He'd been so stupid. Willfully ignorant. He'd been angry with himself, his jaw set, his teeth grinding as everyone else cataloged and bagged and dusted and printed.

The neat notebooks, that perfect, rounded penmanship, bubbly—frozen in tenth grade along with the rest of her. The thickest notebook had been the Dresdens. Edie Beckett had stood outside their house, not just once. She watched them eat dinner and get in a fight, the twins raucous and the young girl despondent. Mrs. Dresden, helpless. They watched television, even got ready for bed. She documented Mr. Dresden's affair, even speculating in the margins (with *!!*) about how and when she would tell his wife. At the bottom of every third page, she'd recorded the daughter's swim times, for fuck's sake.

What could be the logical, sane reason to sleep with a man whose wife had been killed by your own mother? There was nothing to suggest that Peter Lipsky knew who Edie was and yet, a detailed accounting of Peter's life in Edie's hand. She'd *preyed* on him. But why kill him?

Psychosis? Fugue state? What on earth was her angle?

Later, at his desk, he'd look back at that receipt from Lockers and the list of drinks. Four beers and six vodka tonics. When asked, his buddies would say that Lipsky drank the beer. Which means Edie had six—*six!*—vodka tonics. A good amount for anyone, but she was a buck ten soaking wet. She would have been out-of-her-mind drunk. Would she have even known what she was doing? Could she have killed him in a blackout? With whose gun?

He looked over at Merket, chewing like cud and clicking around his computer, his eyes glazed and bloodshot.

If Brandt walked away now, took another case, begged a full plate, she'd be in the wind. Gone. Edie was smarter than any of them, even Brandt. His only advantage was that he knew her. Or he used to think he did.

When the condom in Peter Lipsky's trash came back positive for Edie's DNA, he felt the pain right in his side.

He had originally wanted in to save her. That was hardly an option anymore.

Dear God, Edie, what have you done?

CHAPTER 9

Day 2: Saturday, August 6, 2016

The best thrift store in Philly is two blocks from my apartment, which immediately discounts the place. Who knows how many guys Brandt has staking out my street. In addition, the clerks there know me. You can fool a camera with some hair dye and fake glasses but not a person. Instead I take the 23 bus to the store in Germantown and hope they have a fraction of the inventory.

In every doorway, I make sure to keep my head down, looking at my phone, digging through my purse. Anything to avoid the cameras that are positioned at every storefront.

Inside the racks are stuffed with clothes, and the furniture is positioned in the back. I make my way to the Misses Professional Wear section. The plastic yellow sign is faded and old, perched on a rack overstuffed with black and beige. I find a tan, nicely cut jacket, a few pairs of black pants, some white button-up shirts. A pair of black women's loafers in reasonably good shape. I throw in two pairs of khaki shorts, a few tank tops, and T-shirts. My total comes to $78.

At the back of the store, I change in the restroom. A black

T-shirt under the tan jacket and a pair of black pants. I roll everything else up in tight camping rolls, and store it all in my messenger bag. When I leave, the clerk behind the desk doesn't even look up.

I board the Broad Street Line at Erie Station. The train is only half full and I'm able to snag a seat.

"Excuse me, but mind if I sit?" The man is middle-aged, gray, dressed in jeans and a Phillies T-shirt. He has a soft scruff around his chin and his face is flat, his nose pressed and mouth pinched, as though hit with a frying pan. His voice rumbles, throaty and deep.

"I'm so sorry, but would you mind?" I gesture to the empty seats in front of me. "I'm not feeling well."

He nods good-naturedly, but takes the seat directly across from me.

"Is your name Delilah?" he asks, leaning over the aisle as the train lurches forward. I shake my head and pretend to be involved in my phone. I type furiously in the notes section, hoping he'll think it's a text to a friend and leave me alone.

"You look like a friend of a friend, are you sure you're not Delilah?"

"No," I say shortly, and pull out Peter's Moleskine and flip through it, feigning absorption.

"Do you think they'll strike next week?" The man is talking again, amiable. "Seems to be an every-other-month threat lately."

"Yeah, I don't know," I mumble, and the train lurches to a stop, then starts again. Out of the corner of my eye I watch him, and he's studying me. He clears his throat a few times, a low, garbled sound, like he's trying to get my attention.

When the train stops at City Hall, two stops before mine, I get off, unnerved by the gray man, despite the fact that it's a block from my old job—one can only assume I've been fired—and despite the fact that if I were Brandt, searching for me, I'd hover around the CJC. I duck into an alleyway and make my way south, checking the address I'd looked up and jotted down in Peter's Moleskine. I pass no fewer than four uniformed police officers on my walk, and my heart hammering at the sight of every one.

I don't look up. I don't look in the direction of the CJC. I don't look as I hustle past Lockers. I just move as fast as I can, with the flow of foot traffic through Center City, my eyes on the pavement.

The apartment building has a green awning, boasting "Eagle Green Apartments," and the front door is locked with a security code. Fortunately, the place is busy. I stand on the stoop and pretend to call someone, muttering "Damnit, pick up" over and over. In ten minutes, three different tenants enter, backpacked young kids, barely twenty, and a tall, raven-haired girl dressed in an eyelet dress.

"Do you need to get in?" she asks, her eyes dopey and mouth slack, expressionless. She looks past me, back out onto the street.

"I'm looking for Lindy Cook. Do you know her?" I ask.

"Nah. But we all keep to ourselves here." She punches in the code—1415—and holds the door open with the guileless trust of a kid whose life has been bankrolled.

The lobby is filthy. It hasn't been cleaned in years. Dust and dirt gather along the edges and a small collection of take-out bags are crumpled into the corners by the flow of foot traffic, rather than the deliberate push of a broom. There are thirty-five units, and Lindy Cook's mailbox is labeled #17.

I take the stairs to the third floor, figuring five floors, seven units on each floor. I guess correctly and I'm standing in front of #17, preparing to knock, breathing in and out, when the door flings open.

Lindy lets out a small scream. "You scared the living crap out of me," she says with a laugh. If I'd been a man, she would have called the cops already, but I'm a woman, so maybe I'm selling something. Avon or whatever.

"Are you Lindy Cook?" I deepen my voice, going for authoritative. For a minute I think she'll recognize me: the girl who followed her to work one day. That girl had long light-colored hair. The woman in front of her has dark, choppy hair and black glasses. People are distracted by glasses, the glint of the glass, the way they almost seem to change the shape of your face, your nose.

She steps back, eyes me suspiciously. "Yes?" Her voice tilts upward, an unintended question mark at the end. She takes in my tan jacket, my black pants, my worn professional look.

"My name is . . ." I hesitate because I didn't think about what I'd call myself. Stupidest rookie mistake in the world, I guess, but hey, I'm not *actually* a lifelong criminal. Finally, I introduce myself. "Jill Brand." It's either genius or incredibly stupid, and I guess I'll figure out which eventually. "I'm a private investigator, looking into the death of Peter Lipsky. I was hired by his . . . brother."

She sniffs for a minute and says, "It's so sad." Then she narrows her eyes. "I didn't know he had a brother."

"Oh yeah, from Minneapolis." Maybe when I'm done with this bullshit, I'll become a writer. "He didn't want to count on the cops, so he called me. Said he'd feel better having someone who can dedicate twenty-four-seven to solving this crime."

"You're a woman," she says finally, stupidly. "Do you have like a badge or anything?"

"Miss," I say, condescendingly. "It's illegal for PIs to carry a badge. Could be seen as impersonating an officer. Can I just ask you a few questions?"

"I guess." She looks at the wall behind her; the clock blinks 11:13 a.m. She has a duffel bag slung over her shoulder and is dressed in leggings and a thin T-shirt. Probably on her way to the studio. "I talked to a cop yesterday, I don't remember his name. Do you know him?"

I follow her inside. I don't answer her question about the cop.

"I've only got about five minutes, I'm late anyway." The apartment is dark and small, a little shitty, but it's clean and smells like some kind of flowery candle. I miss my shower, my floral shampoo, air fresheners. I can see into her bedroom, the bed is made, there is art on the walls, a pink shaggy throw rug in the living room to give the place some personality.

The kitchenette and the living room share a space. Between them is a pub table with two high-top chairs. She perches against one, not quite sitting, not quite standing, and looks at me expectantly.

"How did you know Peter Lipsky?" I take out Peter's Moleskine and dig for a pen. For a heartbeat, I think that she might recognize it. She blows her blond bangs up out of her eyes.

"We dated for a while," she says. *Dated*. I knew they'd bonded, but hadn't known it was romantic. It's not as unusual as it sounds. Victims of violent crimes often feel isolated from the rest of the world and find an affinity in each other. I should know, after all. I wait for her to elaborate. After a few seconds, she goes on. "We broke up a few months ago. I haven't talked to him much lately." She stops, grabs a tissue from the table, and wipes under her eyes. "I'm sorry, it's weird. We broke up, I didn't think about him for days at a time, but then I heard on the news he was murdered, I mean *shot*, for God's sake, it gets to you, ya know? I never knew anyone who was shot before. I mean, it's so crazy, especially because of his wife and all."

"His wife? He's married?" I ask, pretending to write, avoiding eye contact.

"No, his wife was murdered maybe fifteen years ago. So

they were both murdered. Isn't that odd?" She is folding the tissue into tiny squares.

"Do you think they're connected?" I ask.

Lindy pushes herself back onto the high-top chair, her bag falling at her feet. I know the interview is going to be longer than five minutes. "No, God, no. His wife's murderer is in prison for life. She was that famous serial killer from 2001. There was a book on her."

"What book?" I ask and my voice cracks.

"*The Serrated Edge.*" She practically spits the title out. "Lilith Wade. Know her?"

I almost choke, but recover. "Of course." I force out a little laugh. "Doesn't everyone?"

She makes a face and gets up to get herself a bottle of water from the fridge. She brings one back to me and takes a long drink. "She killed my mother, too." She says it so casually, I think at first that I've heard her wrong.

"I'm so sorry," I say automatically.

She shrugs. "I hardly knew her. I certainly don't remember her. But that's how Peter and I met. In a grief forum for people who are victims of violent crimes."

"Oh." I write *murder from 2001?* in the notebook, but only because Lindy's watching. "So, why did you and Peter break up?"

"Oh, I don't know. We're both in different places. I'm trying to have a career. He's . . . stagnant. He doesn't want to change or grow or do anything interesting with his life. Ever since that book came out, he's been unstable or something. He said he thinks someone's been breaking into his house."

"Breaking into his house?" I think of crime track. Only one report. Who would break into Peter's house?

She gives a big sigh and tears the tissue in half, then in half again. She stares at her hands, her fingers flexing while she talks. "He said he didn't think his wife was killed by Lilith

Wade. That someone else did it, and now they're after him and the book was the . . . impetus. That's the word he used. *Impetus*. I mean, who says that?" She shakes her head. "I just couldn't deal with it anymore. I had my own shit going on, my own life to get together. But now . . . maybe someone really was after him. Maybe I should have taken him more seriously. But honestly, we should never have been a couple. He's old anyway." Her eyes flit to me. "Sorry."

"That's fine. Peter was fifteen years older than I am," I say mildly.

She looks surprised. "Really? Oh, I thought you were older." She studies me for a minute. "Maybe it's your hair or something."

"Who broke up with whom?" I feign boredom, as if this whole line of questioning is mundane. But I'm fascinated, this too-young girl and Peter, she so naive and half-dumb and he so rigid and unyielding. They made an unlikely pair.

"I broke up with him. He cried about it." She shrugs. "I felt bad, I really did. I liked Peter, but we didn't love each other. I didn't love him, and he only loved his ex. He was like *obsessed* with her."

"The wife who was killed?" I ask, my head tilted.

"Yeah, that's what I meant." She stands up. "I should really go."

"Okay, just a few more questions?" I stand up, too, but make no move toward the door. "Did he say anything else about the break-ins?"

"There was only one definitive one, he said. He said he *thought* someone had been in his apartment other times, but he couldn't prove it. One of our last dates was absolutely terrible. We bickered the whole time. I gave him a blow job in the parking lot of the movie theater, in his car. He took me home first, and then called me hours later saying his house was wrecked." She looked around the room, lost for a moment, her eyes settling on the far wall: a collection of black-and-white photographs hung in plain black frames. "I thought he'd made it up, honestly. Like he wanted to come here to stay. I told him to call the police, but that I had rehearsal in the morning and had to go to bed. He said I was insensitive. I broke up with him a few days later. I never figured out if he was unstable or telling the truth or what." She sighs dramatically. "I guess we know now. Who would be after him? It makes no sense."

"When did you talk to him last?"

"You know, it was the weirdest thing. He called me. The day before he was killed."

"The day before?" My voice is sharp, loud, and my heart picks up speed. She looks at me oddly.

"Yeah, at like four in the afternoon or something. The cop who came here and questioned me said it was before he went to the bar. He said he was so happy to get my email. I told him I never sent him an email and then he got pissed and accused me of playing games and said he had to go. I told that detective."

My email. From the fake Lindy account, to get his password. Brandt had been here. Already.

"Can I ask where you were the morning Peter was killed?" I ask.

She laughs, a brittle, hollow sound. "Sure. I was at the studio where I train until late the evening before and spent the night at Alek Romanov's apartment. I was still at his place until eight that morning, when we left for the studio."

"Alek Romanov?"

"One of the principal dancers in the company." She stood tall, straightened her shoulders. "My new boyfriend." She slings her bag up over her shoulder. "It's just so bizarre," she says, finally, her teeth biting her lower lip.

"What's that?" I put the Moleskine and pen back into my messenger bag.

"He calls me a little over twelve hours before he's killed? We hadn't spoken for weeks." She shakes her head. She opens the door and gestures for me to walk through. Behind me, she locks the door, the deadbolt. The hallway smells like marijuana. I think of the black-haired girl from the lobby. "It almost makes me look like I had something to do with it."

"Did you?" I force my face impassive, like it's a joke.

She smiles then, but her gaze is fixed out the window, down the hall, behind me. "No." Her eyes snap to mine and she brushes her hair back from her shoulder. "Of course not."

• • •

I wait around the corner. Lindy rushes off toward the Pennsylvania ballet building, only a few blocks from Eagle Green Apartments. I punch the key code, 1415, and I'm back into the lobby. I take the steps two at a time until I'm back on the third floor, standing outside #17 again.

I retrieve my lock pick kit from my messenger bag, and for show, I knock on the door. There are no apartments across the hall, Lindy's apartment faces the stairwell, but you never know. I angle my body away against the side of the door, and work the tension wrench with my left hand and the pick with my right. When I feel the locks click, the deadbolt turn, I flick open the door and shut it quickly, but quietly, behind me.

I head straight for the bedroom. Her nightstand holds no surprises: a box of condoms, a nail file, hand cream, and a vibrator. Her room is neat and I sift through the clothes in her closet, haphazardly. I lift the mattress but it's bare.

In the bathroom, I rifle through the drawers: shampoo, conditioner, Vaseline, and hair gel. A small bag of makeup. I recall the dew of her skin, fresh with cold cream.

Her living room is sparse, all IKEA coffee tables and end tables and no hidden drawers anywhere. I turn over the couch cushions, all the while asking myself, *What exactly am*

I looking for? I don't know, but I know whatever she said to me wasn't exactly the truth. I could tell in the way her eyes slid sideways, in the twitch of her mouth. I could see it in her face, like a rearrangement of her features when she said *of course not*, as though she were happy to get away with something. But what? And did I think a full written confession would be found here, in her apartment, between the high-fiber pasta and a box of quinoa?

The kitchenette is small, the stove half the size of a standard stove, the oven barely large enough for a brownie pan. Her refrigerator is almost empty, except for a half gallon of skim milk and an apple. Some leftover takeout. I slam the door shut, frustrated.

She still owns a landline phone, odd for a millennial. The drawer under the phone is filled with junk: pens and Post-it notes, old performance programs, and a mess of business cards for restaurants and bars, some with phone numbers scrawled on the back, some plain. At the bottom was a Chinese menu, torn in half. Scrawled across the top were the words *Lockers @ 4.*

My heart thuds in my chest. Had Lindy been at Lockers on Thursday? I would have noticed her. It could, of course, have been another day, another date altogether. Hardly seemed feasible. I remember Tom's email to Peter: *Lockers, ok? Everyone's going at 4.*

I clicked through her previous calls, all 1-800 numbers, seemingly telemarketers. Until Thursday afternoon, then three calls to Peter Lipsky's cell phone (3:45 p.m., 3:50 p.m., 4:01 p.m.). Lindy lied. Peter hadn't called her.

Lindy had called Peter.

I fold the Chinese menu and stick it in my bag. I scan the apartment, making sure everything I had touched was back the way it should have been. Back out in the hallway, I use the lock pick kit to relock the deadbolt.

"Did you find what you needed?"

The tall, dark-haired girl is standing behind me again, her eyes scanning up and down, alert this time.

"I did, thanks!" I say, too brightly. "Just on my way out."

"The girl who lives here is hardly ever around," she says, blocking my way to the stairwell.

"Oh, really? I got to talk to her quickly, but she had to run out. I left my notebook in there, but I guess she's gone now. I'll call her later," I say, and take a step forward. The tall girl doesn't move.

I have a thought and retrieve my phone from my bag. I flick to Peter's Facebook page and blow up his profile pic, standing next to a bike on a mountain, white peaks behind his head. "Have you seen this guy here?" I ask her. She takes the phone from me and blows it up. Her nails are purple, glittery, and filed to sharp points.

"Oh yeah. I think he was her boyfriend for a while. Then I didn't see him for a few weeks, and then he was back. Last week sometime. Banging on the door. Begging her to let him in. I don't even know for sure if she was home." She pointed down the hall. "I live right there. I cracked the door to see what the commotion was. He seemed pretty fired up."

"Then what happened?"

"I don't know. I guess he left. I haven't seen him again."

"Thanks, you've been helpful," I tell her, and her face breaks into a smile. She moves to the side and lets me pass.

"You a cop? Is she in trouble or something?" she asks me, motioning toward Lindy's door.

"No, why?"

"The cops were here yesterday, waiting around for her." She gives me an appraising look, and in a flash I realize that this girl is far from a dummy. "They asked me the same question, you know? About that guy?"

"Oh yeah?"

"Yeah, I told them the same thing I told you. But then they said he was killed. Do they think she did it?"

"I don't know. Listen, thanks, okay?" I edge past her and jog down the steps. When I turn on the landing, I can see her above me, looking down, her hair curtained over her face.

She laughs, and the sound echoes in the empty hallway. "I never liked that stuck-up bitch anyway," she yells down, and laughter follows me into the lobby and out into the street.

CHAPTER 10

Day 2: Saturday, August 6, 2016

I hail a cab. The events of the past few days are starting to exhaust me. In the faux leather backseat, I feel my chin dip to my chest. The driver is mangy, pale as a whitefish, his white-blond beard patchy as he talks to me with a thick Eastern European accent, his eyes skipping to mine in the rearview mirror. He is young. Maybe twenty, maybe even younger. I turn my head, watch the cars slide by out the window instead, trying to become unmemorable. At Trent's apartment, the driver puts the car in park and eyes the street.

"You be okay here?" he asks skeptically, taking in my nice-as-new jacket, the black pants.

Trent's apartment is on a block where people don't go outside. Where the sounds of gunshots are regular and almost unnoticeable. Where half of the buildings are abandoned, filled with squatters or addicts, and the other half are crack houses. I lean forward to pay him cash before I see it on the passenger seat. It's a thick hardcover, the jacket bright green slashed through with white and gray superimposed with a grainy, artsy photograph of Lilith. Her stringy hair. Her watchful eyes.

I suck in my breath so hard that he hears it. He lifts up the book, fans out the pages.

"You read it?" he asks me. "So interesting. Not too many . . . ah . . . women who do these things."

"No, sorry." I shove the folded ten at him, jabbing him in the shoulder with it, and he pinches it between two fingers, still talking about the book.

"She killed women," he's saying. "But she had a family. A husband. Children. How do you do that?"

I open the door and step into the street, and I see him shrug and toss the book back down on the passenger seat.

In the apartment, I'm hit with the smell anew, a mix of old food and garbage and rotting dead things. There is a dusty roll of garbage bags on the cheap wooden table and I begin to fill them, breathing through my mouth but still tasting the sourness on my tongue. Everything goes in: dishes and trash, pots and pans crusted hard with food. Under a pile of clothes, I find it. The remains of a rat, its belly gelled and hardened to the floor, in mid-decay. I gag, but I've got nothing in me to bring up.

I put four bulging garbage bags on the fire escape and find a dirty mop in the kitchen pantry. The only cleaning product I can find is Clorox. I do a wide and rough sweep of the floor, scrubbing at the corners, the dark black patch where the rat lay. I scrape it into the plastic bag using a cheap frying pan.

The bleach stings my nostrils and I think of my childhood, Lilith's obsession with bleaching things: from her skin to her clothes to her bedding, her whole house smelled like a hospital. I have a partial memory, a slip of a moment, Dylan and I submerged to our bellies in a bleach bath, the water so hot it scalded his thighs, the skin of his buttocks. She'd scrubbed at us with a loofah, her fingertips raw and ragged, her eyes wild, until my arms were scratched and bleeding. I remember crying, but Dylan was stoic, staring past us at the wall, checked into some world in his head, the way he always coped with Lilith's episodes. Later, she rubbed Vaseline on his burns, not even remorseful, never apologizing. Instead telling us over and over that it had to be done. That we were clean now. By the time we went back to Pop at the end of the summer, we would be healed up. No evidence on our skin, nothing for him to worry about. He always worried about us in Lilith's care. We'd come home and he'd shake my shoulders, brushing the hair out of my eyes, his voice rough-hewn, and rumble, *Was she okay?* Not *Are you okay?* But *was she okay?* I'd never known what he meant: As a mother? As a person?

I knew then, even at eight years old, not to tell Pop about Lilith. Not to talk about the bleach baths, the frantic, frenetic pace of her speech or, days later, the slow unraveling when she wouldn't get out of bed and come downstairs, instead leaving Dylan to care for me. He cooked, I cleaned. We performed as a married couple, huddled together in the same single bed at night, freezing while the window unit blasted out nonstop frigid air; we didn't know how to fix it.

These are the things the book never got right. They didn't know about the bleach.

The Serrated Edge was released in June, authored under a pseudonym: E. Green. It only took me a week to break down and order my own copy. I saw it everywhere: talk shows, papered on the sides of buses, even television commercials. Commercials! I'd never seen a commercial for a book before. Dylan wouldn't even discuss it.

It had arrived at my apartment two days later in a brown cardboard book-shaped box, so innocuous compared to the time bomb that was inside. I skimmed the whole thing at first, in a frenzy. Looking for pieces of me: Chad Fink. Faithful. *Hazel.* There was nothing. Then I went back, read a chapter a day, slow and methodical, dissecting them. Highlighting truths and writing notes in the margins.

The book itself was narrated like a novel, with snippets of interviews from people in Lilith's past. Compelling, even if I held my distance I could see that. Everyone wanted to know: What would make a woman kill with such seeming abandon? Parts of it were maddeningly accurate, while others felt foreign to me. I hadn't known about Lilith's childhood. Never knew she'd been in the system, run away at thirteen. Her only mention of her father was the knife, her "daddy's knife." I learned so much about Lilith as a person.

When the author talked about Dylan or me, he spoke only of our irresponsibility. He devoted a few paragraphs to the day in the woods, right before Pop had her committed. It was like holding up a funhouse mirror: the image nothing like you remember.

When I tried to talk to Dylan about it, he'd snapped, "How would I know any more than you, Edie? Why do you insist on rehashing this?" We were always just trying to move on.

And yet, the author knew so much. How did they know so much? The question never haunted me, keeping me awake at night. It was more like sand in my shoe. A skin of popcorn in my tooth. I'd think about it at odd moments, almost reverently: Who would devote this much time to us? Our family? Our lives?

Dylan sent me an article last week that said they were making the movie. Two months after the book's release. *Green-lighted*, was all the subject said. Lilith would be played by Kate Hudson, which was an unusually perfect fit. Lilith used to be beautiful.

* * *

It's so odd how time can become elastic. I have been in Trent's apartment for three days now, and I can hardly remember not living there. I wonder how my own apartment was faring and I picture it speckled with fingerprint dust, the dresser drawers overturned, the couch cushions ripped open, stuffing exposed. I imagine the shower curtain pooling around the stained ceramic tub, the sink plug extended, a slow drip filling the bowl. Later, I'd learn reality was considerably less violent, more subtle: the way my undergarments were pushed to one side of the drawer, the closet emptied, neat stacks of jeans and sweaters piled in the middle of the room.

Today, I shower. Trent had no curtain to keep the spray from the bathroom and the linoleum turns both slick and still somehow sticky when I am done. I rinse the three days of city grime from my arms, the dirt from beneath my fingernails, the smog from my short hair, once so soft, now stiff and brittle from drugstore dye. I run my fingernails against my thighs using hand soap I found under the bathroom sink. I'll pick up shower gel later today, when I'm out. My nails leave red tracks up my legs, skin prickling like chicken flesh, purpling and blotched, until I feel clean.

It had to be done.

In the living room, the shades drawn, I'm toweling off my hair when the knock comes, swift and angry and the wood rattles in the frame.

"I know you in there." The voice comes from the hallway, loud and low, and I immediately slide sockless feet into my sneakers, throwing my laptop, my current phone, and the power cord into my oversized messenger bag that sits by the fire escape.

Another knock propels me forward, this time the door handle jiggling, shaking so hard I'm afraid it's going to shake loose. The door itself is cheap pine, more suited to an interior door than an exterior. The deadbolt rattles. I throw one leg out the window, into the narrow alcove between row buildings.

"TP, man, I'm gonna shoot the door in. Fuck, man. I need that money." TP. Trent Porter.

A shout and a burst of conversation from the hallway, followed by a slamming door. "He locked up, you ain't gettin' no money now."

I pull my leg in, the black jean streaked with dirt, and sink down, under the window, my heart hammering so loud I can hardly hear.

Complacency will kill me. Caught fugitives are brought down by a single tenet: comfort. They get too comfortable, too easy, too sloppy. They order pizza. Take out their trash. Use an old name. They evade capture and post a picture to Facebook. They start to live normally again, wrongly assume the world has moved on. Forgotten them.

I could just run. It wouldn't be impossible: a new identity, a new name, a new city. What would that do to Dylan? I imagine him panicking, sweating, scouring the internet in an insomnia fugue. For what? How long before I signed something *Edie Beckett* by accident? How much of my life would be devoted to staying underground. Not making a mistake. I already spend most of my life under the radar, trying to dodge the Lilith Wade spotlight. Running away would only cement my guilt in Brandt's eyes. So now I'd be a serial killer's daughter and a wanted murderer? Not likely to be forgotten.

So I stay. I figure out what happened to Peter before Brandt finds me.

I run some calculations. I have enough money to last about three weeks. Maybe four if I stretch it. I cannot cook, or rely on a running refrigerator. All my meals will have to be takeout. Which is fine. I can eat one, maybe two meals a day. I predict I'll be walking quite a bit.

Eventually, I will run out of places to go and opportunities to obtain cash. My disguise will inevitably become compromised.

Three weeks isn't a firm deadline, but it helps if I frame it that way. I have three weeks to find who killed Peter.

I'm only three days in.

Three days. I'm no closer to figuring out Peter's murderer than I was three days ago. I think, briefly, about turning myself in to Brandt. He might arrest me. He also might believe me. I'd never know which way it would fall until it happened. There is nothing Brandt likes to do more than save someone. I am his hobby, his professional touchstone. When he has a bad day, a bad call, a lapse in judgment, at least he helped that *poor, lost girl.* Now, here I am, in trouble again, and it's me against his career.

Lilith made him and I would break him, is that how this would play out? Would he stick his neck out to save me? Even after finding my journals in my bedroom, my DNA at Peter's, my scrawl at the bottom of the Lockers receipt? There is no believable explanation for any of it.

Brandt held everything close to the vest. I'd never known his real feelings, his thoughts. Only glimpses here and there of a detached type of kindness, almost an olive branch, since the night of Pop's funeral. I couldn't even think about it, much less talk about it. And yet, my face flamed whenever I saw him: on the other side of the street, on the subway platform as the train pulled away. My body, in reckless defiance, would viscerally recall what I had mentally sequestered.

When I'm sure the hallway is empty, I retrieve my hastily stored laptop and open my email. I have three waiting from Brandt, as I'd suspected.

Edie, call me. I can help you. I've done it before.

Edie, please.

Edie, whatever happened, we can talk about it. I know you're still here, somewhere.

Goddamn Brandt.

To be safe, I use the window anyway. I pop out between two row buildings, the alley as narrow as a metal trash can and littered with garbage. A hypodermic needle glitters in the small patch of sunlight.

In the street, I walk fast for five blocks north, until the peeling asbestos siding turns to solid brick, and the broken glass windows give way to barred ones and row homes turn to duplexes. I duck into the space between two office buildings, a cement bower, and dial Brandt's number.

He picks up on two rings.

"Brandt, can you stop emailing me?" It comes out with more fire than I mean.

"Beckett," he says, calmly but out of breath like maybe I took him by surprise. When he first picks up, it's loud over the line, blowy like he's outside, the wind whipping through the mouthpiece, and then it suddenly goes silent, the house landing in Oz.

"I only have a minute, you can try to track me but you know it won't work."

"You're using a burner phone," he says.

"Sure."

"Beckett, this is silly. Come talk to us. We're wasting a ton of time trying to track you down. If you're not guilty, we could be finding the real criminal here."

I stay silent. He hasn't indicated how he feels either way, what he thinks.

"Edie," he says. He never calls me Edie. "How drunk were you? Blackout? Were you night-at-the-tree blackout drunk?"

"Fuck you, Brandt. Do you really think I did this?"

"I'd know more if you'd talk to us."

It's a bullshit answer. "Who is WinPA99?"

"Who?"

"Who does the internet handle WinPA99 belong to?"

A pause. A sigh. "I've never heard of it."

I press the phone to my forehead before bringing it back to my mouth. "Do your job and you won't need me. Okay? Okay."

I hang up. I want to scream *fuck* as loud as I can. I just wasted a call; I wasted the whole phone. In the main menu, I click reset to factory settings and run it through the deletion cycle. I wipe the whole exterior down with the hem of my shirt—the second black T-shirt today, this time no jacket—and using the fabric, I tuck it into my jeans pocket.

Ten blocks northeast, I pull it out and hand it to a teenager walking past me on the sidewalk. Her gaggle of friends behind her laughs.

"Go on, take it."

"Lady, this is a flip phone."

"So sell it," I call to her, and jog across the street. My stomach rumbles. I know a taco truck parks two blocks from here. One of her friends hoots something at me, but I don't care. I don't care what she does with it, as long as she keeps walking in the opposite direction. I don't look back.

CHAPTER 11

Day 3: Sunday, August 7, 2016

Tom Pickering is forty-six, but he looks sixty. His face is scraggly, creased and pinked like he'd just been asleep on it. He thumbs through his phone as he walks and doesn't notice, or maybe doesn't care when people dodge him on the street. I follow him for a few blocks before I catch up to him.

"Tom? Are you Tom Pickering?" We stand at the corner of Arch and 18th and Peter's work buddy turns to face me, his features rearranging into something feigning recognition.

Before he can speak, I say, "You don't know me, but I'm a private detective. I was hired by Peter Lipsky's brother. He doesn't think the police are working hard enough on his brother's case. Can I talk to you for a few minutes?"

"Uh, sure. Here?" I look around, there is a corner store across the street with a bench in front of it.

I point to it. "Can we sit? Just for a moment, I promise."

"Sure. Anything for Pete. Jesus Christ, it's horrible." We walk over and he flops onto the metal bench with the same abandon as a sullen teenager.

"Yes, it is. What can you tell me about Peter?" I ask, and

pull out Peter's Moleskine. I open to the page after Lindy's interview, pressing the binding down with an index finger, and I wait for Tom.

"Truthfully, we weren't all that close." His mouth folded down, distancing himself from Peter. From the investigation, the drama. His life, already exhausting for one reason or another, whether it be baseball practice for his son or field hockey for his daughter or just a long litany of carpools and teenaged histrionics.

"You were in his phone as one of his most texted contacts." I frown back at him, pretending to check my notes. I'm taking a gamble, because of course I don't have his phone, but they'd at least exchanged emails more than anyone else.

"Yeah, I know." He runs a hand through his hair. "He didn't really have friends. He had me. We talked about Philadelphia sports. We didn't usually get superpersonal. I didn't even know he had a brother."

"They weren't close," I say. "He lives in Minnesota." Tom doesn't reply, he just stares out at the street. I continue, "Did Peter have a girlfriend?"

"Why? Do they think she did this?" His eyes snap back to mine and I can see the sweat beading on his forehead. The sun hits our bench directly and we bake here.

"Who was she?" I reach to tuck my hair behind my ear before I forget that it's short now.

"I don't know. Some ballerina. Peter said she was crazy." Tom sets his black leather computer bag on the ground against his feet and pulls his short-sleeved dress shirt away from his skin.

"What does that mean?" I try to act like this is not new information.

"He said the girl, Lindsey or something, wouldn't let him breathe. She wanted to be over every day, every night after work. She wanted to move in."

I imagine Lindy's apartment, the bare, temporary feel of it.

"Were they serious?" I ask.

"I don't know. At first he liked her. He liked having a girlfriend. But you know, Pete didn't . . . talk about much. Even to brag or whatever. Not that guys our age really do that anymore. But he didn't talk about her at all." He rubbed his palm against his forehead and lurched forward, like he was going to bolt at any minute. "I mean, I bitch about my wife. We all do, in one way or another. But Pete was just mum at first. That's how you know it's good, you know? When we say nothing."

"So when was it good?"

"Maybe January?"

"So, eight months ago? When did they break up?"

"The beginning of summer, I think. Not that long ago. They had tragedy in common. His wife was murdered and I think her sister was, maybe? Not sure. I think it was a bond."

"You seem to know a lot about a guy who didn't talk," I crack, but then I give him a smile. He hesitates then smiles back.

"Yeah, well, he says more when you get him out for drinks. Which we did sometimes. Not a lot. My wife, uh, she gets mad." He smiles apologetically. His hair is gray around the temples, and he'd be good-looking if he didn't look like he'd rather be asleep. "I don't blame her. I work a lot."

"So who broke up with who?" I ask.

"Oh, Pete broke up with her. There was something not right with that girl. One minute she loved him, then she hated him. He's not into that. He's like the most even guy I know. Practically comatose, really."

"How did she react?"

"He said she hit the roof. Accused him of using her. You know there was one weird thing." He snaps his fingers. "In the spring, we went to a ball game. You know, block of tick-ets. Some of us brought our families. I brought my son. Pete comes with his girlfriend. She's young, you know? Closer to my kid's age than Peter's. Anyway, she spent most of the time on her phone. Hardly watched the game. Pete tried to say something to her about it, I heard him, and she shot him a death look. We were all having a good time, Pete even bought Scotty—that's my son—a beer. He's only eighteen, but it was that kind of easy afternoon. Except she was like a black mark on the whole thing. She was just pissy the whole time. So, they pan to her on the Jumbotron, you know? Everyone waves at that thing." He splays his hands wide. "Everyone! No, she just looked up, shrugged, and went back to her phone. So, the whole place kinda blew up and they kept coming back to her, just like making fun of her. Because like who gets mad at the Jumbotron? So then the Phanatic—you've been to a game right?" I nod and he continues, "Okay, he's kind of a jerk, that's just his thing. So we were right on the third baseline. He comes right up into the front row and he gets in on it, pretends to try to climb into her lap, that kind of thing, just trying to get a rise out of her. The crowd is laughing. She's getting madder and madder, I can tell she's gonna blow. Pete doesn't know what the hell to do; he's such a quiet kind of guy. He tries to shoo him away, well, that just makes it worse. The Phanatic starts sashaying around, flinging his hands around like *shoo, shoo,* and meanwhile, they're putting this all up on the big screen. Honestly, it couldn't have been more than a minute or two. The game starts back up, the Phanatic goes away. Pete tries to make her feel better but she storms out. She screamed something at him, like maybe he should have done something different? I don't know, but then she left. He didn't go after her." Tom rubs his palm along his chin and half-laughs. "I told him that day, *you can't date someone half your age.* I mean, I'm raising someone almost half my age.

I think he agreed with me. He broke up with her maybe a month or so later."

"Okay, so maybe she doesn't like baseball games?" I suggest.

"Yeah, sure. Or was having a bad day. Whatever, coulda been anything." He runs his arm along his forehead. "I saw her maybe five days ago? Ran into her coming out of my gym. She was nice, normal. So it could have been the day."

"Wait, you saw her? Did she recognize you?"

"Yeah, we exchanged pleasantries and went on our way."

"What kind of pleasantries?"

"I asked if she'd seen Pete, she said no. She asked if I had, I said no, we'd both been busy with work but we were meeting at Lockers on Thursday for a coworker's retirement. She said tell him I said hello . . . you know, that's it. Oh, she had a Chinese menu in her hand, made a joke about eating junk while I went to the gym, something like that."

Chinese menu. *Lockers @ 4.* "Okay, so all that seems normal," I say, scribbling it all down.

"Yeah, sure. I don't think she was crazy to anyone else. But the way Pete acted, her antics weren't a onetime thing, you know? He was too casual about it, and also somehow, too miserable. That was just her."

"What did she do when he broke up with her?" I ask.

"I'm not sure. After that incident, Pete was careful. Protective of her, almost. He said he broke up with her and I said good, and he said well, we'll see how it goes. He said she kept coming over to his place, sometimes uninvited. That kind of thing. The first month was rough. But last week he seemed to hint that he hadn't heard from her since June. Which was a long time in that chick's world."

"Did he say anything else about her?"

"The only thing he said was that he never expected to have a normal relationship."

"Oh yeah? What does that mean?"

"I was never sure. I think he was talking about his wife. The one that was killed?"

I write in the Moleskine and ignore the pop of goose bumps on my arms, despite the ninety-degree heat. "What did he say about his wife?" My voice cracks over the word *wife*.

"He came to work at True after she died. I didn't know him when all that went down. He hasn't mentioned her very much over the years, but from what he has said, I don't think they were happy."

"Really?" I pause, considering it. "His brother never indicated that." Tom isn't even looking at me anymore, he's watching the street.

"Yeah, you know? Maybe it means nothing, but I always got the impression . . ." He stops talking and I wait. He sighs. "I got the feeling he was relieved, you know?"

"Relieved?" I ask.

"Maybe not relieved, but you know, not broken up that she died."

"His wife?" I can't keep the incredulity out of my voice, thinking of his long nights on Healing Hope, his rambling posts about missing her, loving her, how he can't sleep anymore, hasn't slept in fifteen years. Still thinks about her. Even Lindy thought so.

"Yeah. Don't quote me. It was just an impression. He said once, after a few beers, that her death solved a problem for him. What the hell did he call it?" Tom looks at the sky, the patch of blue slung between the shadowy buildings. "A quandary." He laughs then. "That's how Peter talked, you know? He used these big words in casual conversation. People never knew what to do with him. But yeah. He said her death 'solved a quandary.'"

"Any idea what he meant by that?"

"Nope. I tried to ask him later, too. He tried to play it off. He said, 'Don't listen to me when I drink, man.'" Tom stands. "Listen, I should go. My wife makes dinner for me and the kids. I gotta get home. I gotta get the train."

I stand up, too. I shake his hand, watch him blend into the crowd, the dark shirts, dress pants, the other commuters. I hitch my messenger bag back onto my shoulder and head in the other direction.

A quandary? What the fuck is that supposed to mean?

Excerpt from The Serrated Edge: The Story of Lilith Wade, Serial Killer, *by E. Green, RedBarn Press, copyright June 2016*

Lilith Wade was thirteen when she ran away. Everyone who had tried to help her was at their wits' end. She was defiant, truant. She was in the sixth grade because she scored so low on her exams when entering public school for the first time at ten. Betty Putnak had no idea how to mother a child like that. Bill Putnak only knew how to discipline with his belt. By all accounts, she wasn't beaten with any regularity or vengeance. Willa Price was Lilith's sixth-grade teacher.

Willa Price: There was no oppositional defiant disorder at the time, but that's what she had. I've never known a child so full of anger.

Interviewer: She'd lost her parents. Did you try to get her counseling?

WP: We had a school psychologist. We had countless meetings with the Putnaks. Things were different then. You were either in the classroom with everyone else or you were in IU. Lilith was in the IU.

Interviewer: Did you ever get the sense that Lilith was abused?

WP: I have no idea. Not by Bill Putnak. Sure he whipped her bottom with a belt, but that child needed it.

Interviewer: She was still just a child.

WP: Everyone thinks that. Children, and especially little girls, can be bad. People are born bad. It happens. I was a teacher in the public school system for over thirty years. If she was a boy, no one would think twice about a heinie-whupping. In my day, the nuns would do it to you, rap those knuckles with a yardstick.

Interviewer: You think Lilith Wade was born bad?

WP: I'll tell you a story. I wasn't there, and these things have a way of taking on a life of their own, but this is as accurate as I remember it. Judy, she was the school guidance counselor and psychologist, had Lilith down in the office for a visit. She gave her an evaluation, a series of questions. It was an IQ test. Judy was always giving that girl evaluations, like evaluations could save her. Like if Judy could just help her, figure her out, then she could sleep again. So Judy gave her the test and then left her alone, kind of a show of trust, you know? She was in the guidance room, it had a big table and Judy's office was off to the left, with a door. She shuts the door. The next thing you know, she smells smoke and rushes out to see Lilith holding that assessment packet in one corner while she sets the other corner on fire with a lighter. When she asked her why she'd do such a thing, she just said she wanted to see it burn. That's it. Just see it burn.

Interviewer: Do you think Lilith was smart?

WP: Well, now, everyone assumed she wasn't. But you see, she'd never been to school. How did anyone expect her to know how to act?

Interviewer: Well, you'd have to know not to set school property on fire.

WP: Sure. But Judy said when she grabbed the paper and stamped it out with her foot, she wasn't interested in the test anymore. She wanted to make sure no one got hurt. But Lilith was smiling the whole time, like she thought it was funny. The child hardly smiled. Almost never.

Interviewer: So then what happened?

WP: Judy sent her back to her classroom. But don't you know? The kid had filled out the whole thing. I mean Judy could only read half the test, the rest had disintegrated into ash, but the half she could see? Lilith didn't get one question wrong.

CHAPTER 12

Day 4: Monday, August 8, 2016

A sports bar on a Monday night is less crowded than a Thursday night, but it's trivia night, so the place is still half full. There are two speakers on the sides of the room, and a woman with a microphone is setting up in the front, under the televisions.

I half expect to see Brandt coming or going, but then, I suppose he's already been here. How many times can you shake out the same joint, talk to the same servers? It's a risk coming here, sure, but hell, this whole endeavor is a risk. Frankly, if Brandt comes up behind me right now, his wide palm on my shoulder, whispering *got ya* into my ear, I don't know what I'll do. I do know that my hair can't get any shorter and I'm out of money—and time—to find a good wig. But then I remember the sound of his voice: *Blackout drunk, Edie?*

I recognize the bartender from Thursday night and hope that Brandt hasn't shown him my picture. I realize then that Brandt would have gotten my name from the bill. That's how he found me in the first place. I wonder how many bricks he shit when he saw *Edie Beckett* at the bottom of the check.

Just being in this place is making my teeth sweat.

I sit in the corner, the last chair before the service bar, and pretend to scroll through my phone, making periodic notes in the Moleskine. When there's a break in activity, the bartender asks me, "What can I get ya?" and I ask for a Diet Coke just to run a tab.

He sets it in front of me, on a napkin, and the glass is already sweating.

"Hi, can I ask you a question?"

"You just did, I think." He gives me a wide smile, and in another life, merely a week ago, I might have smiled back the same way.

"Very funny; a second one, if I may?" I hold out my phone. "Have you see this woman?" I pull up the filtered, filmy image of Lindy's Facebook profile picture.

He squints at the phone. "Yeah, you know, she's been in here a few times, I think. Last week, maybe?" He studies me, showing no signs of recognition. I wouldn't expect him to; he didn't wait on me.

"Did she come in alone?"

"Is this related to that guy that got killed?" He turns his head toward a yell at the other end of the bar and gives them the one-minute sign with his finger. His dark hair isn't short, like I'd thought, but rather pulled into a tight, low ponytail. "She came in earlier than him, sat at that table." He points to the corner where Peter was sitting when I first saw him. "Then the guy who was later killed came in, sat with her, but he didn't look happy. They talked for a few minutes and she left, quickly, with her head down. Like she was crying. He yelled something after her, coulda been *come back!* But he didn't get up to see if she was okay. Kind of a dickish move, in my opinion." He shrugs.

"Okay. Did he stay much longer after she left?"

"I didn't see. I went downstairs to change a keg. When I came back up, he was sitting over there"—he points to the other side of the bar, at the table we'd occupied with Peter's coworkers—"and his whole party was here. Then the bar itself got crowded, and Sandy handled the tables, and I didn't give them another thought."

"Did you see her come back?" I ask.

"Nah, but I can't be sure. It gets busy on Thursday nights around here."

"Had you ever seen her in here before?"

"I'm not really sure, I'm sorry. You can ask Bert, he's almost always here. Hold on." The bartender disappears through a swinging door and comes back out a minute later with another man, older, with white hair and bright blue eyes.

"Bert, this lady is looking for someone and wants to know if you've seen her."

I introduce myself as Jill, after a pause, and make a mental note to please come up with a decent alias once I'm home. *Home.* How easily that word rolls off the proverbial tongue, as if the rathole I'm crashing in can be called a home.

I show Bert the phone with Lindy's picture.

"Yeah, she's been in here before with a guy."

I navigate to Peter's Facebook, blow up his picture, and turn the device toward him. "This guy?"

"Nope, not him. Another guy. Dark hair, kind of short, a flat nose, a tattoo right above his collar. Hard to tell what it was, but I noticed it."

I thank him and he shrugs and heads into the back room. On my phone, I pull up the ballet website, find Alek Romanov. I ask the bartender if he can grab Bert again for me. When I show him Alek's picture, he shakes his head. "No, that's not him, either."

I thank them both, throw a five on the bar, and head home. The air is thick, the streets are getting dark. I take the train back to Trent's place, happy to be inside with the chain latched before it gets fully dark.

Before bed, I boot up the computer. I've discovered that in the kitchen, if I drag a chair under the single square window above the counter, I can get a Wi-Fi signal. I check my email.

To: Edie Beckett
From: Gil Brandt

Where are you? Beckett, I swear to God, I've never met a bigger pain in the ass. Get in touch, ok?

My heart surges, a shot of adrenaline travels up my chest, and I shake my legs loose. I hit reply and stare at the blinking cursor for a few minutes before I close the window.

A second one. And a third.

To: Edie Beckett
From: Dylan Beckett

Hey, worried about you. Been trying to call. Please let me known if you're ok. P.S. Camille is worried, too.

Then:

To: Edie Beckett
From: Dylan Beckett

Can you please call me? Email back? Something? I can't sleep.

I close Gmail and click onto the Philadelphia Police Department web page and find Peter's story with one update. A picture of me, taken years ago, a mug shot from my arrest for a DUI. My blond hair, wiry, matted against vacant eyes. There's a thin slick of drool across my bottom lip. I was barely conscious. This is the picture they're using to find me. This, and my county ID. Oh, Brandt.

I log into Healing Hope as Peter and wait for WinPA99. I've been logging on every night, late, just waiting. I remember fishing once with Pop, the canoe bobbing aimlessly around a lake, the line throwing ripples into the flat, glassy surface. Pop laughing, saying, *This is what it's like sometimes, just watching the water. Still a better day than most.*

This is what I'm doing now, fishing. WinPA99 hasn't come back. I read through Peter's private messages, I read about the beginning of his relationship with Lindy. Snippets, in turn inane and maudlin, and eventually disappearing altogether when, I assume, they took up other modes of communication.

> No one understands loss from violent crime like another survivor.

> It's such a relief to have someone to talk to.

> Have you talked to the others, ever?

> No. Have you?

> Is this too weird, us talking?

> It feels natural.

I'm flush with the sense that I am able to see what Brandt won't, what they'll be too far removed to figure out. Their investigation is surface, focused on me, skating through, until the next case takes over, and the next, and the next, and for a second I fear I'll still be here trapped in this cave, clicking-clicking-clicking forever to find the truth. In hiding, waiting for me to come out, get comfortable, order pizza, log into Facebook.

Until whoever wrote *The Serrated Edge* comes back for their other half a million by writing *Edie Beckett: Murderer's Daughter*.

I stay on Healing Hope until after midnight, waiting. When my eyes droop closed, I shut the laptop down.

I keep my bag by the window again, my clothes in tight rolls, ready to go at the first knock. The first shout. Instead I fall asleep.

What I don't expect is a gunshot, right outside the door, in the hallway at three a.m., so loud that it startles me awake. By the time I'm up and looking out the window, the police cars are rolling in, their lights spinning and sirens blaring, the block awash in red and blue.

I smell it then, the wet biologic tang of fresh blood.

* * *

I stand outside the window of Trent's apartment, in the narrow alleyway between the two buildings. In front of me is the street, bathed in red and blue strobe lights, and I hear the *clunk* of metal car doors slamming one after the other, six in all. I have seconds to decide.

At the far end of the alley, a metal chain link fence backs up to another patch of grass, a vacant lot with an abandoned building likely filled with squatters, not empty. I run to the fence and toss my messenger bag up and over. It lands with a soft *thud*. I scale the fence, my feet just fitting in the metal diamond-shaped holes. I land softly on the concrete on the other side and duck behind Trent's apartment building. There is a sweep of a light across the alleyway and an indistinct male shout. I push my palm against my chest, my heart scudding, and catch my breath.

I can't stay here—in this neighborhood, on this block. I could find another empty apartment, but it's too risky. There's too much police activity. I know from working as a clerk that the calls out to this block are almost nightly in a bad stretch.

I cut across the lot, cement and dust and patches of weeds that, in the dim streetlight, could pass for grass. I walk briskly, my head low, for seven blocks south on 6th Street. I can't call an Uber, it's too traceable. With the built-in GPS, I might as well just send Brandt a personal postcard. If I stay on 6th Street, I'll eventually find an on-duty cab, even if I have to hike all the way to Center City, which is only about three miles. That's fine, it'll take me about an hour if I move.

But where am I going? I can't go to my own apartment, I'm sure it's still under surveillance. I can't go to Dylan's or Tim's. I can't squat in an abandoned building; they're already occupied by drug dealers, so I'd have the same issue with regular police encounters. There's only one option, and it's a risk. Honestly, I'm either ingenious or indescribably stupid and only time will tell.

Twenty minutes later, I pass a red-and-white cab with the center number lit and I lift my arm, waving. It blows past me, horn blaring. Five minutes later, I see a yellow cab, and this time he stops.

I climb into the back seat, which reeks of cigarette smoke, perfume, and beer from the barflies, and the cracked leather scratches my jeans.

"Where to?"

"Willow Grove Avenue," I tell him.

He balks. "Too far!" He needs to stay local for the bar pickups. I get it. I reach into my pocket and pull out a hundred-dollar bill that I drop through the plexiglass partition.

"Please?"

He grumbles and puts the car into gear, tucking the hundred into the envelope between the seats, but he doesn't turn off the meter. He'll take my hundred plus the fare.

Before I know it, we're on the Schuylkill Expressway zooming north to Peter's apartment.

• • •

While the cab speeds through the dark streets, I use my phone flashlight to flip through the Moleskine, where I've been keeping notes on Peter's life. I remember, in my drunken haze, the front door to his building had a keypad. The number would have been given to him by the building manager, and Peter, being the attentive tenant he was, would have wanted to write it down, but not on a slip of paper or something that could flutter out of his wallet while paying a restaurant tab. No, Peter was the kind of pedantic, plodding soul who would have written it down in his trusty Moleskine, but of course, without commentary. Just a harmless four-digit code, plunked right *there* between the bulleted items of *Pay internet bill* and *Cavalleria rusticana, Pietro Mascagni.*

75992.

Bingo.

God, people are worse than predictable. Okay, so it was five digits, not four, sue me. But I would die if any stranger could step into my life like this and just figure me out, from a simple notebook and a cursory glance at my online habits. It is so disheartening. With the world being so focused on *celebrating our diversity*, you're led to believe that people inherently are all different and that heterogeneity is magical and wonderful and it's all such fucking bullshit. When you boiled everyone down to their habits, to their simple ways of existing, there it was. A simple five-digit code penned, neatly, in a worn notebook, exactly like I predicted it would be. Like anyone would have predicted.

We don't put a show on for the world, we are the show. Peter was as empty as his Facebook timeline, a daily horoscope check, a spotty sports reference, the rattling inside of a sterile apartment. It reminds me of Brandt's theory about shower drains and microwaves. Peter's apartment was cleaned for himself.

Peter doesn't have next of kin. There's no brother in Minnesota. His parents are dead. The only person he had in the world was Colleen, and she died seventeen years ago. He'd marooned himself on an island of his own making with no interest in pushing off, and now it's too late. Funny thing about isolating oneself—who comes to clean up after you when it's over, especially if no one cares that you're dead? The police care. Brandt cares—arguably too much, now that I am part of the investigation.

The end of any homicide investigation is tracking down who will take care of the victim's property. Many times, it's easy. There's a parent or a sibling or a spouse. But at least half the time, there's no one. There's something hollowly lonely in the idea that finding someone to care about your death could be a task that ratchets up the city's overtime. Brandt used to periodically send me a victim's file when he couldn't find a next of kin. I probably gave him back a name 90 percent of the time.

The worst one, I still remember his name, John Harper, he was fifty-one years old. He wasn't a homicide, he was a suicide, so Brandt was off that case quick, the file shunted to some dusty office of social services somewhere. But Brandt being Brandt knew that in his cursory dig through this guy's life that he had nothing. A tiny box of an apartment, not dirty but not Peter-clean. They found him, a single self-inflicted gunshot through the roof of his mouth. He'd looked up how to hold it so there'd be no mistake. No note. An audit of his finances gave no reason. He worked in a coffee shop and his coworkers said he was nice. Polite. He always received generous tips. Smiled often but didn't talk much. His computer revealed nothing. No recent Google searches, except for how to hold the gun. Not even a porn site. Just one day, a nice, ordinary man in his fifties swallowed a gun and the earth kept on spinning without even a stutter, not even feeling that silent slip of one less person. He was a truly invisible man.

I kept John Harper's file. I don't know why. I never found anyone for him. I assume the building manager emptied the apartment. A social worker would become the estate administrator and pay for Mr. Harper's cremation, his funds would be kept in a living trust indefinitely. If Brandt had gone through my apartment, which he surely did, he would have found it by now. I never hid it, it was just in the back of my desk drawer.

Did Brandt wonder why I'd kept it?

* * *

By the time the cab pulls up to Peter's, it is four-thirty in the morning.

I tap in the code at the front door: 75992. I would have been surprised if it hadn't worked. In the darkened hallway, I work his apartment door open with my lock pick kit. I hear nothing from the other units, but I wait for footsteps. People would be hustling to make the train into different parts of the city, beating the rush. I hold my breath the entire time and only exhale when his door finally clicks open.

Peter's apartment looks and smells like I remember it, a waft of antiseptic, indiscriminate and layered with a mossy odor of something distinctly male. I expected the warm, decaying smell of old blood. The air is cool even though the window unit is off. The streetlights cast a glow into the living room, the furniture all angles and gleaming surfaces.

My footsteps echo in the hall, Peter's bedroom door is closed. The air feels different. I wonder if it is the same air that Peter exhaled. Am I breathing in his dying breath, recycled through the 1970s air-conditioning?

I don't dare flick on a light. Instead, I find myself in the guest room, a single twin bed against the wall facing an IKEA desk. I lie down with my shoes still on, pulling the covers up to my shoulders, the exhaustion seeping in and taking hold and I am dreaming before my head hits the pillow.

CHAPTER 13

Day 5: Tuesday, August 9, 2016

In the dream, I always save the baby.

I've never really thought about what I'd be like as a mother. Motherhood existed as a nebulous notion: a young mom on the train bounces a baby on her hip and I suddenly feel the weight of him against my side. The soft plush of his moist diaper, the sticky heat of his fat legs, the burble of his laugh in my ear. A toddler cries in Starbucks, pulling on her mother's skirt, and I feel the slap of small hands against my thigh.

I was eleven, lonely, skinny. Chad Fink had paid me small pockets of attention the summer before. He seemed to like teaching me to smoke pot until Lilith ruined everything.

He'd grown over the winter, taller, wider. At sixteen, his shoulders looked broad, like a man's. The pimples along his chin line were fading, leaving behind a stipple of scars that made him look tough.

"Well, well, the prodigious daughter returns."

He meant prodigal. At eleven I knew this. Although, later, I'd look it up: *prodigious: adj. Unnatural or abnormal.*

I was sitting on Lilith's stoop. Dylan was inside, the lights dimmed low, his door shut tight. I was bored. Chad and another boy I didn't know stopped in the street. I still hadn't spoken, tongue-tied and not knowing what to do with my legs. Cross them? At the knee or ankle? I tried both, shifting on the step with my feet in the dirt, the dust billowing up.

His friend poked him, as if to say *come on.* They laughed.

"Wait!" I said as they started to walk. Chad turned. "How was your winter?"

They fell apart. Hooted. "How was your winter?" Chad howled, elbowing the other boy. He stood up straight. "Just fine, Ms. Beckett. How was yours?" His voice was formal, as if he were addressing a schoolteacher.

I ignored them, tried again. "Who's your friend?"

More laughter. "This is Johnny," said Chad. "See ya around." They took off this time in earnest, not waiting for me. I watched them go, down the street to the stoplight until a car slowed and they hopped in and disappeared.

• • •

Later, I was watching *The Price Is Right* on Lilith's TV, feeling bored and anxious and restless and hot. Lilith had appeared in a flash, her face a full mask of makeup, telling me not to get in trouble.

"Where are you going?" I asked, and she waved her hand around, a bubble of laughter bursting from her lips.

"I have my shift at the bar, and then well, out for a bit. Your mama has friends, isn't that exciting? I haven't had friends in years. *Years, Edie.*"

I wanted to tell her I understood. As a child, I had no friends. The kids from the trailer park, their families were transient, here one summer but gone the next. I had Dylan, always Dylan. Making dinner together while Pop worked, watching TV late into the night, his finger over his lips when Pop would call home to make sure I'd gone to bed. I felt jealous of her then. With her friends and her laughter and her bright lipstick.

"That's so nice." I didn't call Lilith *Mama* like Dylan did. In my mind I called her Lilith, out loud, I never called her anything at all. "I'm happy for you." I wasn't lying. I *was* happy. I was also miserable, hot, and lonely.

She blew me a kiss and the door swung shut and I heard the rattle of her old car start up and smelled the diesel and she was gone.

I wandered the length of the trailer, all the rooms set in a line: living room, kitchen, back two bedrooms, bathroom so small you had to put your feet in the tub to pee. I was standing at the mirror, staring at myself: the dishwater hair, the tan, dirty-looking skin, when the knock came on the door, quick and frantic.

"Lilith, honey, you in here?"

It was Mrs. Reston from across the street, with her dirty, sticky baby. When I came through the kitchen and stood in the living room, I was shocked to see the baby had grown. She had pigtails now and a bright purple sucker in her mouth.

"She left for work, Mrs. Reston," I said.

She looked panicked. "Honey, could you watch Hazel here? I just had a call from my brother. Mama took a tumble down the stairs, I'll be back in two hours, I just gotta get her to a hospital and wait until Bobby can get there. I don't think nothing's broken, but damn if she can't afford the squad. They charge you, you know, if it's not a 'real emergency.'" She bunny-eared her fingers around *real emergency*. The sheer volume of her words sent me reeling, I hadn't heard much more out of Mrs. Reston than a *Hello there!* ever. Lilith said the baby had made her tired and sad, but that's what babies always did.

She pushed Hazel at me, stuck her fat, gloopy hand in mine before I knew what to say, and fled out the front door. The child watched after her and started to cry. Wail, really.

I banged on Dylan's door and finally just turned the handle until it swung open to reveal a mess of a bed, sheets and blankets tangled among clothes and backpacks and plastic bags and old food and magazines: cars and porn. I knew what porn was, I'd seen his magazines—big, plastic breasts bursting through black netting, their hands between their legs, and I wondered if they ever cut themselves up with those long red fingernails.

No place for a baby.

"Are you a baby?" I asked her, and she blinked at me, the sucker pulsing in her mouth. "Can you talk?" I asked her again.

What do you do with a baby? I gave her a wooden spoon and a bowl, because I saw that on a commercial once for public television: *Children don't need expensive toys! Let them expand their imagination with what's in your kitchen!* She started to cry.

When the door knocked again, I flung it open, saying, "Oh, thank God you're back," but on the stoop stood Chad Fink and "Johnny," his jaw hanging down like a dog's, breathing through his mouth.

"Hey, Beckett, wanna come with us?" He gave me a smile and my heart flipped a little, even though I tried to will it still. They smelled like cigarettes and beer, sour and smoky all at once. Like men.

In the background Hazel wailed again and threw the spoon against the television.

"I'm, uh, babysitting." But I didn't say no. I couldn't let them walk away, the idea of a day stretched out before me filled with nothing but Hazel and her crying seemed unbearable. "I can bring her."

"You want to bring a baby?" Johnny-not-really-Johnny said, his eyes cutting to Chad and stepping back like he couldn't be involved in this horrible decision, which of course it would later turn out to be.

"I don't care, Beckett, just don't let her cry."

And we tumbled into the backseat, me heaving the baby against my hip and the feel of her wet, dewy head against my shoulder and I briefly thought about buckling her in—*shouldn't she have a car seat?*—but I was too caught up in the moment. Where were we even going? Chad turned and grinned at me, and just like that, we took off: me in a gleeful little swoon, the car a hot cocoon, the engine running, the air conditioner blowing a cloying antifreeze smell before we took off onto the highway and out of Faithful.

• • •

A few towns over, as far as I could tell, the homes were lined up like straight soldiers and we rolled to a stop in front of a brick mess, the grass nonexistent, the dusty pavement littered with garbage and old cans.

"Come on, Beckett."

"I'm not taking her in there, it looks like a crack house," I said. Chad and Johnny-not-really-Johnny shrugged and ambled up the walk.

"Stay in the car, okay?" I told Hazel, her eyes wet and blinking. She didn't nod or cry, she just stared.

I'd always been left in the car, for as long as I could remember.

Chad stood on the front porch, his hands in his pockets, and tossed his head, to get the flop of blond out of his eyes. I climbed out and scrambled after him, hating myself, the need coming off my skin had a smell. In the background, I heard a wet bleat, the crumbled cry, but I ignored it. Later, it would be all I could remember with any clarity.

Inside, the house stank. Like wet towels and fast food and garbage. I breathed through my mouth and saw Chad do the same. When he reached out and took my hand, his eyes conveying an unexpected fear, regret, maybe, I forgot about the smell. The car. The baby.

Johnny took the steps two at a time and Chad and I stayed in the darkened hallway. It was dark, and I felt him before I saw him, the puff of his breath against my cheek, his mouth on mine, his hand sliding under my shirt, across my belly. His tongue slipping along my teeth and I did the same. I felt both breathless with need, my heart pounding against my rib cage, and childishly removed, imagining what other girls would do: The pretty lip-glossed girls at school, would they put their hand here?

Time passed. I don't know how much. Could have been twenty minutes, could have been longer. There was shouting from upstairs, a thud like a body hitting the floor, and then Johnny-not-Johnny came running down, stumbling against the railing so hard, he cracked it. Streaking past us and out the door to the car. Chad and I followed, and I wiped my hand across my mouth, wanting to pull him back against me, the warmth and the kiss and his hands against my skin.

I saw the woman—it would later turn out to be a neighbor—before I saw the baby. Then I saw the baby lying on the dusty lawn: red skin, shining and stretched, puffed face and closed eyes, limp and fat, her feet splayed apart, one white sandal missing. It took me a moment to recognize the pink bow, the purple sucker.

The woman was talking to me, yelling, and giving the baby CPR, but I couldn't hear her. All I could see were toes, painted pink.

There's much of the day I don't remember. I don't really remember the police, the questioning, Lilith coming to get me. I don't remember how I got from one place to another. I don't remember going home, I don't remember ever talking to Lilith or Pop about it. I don't remember anyone shaking my shoulders, asking me *What were you thinking?* Although they must have. Someone must have.

The baby would live, I learned later. Her body would

continue to grow, into a child, then a teenager, then an adult. But her brain would not. In her mind, she'd stay a baby. Mrs. Reston would blame herself—eleven years old was far too young to be in charge of a toddler, she'd say, her hands twisting. Caring for Hazel would become a lifelong job, a penance for her one lapse in judgment. I would be simultaneously dismissed, perhaps forgiven, and entirely forgotten.

I've never had any doubt that I am missing a maternal gene. Anyone else would have known, instinctively, that what I did was not okay. Anyone else would have cracked a window, left the car running with the AC on, even taken Hazel with them. Not only am I defective, down to my bones, but I've never been taught. How would I have known? I'd been alone—in cars, houses—my entire life. Alone was a default state.

I have many excuses.

I have one recurring dream. The car, Chad, the garbage house. In the dream, I run from the hallway, pull Hazel from the car, and she is fine, wet and shaking against my arm, and she smiles at me. She has both shoes on. And I save her.

• • •

In the light of the next morning, Peter's apartment looks different. Brighter and less sinister. I eat three slices of stale rye bread, so happy to be living out of squalor, and I roll the cold butter around my tongue. I consider making coffee but worry that a late-to-work neighbor will smell it wafting across the hall from the dead guy's apartment.

I stand in his bedroom doorway. The mattress has been cut apart and the center removed, in the shape of a giant, off-kilter rectangle. The room is in disarray, but in a respectful way. The dresser drawers have been pulled open and shut again, but not fully. Fabric is exposed in a way Peter never would have allowed, which is how I know the police have gone through everything.

I know how long it takes to release a crime scene—anywhere from one day to a week, depending. I know that police, overworked and racking up their overtime, will rarely return to a scene once they cut the tape off. There's no time. Case turnover is too high, the lab has all the physical evidence and is now combing through for fingerprints or DNA, processing every fiber, every hair, every microdrop of skin oil that will tell them I was here. That I am Peter's murderer. The file will be passed to a social worker or a lower-rung detective to find next of kin and will sit, accumulating dust, until the landlord calls the cops, ranting about the rent.

I wonder if they found the gun. I wonder if Brandt swabbed it, if they were able to find DNA. Sometimes if the shooter is new at shooting—funny that's a thing, an experienced shooter or not—the slide can clip the web between the thumb and forefinger, leaving a few cells, a little memento of their crime. Unlike in the movies, it is hard to pull prints from a gun. There's not enough flat metal surface, not enough steady contact with the contours of finger ridges and often, a killer's hands are sweating, shaking.

Which means that the gun not having *my* prints wouldn't exonerate me, whether Brandt had the weapon or not.

I start to feel sick, woozy in the head, the bread balling up in my stomach, and I sit on the floor, on Peter's soft Pottery Barn braided rug, and sift through some of the papers under his desk, filed in a gunmetal gray filing cabinet. Taxes, estate settlements from the late nineties, and a sale of property I assume to be his mother's estate. The edges are curled and brittle. Bills from the previous year. Paycheck stubs and receipts for direct deposit. Peter Lipsky was being dragged kicking and screaming into the paperless age. Who prints receipts of electronic deposits only to file them?

In his closet there are shoeboxes with receipts, marked with blue pen checkmarks. In the bottom, tucked under the shoe rack, is a wide, flat shoebox, originally meant for women's boots. I open the lid. Loose photos of her at various stages of her life, long, flowing dark hair, streaked with blond in the late nineties. Intelligent green eyes, a round, happy face. Laughing in a forest. Sitting with a cocktail by a pool, a sun flare in the corner. Photographs taken with disposable cameras and developed, before cell phones. A close-up of her kissing Peter's cheek. In another, her arms flung around a waifish blonde, both of them smiling broadly with bright red lips, big bangs, and overly lined eyes. I flip it over and find a caption: *Burrows and me, 1996.*

I replace the lid, feeling dirty. Over the green boot emblem, the word *Colleen* is labeled with a black Sharpie. I feel a sudden loss that this man, this meticulous, pleasant, slightly tedious but perfectly kind man is dead, and not for the first time, I consider that it's my fault.

I try to remember more details from the evening. Were there people in the lobby when we'd stumbled home? I have a vague, nebulous recollection of a rustling, perhaps a banging outside his window as I slept fitfully, half in and half out of a boozy dream. I hadn't thought much of it, that kind of sound; it's so common in the city. A garbage can lid. Rats. Raccoons. A drunk. I can't say if this was any different.

In Peter's desk drawer, I find a neat stack of unused wire-bound notebooks, all blue. I can't keep everything in the Moleskine, and if I'm going to exonerate myself, I need to start thinking like a detective. Like Brandt. What would Brandt do? He'd write it down. The man writes everything down.

My list starts simply, and pathetically: *Peter's friends— Tom, Lindy Cook, neighbor who found him?*

Should be easy enough to figure out. I scan Peter's room for a calendar. He was a paper kind of guy, not the kind to schedule on his smartphone. When I don't see anything,

I check the living room, then the kitchen. Bingo. Tucked behind the landline phone is a 5 x 7 calendar. Mondays, Thursdays, and Fridays are marked off: *Running with Liam @ 7AM.*

When I pull open the drawer under the phone, I find an address book and fan through it. Liam Hofstettler. A phone number and an address. Ah, Peter's neighbor, in this building. Easy peasy. I'll wait until later, after everyone is likely to be home from work, to pull my PI act again.

I sit on the floor and retrieve my laptop. Peter's internet may or may not be connected, but I'd bet everything I own—which isn't much these days—that it's password-protected. There's a strong unlocked signal that I hop onto and then I log into my email. One new, from Dylan, *I'm going out of my mind sis, please be in touch*, and I realize that I'm going to have to make time to see him in the next day or two. I write back, *Dylan, please don't worry. I'm fine. I'll be in touch.* I can't give him any warning—I will never fully trust Camille.

I click over to Healing Hope and wait. WinPA99 has not been online for three days, according to her profile. Frustrated, I slam the lid shut. In the corner of the room I see it, on the bottom shelf of his built-in bookcase. The bright green spine, the jagged lettering. *The Serrated Edge.*

Peter has a copy of the book. For a moment, it strikes me as incongruous, the feeling of the floor moving under my feet like a listing ship. But then, of course he would. How could any of them resist buying a copy? I imagine Eileen Dresden, those chicken bits and gravy in her hair, cradling that deep green cover, fanning the pages over her face.

I flip it open and scan with my index finger until I find what I'm looking for. There is an entire chapter devoted to Colleen Lipsky. She was a nurse; she was well liked and active in the community.

The chapter is heavily highlighted:

The profile of Colleen Lipsky does not entirely match the profile of the rest of Lilith's victims:

1. *Lipsky was found outside, all other victims were found in their homes.*
2. *Lipsky had three stab wounds, two surface or hesitation wounds, and one mortal wound that nicked the carotid artery.*
3. *Peter and Lilith did not have a confirmed relationship.*

That part is true. The police never found any connection between Peter and Lilith, no torrid affair, not even a trace of Peter's credit cards being used at Drifter's. Of course, investigators argued, he could have paid cash. When asked, Lilith had laughed, *Peter? Oh God, what'd I want with him for?* She hadn't denied knowing Peter—or at least knowing *a* Peter—although she had said, *Don't know no Colleen, though.* But then she'd clammed right up, wouldn't answer another word, not one more question, and the detective in charge of the investigation at the time, the official lead—not Brandt—had taken her silence as acquiescence and pushed Colleen to the *Solved* pile. When Lilith was tried, she was tried on a total of six counts of first-degree murder.

When asked, an anonymous source within the PPD had this to say. "Lilith Wade was tried by a jury of her peers and convicted on the evidence available at the time. If she were to appeal the conviction of one murder, and win, it would not change her sentencing or her fate."

Interviewer: But do you believe that Lilith Wade killed Colleen Lipsky? Despite the case anomalies.

Anonymous: I believe the right person is on death row for the murder of Ms. Lipsky, yes.

Interviewer: But what do you say about the anomalies?

Anonymous: Are you insinuating that there is a copycat killer? Or that Ms. Lipsky was killed by someone else and staged?

Interviewer: Neither. I'm researching the truth. Ms. Lipsky does not seem to fit Wade's profile, that's all.

Anonymous: Murder is not a neat, well-thought act. Crimes are not by the book. They are committed by people in their most desperate moment.

I can't believe I hadn't realized it earlier.

Brandt was their source. I heard him say it a million times: *Murder is a mostly stupid act committed by mostly stupid people in their most desperate moment.* But why would he talk to a tell-all unauthorized biographist? They are glorified tabloid reporters. I skim down until I see another highlight.

She died of three stab wounds to the chest at approximately 9:50 in the evening on October 15, 1999.

October 15, 1999.

A ping across my consciousness. Something I hadn't noticed when I read the book the first time. I tap my fingers to my lips, try to catch it, and can't. Something about that date scratches at my mind. *Something. But what?*

• • •

I knock only once and Liam Hofstettler flings the door open, his keys in hand; his sunglasses fly off his head and clatter to the gleaming hardwood floor behind him. He laughs nervously and bends over to retrieve them while he asks me, "I'm so sorry, I was on my way out and had no idea anyone was here, can I help you?"

I smile blandly and extend my hand. I introduce myself as Jill Brand again, thinking I'll just stick with it. I like imitating Gil's name, even loosely. Later, if asked, they might confuse the names. *Yes, I spoke to the detective, Gil something, was it?* I imagined him finding out, and being needled, even irritated. It was both emotional and utilitarian.

I give Liam the rundown: I'm a PI on the case, hired by Peter's brother in Minnesota.

"Shit, I had no idea the guy had a brother." Liam scratches at his head and holds the door open for me, his hurry-up-and-leave plans abandoned.

"They weren't close. Estranged," I say, and shake my head like it's all very sad about Peter and this nonexistent brother and I wonder if I'll be forced to invent a name for him, too. I briefly wonder if I should just go all in and call him Gil, too. Why the hell not?

He invites me to sit, clearing away magazines and an errant paper plate on a butter-soft cream-colored leather sofa, and I realize that Liam Hofstettler is likely gay. The apartment is too bright, too airy, too something. I can't put my finger on it.

"I'm just looking for information on Peter. His brother is unhappy with the police investigation. It's been five days, you know?" I pull out the Moleskine and write the date and time and underline it all definitively. Underneath I write Liam's name and he watches me, interested.

"Peter had that same notebook," he comments, and I smile again.

"Really? What a coincidence," I say. "So you were the person who found Mr. Lipsky?"

Liam, startled, stares out the window for a second. A car horn blares out the window and he jumps, or maybe that's my imagination. Hard to tell.

"We run together, a few days a week. Usually Mondays, Thursdays, and Fridays, but Pete always has to switch it up. Which is fine. I, uh, work from home." He pauses. "Anyway, I knocked. No answer. Called for him, nothing. He's a straight arrow. He's never forgotten to call me, not once, and we've been meeting for a few years now. I knew his bedroom window bordered the alley. When I looked in, he wasn't moving. I knocked on the glass a few times, nothing. It was mostly dark, so I could only see a faint outline of him. I called 911, thinking he'd had a heart attack or something." He twists his lower lip between his forefinger and his thumb. "I never thought . . . this. Like, who would kill Pete? The guy was so mild, he barely fogged a mirror."

"Did you hear shots fired at all?"

"No, I really didn't. I have trouble sleeping, though. I use earplugs and a white noise machine. I don't know that I would have heard it."

"What do you know about his friends, girlfriends, anything at all?" I change direction.

Liam leans forward, resting his elbows on his knees, and the metal from his wedding ring glints in the sunlight. On the side table next to the sofa is a photo, Liam and another man, hugging in a bright spot of dappled sun between two trees on the edge of a golf course. I'd guessed he was gay from the leather sofa, not the ring and prominent wedding photo. I hope to God when all this is over I can have my job back, because I'll never eke out a living as an actual private investigator.

"He had a few girlfriends here and there. I mean, there was Lindy Cook, but she was kind of a mess. We always had him over for dinner, tried to set him up a few times with friends or my husband, Greg's, cousin, but nothing ever took. Pete's a strange dude." Liam pauses a moment and winces. "Was."

"I know it's hard," I say. "What did you think of Lindy Cook?"

"Oh, that girl. She wanted him. She didn't want him. She wanted to own him. She wanted nothing to do with him." He laughed a little and sat back. "Had him spinning circles. She was just young, you know?"

"Could she have killed him?"

He blew out a breath. "No. I don't know. She wasn't all there. But I wouldn't have thought she was a murderer. They came to dinner one night. She fell all over herself for him. Got him drunk. Pete wasn't a huge drinker."

I duck my head to hide the blush up my cheeks, thinking of Lockers, that moment in the alcove, the liquor on his breath. How quickly he'd gone from sober to stumbling.

"Can you think of anyone else I can talk to?"

"He hung out with our neighbor sometimes. I think across the hall and one over, apartment two, maybe? His name was Randall something. Seemed like a decent guy, but he might have seen someone that night. I wish I could help, really. I've known Pete for a long time. Since right after his wife was killed. You know about that, right?"

I nod.

"Craziest thing, the most unassuming guy in the world. To be this close to violence not once, but twice." He looks up at me, his eyes widening. "Could it be related?"

"I'm not sure," I say honestly. "We're looking into that."

I stand and shake his hand, thank him for his time. He's nice enough, walks me back to the door, shutting it behind me. I wonder, briefly, where he was headed and why he's no longer interested in going there.

I also wonder if anyone is telling me the truth.

∙ ∙ ∙

The most effective way to remain buried is to stay in one place. I should hole up in Peter's apartment and leave only when necessary. Unfortunately, I still need food. Shampoo. There are so many little inconveniences to existing.

I've frequented the corner store closest to Peter's apartment a handful of times. Today, I take a more circuitous route. I cut east and shop at Acme: bread, cheese, instant coffee, apples. The aisles are brightly lit and wide and I take my time. It's a weird feeling to appreciate an Acme. What had felt mundane and even inconvenient a mere week ago now feels decadent in its normalcy.

With my bags bumping against my leg, I make my way back to Peter's. It's dusk, the heat has relented, and there's a breeze through the trees. I haven't spent a lot of time in Chestnut Hill, but I always marvel at how pretty it is. Old stone buildings and looming oaks.

There's a man in front of me, his hand in his pocket, his head turning left then right as he scans the horizon in front of him.

I'd know him anywhere, even from the back of his head.

If I know him as well as I think I do, his eyes never settle on one thing, he continues to look at everything all at once: colors and movement and faces and voices. Taking it all in, his mind like a recorder, to be reviewed, examined, and analyzed later. I drop back into an alley between two duplexes and catch my breath.

Brandt. In Peter's neighborhood.

CHAPTER 14

Day 5: Tuesday, August 9, 2016

I follow Brandt all the way back to Peter's, keeping almost a full block and a half between us. If he turned, he wouldn't immediately recognize me, and I'd have time to turn into the next street, the next alley, hell, the next house, if I had to.

It's only five blocks, but he takes his time. He looks like a retiree out for an evening stroll. He's even dressed the part: a golf shirt and a pair of khakis. I've never seen him dress like an old man and it ages him instantly. Somehow, this humanizes him, almost makes me tender. I think about tapping him on the shoulder, asking, *Looking for me?* I'm tempted if for no other reason than to see the shock on his face. It would delight him.

He pauses in front of Peter's building. I keep my head low and lean against a car, pretending to scroll through my phone. I hold my breath, no inkling of whether my cover is going to hold up or not. He looks up, his gaze skips past me and down the street, before turning, continuing on toward Germantown Avenue.

The fact that he didn't stop at Peter's tells me two things:

1. He doesn't *know* I'm here. He's fishing. I bet he strolls past my apartment, Dylan's house, the CJC. Anywhere I could hide.
2. He's gone rogue. He's looking for me during his time off.

I'm grateful that I decided yesterday to leave Peter's door permanently unlocked. The lobby door is still locked with his numeric code. Peter's apartment is the first door on the right, so it's easy to duck into. Avoiding Liam and Peter's second neighbor, Randall, is now my second priority. My first is avoiding Brandt.

I won't turn on the lights, it's too risky. So once the sun goes down, I sit on the guest room floor with my laptop on my lap, waiting for WinPA99, figuring out what I'm doing tomorrow. Where I'm going next, whom I need to talk to.

None of the available Wi-Fi connections are unsecured tonight, so I take a risk and tether to one of my burner phones. I have an email from Brandt.

You're Jill Brand now? Come pay my rent, too, then?

I won't write back when I'm tethered, might as well toss the burner phone—and the data one, at that. I'll wait until tomorrow. The joke tells me that they are reinterviewing people they've already talked to. Which means they haven't come any closer to finding Peter's murderer. They've found no new leads—or few, anyway. No new leads means I'm still their focus. I don't trust Brandt, I don't trust his jokey tone. He wants me to come out, show myself, trust him and the system. He forgets one thing: I'm *in* the system. I've been in the system for a long time, first as a defendant, then as a cog in the wheel, and now, apparently, as a fugitive. My job is long gone; Weller surely cut that cord the first day I didn't show up. The police APB would have only sealed my fate. I have nothing to lose by staying underground.

With my computer screen blinking, I use Brandt's flashlight to explore Peter's bedroom. I keep the beam to the ground; even though there's only one window in his room that faces the alley, I take no chances. In his filing cabinet, I'm working my way through the hanging file folders, but I've started to skim, my eyes aching.

Working in the dark reminds me of Faithful. The summer I was twelve. The worst one, and somehow the best one, too. We'd made it to August, like a final gasp at the finish line, and Lilith seemed to shake with the effort. We hadn't been allowed to turn the lights on at night for most of July, and Lilith would sit, perched at the windows, her thin, knobby fingers working the curtains, rubbing them like a silk as she watched the houses up and down the block light up from within as the sun set. When it was fully dark, she'd check the lock on the front door, turning the deadbolts (there were two), over and over until she was sure—absolutely *sure*—we were all safe. We'd play UNO and the Game of Life by flashlight, cheap dollar-store finds that spit out weak beams and made the greens and blues look so similar we played as if they were the same, rather than figure it out. We knew playing UNO in the dark wasn't normal, but Dylan would save up all his Wild Draw Fours and fire them, one after the other, until you held nearly the whole deck, and we'd howl with laughter, and despite the fact we were sitting in the dark, Lilith felt normal.

We felt normal.

Some nights Dylan would sleep in Lilith's bed and Lilith in mine. She would curl around me, her palm flat on my forehead as she kissed my cheek, her breath sour from the medicine—later I'd learned that I could smell her meds on her. That her dry mouth from the Haldol gave her a fishy smell that, by that point, I'd come to associate with pleasantness.

Life with Lilith would turn from relatively normal—if playing cards in the dark could be counted as normal—to terrifying in the span of a week, the downward slide almost imperceptible until I learned to decipher the signs. Other years, I had called Pop by July from a phone at Mrs. Young's from next door and he'd been on his way. Those summers, I wonder if Lilith even realized I'd been there at all. Had she missed us when we left?

This year, we had hung in, though, clinging to the echoes of laughter by candlelight, the feeling of normalcy like a high we couldn't come down from. Then one morning she woke us at five, her hair slicked back, dressed in black, sweatshirt and pants, even in the heat. She drove us north, silent save for the rattle of the old Buick, to a state park where we camped for four days before everything slid sideways. The whole trip, I don't remember feeling like things were wrong. Later, we'd ask ourselves if we'd known.

We had hiked up to the waterfall that morning, left her alone, sleeping, and when we came back, she'd covered the tent with leaves and branches. She'd been manic, *they were coming, there was no time to leave*, she had to protect us. I saw it then, glinting in her palm, the flash of light off a small Colt 25.

Dylan ran, left me there, I had been shaking so bad, I'd urinated. We had no idea what was real and what was not, if the impending invasion was Lilith's imagination or based in truth. He said later that he called Pop from the pay phone at a lodge, a mile away. He told me he ran the whole time and I couldn't imagine that: my big-bellied, lumbering brother.

Pop committed her after that, and when she came out, a year later, she was subdued. Pop moved her out of Faithful and back to the city where he could keep an eye on her, into a rattly tin can of an apartment. Easier, sure, but the fire was gone. There was nothing behind her eyes, a bland smile, a slow blink. It was almost worse than if I'd never had her in the first place.

I spent a few years, in my teens, blaming Pop for that. See, he'd given me my mother and then he'd taken her away.

• • •

Randall Reynolds is tall with a long, thin nose and a thick brow, one side melding into the other, his hair grown shoulder length, wild and untamed. His eyes are deep-set, intelligent, but he's a bit manic. When I introduce myself, running through the whole PI bit, he shakes my hand enthusiastically and too long to be comfortable and I wonder if I'm being set up.

It's a gamble. I'd expect Brandt to have already spoken to Randall; the question is if he's been back a second time. If so, he would have warned him. *There's a woman impersonating a private investigator. Call me if you hear from her.*

"Anything I can do, anything. I loved Pete. Weird guy, but would do anything for you. Not superfriendly. Just whatever, man." The room is bare, no furniture, no rug, nothing but a single folding chair, which he offers me while he remains standing. "I'm getting new furniture. The old shit . . . was, well, shit. Well, anyway, you don't need to know all that."

"Mr. Reynolds—"

"Oh, call me Randall. Please. Mr. Reynolds is my dad." He laughs, loudly, inappropriately, and I clear my throat to cover it up. I think he's probably on something—speed, coke, some kind of amphetamine. His eyes skip around the place.

"Can you tell me if you saw anything weird around the time Peter was killed?" I ask gently, hoping to get him to settle, but he remains standing, pacing a little bit, two steps toward the kitchen, two steps toward the hallway, and back again. In the background, toward the bedroom, I can hear classical music. It's not uncomfortably loud here in the living room. But if he'd been in the bedroom, it would have been blasting. "Did you hear the gunshots?"

"Uh, well, I wasn't home all night, I stayed at a friend's house. I came home and was in the shower about 6:00 a.m.

or so, getting ready for work, and I swear I heard *something*."
He scratched his head.

"You didn't call it in?" I ask him, incredulous.

"Well, listen, there's always something in the city: a car, a
firework, construction. I wasn't sure what I heard was a gunshot. I didn't hear anything else after that, no screaming or
whatever, so what do you do?"

I want to say, *You call it in and let the cops handle it.* I write
down everything he said in the Moleskine on his own page.

"Did you notice anything else, either the day before or
later that same day? Anything at all?" I ask finally.

"Yeah, I told the other detective this. Two nights before
he was killed, a woman was pounding at his door. Yelling to
open the fucking door."

"Who? Who was it?" I ask sharply. I hadn't been expecting
a real answer, not like this.

"I've got no idea. She was pretty. Younger, I think. That
orangey-red kind of hair. She was swearing, demanding Pete
let her in. But you know, Pete wasn't there. She did leave, eventually. Listen, this is a nice section of town. These apartments
are big, cost a lot of money. We can't have that kind of thing
going on. The next day, the other neighbors talked about it."

He starts picking at a scab on his arm, scratching at the skin.
Red hair. "What did you do?"

"Nothing. I didn't do anything. He wasn't home." His
voice is defensive. "I should have called the cops, but I didn't.
I didn't even talk to her. I should have. Did she kill Pete?"

I open my phone and pull up the picture of Lindy and
show him. "This her?"

He takes it, squints. "No, but I know her. That was his ex."

No? Who else would it be if not Lindy? "And then what?
Did she leave?"

"Yeah, she kicked at the door first. I remember the next morning, before Pete was going to work, I grabbed him in the hall and

said, *Hey, buddy, you had a girl here last night. Redhead.* He seemed confused for a second, then pissed. He said, *Jesus fucking Christ,* and I'd never heard him say that before. He's a level guy."

"All right, you said you knew his girlfriend?" I ask.

"Oh, Lindy? Yeah, I knew her. She was okay. She's just young, you know? When everything is such a big fucking deal? She was like that. But overall, a good kid. Peter was a little old for her. I told her that." He coughs. "He was in over his head. She has daddy issues and she's trying to work them out and I don't think Pete's the guy for that."

"So you knew her outside of Peter?" I'm surprised.

"Oh yeah. A friend of a cousin. I met her at a party years ago. Then she shows up in my building with my neighbor. We laughed about it. Small world and all."

"What kind of daddy issues?" I shift and cross my legs, balancing the Moleskine on my other knee.

"I'm not sure, but her home life sucked. Her mom was killed, her dad was a drunk. She was on her own a lot from the time she was too small. I heard she has a new boyfriend now. Some Russian guy from the ballet. Pete told me about him; he seemed less than thrilled. She always dated old guys, I think."

Randall looks the same age as Peter. Does he consider himself in that category?

"One more thing: Did Pete ever mention a break-in to you? That someone was in his apartment?"

"A break-in? Here? When?"

"It would have happened about two weeks ago."

"First I'm hearing of it. You'd think he'd tell us, at least to warn us, neighbors and all." He rubs his jaw, thoughtful.

I stand and shake Randall's hand. I thank him for his time. Randall walks me to the door, and I leave and amble around the block, take my time. At this point, running into Randall again might put me back out on the street. I'm going to have to be extra careful.

Excerpt from The Serrated Edge: The Story of Lilith Wade, Serial Killer, *by E. Green, RedBarn Press, copyright June 2016*

Lilith left Faithful behind for Philadelphia at thirteen. She would later return, as an adult, because it was all she knew. It was familiar.

When she left, she had no plan, only a few hundred dollars that she'd stolen from the Putnaks. She took a train forty minutes into the city and lied her way into a busboy job at a diner. She slept at night in an abandoned building, fashioning an apartment out of what she'd stolen from Dumpsters in alleyways behind hotels. She ate from the diner where she worked, stealing the food from leftover plates while her supervisors pretended not to notice. Her coworkers knew she wasn't seventeen.

She lived like this for almost a year. Even through the coldest months, despite the unheated building.

When she was almost fifteen, she was arrested for trespassing when the building she was staying in was raided. She wouldn't give her age to the authorities, and she was put into the foster care system. She was shunted to a group home for troubled teens, a place she'd dubbed The Nightmare in all her interviews. Group homes for kids were transient, chaotic places. Crime was rampant, the living conditions weren't always clean or orderly. For kids with mental health problems, they were an accelerator, a catalyst.

We were able to connect with Lilith's social worker, who wished to remain anonymous.

Interviewer: What can you tell us about Lilith as a teenager?

Social Worker: She was defiant, sure. But most of them are, they're system kids. She wasn't worse or better than most. She was only with us for three years. She aged out and took off. She didn't finish high school, but that's not unusual, either.

Interviewer: Did she move a lot? Placement wise?

SW: Do you mean, did people give her back? Yeah, sure. She had a penchant for violence that was unsettling. She was angry, moody, and manipulative, but that wasn't the worst of it. What she did to anyone else was nothing compared to what was done to her.

Interviewer: What do you mean?

SW: There was an investigation, I'm sure you've seen it.

Interviewer: I haven't.

SW: One day, Lilith just shows up at my office. She's not crying, nothing. Listen, kids don't just show up at the Department of Child Services building. She must have taken two buses just to get here. She's got a bag with her and she says she's leaving. She'll be eighteen in a few months and she's just out. Can't live with this family anymore. So I calm her down, get her a sandwich. She bitched because there were pickles. Made the bread soggy. Funny, how I re-

member that. That's just how she was, though, you know? You'd do something nice for her and she'd needle you just to see if she could get a rise out of you. I didn't mind. I didn't have any certain affection for her, but her brand of personality didn't bother me, that's all. So anyway, anytime a kid requests to leave a placement like that, there's an investigation. We go over there and the foster parent, the woman, I forget her name now, is just furious. Ranting and raving and carrying on. Calling her a whore and what have you. I stopped her right there, I said Ma'am, she's seventeen years old. She's a child. *She hollers at me that no child ever did what she did.*

Interviewer: What did she do?

SW: There is nothing I haven't seen before. Nothing. But this one, well, I remember it, I'll just say that. She said Lilith seduced her boyfriend. Now, she didn't use that nice of a word, but I'm sure you get my point.

Interviewer: This isn't uncommon?

SW: Well, it's not common, *but it's not unheard of. Here's the thing. The "boyfriend" was almost fifty years old. I told the woman, that's not [mouths the word* fucking*], that's abuse. That's statutory rape.*

Interviewer: Then what happened?

SW: She lost her damn mind at me. Carrying on and screaming about that little bitch. She had no other kids in placement at the time. I placed a hold on them and filed a police report for statutory rape. They said they'd investigate, I don't know if they ever did. I'm guessing not. I pulled the couple from the system, though. They can't have any more kids, teenagers or not. When I looked back at the file, they took in all teenagers. Requested it specifically. That's an odd thing, you know?

Interviewer: *Did you ask Lilith what happened?*

SW: I did. She wouldn't answer me. I said, do you know that when a fifty-year-old man has sex with a seventeen-year-old girl, it's called statutory rape? It wasn't much enforced in the eighties, though. She wouldn't tell me anything, so I just kept talking, trying to get her to talk, you know? I said, listen, sex isn't some dirty, awful thing. But you have no business doing it with a man that age, that's all. The law says you don't know any better. I felt bad about saying that stuff, I do. She got so mad, I remember she picked up her chair and threw it across the table we were sitting at. She got so close to my face, with the flattest eyes I've ever seen, just nothing there. Scared the dickens outta me. She said, "I never fucked anyone." Screamed it, just like that, and I knew it then. That wasn't statutory rape, that was rape rape. That kind of violence kills the light and I'd never seen such deadness. She said, I ain't going back to The Nightmare neither. Then she sat back down, never said one more word. I put her up in a hotel that night—shame we gotta do that sometimes, but we do. I stayed in the room next door. She was in that room at ten o'clock. We watched some sitcoms, you know, with the laugh track? Then I went to bed. When I woke up the next morning, she was gone. That was the last I ever saw of Lilith Wade. But I never forgot her.

CHAPTER 15

Day 6: Wednesday, August 10, 2016

Alek Romanov lives in a brick condo complex with a wide, grassy courtyard dotted with trimmed pear trees and towering maples. The complex looks expensive.

I find Alek's name easily from the lobby mailboxes (4E) and buzz his apartment. He answers, "Yes?"

"Hello, Mr. Romanov, my name is Jill Brand, I'm investigating Peter Lipsky's death. Can I come up for a few moments?"

Silence. Then, "Are you the police?"

"I'm an investigator."

"I'm very busy, Miss."

"I understand that, but I just need ten minutes of your time."

I wait and it takes him about two full minutes, but he does eventually unlock the door. I hear the click and release of the lock and take the steps two at a time.

He is standing in the doorway of 4E when I come up the stairs, out of breath. It's only four flights, but I'm still huffing and puffing by the top. I should consider the gym when this is all over. Or maybe I can just use the one in prison.

"Ms. Brand, did you say?"

"Yes, are you Mr. Romanov?" I recover and extend my hand. He takes it gently but doesn't shake it, rather, he holds it between his two hands. After a few seconds, I pull back. Alek is taller than I'd expected for a dancer, thin but solid, his arms veined. His face is pleasant, deep-set lines around his mouth and dark brown eyes. He appears to be laughing at me, mocking, and I've hardly said a word. The effect is deeply unsettling.

"As I said, I'm a private investigator, Jill Brand. I'm investigating Peter Lipsky's death."

He leads me from the hallway into his living room, which is bright, floor-to-ten-foot-ceiling windows. If Randall's apartment was bare, Alek's is overcrowded with large black leather furniture, and ornate end tables. Carved stone elephants big and small rest on every surface. The whole apartment has a smoky smell. He settles himself into a chair and picks up a clove cigarette. "Do I know Peter Lipsky?" He gestures toward an oversized plush couch opposite him.

"I think so. Your girlfriend certainly knew him. She claimed he was stalking her." I sit on the edge of the seat and pull out my Moleskine. I'm getting tired of this drill. I wonder if Brandt ever gets tired of interviewing people, watching their reactions, trying to ferret out the truth from unsaid words and subtext, or if this is where the thrill lies for him.

"Ah yes, him." He gives me a banal smile.

"What do you know about their relationship?" I ask, suddenly unsure of how to proceed.

"All I know is that it is over, Ms. Brand." He flicks the cigarette into the ashtray next to him. The way he speaks, soft and affecting, is undeniably attractive. Soothing. The filtered light of late afternoon through the gauzy curtains makes him look exotic, almost dazzling. He isn't particularly good-looking, and yet something about him ties my tongue.

"Where were you the night of August fourth?" I ask him.

He stares at me for a moment before bursting into laughter. A hard, rocking laughter I wouldn't have thought him capable of. "Are you suggesting that I killed your Peter?"

"Sure, why not? Someone did. The jealous new boyfriend? It works on television." I scribble in the Moleskine, thinking about how half my notes are made up, fake or written down to buy myself time, not of any real value.

"No. I did not kill your Peter. I'd never even met him. He was hardly a blip on my radar."

I generally enjoy thinking on my feet, manipulating facts, bending the truth, to get what I want. I have the sensation that Alek can see me in my entirety, skin as transparent as cellophane. He sees all of me and finds me not only lacking, but amusing. I straighten my spine.

"Your girlfriend says he was stalking her. Doesn't that make him more than a blip on your radar?" I ask. He looks at me evenly.

"Lindy is a grown girl. She can take care of herself. This man, he was hardly a threat. He wanted her back. She's happier with me." He lets out a sigh. It has darkened, somehow, just that quickly. The burgundy glow of the carpet and the drapes cast an eerie pall over the room. "But to answer your question, yes, he was terrorizing her."

"Terrorizing?" I ask. I can feel the weight of the word and am certain that Peter was doing no such thing. "A minute ago, you pretended to not know who he was. Strong language, isn't it?"

"He calls her many times a day. He shows up at her work—our work—uninvited and unexpected. This is frightening for a woman, is it not? He's frightening her. He's terrorizing her." Alek leans forward, and exhales a sweet plume of smoke out the side of his mouth, away from me. "Or, he was."

"You saw him do these things? Show up uninvited? Call her?"

"Yes. A week ago. He showed up at the studio. They got in a fight in the lobby. He told her to leave *him* alone. See? He was delusional. Out of his mind."

"Or maybe she was stalking him and he'd had enough."

"Ha." His laugh is soft, lilting and feminine. Unexpected. "No. He follows her. She's called me, frightened, from the subway, the corner market, the street."

"Why?" I ask sharply.

"Why else? Why does any man do these things?" He lifts his shoulders once. "Love, of course. Always love. Men fall in love so much quicker, faster. It's been proven."

"Did she love him?" I pick a pretend bit of lint from my black pants and write something in the notebook.

"Ah, well, you'd have to ask her. They were lovers at one point. Bonded in shared tragedy, I'm sure you know. But now, she's moved on from him. He's too immature for her. Too pedestrian."

"Pedestrian?"

He laughs then, the sound unexpectedly loud. "Yes! Have you met him? He seems as dull as they come." His voice jumps up now, animated. He stands, crosses the room, and seats himself on the opposite end of my couch. The light outside the window is beginning to fade, the room is darker than when I'd first arrived, the twilight light casting a bluish glow onto his face. He leans toward me and I try not to lean away from him. "You have a beautiful face, you know that? Beautiful cheekbones, jawline."

I say nothing at first, his voice both mesmerizing and uncomfortable. Then, "Mr. Romanov, did you kill Peter Lipsky?"

He is undaunted. He even smiles, barely noticeable. "No. But why should you believe me?"

I have the sense that I've lost any notion of control. It

seems that since I've stepped into Alek Romanov's apartment, he's been in the driver's seat, and he seems completely, utterly unconcerned by any question I ask him.

He inches closer to me. "Let me ask you, are you working with the police?"

I hesitate. "I keep in touch with an officer on the case, yes," I say truthfully.

He reaches out and rests his hand on my knee. I stare at his long, knuckly fingers, his short, square nails, clean, and the loose, gathered skin above his wrist. The cigarette burns alone, resting in the glass-cut ashtray on the other side of the room, and I watch a curl of smoke lazily dance toward a window that has been cracked open, the August breeze pulling it gently outside.

"When did Peter show up at Lindy's work?" I ask him softly.

"Beg your pardon?" Finally, an indication of surprise.

"You said Peter showed up at Lindy's work. The ballet? When?" I subtly shift my weight and his hand falls away. He leans back against the arm of the couch and crosses his legs, gives me a wide smile.

"Three weeks ago. He was wild. Shouting. They went outside and had an argument. It was undignified and Lindy was shaken up."

"Did he threaten to harm her?"

"No. He accused Lindy of following him. He said he wanted to be left alone." Alek stops talking abruptly. "I do think he was a bit out of his head. Accused her of breaking into his apartment."

"Did she? Follow him, I mean?" I let the break-in question lie. Lindy had said something similar, too.

"Of course not. Look at Ms. Cook and look at Mr. Lipsky. Who would be chasing whom in this case? He was too old for her."

"Are you too old for her?"

He laughs. "I am a hundred years younger than Peter Lipsky, I assure you." The way he lowers his head. There is something otherworldly about Alek Romanov, as though he's stepped from the black-and-white screen of a Cold War–era movie, his villainy a near parody. He's putting on an act, and I realize too late that I've read him wrong, but I have no idea in which way.

I stand. "Thank you for your time, Mr. Romanov. I'll see myself out." I tuck the Moleskine back into the messenger bag. I brush past him and his hand encircles my wrist, so soft and gentle that at first I have to stare at it to understand what he's doing.

"Ms. Brand, it was an absolute pleasure." I expect him to kiss it, some weird throwback maneuver, but he doesn't. He lets me go.

I let myself out.

• • •

Wednesday morning, I am back at the Wayne Junction platform waiting for the train to Hatboro. Camille is at work, the baby is at daycare, my brother is surfing the internet under the guise of working. I study my phone, avoid looking at the cameras I know are pointed at the platform, inside the door.

The city cameras record on a constant loop, the hours feeding over one another. If there is an accident, or an incident, the engineer can press a button and the recording saves. As long as all goes according to schedule, the hour I spend on this train will be replaced with a new tape. Like I was never here. The city recording system is set up to catch pickpockets and bar fights, not fugitives.

The train lets me off at a station about a mile from Dylan's. Their house is small, a low-slung rancher on a tiny square of green with a short driveway and a brick walk. Camille works at a bank—a personal loan auditor. She spends her days deciding who is responsible enough to handle five and ten thousand dollars, based on their paper qualifications. She is generally haughty when she talks about her job—stuffed with self-importance, convinced she is the correct person to make these judgments. I asked her once if she'd give Dylan a loan and she smiled at me, tight lips stretched over teeth, and would only say, *Well, he has me.* She'd give herself a loan.

Listen, I wouldn't loan Dylan money, either. That's not the point.

A block before Dylan's, I cut through someone's driveway and walk up the yard. I'm not dumb enough to stand on Dylan's front porch and knock like an idiot. If Brandt was trawling Peter's neighborhood, he likely wandered around Dylan's, too. Visiting my not-altogether-stable brother could very well be the thing that does me in. Complacency. Ignoring the details.

Dennis Nilsen strangled fifteen boys in London in the early eighties. He cut up their bodies and flushed them down the toilet. When his drains got clogged, he had to call a plumber who found the pieces in the pipes. Details.

Here's the thing. No matter how hard you try, you can't escape who you are. In 1971, John List murdered his entire family and moved from New Jersey to Virginia. When they found him, he was remarried. *America's Most Wanted* aired an uncannily accurate aged-progressed model of List, including his signature horn-rimmed glasses. He'd spent his whole life longing to be an intellectual, an academic. It was part of his base makeup. He reinvented himself and could have been happy with that. He could have been just fine with everyone assuming he was an accountant; he was smart, he was part of a club he'd previously had no access to. But no, he needed to have the accessories. It wasn't enough just to *be* the part, he also had to *look* the part. The accessories are what ruin people; authenticity isn't enough, you must also prove that you're authentic.

You might ask how I know so much about serial killers. Call it another hobby. I must know them all: how they killed, how they were caught, and most pertinent to me right now, how they evaded capture. I knock softly on the back screen door (Camille hates air-conditioning, she says it inflames her sinuses and the fake air isn't good for Baby Matty) and when no one answers, I let myself in.

"Dylan?" I stand in his kitchen, shining and pristine and smelling like cleaner. I make my way to the living room, bright and airy.

"Edie?" When I spin around, Camille is holding Baby Matty tight to her chest, one arm under his bum, the other around his back, his head pressed into her shoulder. He's as still as a doll, and for a moment I think he's dead. Then he lets out a squawk and she loosens her grip, her eyes wild with fear. She wears a faint slip of a tank top and a pair of cutoff jeans. Her feet are bare and her toenails are painted bright pink, dusted with glitter. She's had a pedicure. She looks fresh, young, even.

"Where's Dylan?" I ask her, and she glances out the window, then back at me.

"He . . . ," she falters, and shifts the baby onto her hip. He's fat, with dimpled cheeks and thighs and I want to hold him, to kiss his forehead and blow raspberries against his belly. I imagine his baby skin on my lips. I've never held him, not once—never even asked, assumed I'd be denied even if I'd wanted to. I haven't held a child since Hazel. "He's not here. He got a new job."

"Not at 8A? Where?" I ask immediately. He would have told me. I think. 8A was entirely remote. His promotion would never have taken him away from the house.

"You have to leave. You can't be here." Her tongue runs

along her bottom lip, quick and darting like a snake. She holds the baby's head against her shoulder and shields him from me.

"Camille," I say, stepping toward her. "What's going on? Where is Dylan?"

"I told you. He got a new job. You have to leave. I don't know what you did, and I don't want to know. But I have a baby here. I will call the police if I have to." I see her eyes dart to her cell phone lying on the end table, next to a sweating glass of water. I can picture her there, holding the baby (I wonder if his feet have ever touched the ground?), scrolling through her Facebook, sipping on a cool glass of water after cleaning the house. For the first time, I hear music—a country twang from a radio—playing from somewhere in the back of the house, toward my brother's office. Dylan hated country, he'd never sit in his office and listen to it. The living room is different—not just brighter. They've gotten new furniture.

"Where did he get a job?"

"I can't tell you that, Edie." She gives me a pitying look, her eyes slanted. Shuffles sideways and picks up her phone, all while keeping her death grip on Baby Matty.

I take a step toward her. "Hey there, Matty boy, how are you?"

"Get away from my kid." Her voice is low, cut with warning.

I back up and put my hands up. "Camille. I didn't kill anyone. He's my nephew, I can say hello."

"I want you out of my house." Her face is going red with the effort of holding Matty, her muscles straining in her pale pink tank top, her toes flexing on the lemon carpet.

"Where's my brother?" I ask again. "He didn't get a job, he would have told me. Where is he?"

"He's not supposed to be talking to you. He promised he—" She cuts off, her eyes squeezing shut and her mouth pinched. "He *promised*."

"Where is he, Camille? Tell me now or I'll—"

"What? What will you do, exactly, Edie? Call the police? Report him missing? Go into the station, file a report?" She lets out a laugh, but it comes out like a yelp. She steps toward me, the baby between us. She narrows her eyes, and her voice goes honey sweet. "You look different, Edie. Is your hair much shorter? And brown now? You have glasses? And are you . . . Are you tanning?"

I'd found an old, crusted bottle of self-tanner in the back of Peter's bathroom cabinet. I used a dab on my face, just to take the bluish-white tint off my pale skin, figuring any measure would help. It gave me a faintly healthy glow, like I'd just run a 5K in the hot August sun. Underneath the tan, I feel my cheeks flush. She's trying to make me feel stupid, but also, discovered. Camille bounces the baby on her hip now, more in control, less scared.

Before I can say anything, she continues, "You should just go back to wherever you came from, Edie. Don't come back, okay? There's really no reason to." Matty grabs a fistful of her shining blond hair and her blue eyes blink at him, a quick second of hot anger before melting to something softer and more pleasing. She pushes his chubby hand back against his side, holding him still while he squirms, and tilts her head at me. "Anyway, honey, your brother doesn't live here anymore."

CHAPTER 16

Day 7: Thursday, August 11, 2016

People have never understood that Lilith could be normal. Not just normal but motherly. I wouldn't say loving; but then again, I'm never sure what loving actually means. She could be tender. Her brand of tenderness, in retrospect, seems as contrived as playacting. But as a child, I ate it up, tucked into the sour curve of her armpit, anxious for her affection, her touch.

I'd gotten scarlet fever when I was thirteen. My body had been covered in red, scaly patches and welts, itchy and stinging. I remember lying in bed, the sheets soaked beneath me, thinking I could die.

Pop was still working in those days, at the wastewater treatment plant in West Philly, he'd come home smelling like rotten eggs and onions, a warm body smell that was both repulsive and comforting. He had little vacation or sick time, so he hadn't known what to do with me, my hair matted to my face, the sweat pooling beneath my scalp.

Lilith came to stay—the only time I could remember them living under the same roof. At the time I thought she'd come on her own, a siren song sent out into the night: her child in trouble, a motherhood bat signal. The idea that she could be intuitive, that we were in tune, pleased me. I had always loved her attention. When I would later sift through my childhood memories, putting together the story—how Pop loved Lilith but couldn't live with her, how Lilith may have loved Pop—I'd recall a phone conversation in hushed whispers, with his rough hand on my cheek and two words, *please come.*

She did, because ultimately, she did what he'd asked of her and always would. She'd brought me ice chips, rubbed alcohol and cold water across my face, changed my sheets. She'd taken care of me, singing Nina Simone, "To Love Somebody." I've thought about this day, the sultry rasp of her voice, the small rock of her hips, countless times as an adult. She wasn't singing to me, she was just *singing.* She didn't love somebody, the way she loved me, because I've become convinced—maybe accurately, maybe through delusional self-preservation—that Lilith didn't know how to love. That love is taught, not born. If I think about it long enough, I end up wondering who taught me and the answer is both obvious and surprising: Dylan.

Lilith would go to work at night, bartending the way I'd always known, sometimes leaving with a quick kiss on my forehead and sometimes not, smelling like cheap perfume, her lipstick fanning into the creases around her mouth. As Pop took her place, they'd talked about me at low volume in the hallway, just beyond my bedroom door. Exchanging information, sharing the details of my sickness.

I'd regretted getting better, even stringing it along. Answering *How do you feel today?* with more frailty and apprehension than I'd felt. Until I couldn't drag it out any longer. When it was gone, I missed it: the wet pillow beneath my head, Lilith's cool, frail fingertips twisting a knot out of my hair, grazing the back of my neck, the stilted way she sometimes moved around, unsure of her place in Pop's home.

I had no memory of Dylan being there at the time, until he'd mentioned it when we were out to dinner one night.

"Do you remember when you were sick?" he asked. "And Lilith stayed with Pop?"

I'd nodded. *To Love Somebody.*

"I saw them dancing, in the living room."

I didn't tell him that I don't even remember him being there. That I assumed he'd been sent to stay with a friend to avoid contagion.

"Edie." Dylan had leaned in with urgency. "I saw Pop cry."

My bighearted but stoic, somewhat lumbering father mourning the woman he wanted Lilith to be. The woman she would never become. Her mental failures. How many times in his life had he questioned himself? His decision to leave? It would have been endless. I didn't tell Dylan about Pop on the porch, right after Lilith was arrested, weeping. I felt proprietary over the memory—that it was mine alone.

All this happened during the time that Lilith was killing. Maybe not the days, or even the months. But the years. She'd started when I was twelve, and was caught when I was fifteen, all after Pop moved her back to the city. Out of Faithful, away from the trailer park and back to the city. When she started working at Drifter's, and we stopped going to see her in the summers.

We thought she was better here.

I was sick in October, right in the beginning of the school year. My first year at a charter school. I was gone for a month and no one even realized it. When I came back, some kids called me the new girl, and I'd never corrected anyone. I can't remember how long after that I'd met Mia, then Rachel, and their twosome became three and I nearly forgot about my illness, the memory pulling at the corners of my mind, and only in the darkest part of the night.

Everyone wanted a piece of this, to know: *What was it like on the inside?* This is the one thing that people never understood, even after the documentaries and the think pieces when they asked, *How couldn't they have known?* Sometimes, Lilith was just my mother.

* * *

It seems ridiculous that Dylan wouldn't live at his house anymore, but why on earth would Camille lie? The answer is obvious: so that I would leave. Maybe for good. She's never liked me, never trusted me. She's always treated Dylan like a bothersome, yet lovable, pet—a cat who keeps getting underfoot, a dog who barks a little too loudly. Unless, unless. She's kicked him out. Where would he go? He has no job. He can't be alone, never has.

Dylan hopped from college to college—a stutter-step affair of three different universities, finally graduating but barely, with a degree in some kind of business administration, which was actually a fairly hard degree to obtain and reinforced my idea that they'd passed him through more on some combination of pity and exhaustion—Dylan could be exhausting. I guess he could have gotten through on merit, but it always seemed to me that he bumbled his way. Later, he held various jobs for the short term, but always had trouble with a boss, a coworker, *something*. He'd been laid off twice due to resources and once he just up and quit (a coworker had accused him of sexual harassment because he'd bought her a drink at a company happy hour, his story), and ever since that job—at a tiling place where he did the books—he'd been job searching and holding out for his middle-management position.

It's not that I blamed him, but after graduation, he

moved in right away with Camille. They were married for years before Baby Matty came along. They'd had trouble, Camille grew obsessed, and Dylan seemed in a constant state of fret. Still, it seemed like Camille was born a mother and she tended to Dylan like he was her responsibility. She was always furious on his behalf when he was laid off, and indignant when he quit. When Pop was still alive they'd have hour-long dinner conversations about all the injustices in Dylan's life, and I always shrank back against the seat, feeling like it was some kind of big production so that no one would have to talk about the mess that was my life—living with Pop at the time, a pending DUI, an obvious alcohol problem, and a short-lived stint in rehab, followed by a retail job that I'd forget to show up for once I dipped back into the vodka.

Dylan had no idea how to live alone. I mean, I guess no one does, but he'd never learned. He'd never had to. Even their house was Camille's before they'd gotten married. I remember once, years ago, being there for lunch and Camille had made sandwiches. She'd cut his on a bias, the way Mia's mom had cut hers in high school. He'd nibbled on his white bread triangles and talked about his latest hobby. Actually, Dylan didn't have hobbies; he courted obsessions. He spent massive amounts of money, racking up credit debt only to have the interest fizzle out in months. He'd gone through model trains, craft beer making (in that small kitchen, too, the only time I felt sorry for Camille), the guitar (he later switched to the trombone). The beer made the whole house stink like a locker room—a hot, yeasty smell that clung to the drapes.

My point was, he didn't move out of his own accord. There was no way. I tried to recall the living room: the television, Dylan's chair—the soft puddling of loose blue fabric in the middle where he sat for hours at night skipping through cable channels trying to find something to settle his mind—mostly picking true crime shows that he'd tell me about later. Once even finding one on Lilith Wade and calling me at midnight, gleefully frantic.

I pulled one of the burner phones out of my bag and sent an email to Dylan, one line: *Where are you?*

On a whim, I navigate to the website for 8A Games.

On the company website, I find a list of options and click the support button. There are selections for email, form letter, live chat. I click the live chat and it asks me for my phone number. I hit the info button on the burner phone and type the phone number into the box. It's a stupid move, but I have to do it. A dialogue box returns that says someone will call me in approximately six minutes.

It's a long six minutes.

When the phone rings with an Arkansas phone number, I pick it up, cursing myself the whole way. Something so innocuous as answering the phone could be the thing that undoes this whole mess.

"Hi," I say to the support technician, before he barely has a chance to say hello. "I have an odd question, but I'm looking for Dylan Beckett. I think he was a service rep for you guys?"

"Who?" the guy asks, suddenly leery.

"Dylan Beckett," I repeat.

"Listen, I don't know. We all telecommute. There's probably a zillion of us and it's not like we have office Christmas parties, you know?" His voice is nasally and he snorts at his own joke.

"Sure, I understand. Do you all report up to the same supervisor?"

"Yeah," he says slowly. "But I'm not sure what this is about. Is the dude in trouble or something?"

"No, not at all. He's actually missing and this is listed as his last place of employment, so it will help me verify the timeline if I can find out when the last time he logged into work was, you know?"

"Oh shit, that's crazy, um, let me have someone call you back okay?"

The guy hangs up and I bang the phone against my forehead. I am fucking this all up.

It rings back and I answer.

"Yeah, so I hear you're looking for someone who works here?" It's a different guy, a deeper voice, his voice echoing as if through a tin can. I'm being recorded, I realize, too late to do anything about it.

I repeat the story I told the first guy. "If you could just tell me the last time he logged into work, that would really help us out, you know?"

"Yeah, I hear what you're saying, but I can't do that." He coughs into the phone, thick and hesitant.

"Listen, I get it. I know customer service personnel sometimes use alternative names for privacy and identity, but all I need is a last login—"

"No, ma'am." He cuts me off. "I mean Dylan Beckett hasn't worked for 8A in six months."

• • •

I call Brandt.

He picks up on one ring and I don't even bother with a hello.

"Brandt. Listen, my brother is missing."

"Come in and file a report, then." I can hear the sardonic tone of his voice, a slight teasing edge.

"I mean it, Brandt. I can't get in touch with him," I said, impatient with him. "And he was fired from his job about six months ago. He never said a word about it."

"Okay, I'll send a guy over. Are you, uh, there now?"

He was going to try to triangulate me. With a phone number, he can ping it off different cell towers and figure out a location within a block or two. The phone I was using was dead.

"No, I'm not there now. Am I an idiot?" I'd taken the train back to the city expressly to make this call. I'd start the long walk back to Peter's as soon as I threw away this phone. What a waste. Through the line, I think he laughs.

"Okay, I'll check on your brother. Hey, while I have you . . ." He pauses then, talking in the background. I stomp my foot impatiently. He can't keep me on the phone just to trace me.

I say as much. He sighs and comes back on the line. "What do you know about Peter's coworker Tom Pickering?"

"Nothing. I don't even think they were that close. Why? Is he a suspect?"

He pauses for a second and I contemplate just hanging up. The longer I hang on, the more danger I'm in. Come on, *come on.* "Brandt! How many suspects do you have? Officially."

He sighs into the phone. "Officially? Just the one."

Goddamnit. "What about Lindy Cook?" I ask. "The girlfriend? The crazy one? Have you really looked into her? She knew where Peter was going that night." Her chance meeting with Tom Pickering. *Lockers @ 4.*

I hear a rustle. A sign. Then he says, "Edie," and he never calls me Edie.

Fuck.

I don't hang up, but instead throw the cell into the nearest garbage bin and jog uptown, putting as much concrete between myself and that trash can as I can.

• • •

The walk back to Peter's takes me over two hours, more time than I planned. It's past eleven when I punch in the key code and let myself in.

My brother is missing. My ungainly, slow-blinking brother, with all his get-rich-quick schemes that never had a shot at working. The way he was convinced, in childhood, that he protected me. Saved me from Lilith and that saving me was all that mattered. His own childhood had been indispensable to me later, or at least this is how he saw himself: as the hero of his own story. His emails had become more urgent and frantic the longer I stayed under.

He lied about a job.

I should have written him back. Technically, I did, once. But once is never enough for Dylan, he doesn't do subtlety. In order to assuage his fears, I would have had to call him daily.

Camille could have killed him. That serene, plastic smile, bouncing Matty against her thigh. I imagine her stabbing him, her hands slick with blood. Maybe shooting him. In my frame of reference, with only the mildest of inclinations, people can kill.

But I'm self-aware enough to know that regular, normal people do not kill each other.

In Peter's room, I string a blanket up against the window, pushing it down around the curtain rod and taping the edges to the wall with duct tape I find in the kitchen. I refuse to sit in the dark every night.

Why would he tell me he had been promoted when he had been fired months before?

My worry for Dylan is a tightly held fist inside my chest, a panic I can't give in to. I long for my apartment, fresh green-striped sheets, my patchwork quilt, mohair throw pillows, and clean gray bedside table. The things that were mine; I'd worked so hard in my life to have things that were mine. I'd always felt like I'd worked harder than anyone. I should have just done what Dylan had done. I could have sunk into some stagnant, stale life with a husband—anyone I'd let myself get close to. Spent my days being cared for, catered to. There is no shortage of men who want to care for a helpless woman. Instead, I'd pushed forward, through alcoholism and legal trouble and Brandt and Lilith and even Tim. I'd resisted Tim, all to be this person—my own person who needed no one, the opposite of Dylan, who seemed to need everyone—and now I can't help feeling, in this walled-off cave of Peter's bedroom, like it was all for nothing.

With the only window sealed tight, I flick on the lamp. Peter's room, despite the missing square of mattress and hot, sour undertone that I realize is dried blood, is actually pleasant. Deep grays and light blues, almost the color scheme of Matty's nursery. His desk is organized, his files in a row.

This is so pointless. What am I doing? A reasonable person would turn themselves over to Brandt and let him do his job. But I was the last one to see Peter alive. My DNA is at his apartment. My apartment is filled with notebooks, startling ramblings, observations about the families of Lilith's victims. To all outward appearances, I followed Peter to Lockers to kill him. I am my mother's daughter.

Officially? Just the one. If I don't want to be arrested, I have to lead the police to another suspect.

In Peter's closet, I return to the shoebox, pushing through the glossy, faded photos aimlessly, marveling at Colleen's effortless, insistent beauty: straight white teeth and wild, blowing hair. When I try to return the shoebox to the shelf, under all Peter's sweaters, it won't slide easily. I lift the stack of various colored cable knits to see what the issue is.

A manila folder has slid out from underneath the clothing stack to the left. I pull it out and leaf through it.

Case Report, Philadelphia Police Department

LAST NAME: Lipsky
FIRST NAME: Colleen
PLACE OF DEATH: Philadelphia, PA

Autopsy Findings
Cause of death: Multiple sharp-force injury stab wounds to chest. Significant hemothorax. Severed anterior descending coronary artery. Two superficial or nonmortal wounds.

Mortal wound is located 16 inches below the top of the head and 2 inches from the back of the body. After approximation of the edges it measures 1-1/2 inches in length and is diagonally oriented; the posterior aspect is dull or flat, measuring 1/32 inch, and the anterior aspect is pointed or tapered. Estimated minimum total depth of penetration is 3–4 inches.

Description of weapon: Smooth blade, 8–12 inches in length, clean exit.

See diagrams on page 4.

Peter had Colleen's autopsy report. Why? In my years working for the city, I'd never heard of a victim's family requesting to keep copies of the report. Most people avoided the idea of autopsy, their loved ones being cut into and splayed open on a steel table almost too much to bear. And here is Peter, his wife's formal report hiding in his closet. Did he pull it out, thumb through it at night? The edges look crisp, barely glanced at.

I read over the report again, my eyes skipping around at

the medical jargon, *hemothorax* and *anterior descending coronary artery*, and note a few things. First, there were only three stab wounds. *The Serrated Edge* had covered that, casting doubt and stirring controversy. At least the report and the book check each other out.

Lilith was tiny, but strong. Her physical strength was a gift from Mother Nature, a tacit apology for all her mental deficiencies. I'd watched her once, in a fit of rage, topple the sofa, a seventies monstrosity before they used pine and balsam, stuffed through with old damp foam, heavy with years of absorbed sweat and microscopic flakes of skin. Still, her victims were all stabbed sixteen, seventeen times. Some wounds deep, fatal, others tired, surface, like her rage had just leaked out mid-frenzy. At autopsy, it was discovered that Annora had suffered through a record seventeen fatal and surface wounds. God, Lilith had really loved Quentin. But here there were just the three.

Colleen, again, was the outlier.

See, Lilith had come home from the state hospital back in 1998 and gotten assistance, Pop even helped her fill out the grant paperwork. She was better now, he'd promised. She moved a few blocks away, Pop said we weren't going to be allowed back next summer, not alone, anyway, but she could live where he could keep an eye on her. He brought her dinners a few nights a week, checking her med levels while she tinkered in the living room. She'd gotten a job waitressing at a run-down bar, and the tips weren't bad once Lilith learned to smile at the men.

By 1999–2001, when the bulk of the murders happened, the city had been printing monthly reports on the Serial Killer—they hadn't given him any kind of sensational name yet, and of course, everything pointed to *him*, no one even considered the possibility that the murderer was a *her*. On the next page were the overtime reports for the city employees, with the homicide detectives at the top. *Solving fewer crimes with more of your money.* There were town halls every year on it, there still were, the mayor flapping his hands at an overrun crowd murmuring about unsolved rates. The headlines varied, but they were cohesive in their theme: "There Is a Serial Killer and Your Cops Don't Care." It was a wonder that more "Unsolveds" didn't get swept under the Lilith Wade rug.

Sometimes I try to look back, see the signs, but even now, I don't. Lilith's unraveling, her descent into madness that summer she was finally caught in 2001, was no different from her wild swings with sanity before it. It had become normal. And yet the press, the book, my former friends, all couldn't stop asking: Why hadn't anyone seen what she was doing? Why hadn't we known? If we'd paid just a little more attention, would anyone still be alive? Would Colleen?

I summon the words from the book, what had the author called it? *The jagged edge of torn flesh.* Murder is a sloppy act. If the blade had a serration, it was all but guaranteed to tear the skin loose, ripping. Lilith's knife: three inches of plain blade, three inches of serration. A countryman's tool, not a city dweller's weapon. When she'd tucked us under that tent covered in branches and leaves with a gun in one hand, in the other, she'd held that knife.

I skip up to the autopsy report's description of the knife and wound: *Smooth blade, clean exit.*

I think it's long been assumed that she'd stabbed Colleen with the smooth edge of her knife. It's so much easier to assign blame, apologize, retract, drop charges later. After all: Six murders or five? It's all the same to the murderer. But to the police? One less headline.

Which, technically, is still possible. But I'd spent my childhood looking at that knife, clattering around a drawer, sawing through a loop of cable tie. I used it myself to whittle a stick—dangerous, but who would have stopped me?

Estimated minimum total depth of penetration is 3–4 inches.

A good lawyer would have had to argue the point, it's a difference of less than one inch; perform a sensational demonstration for a jury. I think of the stacks of evidence that must have existed. Hundreds of files, investigation and autopsy reports, just like this one, for six women. I think of the public defender—we had no money for a real defense and even if we had? Who's to say if Pop would have used it to defend her? Three inches of blade, three to four inches of penetration, smooth blade entry and exit.

CHAPTER 17

Gil Brandt, Philadelphia Police Department, Homicide Division,
August 2016

A week in and they had another body already. Not the same killer, not connected in any way, but Brandt was up. His turn to be the lead on a new case. The DOA was a street shooting, a young kid, found with drugs in his pocket. Brandt didn't care about any of that.

"Switch leads with me?" Brandt asked Merket, but knew it didn't work that way. The other guys switched, but Brandt never did. He played the hand he was dealt, always. Plus, the captain didn't have a lot of patience for detective shenanigans, and Brandt was mostly a rule follower. At least in-house. On the street, he tended to think the rules shifted depending on the day, but that was more natural law than anything else.

Merket gave him a long look. "You've never once asked for that. Listen, we have her on motive, means, opportunity, and now we have physical evidence, her DNA all over the scene."

"You barely have motive—claiming she's batshit crazy just because her mother was doesn't hold water, and if you can't connect her to the gun, you don't have means, either.

You have physical evidence of sex, not of murder. C'mon, Merket, there's a difference. If there wasn't, Klipper'd be arrested every Friday night." Lance Klipper, who was sitting across the aisle, looked up and smirked. Brandt knew he'd been listening. He lowered his voice. "I've never asked for a favor."

"And if I give you this one, Potts'll be all over it. It doesn't pass the smell test and you know it. You got something going on with this girl?" Merket raised his eyebrow and Brandt wanted to sock him. Captain Potts liked the internal regs more than he liked the law itself. He was a *t*-crosser and an *i*-dotter.

"Of course not, but I *am* personally invested. I arrested her mother. I knew her father. I helped her get a job. Isn't that what we're supposed to do as *police officers*? Help the members of the community?" Brandt coughed; he almost couldn't eke the next words out. "She's like a daughter to me."

There was a lot more leeway for a cop who was led by his heart rather than his dick.

Merket sighed. Tapped his pencil.

"Look. You don't have shit and you know it. You know who can find her? Me. I know that kid like nobody, and I really mean nobody, else. She'll never trust any of you, but she might trust me." Emphasis on the *might*.

Brandt was making progress. Finally, Merket said, "You know it won't fly. Work it on the side. Log the interviews and let me know. But don't take the whole thing off on some un-beaten path. We'd have to prove pretty squarely that she didn't do it for the DA to take it. With a shit ton of evidence and a confession from someone else. It's just too much to counter otherwise. Could you really get that? You don't even have a theory."

Brandt nodded, sat back at his desk, and tapped the eraser end of a pencil against his knuckles. More overtime, but people hardly questioned that anymore. The clearance rate had dipped below 50 percent. People were antsy, citizens and the department alike.

Problem was, he had no other theory in mind. Brandt thumbed through his copy of the file. He was getting to be the only guy in the office that kept manila folders around. Clipped to the inside was a photo they'd found in the kitchen trash at the scene. Lipsky's wife, a picture from college. Ripped into two pieces, the other half of the photograph missing. They'd dusted and released it, finding only Lipsky's prints. Why had it been torn up? Where was the other half? His wife, that he'd loved and missed so much. Hell, not like he truly understood marriage. He'd probably rip up a picture of his ex on a good day. But still. He wondered. The Cook girl seemed fine, just skittish and nervous, with an overprotective new boyfriend. Both had alibis and Brandt just never got any vibe from either of them. The boyfriend was an odd bird, but they were rehearsing all night and then the two of them were together. Not airtight by any means, but a neighbor had seen them leave the Russian's apartment at six-thirty in the morning. They were at the studio by seven. Hard to kill a guy between five and six, almost an hour away by train, and get back in time to pirouette with your girlfriend.

When his phone rang with an unknown number, he answered it. Merket didn't glance up.

"Brandt. Listen, my brother is missing." Her voice was low, urgent, and cut through with panic.

Brandt stood up with forced nonchalance and made his way across the squad room, the thin paper case file in his hand. There was an unused conference room in the corner and he shut the door behind him. "Come in and file a report, then." He said it tongue in cheek, hoping to get a rise out of her. It didn't work. She says something about him being fired but her voice is drowned out by a car horn.

"I mean it, Brandt. I can't get in touch with him." A shuffling of papers, the soft click of a door, and then a deep-welled silence.

Missing brother. Brandt's first thought was that someone was picking them off, the leftover Becketts. Some copycat serial killer, or a tormented family member. They could easily pin the whole thing on Edie—take down the whole family. Brandt almost opened the door, waved to Merket to come in. They could have worked the phone, tried to keep her on the line. The thing was, Edie was too smart for that. She'd be gone by the time Merket lumbered his big ass over here.

Brandt went for the stall, tried to listen but only heard the sounds of the street: cars, horns, a whoosh of air. "Okay, I'll check on your brother. Are you there now?"

She cursed him out, and he almost laughed. He tried to keep her on the line, and flipped through the interviews. "Hey, while I have you, what do you know about Peter's co-worker Tom Pickering?" he asked, working through his next move and drawing a blank. She saw through him in no time.

"Brandt! How many suspects do you have? Officially."

He sighed, rubbed his eyebrows together. "Officially? Just the one." Her.

He wanted to say so many things: that if she talked to him, he'd help her. That he would help her again, and again, probably for the rest of his life. Why? He wasn't in love with her. That was insanity. He wasn't so far wrong when he'd said she was like a daughter to him. He also wanted to reach through the phone and knock the sense into her. She started talking about Lindy Cook, her voice laced thick with panic. Maybe that was how he could get to her. Get her to come unglued, push against the wound.

"Edie," he said. He never called her Edie. Always Beckett. "What are you doing? What were you doing? Standing outside their houses? Writing down the intimate details of their lives: affairs, meals, internet habits, swim times, for God's sake. Do you know how that looks? You seem unhinged. That's not normal, justifiable behavior. Let me help you. I will, you know? Meet me. I want to know the truth. Do you trust me?"

Brandt knew he'd never log the call. Never write up the meeting. That not doing so would violate every reg he could think of. Fraternization was the least of it.

She hadn't hung up, but it had gone silent. "Edie?" he asked again. She wasn't there. He looked at the time, the seconds counting up. He'd only been on the call for three minutes.

He stood, walked back across the squad room, and handed the phone to Merket.

"It's Edie Beckett," Brandt told him. "Called me from a burner phone, said her brother is missing. You can track the phone, it's still connected."

Merket lit up like Christmas and Brandt left him with his present and went outside. The heat off the pavement smacked him in the face.

He knew Merket would ping the location and peel out of the garage in an unmarked car. He'd chase that call all the way to a corner garbage can. It would keep him busy for a while, as it was intended to do. If he was smart, and he was, Merket would pull the video surveillance footage in the stores and businesses around the corner.

If Edie was smarter, and she was, there wouldn't be any.

CHAPTER 18

Day 8: Friday, August 12, 2016

I wake up on the floor, not knowing where I am and forgetting for a moment why I'm there. Peter's area rug has worn a pattern into my cheek and my forearm and I hold my palm against my stomach, which is rumbling and hungry.

The loaf of bread I've been eating has gone stale but has not yet started to mold, so I use it to make toast, which I load with peanut butter to make it more palatable. While I chew, I think.

I'm not only one who thinks the autopsy report doesn't add up, that the math was too neat. In the book, the Colleen chapter delved into this: no link from Lilith to Peter, no confession, no memory of Peter, and then the knife. Three inches. No serrated edge.

It's possible that Lilith didn't kill Colleen.

This is both interesting and terrifying and somehow satisfying, and I mull it over—the satisfaction part, trying to figure out the root of that feeling.

There is not a lot of tolerance for people who aren't heroes in times of crisis; for people who are instead scared or in denial, or, as in my case, self-involved teenagers. The papers and magazine articles, and even the book, have spent an inordinate amount of time focused on why no one in Lilith's life could see what she was doing, or suspect her of anything, for so long—years!—enough to call the cops, prevent just one death. There is no shortage of people who believe they wouldn't have done the same, who are convinced of their instincts, and their moral superiority.

I spend a few minutes prodding the vaguely positive feeling. Instead of actual, effective therapy, I've researched how to mentally heal myself, and Dr. Dole, a famous (or infamous) internet psychologist, has stressed the need to stand still. Acknowledge the feeling. Press against it in your mind, blow it up, find the root. It's a visual exercise—one that Dylan had called a "lot of hooey," but it seemed to work for me. Sometimes I could visualize my fingers stretching apart inside my brain, the way you blow up a picture on a tablet or device, and visualize the expansion of my emotion.

Relief. I feel relief.

If Lilith didn't kill Colleen, then Peter's death wasn't related to Lilith at all, and I couldn't be responsible. Except, of course, the fact that Colleen was *thought* to be killed by Lilith and that I was in Peter's apartment mere moments before he was killed couldn't be ignored. If anything, I was only slightly less responsible.

I live under the radar on a normal day. I had assumed there was office gossip at the CJC, but their scale of normalcy was skewed. We worked with criminals and drug addicts every day. It was likely that they knew who I was and didn't care. Or kept their distance. Or even, because of their jobs, avoided true crime documentaries and tell-all biographies.

Still, it wouldn't be impossible for someone with an ax to grind to find me. I never changed my name, or altered my identity in any way. As a minor, my name was kept out of the newspapers for a time, but any anniversary story mentioned me by name, just stating that I lived in the Philadelphia area. I was inextricably tied to Lilith.

It also stood to reason that Peter's death may be related to Colleen's death. I suspected they were connected. Otherwise, there were three coincidences: a) I was in Peter's apartment prior to his death, b) I was Lilith's daughter, and c) Peter and his wife were both murdered seventeen years apart for completely different reasons. No, the connection is undeniable.

I suddenly had two murder investigations on my hands when I had been feeling ill-equipped to handle one. If I start with Colleen, I'll end up at Peter.

I think of the crash then. The tinny banging outside Peter's bedroom window. The raccoon garbage can. The drunk vagrant. Could have been the real murderer. Could have been any number of things.

On the Healing Hope website, he'd complained of insomnia, headaches, that his grief wasn't lessening. Telling stories about Colleen—how she liked her eggs or what she ordered at restaurants, how she cut her hair short right before she was killed and how that made it easier somehow, that she looked like a stranger to him, lying in the casket, and when he thought about it, which he did every day, he could pretend he hadn't known her at all and that she was just maybe a coworker's wife or something, and did that make him a bad person? How many times in the past fifteen years had he pawed through these photos, looking for the clues that would tell him who his wife really was, the signs he had missed that had gotten her killed?

Tom Pickering had said Colleen's death had solved a quandary for Peter. That he'd seemed relieved. And yet, he kept this box. Seventeen years, these glossy, dog-eared photos had been thumbed over. If Colleen wasn't killed by Lilith, then who did it? And why would Peter feel relieved by it? Was Peter having an affair?

I think of his absence on Healing Hope, his breakup with Lindy, the break-in at his apartment, the redhead banging at his door.

I dust the crumbs into my palm and put away the peanut butter, ball the napkin in my hand. On my way to the garbage can, I open every drawer in the kitchen. Call it curiosity. Silverware. Large utensils: spatulas and wooden mixing spoons. Batteries, organized by size. Rubber bands. Someone else's mother would be proud.

A small pocketknife occupies the slot next to the paper clips. I retrieve it, setting the balled-up napkin on the counter. I open and close the blade, remembering the knife that rattled around Lilith's drawers for years. This one is so small and clean. Lilith's had been huge, practically obscene.

I flick it closed and it almost nicks my thumb. The knife clatters to the tile floor, knocking against my shoe and skids neatly under the stove. I sink to my hands and knees, unclip the carabiner from my belt loop and shine Brandt's flashlight under the appliance. Jesus, even under Peter's stove is clean.

I find the tape in the rubber band drawer and carefully fit the pieces together. A girl, with her arm flung around someone else, only a pink T-shirted shoulder visible along the torn edge. She is laughing, and in the background, I can make out the Greek letters emblazoned on the wall. She must be in a sorority house; the invisible girl must be her "sister." They're having the kind of silly, spontaneous moment I've never had. I leave the taped photograph on the table and sink to the floor again. I run my hand under the stove, under the cabinets. Where is the other half? There's nothing on the floor. I check the trash can, but it's empty, the bag gone. The police would have taken it. The girl is a redhead. *That orangey-red kind of hair*, Randall had said. She is holding a stuffed animal.

A golden owl, its eyes large, unfocused. There's something about that owl, its vacant expression.

I pull out my laptop and navigate to Healing Hope, searching through the forum users. She's offline: *WinPA99, offline for over 3 days.* But it's there: her avatar. A golden, wide-eyed owl.

Why is it under the stove? And why was it torn in pieces?

* * *

Friday morning, I email Dylan again: *Please be in touch. I went to your house. Why aren't you there? Why did Camille tell me you no longer live there?*

I wait for a full five minutes but nothing comes back.

I fish through the internet: marriage information, last known address, date of death. *Peter Lipsky married Colleen Paulus in 1997.* With Colleen Paulus, I find her obituary. *Colleen Paulus is survived by her father, Richard Paulus; and sister, Amanda Paulus; and her husband, Peter Lipsky.* I find an article in the alumni magazine at Lehigh University: *Colleen Paulus was a member of Theta Kappa Sigma.* In the photograph, I can make out the blurred but readable letters: $\Theta K\Sigma$.

Twenty-three-year-old Colleen Lipsky, née Paulus, died behind a Dumpster in back of her apartment in Upper Darby almost seventeen years ago. And now, WinPA99 has been chatting with Peter on a grief forum about her murdered sister. I had assumed biological sister. And yet, her avatar is the mascot of Colleen's college sorority. *Sister.*

When I had logged on as Peter, she knew it was me. She'd said, *Hello, Edie.* How? Before Peter was killed, before Thursday, on paper, I barely existed. For all my false pretenses, I didn't have a Facebook account of my own. Not a real one. Edie Beckett didn't have an email address registered to her name. My street address was listed as E. Beckett. Yes, the book had named me, Edie Beckett, as Lilith Wade's daughter. No one but Brandt, and the rest of the PPD, would connect *me* to *Peter.*

How did a ripped-up photo get under the stove? Or part of a photo anyway. Where did the rest of it go?

I take inventory of what I've got left: one Trac phone, one smartphone, and—I sift through my money pouch—four hundred and seventy-two dollars.

If my time doesn't run out, my money will. I've been running for eight days.

• • •

The first time I broke into Tim's apartment was last December. The heat had gone out, and at two a.m., I'd woken up shivering and sweating at the same time, feverish from the cold. Tim had a thumbturn deadbolt and a knob lock. After I slid under his covers, pressing against his hot back, he'd turned and sleepily pulled me against him. I'd found his mouth in the dark, whispering only that he should consider a jimmy-proof deadbolt and probably a door chain.

"Why?" he'd murmured, his hands sliding beneath my sweatpants. "This is the hottest thing you've ever done."

I doubt I'd get the same reception this time, but Tim could be unpredictable.

I wait until eleven and cut across to my block from the back side, through the fenced-in plots of grass and gardens. I don't doubt that Brandt would have my apartment under surveillance, but for a week? Probably a drive-by at this point, certainly he's not staking it out. The department gets forty-eight hours of surveillance resources if they're lucky. There are always fresh bodies, new cases; people get pulled away.

I see the lights go on in Tim's room and then blink off. He falls asleep hard and quick, one minute he's up, scrolling through the news on his phone, the next he's rumbling softly next to me. Generally, I wait for that moment to leave. Tonight I'm waiting for that moment to arrive. But first: an errand.

I hunker between the buildings. I count slowly, not wanting to illuminate the light on my phone. When I reach three hundred, I let myself in the front door of my building with the key code. I can't believe it hasn't been changed.

Inside, the apartment smells musty, like it's been locked up for months, not weeks. The smell of garbage permeates, and I remember the last night I was there I'd cooked chicken. I check my bedroom. The drawers have been emptied and the contents remain spilled on the bed. The desk is in disarray and the clothing from the closet is stacked up in piles on the floor. A section of the carpet has been cut free, and black fingerprint powder dusts every solid, flat surface.

The notebooks are gone, as I knew they'd be. I imagine them stacked in an evidence box, individually bagged and tagged, the contents scanned in the system, attached to my name in the electronic evidence file.

In my closet, in the back, behind a file box, I find them. My old journals. From childhood, from Lilith's, from Faithful. I haven't thought about them in years. Wire-bound, cheap notebooks I could get from the corner store in Faithful or the one near Pop's for a quarter. I count them. Twenty-six.

There was no rhyme or reason to my journaling. They aren't externally labeled, or organized in any particular way. When I filled one, I started another. Some years I was more vigilant than others. Did Dylan, Pop, or Lilith know I'd kept them? I don't know. I never talked about it—but then, I'd hadn't talked much about myself to anyone. They'd never asked.

With the beam of Brandt's flashlight trained on my lap, I pull the top book from the stack and flip through, finding a year. I dated every entry. Some entries were fiction, some were details of my day, some were merely stream of consciousness. I've never reread them.

August 2, 2000: I will leave here when I'm 18 and never come back. Pop will sit on his porch and rock forever.

Lilith will talk to herself until she is old and crazy. I will miss my brother.

I was fourteen in 2000. Two years after Pop brought Lilith home. After her commitment, and her return to Philadelphia. We saw her only intermittently after that, and Pop rarely let us be alone with her. She'd started working at Drifter's. She'd seemed calmer. I'd met Mia, then Rachel. I wonder what had prompted the entry. What had made me so angry.

The date I am looking for is almost a full year prior. I flip through the pages: January 3, 2000; November 27, 1999.

October 15, 1999.

Lilith is here. Staying with Pop and me because I'm sick. I could die, I heard them talking about it. Lilith said I could die, and Pop told her it's not like it used to be. I have something called scarlet fever, which I remember from The Velveteen Rabbit. Mrs. Westley read that book to us in second grade, and I only remember it because they had to burn all the boy's things. I have nothing they can burn, not really, but I don't think they still do that. Or at least not in the city. Anyway.

I am sweating and hot and freezing cold and my skin is like sandpaper, but it doesn't itch, which is weird. My throat is scratchy and I've never been THIS SICK EVER IN MY LIFE. Lilith is giving me medicine and singing. I've never heard her sing before. I didn't know she could, but she really can. She should go on Star Search, too bad it's not a show anymore. If it was, maybe she'd win and become famous and we could move OUT OF HERE because I hate it here. HATE HATE HATE. Maybe I'll be sick forever and never have to go back to school and Lilith

*can stay here and BE NORMAL and her and Pop will
be married again.*

That night, Lilith slept with me. Her body, tiny and frail,
curled around mine. I was taller and broader than her. She
smelled like sweat and cloying sweetness, her hair was pulled
into a stringy ponytail, and her elbow dug into my back. She
slept deeply and I slept fitfully. I stared at her face while she
slept and I remember begging her to stay this way. Calm.
Normal. Medicated.

I remember the silence of the house with Pop working the
night shift. I remember Dylan leaving for his best friend's house,
a guy we just called Gibble, the door slamming. Yelling about
something, but I didn't know what. There had been a fight.

I remember being so happy to have her to myself. To
have my mother. Knowing it would all vanish, that it might
never happen again, dozing in and out of consciousness and
waking to find her next to me. Every time. Memorizing the
lines around her mouth, the lipstick smudged on her teeth,
the puff of sour breath.

She never left the apartment.

October 15, 1999. The night Colleen Lipsky was stabbed
and left behind her apartment Dumpster.

Lilith didn't kill Peter's wife.

• • •

Working a lock-pick kit in near-total darkness, just the low-
level buzz of the lobby light, isn't impossible, but I'll tell
you what, it ain't easy. I fumble twice and drop the tension
wrench, and have to start all over again. I know the mechan-
ics of Tim's locks now, which makes it only slightly simpler.
When I feel the soft click, the tension lessening, and a loose-
ness in my fingertips—it's more tactile than technical—I
silently turn the knob and let myself in.

The hallway is dark, but a soft kitchen light glows from

the back of the apartment. Tim's room is to the right and I feel along the wall he'd so deftly held me against and feel the backs of my thighs tingle, a skin memory of his touch.

I sit on the edge of his bed, for a moment, and watch him sleep. His face is smooth, unworried, his mouth turned slightly up. He breathes in and lets out a soft sigh. I place my hand on his stomach, soft beneath my palm but then it goes taut with alarm as he starts to wake up.

"Jesus, Edie, what the fuck are you doing?" He scrambles to sit up, and I move my hand up to his chest, his heart thumping hard beneath my fingertips. When I straddle him and kiss him, he kisses back, hungrily, his hands running up and down my back. He stops, pulls back, and studies me in the streetlamp glow from his window. "I thought you were dead. Where have you been?"

I kiss him hard. "Shhh."

He smells better than I remember, something soft and mossy. I press my face against the dewy skin of his neck, the salty tang on my tongue, and he groans.

"What did you do to your hair?" He leans back to get a better look at me. "The police are looking for you, you know. They've been here three times, asking if I've seen you, been in contact."

I peel off my clothes and lie flat, pulling him down, between my legs and inside me. He's still talking. "What do I say next time? She came here, seduced me, and left?" He lets out a soft moan and licks my nipple. "Are you?" he says softly. "Are you just going to leave?" He shudders and bucks against me twice and I wrap my legs around him tight, like a vise, until he's deep, and I hear his breath come in gasps in my ear.

"Yes," I whisper. "But you're going to come with me."

Tim lies half on top of me, panting hard, and I don't want him to move. I like how this feels, the weight of him, his solidness, his dependability, the pressure of his body between my legs. I kiss along his hairline, something I've never done.

"Hey, now, are you okay?" He traces my collarbone with his mouth. "This isn't like you. You fuck, get up, make a joke, and leave."

"Don't ruin it," I say, smiling into his skin, his hair. I take a deep breath. "I need help. I didn't come to bribe you with sex and ask for your help. I came because . . ." I pause. This is true, but also, partially, I know it will get to him. "I trust you. Can I trust you?"

He pushes off me, the air frigid, our intermingled sweat on my skin drying and going to clam almost instantly. He fumbles around in the dark, swearing a little before finding his boxers and pulling them on. I pull the comforter across my chest and turn on my side, giving him room to lie down. Instead, he sits on the edge of the bed.

"I'm glad you're safe, Edie, but if I help you and it gets out, I'll get fired. Charged as some kind of accessory, maybe. Do you get that?"

"I do. I do get that," I say, nodding emphatically. I know this is unfair. "You can say no, and I'll leave. You can even tell the cops I was here."

"You're wanted for murder." He lays his hand out, palm up, and I take it, tracing the lines with my index finger.

"I know. I didn't do it, Tim."

He inhales and pulls his hand away. Stands up, goes to the dresser, and pulls on a T-shirt. He flips the bedside light on. When he sits back down, he looks at me seriously for a long moment before shaking his head. "You're going to have to tell me everything."

"I know." I nod. "I will."

"Everything," he says again, and leans closer. "And you can start with your mother."

• • •

So I tell him about Lilith. He knows who she is, of course, almost everyone does. I tell him about the miniseries (there were two), the countless news articles, the magazine think pieces, when budding journalists had knocked on my door for hours, staking out Pop's house, following Dylan and me to school. Just to get one question answered: Did we know anything?

I click off the bedside lamp and he lies beside me. I tell him about my timeline. How I've matched up—as much as possible—all Lilith's murders with my life. I tell him things that no one else knows: that the night Eileen Dresden's sister, Annora, was murdered the phone rang, clanging next to my head at one in the morning and I picked it up to Lilith's rapid breathing and I *just knew* it was her. I said her name, *Lilith? Lilith?* Twice like that and she'd laughed a little, a burble in the phone, but one that I recognized, and hung up. I went back to sleep and never thought about it again. Until I wrote the timeline and vaguely remembered that phone call. I have no proof that they were the same night—all I have is my memory. But if I was ever asked, I would easily swear to it. Did she call me before? Or after? At what point during the murder of another human being did Lilith think of her teenaged daughter?

It wasn't until later that I realized how much Pop protected us. We weren't with her when she *was really bad*, which was how Pop talked about her. He made excuses, invented code words, talked around her illness. It's impossible to explain that the day-to-day was fine. It's only when you pulled the lens out, saw our lives in panorama, that her deficiencies became so striking. That's all hindsight. In the thick of it, *she was going through a spell, you know your mother. She's having an episode.*

I tell him about Dylan. How when the reporters came, and our friends vanished, all we had was each other. We'd stay up late every night and watch old black-and-white movies: *Topper Returns. His Girl Friday. The Maltese Falcon. High Noon.* (How even now, when we'd meet up, I'd say, *Am I glad to see you!* and Dylan would say, *Why, did you forget your wallet?* like we were Gregory Peck and Eddie Albert in *Roman Holiday*.)

The magazines and newspapers completely eviscerated Pop, which contributed, I think, largely to his stroke. They claimed he knew what Lilith was doing and covered it up. That he was *just as responsible*—this is the phrase that did him in—by not getting Lilith the help she needed. What no one acknowledged was all the times Pop called the police, or the one time he'd had her involuntarily committed. It's damn hard in this country to get help for the mentally ill when they don't want to help themselves. Especially when the vast majority of mentally ill adults are not violent. Especially when we had no idea she was. It didn't help that Lilith was undiagnosed for much of her life, and being poor, her help and medical care, as well as her medication supply, were inconsistent and spotty.

I tell Tim all of this under the cloak of darkness, my cheek pressed against his shoulder, my arms tight to my sides, rigid, like a corpse. His breathing is even and steady, seemingly unaffected by everything I say. I wait for his words to come: that our relationship would be too public, or whatever the fuck Brandt had said. I know that Tim isn't Brandt, but he's in the system. I doubt I'd be welcome at office holiday parties.

The facts are easier to lay bare to Tim. Lilith did these things, she was who she was. It's much harder to tell him about the things I did, so I don't. I leave out the details: Chad Fink. Faithful. Hazel.

I do, finally, tell him about Brandt.

Excerpt from The Serrated Edge: The Story of Lilith Wade, Serial Killer, *by E. Green, RedBarn Press, copyright June 2016*

James Beckett Jr., sometimes called Jim or Jimmy, grew up in the city. He got a job right after high school at the wastewater treatment plant and stayed there until he retired. When he was twenty, he wandered into a bar with his friends and reportedly fell immediately for the bartender. Lilith was pretty, jaded, a little wild. Jimmy was quiet, even. Jimmy hardly ever drank, but he went back to that bar every night for two weeks until she agreed to go out with him.

They dated for six months before Lilith became pregnant with her first son, whom they named Dylan James. They were married at the courthouse. [*image, Lilith and James, at their wedding in 1985*] There was only one witness to the nuptials, a school friend of James's, a woman named Carol Rodrigues.

Interviewer: Did you know Lilith Wade well?

Carol Rodrigues: Listen, no one knew Lilith well. I don't even think Jimmy did. She didn't let you in. She could be charming sure, and I tried with her, I really did.

Interviewer: Do you know how they met?

CR: At a bar. She knew how to make drinks and smile at the men and ratchet up tips. She knew how to wear the right kind of jean shorts, with the rips at the bottom. She'd flash a bit of skin and turn fives into tens. She wasn't afraid to go home with the patrons, either, which I heard got her fired more than once and ended up being her downfall, I guess, all them men.

Interviewer: Did you ever see them fight?

CR: Oh, sure. She was always mad at him for something. Mostly related to other women, she had a jealous streak like I'd never seen before. You couldn't tell her no different either. Jimmy asked me to talk to her once, and I tried. I told her, Jimmy's like my brother. She said, nobody looks at their brother like that. You're in love with him! I couldn't believe it.

Interviewer: Was it true?

CR: No, of course not. I was married. Well, I guess that doesn't always matter. It matters to me, though! No, Jimmy was my neighbor. Our mamas used to be best friends. Both died young.

Interviewer: When did Jimmy and Lilith break up?

CR: You know, they couldn't have lasted five years. We weren't on speaking terms much at the end there. I know he moved out, got his own place. Stayed there, too. Jimmy is a man of habits, you know? He's as stable as they come. For her to rattle his cage? She must'a been doing something to him. We got friendly again after they broke up. Bill and I—that's my husband—would come over

*for cards sometimes. He kept the kids for the most part;
she didn't even try to fight him. He paid her money, he'd
grumble about it sometimes. She made more tending bar
than he made at the plant, you know? It was all tips,
under the table. Then she got sick.*

Interviewer: What do you mean sick?

*CR: She was in an institution for a while, I think. Jimmy
put her there. It was sad. She was so beautiful. No one
thinks about that, that a pretty girl could be not all there
like that. I think that was hard for him to wrap his head
around. He was worried about those kids all summer
with her. They wanted to go, though. He said it was the
right thing to do, for them to see their mama. Sometimes
he had to go up and get 'em early, she got so bad. I think
he was lonely all summer. He never married again. Hell,
I never even heard of him dating anyone.*

Interviewer: Why do you think that is?

*CR: He only loved one woman his whole life. He just
couldn't live with her.*

CHAPTER 19

Day 9: Saturday, August 13, 2016

When the sun rises, slanting through the window, bathing the room in soft pink light, Tim stirs. My eyes are scratchy and blurred and I pad to the bathroom, naked, to shower. I use Tim's towel.

He's agreed to drive me to Bethlehem in his car—mostly a tacit silence, a nonprotest when I asked him, than an actual agreement. It wasn't the sex that did him in; it was the talking. I let him in, I told him about Lilith. I let myself become vulnerable. Even in sleep, he was gleeful, the smile playing at his lips.

Under the hot steam, I think about everything I avoided: mainly Peter. He has to know I was at Peter's that morning, that I was the last to see him, maybe even that I went home with him the night before. Yet, he asked no questions. Brandt would have told him. Maybe saved it for the last moment, as an aha. A *gotcha!* Hoping to trip him, make him mad enough to give me up. I try to imagine his reaction. The slow realization that I slept with someone else, the self-awareness to know he couldn't be mad at this, the questioning of how many times it's happened before (none, if he'd asked).

In my head, I defend myself: Tim and I were never exclusive. He could have any number of women, and surely has. Women love Tim. He is tall, dark, handsome in a slightly less than conventional way: his nose a bit too sharp, the slope of his jaw just a bit too soft, intimidating at first until he smiles, inside he's a cream puff. Overly in touch with his emotions. Women love that shit, they all eat it up.

Still, I have guilt. Which is silly. Men never have guilt. Men sleep with women all the time—multiple women, hell, multiple women at once. They don't have guilt for it.

When I come back to the bedroom, he's awake. Sitting up in bed, reading on his iPad, a steaming cup of coffee on his nightstand.

"Look how domestic we are." He grins, gesturing to the nightstand on my side. A matching mug of coffee sits, waiting. Light and sweet. Tim pays attention.

I sit. Blow across the top of the mug. Try to think of something to say.

"So." He raises one eyebrow at me. "All it took for you to stay over was to be wanted for murder?"

"I guess so," I say, but I smile.

"I've been thinking," Tim starts, hesitating. "Why not just leave? After all this? Everyone in Philly knows you. They know your family. Why stick around here? You could just take off. Change your name, become someone entirely new in an entirely new place." He runs a thumb up my arm. "Not that I'm saying I want you to. But why wouldn't you?"

"I've thought about it, but you know Dylan is here. Philadelphia is the only city I've ever known. I've never lived anywhere else, unless you count Faithful, which I don't." I pull the towel tighter around me, tucking the corner into the top tightly. I think of my journal entry, *HATE HATE HATE.* I can't remember feeling that way. "Maybe because I have my shit together for once. Or had. I had a job. I was mostly sober."

What I don't say is that I've lived my entire life flying just under the radar and it was exhausting. The idea of fully hiding, of becoming an entirely different person, sweating every time I saw a cop, checking behind me for the rest of my life, staying completely underground, held no appeal. Some people might have looked at that and seen freedom. I saw a prison. And if I eventually got caught? Then what? Wouldn't running have made me look guilty? All that work, for nothing. Besides joining Lilith upstate, anyway. Disappearing forever wasn't an option, not now.

What I say instead is, "Are you going to help me? Drive me?"

"I think so. Can you tell me why we're going to Lehigh University?"

I stand up, towel-dried, and start to get dressed in my private investigator outfit. Khaki pants, black T-shirt.

"Nice getup," he says.

"Thanks," I say. Then, "Lilith didn't kill Colleen. Someone else did. I found my childhood journal. She was with me." I wait for him to ask to see it. I can see him dying to ask, the spark in his eye lights immediately. He doesn't. "But Colleen had a friend from college that goes by WinPA99, who has spent a lot of time talking to Peter in the past year or so. When I logged on as Peter the other day, she knew it was me. I'm going to find her." I pause. "*We're* going to find her."

"Oh, is that right?" He looks curious now. "This was fifteen years ago. What do you plan to do, show her picture around to old professors?"

If he wanted to get in on the investigation, he was going to have to do better than that. "Nope. Colleen was in a sorority. I think WinPA99 was, too. You know how sororities hang those big pictures on the wall? Composite pictures? I want to look at Colleen's."

"It's not online?" Tim asked.

"It's from 1997. Come on, Tim." I toss a pillow at him.

"Okay, okay. I have to call out sick from work." He's slow to move.

"Will you get in trouble?" I ask, a passing worry that I may have put him at risk, more than I already have.

"No. I'm never sick." He shrugs and makes the call while I finish getting dressed. I hear him on the phone, "No, just a twenty-four-hour bug. I'm sure I'll be in tomorrow."

He hangs up and turns back to me. "Ready?" he asks.

"Yeah, but you're not. Get dressed. You're my Watson now."

"Oh, is that what you call me, Beckett?" I can still hear him laughing as he walks down the hall.

• • •

Lehigh University is a school for smart kids: engineers and business and economics majors. Future inventors and world leaders. Past Nobel Prize and Pulitzer winners. This is what Wikipedia tells me on the ride up there. I scroll down and click through to their campus website on Tim's phone. When we reach the picturesque hills in Bethlehem, Pennsylvania, I'm reminded of eighties movies and ABC after-school specials about eating disorders and suicide. The buildings are stone, regal, shrouded in aging oaks and lush green maples. The school is nestled among rolling hills, and it seems impossible to me that people live this way. That families send their offspring to places like this, so idyllic it almost seems sinister, an ironic, kitschy backdrop to a horror flick.

Tim is quiet while I rattle it all off, half astonished: a legendary football rivalry, a thriving Greek life.

The campus is lazy, still sleeping from the hot summer, a few students milling around, those who have come back early and those who never left.

"You don't have to hate all things conventional, you know?" His eyes flick to me momentarily, and he's smiling, but I know it rankles him.

"I don't hate it," I protest, not entirely sure that he's wrong. "It just makes no sense to me, that this isn't a Hollywood set."

I'd taken three semesters at the Community College of Philadelphia before I quit and smashed my car into a tree. I'd paid for the classes myself, mostly, except for the two that the city covered. Two years ago, when I started to realize I might be interested in hacking, I'd taken a beginning coding class. I stopped going halfway through the semester. It all felt so aimless, the idea of having direction—a piece of paper just in case I wanted to better myself. I already knew how to code, the language itself felt instinctive, and I could get basic commands from Google if I ever needed them. And really, it had been far easier to socially engineer information out of people than it was to code trick sites and password-grabbing schemes.

My cobbled-together secondary education had always felt beside the point, and yet to everyone here, among the sprawling buildings and ornate stone fountains, it was the only point. How many students committed suicide over grades? How many found the sheer regality of this campus oppressive, pressing down on their sheltered lungs until they just couldn't take one more breath? The setting, no matter how idyllic it was, became your entire life. I couldn't fathom the feeling.

I feel wildly, ludicrously out of place: a fraud, a poser. The sense of being naked at work, like the dream. I'd smoked shitty pot at a party once, inches from being blackout drunk, and the pot counteracted the booze. I'd sobered up, quick, my mind going straight to paranoia. I felt like that now, heavy, my limbs burdensome, my tongue stuck to the roof of my mouth. "We should go home."

"You're being ridiculous. We're here now and we might as well knock."

Tim had found the Theta Kappa Sigma sorority house: a monstrous brick revival-style with gleaming white Greek columns. My morning bagel and Tim's coffee form a hard lump in my stomach.

He's up and out of the car, at the base of the concrete steps, stretching, before I can stop him.

"Are you coming? This is your gig, you know." He holds out his hand and I swat him away. He shrugs and takes the steps two at a time ahead of me.

"It's possible there will be no one here. It's still technically summer." I say it hopefully.

"Everyone comes back to college in August. It's the best partying of the year." He doesn't even slow down and I can't help but appreciate the view of his backside, even in baggy khaki shorts. I wouldn't know love if it came up and introduced itself, but God was I well versed in attraction.

Tim knocks on the door and from somewhere inside, I hear the *yip-yip* of a small dog. The woman who answers is tall, striking, with straight, blunt-cut black hair and smooth skin. Her smile is tentative and her eyes narrow slightly at Tim, who I realize in retrospect looks too casual. Rumpled and unprofessional. He'll get a pass, I can tell, the way her eyes flick over him.

I step forward. "Hi, my name is Jill Brand and I'm a private investigator from the city of Philadelphia." Most people, I've realized, associate private investigation with police, and while that couldn't be further from the truth, it has been serving me well.

She shakes my hand cautiously, and her eyes widen in alarm. "Hello, I'm Maura Wu."

"Don't worry, everything is fine. I'm investigating a recent murder, which has called into question a cold case." I clear my throat. "As it turns out, a murder victim from fifteen years ago was a member of this sorority. I was hoping you might be able to help me locate the people she graduated with?"

"I probably could, yes. I've heard of this before. Do you

have identification or anything?" She pulls the door in front of her, hiding half her face, and she shrinks behind it. I get it: people don't like the words *murder* and *investigation*. They're especially trepidatious when it shows up on their doorstep. I straighten my shoulders and give her my best, most winning smile. She smiles back. Out of the corner of my eye, I see Tim cross his arms over his chest and watch me, grinning a bit. I feel silly, all of us standing around smiling at one another.

"Unfortunately, it is illegal for a private investigator to carry a badge. I'm not a police officer." I cough and fish through my pockets until I come up with a homemade business card I'd cobbled together one night at Peter's. It's printed on card stock and cut with scissors, but I hope she won't notice or care. It reads *Jill Brand, Private Investigator* with a made-up phone number and website.

She barely glances at it and hands it back to me. She hesitates for a moment, then opens the door wider. The foyer is cavernous, with a wide, sweeping staircase. A blond girl appears at the top, a Blow Pop in her cheek.

"Hi, y'all." She giggles and Tim gives a gentlemanly wave. I shoot him a look and he shrugs, with one raised eyebrow. I shake my head in his direction and roll my eyes and he can't help himself, he laughs at me, the fucking idiot.

We follow Maura through the downstairs. There are large sitting rooms with mismatched oversized furniture, a big-screen TV, and burning vanilla candles. The whole house smells like perfume and cigarettes with the slight tang of old beer. Maura pads barefoot on the shining hardwood, leaving footprints without a second thought. She leads us into an almost empty room, the walls adorned with large composite pictures, each sister with her own oval, shoulders draped in the same black velvet, identical bubbly smiles in each photo. They look so happy, it takes my breath away.

"What about 1997?" I ask, and Maura shakes her head.

"There just isn't the wall space in the room." She brightens. "I think the old ones are kept in the basement. Let me find out. I just moved in this summer. There aren't a lot of us here, though."

She double-steps out of the room, back through the hallway we came in from, and I hear her call up the stairs to someone, "Do you know where all the old composites are? Are they in the basement? Did someone fix the light down there?"

Tim says, "You know, if I didn't know you, I'd think you were really a PI."

"Shhh, you'll give me away."

When Maura returns she motions to us from the doorway. "The rest are down in the basement, like I thought." Her voice is deep, intelligent. "Honestly, I had to ask where the basement was. Like I said, new to the house."

We follow her through a formal dining room with mismatched chairs. An impressively sized industrial kitchen, with a six-burner gas stove and stainless steel appliances. An eat-in space with long tables and folding chairs, like a cafeteria.

"How many people live here?" I ask.

"There are about twenty-seven of us living in the house this semester, but it's the summer, so only ten or so have come back. Next week should be a big move-in week."

"Twenty-seven?" Tim breaks his silence. "That's a lot in one house."

"Nah, there's ten bedrooms, and we're two to three per room. They're pretty big. I'm lucky, it's a beautiful place to live."

She wasn't kidding. I fought off the envy creeping up my chest.

The basement is finished, dark leather couches border the room and another huge flat-screen hangs above a faux fireplace. Two girls are lounging and watching a reality show, I can tell by the voice-over, and their eyes follow us curiously.

On the wall opposite the couch, a giant wooden yellow owl hangs, its eyes beady and unfocused. I stare at it for a moment and then ask, "What is that?"

"Oh, that's our mascot. His name is Winston."

"Really? He has a name?" I ask. I nudge Tim and point at the owl. He shrugs and opens his hands in a gesture of incomprehension. I shake my head and mouth, *Tell you later.*

"Of course, it's tradition!" Maura burbles. She leads us to the back of the basement, and through a door to the unfinished side. Large framed composites are stacked against a steel wire shelving unit.

"I think these go back pretty far, maybe even to the eighties." She says *eighties* like it is so ancient she can hardly envision it.

I flip through the first set all the way back to 2005, and then move on to the second set. It looks like there are two for each year, and I ask Maura about it. She tells us they take a new one for each pledge class, spring and fall. I nod like I understand what this means.

I find 1997 and scan it until I see *Colleen Paulus* under a photo. I pull the frame up and rest it on my knee, leaving a streak of dust and basement floor dirt on my pants.

She was beautiful. Light, wild hair, dark eyes framed in long lashes. A slight rosy-pink dusting across her cheeks, a shimmery lip gloss. I skim the rest of the photos and nothing jumps out at me. I don't know what I was expecting, I had hoped what I was looking for would make itself apparent.

"Do you know who Colleen Paulus Lipsky is?" I ask her.

She thinks for a moment, brushing her black bangs out of her yes. "Wasn't she killed by that serial killer woman? In Philly, right? They came here and did a thing on her once."

"Who's they?" I ask. I can feel Tim hovering behind me.

Maura shrugs. "It was last year, some anniversary special. That *Nightline* show, I think."

This was news to me, that *Nightline* had been preparing an anniversary special. Last year was fifteen years. There'd been nothing on *Nightline*.

"Who was it, do you know?"

"Nope, just some guy, interviewing people. Asking around. He came down here, like you, and looked at the composites, now that I think of it. I wasn't here. I heard about it second-hand."

"Who was here? Anyone who would be here now?"

She thinks for a moment. "Nicole would have talked to him, I think? She was the president at the time. She graduated in May, though, so no."

I tilt the large frame in her direction. "Do you know any of these people?" I ask, and she shakes her head.

She snaps her fingers. "Though, our chapter advisor graduated in 2000. Candace Ontero. She lives around here. She might know the girls from that year better than anyone else. Do you want her contact information?"

"Yes, please." I place the glass back down on the floor and pull out my phone. I take pictures of the 1996, 1997, 1998, 1999, and 2000 composites, ten in total. Maura starts to look nervous.

"Are you allowed to do that? Isn't this private property?"

"It's just for Candace's reference," I promise.

We exit the basement, heading back up to the kitchen, the way we came in. Maura says she'll be right back and disappears upstairs to fetch the student advisor contact card. When she returns, she's pinching an index card in between her index and middle finger.

"I put Nicole's information on the card, too. Just in case you wanted to talk to her. I think she lives outside of Philly now. She could tell you about the guy from *Nightline*."

Tim steps outside before me and Maura grabs my sleeve. "Are you really a PI?" she asks. I nod my head, but my throat closes up. I cough to clear it. "Your job must be pretty interesting, huh? You get to do all this cool stuff, investigate murders and everything, without having to be a cop."

"Well, it's mostly just insurance claims," I say, and pull my arm back out of her grasp. She smells like jasmine and something sticky sweet, like last night's vodka and Skittles. She eyes me suspiciously, her toes flexing, her toenails shining red. I hold my sleeve where she touched it and Tim pauses on the steps, turns and starts to say something but stops, watching us.

"This is a once-in-a-lifetime kind of case," I say, smiling blandly before turning and walking down the concrete staircase. She watches us go, down the concrete steps, and we climb into Tim's Toyota. We pull away, and as I look back, Maura's hands burst up, into the air, a too-friendly, too-enthusiastic wave.

• • •

Candace lives ten miles away in Allentown, behind a large amusement park in a two-bedroom ranch-style house. Through her kitchen window, I can see the red spiral of a roller coaster in the distance.

Candace pours us two mugs of tea and sets out a plate of cookies, as though she'd been waiting for us. She has long blond hair pulled into a low ponytail, and she wears a cardigan despite the heat. When I introduce us, her eyes flick briefly to Tim, and she gives us both a perky, happy hello. Even when I say the words *murder investigation*, she barely blinks.

"I just love those girls," she says, her mouth twisting wistfully. "I'd give anything to be that age again." She's young, in her early forties, but with the paper-thin frailty of an octogenarian.

"Really?" I say. I have one sharp, pointed memory then: I am nineteen and registering for classes at the Community

College of Philadelphia, Pop standing with his hand on my shoulder in a long line at the bookstore. I am surrounded by Candaces and Mauras: girls for whom friendship and belonging are a given. Pretty. Bubbly. Talking in whisper shouts about who was at what party, even on the first day. They'd all moved into the same off-campus housing complex the previous week. I lived at home. I had worn black. The line was filled with bright pink and yellow hoodie sweatshirts with JUICY and PINK emblazoned on the back. Somehow, they'd gotten it all right; without knowing one another, they'd dressed in the exact perfect thing. They waved and talked to one another with ease, and I assumed for a moment that I'd missed orientation, where they'd all met. Until I heard two of the girls introduce themselves, and then turn and introduce their respective mothers. When I looked up and down the line, it wasn't me who stood out. It was Pop. He'd worn his blue denim work shirt and Dickies, heavy steel-toed boots. He ran his hand nervously through his gray hair, smoothing down the sides and rubbing his jaw. He looked so *old.* There were no stares or whispers about Pop standing out, a line worker among housewives. No one looked at us at all. My black clothes and Pop's denim had rendered us invisible.

Candace would have been one of the JUICY girls, her blond hair in a swinging ponytail, her bright eyes blinking, gazing past Pop and me, onto something brighter, more interesting.

"Oh sure." She nods. "I just love them. They're just so compassionate. Sororities aren't like they used to be, you know? It's so much about the charity now, the giving back. Sure, there's still partying, but many of them are straight-A students. They have such *heart.* I've never seen such heart." Candace's eyes hold mine, so earnest. I can't tell if she's serious.

"Candace, I came to ask you about someone you went to school with? Colleen Paulus? Her married name was Lipsky."

"Oh, Colleen. Yes, of course, I knew her. Such a sweet,

wonderful girl. God, so tragic what happened to her. And random!" Candace sits across from us at her kitchen table, smoothing her skirt and picking off imaginary lint. Tim pulls out her chair for her. There are some men for whom infirmity is a turn-on, a savior syndrome. I wonder, briefly, if Tim is one of them. "That image of her behind the Dumpster." She gives an exaggerated shudder, her shoulders shaking.

"What can you tell me about her?"

"Oh, she was so kind. One of those salt-of-the-earth types. You just knew she'd go far, be successful, keep a head about her. She'd probably never flounder. She knew her own mind and wasn't afraid to share it. I think she pissed some people off with that here and there but I always adored her. And she was so wickedly funny, you know the type? Says the bawdy thing?" Candace looks around the room, gives Tim a tentative smile. "I was a pinch jealous of that. I'm not funny, I never say the wild thing. The thing that makes the room laugh."

"Can you tell me who she was friends with? I think someone knows more about her murder than they're saying. Her husband was recently killed. He was corresponding with someone with the online handle WinPA99." From my jacket pocket, I pull out a printed sheet with WinPA99's avatar.

"Oh, that's definitely Winston." She laughs. *Winston. WINPA. Winston PA 99.*

"Was the owl's name always Winston?" I ask.

"Oh yes, for years and years. It's *tradition.*"

She says *tradition* the same way Maura did, with solemnness and weight to it.

"Was she particularly close with anyone who graduated in 1997?" I ask, changing the subject.

"Oh sure. Her best friend was Julie."

"Julie?"

"Julie Kniper. They were thick as thieves. Roommates,

best friends, rarely saw one without the other. We called them the Doublemints. You know, like that old commercial? It was funny because they looked nothing alike."

"Do you know where I can find Julie now?"

"I really don't. She's gone off the grid a bit since Colleen's death. We send her Facebook invites for alumni events but she never responds. She's never come to anything."

"Do you think she's still in the area?" I ask, biting into a cookie as Candace does the same. It's light and airy and homemade, and impossibly still warm. Her tongue chases a crumb around her pink kitten mouth and I catch Tim watching her.

She pats her lips with a white cloth napkin and when it comes away, there's not a trace of pink lipstick on it. "I doubt it. She really came unglued when Colleen died. There were rumors. It feels wrong to speak ill of the dead . . ."

"Julie isn't dead," Tim says, and then looks surprised that he'd spoken. Candace rewards him with a gleaming white smile, a coquettish look. I swear Tim blushes.

"I know, but the rumors, well . . . people said they were lovers." Candace practically whispers the word and Tim shoots me raised eyebrows.

"Lovers? As in . . . ?" I ask.

"Gay. Yes." Candace stands, picks up our empty tea cups, flustered, and buses them to the sink. She prattles on, "But you know, I never paid attention, and even if they were, who cares? It's not my life. Then they both got married, so who knows? I guess that means nothing, really, lots of married people get divorced and come out. You never know, do you? I grew up Presbyterian." She takes a breath and faces us. "Sexuality and gender wasn't so . . . willy-nilly to me, I guess. It wasn't then, either, back in the late nineties. It was still a big deal!" She says this forcefully, to convince us. "People can't just let women be, you know? If we have girlfriends, we must be lovers. If we are loners, we must be damaged. Women are put in boxes. So who knows? I didn't put much stock in any of it."

"How true," I muse. It's astute observation from this nervous bird of a woman who looks thirty, but acts eighty. Then again, maybe I'm just putting her into a box. Seems we can't even help but do it to one another, ourselves, too.

We say good-bye, and Candace looks deflated. Let down, even. I've left my tea to cool on the table, untouched. In the front seat of Tim's car, I open my photos and blow up the composite pictures, searching until I find her. In my bag, I retrieve the photograph, held together with tape. Two girls hugging, the owl taunting the background.

Julie Kniper. With the bright red hair.

. . .

Julie was banging on Peter's door. Julie killed Colleen, and now Peter. She's unhinged. Jealous. But why? It's a reach, but it's all I have right now. Well, not entirely true. Lindy is a wild card, for sure. But she was a baby when Colleen was killed. The fundamental question then becomes: Are Colleen and Peter's deaths connected?

If so, how does Lindy fit into all this? A loose cannon of an ex-girlfriend who lied to both Brandt and me. Why would she lie? Brandt would know it as soon as he pulled the phone records. Unless she told Brandt the truth and lied to me twice. Again, why?

Women are less likely to kill than men, by almost tenfold. I've looked up the statistics. In the years when I was the most drunk, I researched, quite exhaustively, female mass murderers. Marybeth Tinning killed her children, Nannie Doss killed her husbands, Aileen Wuornos killed men who raped her. The thing about women murderers is that they're bizarrely, coldly, logical. Men kill for sexual satisfaction. Women, by and large, kill to accomplish a goal, and more often than not, their victims include members of their own family. To women, the killing is generally deeply personal, but functional.

All my suspects are women. Hell, all of Brandt's suspects are women.

In the car, as Tim pulls away, he says, "I thought she was just delightful."

"You'll never have to save me, you know," I say, irritated.

"What do you think I'm doing now?" He says it like he's joking, but I'm not convinced.

I change the subject, tell him my theory.

"You think Julie killed Colleen and then came back and killed Peter fifteen years later? Why?"

"That's the part we need to figure out." I pull out my phone and start to search for Julie Kniper. Nothing on Facebook since 2012. A sprinkling of photos: her with a gray-haired man, a climbing wisteria vine, honeysuckle, and strawberry plants. Her Facebook is locked down tight, even her friends list is private.

I run her name through all my search engines. "Aha!" I say to Tim, triumphant. "She married William McNamara in 2008. They live in Bryn Mawr!" I say excitedly, and Tim gives me a thumbs-up.

"You *really* think that this Julie killed Colleen?" he asks.

"I don't know. She talked to me briefly online when I was logged on as Peter and she knew immediately who I was. I've been waiting for her online at night ever since, and she never logs into the forum. WinPA99 must be Julie, or why else would she say that to me? Why else would she have spent the past year only talking to Peter in the grief forum? It makes no sense."

"You've been out-Edie'd," Tim says.

On my phone, I'm able to get William McNamara's address while I talk.

"How can you do that so fast? I'm unlisted, you know." Tim's mouth curls up in a smirk and he taps out the radio beat on the steering wheel.

"You think?" I type in Tim's name and city. Within seconds, I read him back his address. He opens his mouth to say something, then shakes his head.

"That's crazy," he says.

"It takes an incredible amount of vigilance to stay underground these days. You'd have to scour the internet and submit removal notices one by one to each site. They crop back up almost weekly," I say.

He looks impressed and I realize that I like impressing him. As soon as I deliver a killer to Brandt, I need to figure this out.

He reaches out and touches my knee, like he can hear what I'm thinking.

"This has been one of my better days off, you know?" He says it quiet, shyly. The late afternoon sun glints off his arm hair through the open car window. The heat is thick, but today, it's breathable. "And I have to say. I'm kind of blown away that Brandt hasn't found you yet."

"Yeah? He will. He's smart." I turn the data off on his phone and tuck it back under my thigh, the movement dislodging Tim's hand, and I feel a pang. "There are cameras all over Philly, it's true. But most of them are on a loop, and the data never feeds directly to the police station. They'd have to find the property or store owner, get a warrant. It's not as easy as you think."

"Yeah but there's GPS, and you've been using a cell phone. You're on the PPD website. It just seems impossible."

"Well, I'm on the website with long, light hair." I shake my head out, feel the short, choppy wisps against my neck. "It would be hard if I wanted to stay underground indefinitely. It's nearly impossible to bury yourself with any permanence.

I could never get a job or a new apartment or anything. I could never have an actual life, you know?" I laugh. "Not like I really have one now."

"You could have. You still could."

I can't tell if he wants to add *with me*. I want him to, just for a second. I laugh.

"What?" he asks defensively.

"Nothing. I was just wondering how this will all end, you know? Will the cops just assume I killed Peter because they think I'm like Lilith? If Brandt finds me before I figure it all out, will I just go upstate to Muncy with my mother? Then whoever wrote the biography will have a sequel. They seem to know me well enough."

"Don't you wonder who wrote it?" Tim asks.

"I think it was Camille," I say, which has always been in the back of my mind, but I've never actually said it out loud. I've never asked Dylan. "My brother's wife."

"How would she write a hugely successful sensationalized book, with a ton of press like that, and do it in secret?"

"The author has never come forward. Never spoken publicly. Never even given an anonymous interview. Camille has a job that pays for that house in Hatboro, which isn't exactly a cheap place to live, while Dylan sits around holding out for a job in middle management? Only to find out now that he's been fired? I'm not buying it." I feel on a roll now, the words coming fast and furious. "I don't know. I searched his hard drive once and came up with zip. But you know, maybe he even knows about it. Maybe he hid it. Encrypted it. Who knows? He's a computer whiz." I stop, tap my finger against the glass of the window. "You know, Dylan isn't above capitalizing on anything. And now, the house seems redecorated and Dylan is nowhere to be found? Where is he?"

"Where do you think he is?"

"I think Camille kicked him out. I don't know where he'd

go," I say. "But my brother isn't . . . well. He's not normal, I don't think. He struggles to hold down a job. When he can't reach me, he goes out of his mind. He hardly leaves the house. If I were Camille, it would be hard, you know? To stay." Tim rubs the stubble on his cheek, his fingers finding the soft pad beneath the jawbone and massaging it like a headache. I continue, "I'm a lot to handle. My family. My baggage. I know." I've never apologized for my family. I've never had a friendship close enough to feel the need.

Tim reaches out, puts his hand on my knee again. He doesn't say anything for a long moment and he doesn't look over at me. The car fills with music from the radio and for the first time, I realize it's even been on.

"You're fine," he says finally. "You're just fine."

CHAPTER 20

Day 9: Saturday, August 13, 2016

William McNamara lives in a townhouse in Bryn Mawr, a tan brick complex on a main drag, boxy and utterly unmemorable. The area is busy, a Target and a Walmart on opposite ends of the strip mall, competing for clientele. It's the kind of place that couples buy as a starter home, then stay there out of stagnation when the life they'd planned never seems to take flight.

A storm was moving in, the pregnant swell of clouds pushing the heat downward.

I stand on his doorstep, the number three cockeyed and hanging from a single nail. Tim hovers on the last step, trying to look benign, but generally failing. After I ring the bell, a heavyset man in his fifties opens the door. He wears a white ribbed tank top, a shirt that in Faithful we called a "wife beater" without any trace of irony. His eyes, red-rimmed and watery, dart from Tim to me and back again.

"Help ya?"

"Sure," I say, and plaster on a big smile. I act bubbly. "I'm looking for Julie Kniper?"

"Now, what'd you want her for?" He snorts, a heavy blast

of air from the back of his throat, and it sounds almost like a laugh. "She's not here at the moment."

"Can I come in, Mr. McNamara? May I speak to you for a few minutes?" I fish out my crumpled index card and hand it to him. He doesn't take it, instead squints and reads the words.

"Pee-Eye, eh? Well, then." He opens the door all the way and ambles into the living room. He favors his left side, a faint, wobbling limp. Tim and I follow.

William lowers himself to the sofa in a wide-legged squat and motions to the love seat across the room for us to sit. There's no air-conditioning in the room, and the shades are drawn except for one, the window open a few inches. William's balding head is shining with sweat, a few scraps of hair slicked back. "What's this all about now?"

"We're investigating the murder of Peter Lipsky. He was married to Colleen Paulus, who was close friends with your wife, Julie. We have reason to believe that Julie and Peter have been in touch. I was hoping to speak with her."

"I haven't seen Julie in about two months. That's about when she left. We were married for eight years; happily, I thought." He stops and breathes in. "I did get a phone call from her a week or so ago. It was an odd thing."

"What did she say, Mr. McNamara?"

"She just said that she did miss me. And in her own way, she loved me. She was sorry for leaving and knew she'd broken my heart. She'd never said those words before. Just one day she was here, making mashed potatoes from a box of flakes and baked chicken, and the next she was sitting right where you are now, with a single duffel bag, between her ankles, telling me she couldn't continue living a charade." He rocks forward and sits back, soothing himself. "Is it a charade if only one of us thinks it is? Everything felt real to me."

"Did you have children?" I ask.

McNamara shakes his head, his mouth opening and closing like a fish. "Julie never wanted them. She said she hated kids, the crying, the neediness, all the accessories. So much stuff everywhere. Julie was a minimalist. She liked things simple."

"Did you ever hear her talk of her college friend, Colleen?"

He snorts, a low, rumbled growl. "Talk about her? All she did was talk about her. She never got over her death. I never met the woman, she died before I met Julie, but every time they ran a special, did a series on the TV, Julie'd be agitated for days. Then the book. That was the beginning of the end, really." He stood up, left the room, came back with a T-shirt on. "Sorry, was getting a little chilly."

I give Tim a look as if to say, *Really?* I am suffocating.

"So *The Serrated Edge*," I say, not sure where I'm going next. "She had issues with it?"

"Issues! Hell, she lost her damn mind when it came out. Do you know there was a whole chapter devoted to Colleen?"

Of course I do. Out of the corner of my eye, I see Tim's eyes trained on me.

"Julie didn't even know the book was in the works. You'd think they would have interviewed her. Apparently, she was a thorn in the police investigation. Always down at the station, trying to talk to them. They know who killed Colleen. That crazy lady who's in jail for it. Oh, no, not according to Julie. She was so angry about it all the time. I think they were just plain sick of her. This is everything she told me later, you see. I wasn't there, like I said."

"Wait, she was mad?" I ask, and I see Tim's eyebrows shoot up. Tim's become somewhat of a silent partner, not to be confused with a lazy or apathetic one. I was beginning to read his expressions, and see when our thinking was aligned and when it wasn't.

"Sure. She insisted that they got it wrong. That that serial killer lady had nothing to do with Colleen's murder. That it was a cover-up or something. Hell, half the time I couldn't even follow her logic. You couldn't expect the police to."

"Wait, Mr. McNamara, I'm confused. If Julie was convinced that Lilith Wade didn't kill Colleen, who did she think did?"

"Oh, the husband. What's his name? Peter, you said?" His eyes go wide when he realizes what he said. "Did you say he was murdered, too? Recently? My Julie wouldn't have done that, don't go thinking like that, okay?"

"When did she call you last?" I ask. "That last phone call when she apologized, when was that?"

"Let me think." He stares at the ceiling, calculating. "It was about a week ago. I remember somebody shooting off fireworks. I have an old dog, she's upstairs now, but she hates 'em. I remember telling Julie about it. That would make it last Saturday night. That Pepper was terrified. That seemed to upset her. She did love that dog."

"Mr. McNamara, why did you and Julie break up?" I ask.

William leans to the side, against the sofa arm, resting his fist in a divot that seems to be made expressly for this purpose. Outside, the rain starts to fall, beating heavily against the windows. The one open window lets in a swirl of cool air, a wet-pavement fish smell.

"When she left, she said she didn't love me. She'd never loved me." He says it deadpan, like he'd had practice at it, maybe in the mirror in the morning or late at night, just trying to warm to the idea. "That she'd only ever loved one person her whole life and now that person was dead and her whole heart had died, too."

"Colleen?" I ask quietly, and William nods. "Did you suspect that your wife wasn't straight, Mr. McNamara?"

"Not really. I'd always wondered why she married me, of all people. Beautiful, smart, funny girl like that." He dips his chin into his neck, the crown of his head gleaming in the lamplight. "Can't say I was all that surprised that it was a ruse."

• • •

Tim drops me off at Peter's, hesitating until I say, "What?"

"Will you be okay? I feel responsible now." He laughs at the absurdity of it. Being responsible for me.

"I'm fine. Thank you. For today," I say awkwardly. Gratitude takes practice and I've had precious little.

"Really, Edie. Is it so weird that I would care about what happens to you? Today wasn't exactly a favor, you know."

The sky is black, the rain is hitting Tim's windshield in loud torrents. I click the door handle, but I don't open the door.

"What happens now?" Tim asks, and I sigh impatiently. I can't linger outside Peter's apartment building. I'm sure Brandt isn't coming back, but he could easily drive by. I shrug and shake out my foot. It fell asleep on the drive.

"I'll figure it out and let you know." I mean it like a joke but the air in the car feels suddenly flat, netted thick with misunderstanding. "Thanks again, I appreciate it."

"Jesus, Beckett, I try so hard with you." He sits back against the window, blinking.

"What does that mean?" I feel the fire in my voice: instant, full-throttle.

"It means, we spend the whole day together. I agree to *hide you from the police* and all I get is a thank you very much, see ya, Tim, you pathetic dog, I'll let you know?"

"Wait, I don't think that way," I protest, and then stop, the blood filling my ears, my voice echoing back to me. This, this right here, is why I don't get involved with other people. This bullshit. "Do you think I owe you something? A roll in the hay? A good fuck or something?"

"Beckett, no. That's not *at all* what I'm saying and you know it. I'm saying, for the first time, I felt we were on the same team. I actually know something about you and now

I'm just dropping you off at the home of a guy whose murder you're wanted for, and all I get is a formal *I appreciate it*, like this was some kind of contracted arrangement."

"I don't *know* what I'm doing next. I think it's possible that Julie killed Colleen. I have to try to sort it all through. It seems unlikely to me that Peter killed his wife."

"Why?" His response is immediate. He's jealous, I realize, too late.

"I just don't think he's capable. You didn't know him—"

"Well, to be fair, neither did you." He gives me a smirk. "Sex isn't knowing someone. As you're well aware."

I wonder if he's right. I've had dreams about Peter the past few nights, wild, graphic dreams, his teeth biting at my nipple. I've woken up aroused. I wonder if this is grieving. Can you grieve for a stranger?

"Tim," I say, and feel the flush blooming on my cheeks, "don't do this. He's *dead*."

"I just asked why, Beckett. You're the one who gave that meaning. Why couldn't Peter kill his wife?" Tim's leg bounces, a tic I've come to associate with annoyance.

"He was too nice. He was an insurance guy. You didn't see his apartment, you know? It was weirdly clean. Organized. He'd never stab someone, think of the blood." My justifications are feeble. I just know that Peter didn't kill Colleen, call it gut, call it whatever.

"I think you're justifying because you don't want it to be true. You liked the guy. You feel protective of him, somehow."

"I think you're jealous."

"It's possible to be both jealous and right." Tim shrugs. "But for what it's worth, I'm only ever jealous of someone who is an actual threat."

I open the car door. "I have to go, Tim."

He shakes his head and gives me a hollow-sounding laugh. "Course you do, Edie. That's what you do."

• • •

I slip in and out of Peter's apartment, usually at night, by flicking the lobby light off. Usually it's set on a motion sensor, but above the detection panel, there's a simple black switch. In the dark, it's easier to press into a corner, behind a door. I did almost get caught once, the lobby door swinging open just as I was about to pull the handle, and I'd pressed against the wall, against the row of mailboxes. The man had rushed out the front and taken a long stride from the small stoop to the walk, over the broken steps, and whistled as he fiddled with his keys. He'd never even seen me.

Tonight, the whole apartment is silent. I can at least usually hear music or the occasional clattering of pots, running water, something. Not tonight. Everyone is out.

I have a hollow scooping in my stomach that I recognize as loneliness. Usually I'd fill it by knocking on Tim's door or, on a bad day, taking a quick slug off the vodka stashed under the sink. Today I have neither vodka nor Tim and I feel restless, itchy. I'd gotten used to Tim's companionship. Foolish because it had happened so quickly. I'd let myself get so reliant on someone besides Dylan. There was no one outside the two of us who could begin to comprehend our life. Our upbringing. Our flawed decision-making, our quickly changing moods, our obsessive proclivities. Camille was proof of that. Friendship, romance, even love was for others.

The last real friends I'd had were Mia and Rachel.

Mia. She was first.

Mia Packer with the house that smelled like cinnamon and eucalyptus, a gingham checked door wreath, the stained-wood bookcases and dried grapevine garland twined up the staircase.

Her house hadn't been big. She lived only a few miles from Pop, a duplex in a working-class neighborhood. Her mom was single, a nurse, and wore coral lipstick that stuck to bright white teeth. In the winter the house was warm, hot, even. I'd sleep on Mia's floor on top of a borrowed sleeping bag, the air dry and hot in my lungs. I'd never been there in the summer, but I imagine it was kept cool and bright, the opposite of my summers in Faithful.

The days when Pop would work nights, he would be leaving just as I would get home. I would head off to Mia's, leaving Dylan whining behind me, biking through the alleys and along the sides of busy streets. Mrs. Packer would flutter around in a near-constant state of fret, citing bike accident statistics, and while we watched *Maury* she'd smoke Parliaments with her best friend, Molly, at the kitchen table and holler scanner calls into the living room. *Biker down on Broad, see, Edie! See? Take the bus!*

On Fridays we'd play gin rummy at that table, Molly and Mrs. Packer gossiping about the hospital staff—*Celeste Lingess from down the street, remember her? Ginny says they found Frank Lingess passed out drunk Friday morning on the lawn, it's March, fa chrissake*—while Mia and I sucked on stolen bourbon ice cubes from their highballs, until we were drifty sleepy. Molly would crash on Mrs. Packer's sofa; her husband was traveling (she said he was always traveling, *good thing she loved him*) and she felt safer on the Packers' sofa than she did in her empty apartment, *where she could hear every g-d mouse.*

At night, as Mia slept, I'd wonder if Lilith had ever had what Molly and Mrs. Packer had. If she ever had anyone cover her with a blanket while she slept on someone else's sofa. If she'd had friends in high school or even in Faithful, during the winter months, before Dylan and I invaded. Until I'd met Mia, I hadn't thought Lilith's solitude unnatural. I'd assumed adults didn't court girlfriends the way teenagers did, vying for each other's attention.

I loved watching them, Molly and Mrs. Packer, jostling each other for space at the counter, ribbing each other while they made dinner—*honestly, I've never seen anyone chop celery so slowly, are you dicing it or seducing it*—sometimes falling helplessly into peals of laughter and we'd find them slumped against the kitchen cabinets, and each other, until Mrs. Packer would gasp, *Stop or I'm gonna pee.* And Mia would roll her eyes or make a face at me, but I couldn't help but be fascinated. I'd never known adults to behave like children, silly and happy, or to do anything that wasn't rooted in either logic (Pop) or madness (Lilith). I'd never known any adult who didn't guard themselves.

I began to question if anything I'd known my whole life—either Lilith's frenetic highs or the long days and nights she stayed in her room—was normal. I wondered if there was more to life than Pop, and the solitary *crick-creak* of his rocker on the porch as day melted to evening and evening melted to night. Even Dylan's friendships, secretive and hurried, in and out of Pop's front door, felt wrong.

I wanted that helpless, clinging, amorphous friendship for myself—where you couldn't tell where one woman ended and another began. I fantasized that Mrs. Packer was my mother, that Mia was my sister. I showed up at Mia's unannounced, unexpectedly. *Mia's at a friend's house today, honey.* The *honey* was warming, even though it shouldn't have been. I'd been starved.

It's okay, I said, unthinkingly. *Can I come in and wait?* Mrs. Packer exchanged a glance with Molly, and I'd even envied that: the wordless communication. I wanted to be near *them*, Mia was a means to an end.

Not today, I'm sorry, she faltered, her fingers fidgeting with the wreath on the door. *Another day soon, okay?* before squeezing my shoulder and shutting the door.

I was invited over less. Mia introduced me to Rachel, and we two became three. The following year, she grew meaner. Teenagery, moody. Mrs. Packer started working nights and got a boyfriend. When I asked about Molly, Mia would roll her eyes, flick her fingers at me. *God, you're so in love with her*, and Rachel would giggle. Rachel was *in*, sleeping on the floor of Mia's stifling bedroom, while I was *out*, staring at Pop's ceiling wondering what they talked about without me.

I remembered their friendship, that squeal of laughter from the kitchen floor, but Molly's face grew blurry until I forgot it entirely. I saw Mrs. Packer at ShopRite in Glenolden once, years ago, her hair lighter and the skin papery around her eyes, but looking much the same as I'd remembered. I'd ducked behind a rack of bananas, my heart hammering in my ears, until I saw her out in the parking lot, climbing into a brown Buick parked in a handicap spot.

My friendship with Mia and Rachel ended not with a whimper, but a bang. Sometimes I forgot the details, how we talked to each other, what they looked like when they smiled. I've long forgotten any of our inside jokes, if we'd had any. But I've never forgotten Mia's mom, tears on her cheeks as she wilted against her friend, their legs and arms entangled, her mouth wide open, laughing so hard she made no sound at all.

• • •

I drop my stuff on Peter's couch and fish out my laptop. When I flick on the table lamp next, nothing happens. *Click, click.* I try the lamp on the other side of the room with the same result. The power's been shut off. I shouldn't be surprised, it had to happen. I'd been hoping to get a few weeks out of the place, but that means no microwave, and anything I'd been picking on in the fridge would be bad by tomorrow, and the place would start to stink. It also means that Peter's death is on someone's radar: either the building manager or a long-lost family member, and someone would be by to start cleaning the place out.

It also means my laptop has maybe three hours of use left.

I power up and sit in the dark, nursing a mug of room-temperature tap water, pretending it has more bite.

In Healing Hope, I browse through the forum posts,

posing as Peter, waiting like I do every night. Waiting for WinPA99. I don't have to wait long.

Hi. Who are you and what are you doing? The owl avatar blinks at me, a waiting message. Seems as though Julie's been waiting for me.

Hi Julie. I hold my breath.

How did you find me?

It wasn't hard. I went to the Theta Kappa Sigma house. I talked to Candace, your old sorority sister.

I don't tell her about William. She takes a full minute and a half to write back. My fingers hover over the keys. If I ask the wrong question she'll log off. *Who killed Colleen?*

You don't know what you think you know.

The bubble in the bottom corner shows ". . ." But no text comes through. I write again. *Would you meet with me? I'm not a cop.*

Then who are you? No hesitation.

Smart girl, Edie. Then she says something that throws me. *There's a park a block away from Peter's apartment. Meet me there in one hour.*

I think you already know who I am. You're framing me for Peter's murder.

I wonder if she'll admit it.
She signs off before I can agree.

Excerpt from The Serrated Edge: The Story of Lilith Wade, Serial Killer, *by E. Green, RedBarn Press, copyright June 2016*

James Beckett had Lilith Wade involuntarily committed after an incident with her children, in which she believed the police were coming to arrest her in September of 1998. The public would find out, years later, that she had killed her second victim, Melinda Holmes, in June of 1998. She was committed according to the Mental Health Procedures Act of 1976, Section 7301, 302. James had to appear in court and petition for an involuntary commitment, citing that Lilith Wade was a danger to herself and her children. Her bipolar disorder (in 1997, the DSM called this manic depression) had evolved such that she was now mostly manic, with paranoid delusions.

We were able to speak to a psychiatrist who treated Lilith at Norristown State Hospital, twenty miles northwest of Philadelphia. The psychiatrist agreed to give us limited information on record but only anonymously, due to HIPAA restrictions. It is worth noting that the psychiatrist we spoke to is no longer practicing or treating patients for unspecified reasons.

Interviewer: *Were you involved in the treatment of Lilith Wade in 1998?*

Norristown Psychiatrist: Only peripherally. I was a resident at the time and not the primary treatment doctor. There was a rotation of psychiatrists, and turnover is always fairly high here. There were quite a few doctors who worked with Ms. Wade.

Interviewer: How long did Ms. Wade stay at NSH?

NP: The 302 involuntary hold is only for a maximum of five days. At the end, it was determined that hospitalization would be best for her and she was kept for sixty days. She could have petitioned the court for release but she did not.

Interviewer: What was Ms. Wade's official diagnosis?

NP: She was treated as manic-depressive, which is now bipolar disorder, but at the time of her involuntary commitment, she presented in entirely manic mode, which had escalated to include paranoid delusions and irrational fears. She had not taken any medication for a month prior to her commitment because her prescription ran out and she was not able to obtain additional help.

Interviewer: Why not?

NP: This is common, unfortunately, in patients with bipolar disorder. The act of calling or seeing a doctor, filling a prescription, dealing with payment . . . It's too much in the throes of a depressive episode. If the medicine needed titration at all—adjustments up or down—or wasn't working as well as she'd been led to expect, it promoted hopelessness.

Interviewer: Is bipolar disorder related to Ms. Wade's homicides?

NP: No, not entirely. I can't stress this enough. The majority of people diagnosed with bipolar disorder are neither suicidal or homicidal. They are not criminals. Ms. Wade had the coupled diagnosis, not discovered at NSH, of having antisocial personality disorder—ASPD, as it's called now. Back then, she would have just been called a psychopath. Later, it became a sociopath. There's a lot of overlap of these diagnoses, but basically, this is the dangerous piece of the puzzle. Most people with bipolar disorder are still fully functioning members of society. I will say that her disorder was characterized by rage, which, combined with her utter disregard for ethics and morals, allowed her to kill women with unprecedented calculation.

Interviewer: Is Lilith a narcissist?

NP: There is much discussion around the differences between ASPD, antisocial personality disorder, and NPD, narcissistic personality disorder. I'm not able to make a definitive diagnosis, of course, never having evaluated her for them as her primary doctor, but I would expect that Lilith could be either one. Ms. Wade certainly showed no regard for the law, for ethical rights and wrongs, and an inward focus on "what she was owed." Her childhood, from what I understand, was brutally neglectful. Where would she have learned empathy? But again, this is only based on what I've read. I didn't see this while she was in NSH.

Interviewer: Why not?

NP: The 302 is focused only on getting "healthy enough" for discharge. Once her mania was under control, and her meds appeared to be working, she was released. She had discharge instructions for sure. Follow up with doctors, etc. Whether she did them or not was not my concern.

Interviewer: Why not? [Author's note: this seemed horrific to me.]

NP: I can't stress this enough. The mental health system in this country is irreparably broken. We had other, more urgent patients. We triage and treat according to need. Once Lilith was no longer an immediate harm to herself or others, she was released. The bed is needed for someone who is. There's always someone who needs the bed. Who is more urgent. Who is an immediate harm to themselves and others. A state hospital with a forensic wing is not the place for in-depth psychotherapy.

Interviewer: So, in your opinion, where does the responsibility for the murders committed by Lilith Wade lie? James Beckett? The Wade family who neglected and abused her? Lilith Wade herself? Or a broken mental health care system?

NP: [after a long silence] If I had to place blame, of course I'd say it lies primarily with Ms. Wade herself. But to me, it's undeniable. In this particular case, the system failed spectacularly.

CHAPTER 21

Day 9: Saturday, August 13, 2016

The park is empty and the air is cooling. I sit under a copse of trees in the center of the park, hidden out of sight, but conveniently able to see the entrance. A colony of bats swoops in and out of the branches above me. A metal swing set squeaks in the breeze.

I wait about a half hour, which is an hour and a half since our chat room conversation, and I'm just about to get up, figuring she stood me up, when I see her walk through the metal arbor. She hovers there, looking for me in either direction and then back out onto the street. For a probable murderess, she doesn't seem either careful or cautious.

I skirt the shadows, the trees providing cover, and make my way along the perimeter to the front of the park. I trip over a fallen branch and curse and she calls out, "Hello?" with a surprising absence of fear.

There's one streetlight that stands at the north end of the park and the splay of light is weak by the time it reaches me. She still sees me.

"Hi, Julie," I say. Behind my back, I tap record on my phone, and stick it in my jacket pocket, microphone side out.

"Edie." Her voice is soft, lilting, breathy. I stop about twenty feet from her and wait. "Thank you for meeting me."

Her hair is as red as her picture, chopped and uneven, like mine. We're both in hiding, I realize. Hers has been left natural, maybe an error if she's truly trying to fly under the radar. Its carrot gleam is unmistakable. She doesn't look like a murderer; then again, who does? She looks like a kindergarten teacher.

She's slightly built, her arms and legs gangly like a preteen and her freckled face youthful despite the slight tightening of skin around her eyes, the faint etchings of crow's-feet.

"You're older than I thought," she muses. "Then again, tragedy ages everyone who remains, right?"

She's talking about Lilith. She not only knows who I am, *she knows who I am.* She's read the book, seen the interviews.

"Everyone thinks I'm still a kid, right? Like Lilith froze me at fifteen years old, and everyone else forgets that my world kept spinning, too." I think for a minute, watch her foot kick at a pebble. Then continue softly, "You were frozen then, too, right? When you were what, twenty-two?"

She coughs, a deep, rasping sound. It goes on longer than it should. "Colleen. Yes."

"Are you sick?" I ask.

"I have lung cancer. A year, maybe less, left. Who knows? Stage 4, but it's not actively growing. So I wait for death to come to me." She twirls her hair around her finger, her breathing noticeable for the first time. "Ironic."

I'm stunned, but I try to cover it up. It feels inhumane to grill a cancer patient, but then, cancer doesn't pick its victims on moral stature. Cancer patients can still be murderers. The Night Stalker, a serial killer who terrorized California in the eighties, died of lymphoma in prison.

"Did you kill Colleen?" I ask.

She sucks in her breath, but then gives me a smile. "Why are you worried about that?"

"Peter is dead. They want me for his murder, but you know I didn't do it. So now I have to figure out who did or else I'll join Lilith upstate. It's too sensational—the mother-daughter killing team. Can't you see the headlines?"

"The stuff books are made of." She gives me another enigmatic smile, her closed lips curved around her teeth. Clever. I don't take the bait and instead wait her out.

"Look," she says finally. "Peter deserved to die, I'll admit. He was a creep and a jerk. But I didn't kill him." She looks at me pointedly. "And I definitely didn't kill Colleen. I loved her."

"Why did you hate Peter? Just because he married Colleen?"

"Ha." The sound is an actual *ha*. "No. Peter was . . . abusive. Controlling. She was *afraid* of him."

"Abusive?" I feel the hair on the back of my neck rise. Peter? Abusive? Peter was unassuming, quiet, patient. He seemed kind. Even chivalrous, holding doors, that kind of thing. Not in the way that abusive men are intentionally chivalrous—with Peter it seemed habitual, innate.

You knew him for a few hours. It's Tim's voice I hear.

"Manipulative. Not physical, that I ever saw. But sometimes that's worse. Bruises heal, you know?"

"You loved Colleen and Peter controlled her. You killed Peter. Who killed Colleen?" Deliberately provocative questioning might not be the best way to get information, but the time of night, the flying bats, the oppressive heat, Julie's breathing: it's all working a number on me and the trees seem to shift in the wind.

"I didn't kill Peter. Or Colleen." Her voice is loud, forceful. "I'm not framing you."

"Then why are you here? Why are you in Philadelphia?"

"I know Peter killed Colleen, I just have to prove it." She looks up at the sky; the long slope of her neck gleams white in the streetlamp. "The police are sick of me. They haven't listened to anything I've said in years. You put a wrinkle in things because I was hoping to meet with Peter in person. You know, the element of surprise? But now he's dead. I guess thanks to you."

"How were you going to surprise him?" I ask.

"I've been working him for a while. Before I . . . ," she let her voice falter, "came here." Left William. Her old life. Gave in to mortality and vengeance. Maybe that's too dramatic.

"He didn't know that WinPA99 was you, Julie Kniper," I clarify.

"No, of course not." She smiled, the memory of something deliciously sinister. "I was sort of fucking with him."

"You broke into Peter's apartment," I say. She looks startled. I'd almost forgotten about it, it seems like so long ago, that day in Lindy's dark, flowery apartment. The filed police report. *I thought he made it all up.* He hadn't made it up. It was Julie. "Why?"

Her fingers flit around, toward the street, procrastinating. She looks up, then finally says, "I wanted him to be nervous. Scared. Worried about who knew what."

"How many times?" I imagine him coming home, his coat not where he left it, a picture on the wall crooked when it had been straight that morning, the subtle rearrangement of his sparse and meticulous centerpiece.

"Not too many. Five." She smiles then, lips covering her teeth, a slow blink. Positively delighted with herself, happy to share it with someone. "I left him a picture. On his kitchen table. Of Colleen and I."

"You went to his apartment the day before he was killed, knocked on the door." The swearing redhead, according to Randall. "Why?"

She gives me a look. "Same reason as before. I wanted to scare him. I know he killed Colleen. I just can't prove it. No one will listen to me anymore. But I could make him crazy enough to turn himself in. It wouldn't have taken much." She had a nervous habit of pushing her hair back away from her face, behind her ears, with both hands. Her hair was stringy. Greasy. "That's what I was doing. It would have worked, too. He was so close to losing it. He'd never meant to actually kill her that night, I'm sure of it. Then he died."

"Why now? After seventeen years, why now?"

"The book. It was the first time anyone validated it. There were published doubts in that chapter. Clearly, everyone knows your mother didn't kill Peter's wife. But after this long, the only thing that would turn over the conviction is a confession from the real killer. There's no reason to reopen the case. They only do that to exonerate innocent people. Lilith was far from innocent. It would all be added expense and no benefit for the ADA's office. Not to mention, publicly unpopular." She speaks quickly but firmly. She knows her shit.

"So you were gaslighting him into it?"

"Yeah." Her hand goes to her mouth. A giggle. "God, is it wrong that it felt so fucking good? Then you killed him. Fucked it all up. I only half-care, though. He's dead, right?"

"Julie, I didn't kill Peter," I say slowly. "If I did, I wouldn't have taken the time to meet with you. I wouldn't still be in Philadelphia."

She pauses, looks up at the sky. A Medevac spirals overhead; the sound is deafening for a moment. When she looks back at me, her gaze is steady. Calculating.

"It was you or the blonde." She smiles, delivers it perfectly. I falter. Almost.

"What blonde?"

"The ex. The young ballerina." She steps closer to me, into my space. I can feel her breath against my cheek. "Here's the thing. I followed you and Peter home from Lockers that night. See, I've been keeping an eye on him. I don't normally follow him around the city, but I saw you show up and thought, *Well this is interesting.* I know who you are. I've been fairly interested in the murders and your mother for the past fifteen years. I knew it couldn't be a coincidence. What did you want with him? Then you're kissing him in the doorway, following him inside. I have a car, I park a few spots up from his apartment, watch the two of you stumble inside. When you don't come back out, it's pretty obvious what's going on. I'm all ready to drive home—no offense, but I couldn't stay there all night. Except I have a fucking conscience. What if he killed you, too? I won't deny that my perception is skewed. I'm debating all this when up the street comes the blonde. I recognize *her.* Suddenly, it's like my own little reality show." Julie coughs again, her chest heaving. She's slight but she has a toughness to her. I have a vision of her attacking me, clawing at my face. She's the kind of person whose anger seems to bubble out onto her skin. She even smells like rage, something warm and fiery. "She punches in the code to the front door and flings it open. It hangs there, the hinge is broken, and I can hear her screaming. I think I hear her bang on the door but I'm not sure. She comes out, bangs on Peter's front window that faces the street. She storms up the street and she's gone." She stops, her breath heaving. I wonder if she's said this many words in a row to anyone. "I've witnessed this exact scene before. The whole thing felt so surreal."

"What do you mean?"

She rakes a hand through her hair. "I was there. The night Colleen was killed."

"You saw him kill her?"

"No. Yes. No." She shivers, her hands rubbing at her arms, despite the heat. "We'd had a fight. I wanted her to leave Peter. She said she was pregnant."

"There was nothing about a pregnancy on the autopsy report. Or anywhere," I interject.

"No. I think she lied. Trying to end it with me, maybe? Not sure." She shrugs. "Peter was away, we made a nice dinner. Candles and everything. Like a real couple. Made love in the living room." She says it baldly, without hedging. How many times has she said it in her head? Told herself the story?

"Then she picked a fight. I don't know why, none of it ever made sense. I think she loved me but was afraid to be gay. Or she loved both Peter and me. It drives me crazy, not knowing." Her eyes skip past my shoulder, maybe to the line of trees beyond me, or the small stone outbuilding in the far corner of the park. "I left, slamming doors. I walked around the city for a while. Furious. When I calmed down, I came back and he was there. I could see him in the living room from the street. They were fighting. Screaming at each other. I was angry again, but also, kind of happy. Maybe she was going to end it with him tonight? Maybe she'd pick me." Her hand thumps against her chest, her voice strained. "It was maybe eleven at night. I walked down the street, ordered a drink. Paid in cash. Gave it an hour, walked back. The curtains were drawn. They weren't yelling anymore. I had this incredible sense of sadness, like they'd made up. I imagined them making love on the same living room floor."

She blinks for a moment, like she'd forgotten she was talking to me.

"Then what?" My voice is a whisper.

"I sat on the curb between cars across the street, trying to figure out what to do next. I had a cell phone, but Colleen didn't. I called their house, let it ring. I was about to leave, when he comes outside. Stumbles. At first I think he's drunk." She steps toward me and grips my forearm. "He looked like he was crying. He was wearing a white dress shirt, the kind he'd wear to work." Her nails are short but they press into my skin. "They had two cars. He sort of stumbles his way to her car, pulls something out of the backseat. A blanket or something. When he turns, I can see him in the streetlight. His shirt is covered in blood."

"Blood?" I try to envision the streetlamp lighting, the segmenting shadows casting splatter patterns against the white cotton. She laughs and lets go of my arm, makes a stabbing motion with her hand, and then opens her hand wide like a starfish. Or a firework. She takes a step toward me and I have to step back to get comfortable again. "Why wouldn't you go to the police?"

She laughs again. "I have! A million times. I said I saw him that night, with blood on his shirt. They asked the bartender, who said he served me the drink, which puts me a block from the crime scene around the time of the crime. They had phone records of me calling his house, maybe minutes before she was supposedly killed. The detectives in homicide told me they had his alibi. He was at an insurance conference in New York City. His car never left the place. They asked if I had an alibi after I left the bar. They threatened me with arrest."

"Julie, did you kill Peter?"

"No. Until we met, I thought you did. I didn't want him dead. I wanted justice. I wanted him in prison. I wanted to see him miserable. I had fantasies about going to visit him there and *laughing*. Sick, right?"

"If she loved you, why did she marry Peter?" I ask.

"She never loved me the way I loved her. Never. That's the way all love is, though. One person always loves harder." She looks wistful, rubs the bridge of her nose. "William loved me harder. I loved Colleen harder. Peter loved Colleen harder."

"Who did Colleen love?"

"I don't know." She repeats it again, softer. "I really don't." She bites on the tip of her pinky nail. All her mannerisms are that of a teenager: quick, impulsive, uncertain.

There is a sharp, bright flashing strobe of red and blue. A police light flicking on the silhouette of trees. My pulse skips up, my heart pattering in my throat. I back away from her, turn to run, but think better of it and face her again. I don't know what to say.

She talks first. "If you didn't kill Peter, then it was the blond girl. Lindsay or whatever." She takes a wheezing breath. "But if you did, you can say it was me. They'll believe it. I'll be dead before it goes to trial."

• • •

I can't decide if I've been played. I believe her but maybe I'm the fool. *You can say it was me*, she'd said.

I stand in Peter's lobby, listening for the sounds of the other tenants. They are silent. I quickly slip through the door into the hallway and into Peter's apartment. I boot up my computer and discover the Wi-Fi I've been hopping on is now password-protected. I tether to my phone—a risk—and log into Healing Hope.

Lindy was at Peter's. Did she come back? After I'd left, did she come back, kill him in a blind rage? It's the only thing that makes any sense. Julie said she screamed, she heard the yell. I don't remember that. I remember a banging, irregular and loud, thinking it was a garbage can lid. A drunk. A raccoon. But that was later, what did I think in the moment? I don't know, I don't remember the moment.

WinPA99 isn't online. I wait for her. I have to think of more questions. While I wait, I check the recording on my phone. The conversation is an astounding eight minutes. Felt like hours. It's choppy, with a flurry of activity at the end when I ran, but it's mostly salvageable. Too bad Julie didn't say anything incriminating. Not about herself, anyway.

I check my watch. It's 11:30. I skip over and check my email. Something from Dylan. I click it open,

To: EdieBeckett30@gmail.com
From: DBeckett82@gmail.com

Subject: Help

I feel like I've finally lost the thread, Edie. I moved out. I went looking for you and failed. I fail at everything I do.

I pull out my flip phone and call Dylan's house. I let it ring ten times, hang up, and try again. *Pick up, pick up, pick up, PICK UP.*

Finally, a furious *"Hello?"*

"Camille. Don't hang up. Please talk to me."

I have the urgent sense that Dylan's disappearance and Julie's appearance are connected, somehow. But I can't draw a straight line from one to the other.

"For God's sake, Edie. I already talked to you. Do you know how late it is? Baby Matty is sleeping. The phone is ringing off the hook over here." Her vowels are elongated when she's tired, a slow southern drawl that comes out in the most stressed of moments. I've heard her yell at Dylan before, *For the love of Christ Almighty*, her long *iiiiii*s showing off her Alabama roots.

"I just have to understand, okay? Dylan emailed me. Where did my brother go?"

"I already told you this, Edie. He left us. He left me and the baby and went to look for you. I told him if he left, he shouldn't come back. But he knew that already." She blows air into the phone, an exasperated breath.

"How did he know that?"

"Oh, it's no secret. He's been choosing you over me since

we got together. Y'all had some kind of twisted-up childhood and now I'm here, stuck in the middle. I'm sick to death of it." Her voice creeps up until she's almost yelling and I imagine Baby Matty confused by the screeching yowl, a sound he'd never been exposed to. Even when she used to scold Dylan it was quiet, endlessly civil, and ruthlessly unkind. "I loved your brother once, I did. But I didn't know what I was getting myself into with your family. His fascination with Lilith. His obsession with you."

"Fascination?" I cut her off, my own voice creeping up. I can feel the pulse in my neck. "She is his *mother*. God, Camille, I've never known anyone to be so selfish in my whole life—"

"Oh, that's just rich, Edie. Do you even hear yourself? You, your brother, and your mother are the most self-centered people I've ever met."

"How? How are we self-centered? Explain, please."

"Your mother murders six people in four years and you and Dylan never knew anything? I don't buy it. I used to. Not anymore. Your brother knew something, he almost said as much one day. Years ago. I didn't want to believe it, but I'm so over all of you. Your whole family is sick and I don't want my baby to have anything to do with any of you."

I don't even flinch. Fuck her. I've heard it all before and it doesn't hurt more or less coming from Camille's mouth. Her twang is deep now, she's off the rails.

"What did Dylan say that made you question what he knew?" I interrupt her tirade, cut to the rich, beating heart of it all.

"Just that he knew she was off. That something was wrong with her. If any of you had gotten her help . . . well, I can't go down this road again. You've all only had your own interests at heart, that's all. Not Lilith's, not each other's. Certainly not the victims' or their families'. Just your own interests."

She hangs up. *Your own interests at heart.* Such an oddity, like Camille: both charming and cutting at the same time, like a thorny glass rose. The phrase sends warning bells off in the back of my mind, a ringing, niggling feeling.

I stand up, my knees creaking, and move to Peter's bedroom. Using my cell phone flashlight, I scan Peter's bookshelf and pluck it down: *The Serrated Edge.*

I flip through the book until I find it: *Despite contrary public statements, the Wade-Beckett family show very little mercy or kindness to the victims' families and have yet to donate to any campaign or fund. They only appear to have their own interests at heart.*

CHAPTER 22

Day 10: Sunday, August 14, 2016

It's 1:30 in the morning. I'm lying in Peter's guest room bed, an area I've begun to think of as my own. It's starting to feel like home and I'm getting sloppier and lazier with the details. My stuff is strewn all over—not rolled in tight balls in my backpack like it was a week ago. I don't sleep with my shoes on anymore. In fact, right now I'm lying in my underwear and bra trying not to die of heat exhaustion. I'm becoming John List with those goddamn glasses. Getting comfortable is never beneficial, it's only to my detriment. *I know this.* And yet, the idea of putting on my clothes in this stifling-hot apartment makes me want to die.

I call Dylan, over and over again. When he doesn't answer, I call Tim. I know he's mad at me, I know how we left things wasn't good. I've texted him *I'm sorry* in various ways. I've also texted him *What is your fucking problem?* but I'm hoping he can overlook that. My impulse control isn't great.

The biggest problem I have is that the texts aren't even showing as read. Tim is up off and on all night. If I sent him a text, he'd read it. He reads it immediately. Maybe I've lost my shine, I'll give you that. A full day with me is a lot, and in our last exchange, I was a real shit.

I can't sleep, I'll never sleep like this. I get up, slide into shorts and black T-shirt. It's cooler outside than it is in here; at least the almost ten-mile trek to Tim's will give me something to do. Maybe Tim can even help me figure out what to do with Dylan.

I pack my bag: lock-pick kit, flashlight, change of clothes, money. Shit, I need to figure all this out or I'm going to need to get more money. I count the cash from each pocket and the front pocket of my backpack: $114. I've got maybe two or three days left of bus and train fare, food, miscellaneous supplies. I have one phone left. I'll need another one if I'm going to get through another week.

I start walking downtown on Germantown Avenue. I figure I'll walk for about an hour then find a cab the rest of the way.

Walking never bothers me, it's what I've done my whole life. My feet hitting the concrete at a measured clip, the reverberation up my legs, the pulling in my hips after a handful of miles: all these sensations ricocheting around my body give me an unexpected clarity.

I walk and think.

Who killed Colleen? I come back to this question, again. Not Lilith. Either Julie, or Peter. I believe Julie, I do. It doesn't match up with the Peter I knew. But she had nothing to gain by telling me what she did. I believe she didn't kill Colleen. But Peter is another matter.

If Peter killed Colleen, then who killed Peter? Lindy? Lindy with the father figure issues. The furious search for someone to understand her tragic childhood. The combination of the two lethal. Obsessive. I remember desperation. I remember the way I clung to Brandt, pushing my breasts against him, hoping lust could keep him there even if love couldn't. Feeling that wild pull in my chest when he walked out the door, the propulsive desire to chase him down, fling myself at him—the only thing stopping me was pride. Lindy's lies to the police, and later, me. *Lockers @ 4* on the menu. Her banging on his front door the night I'd been with him. Her lackluster on-again-off-again affair with Alek. Lindy didn't kill Peter. She loved him. Do people kill for love? Sure. But Lindy was hopeless and fervid. She wasn't bubbling over with rage enough to kill.

Julie, as WinPA99, was luring him for a *year*. She had nothing to lose. Lung cancer was stealing her life. Why should Peter, if she believed he killed Colleen, her only love, continue to live? Why would she spend a year chatting Peter up online? To kill him or, like she'd said, drive him crazy enough that he'd turn himself in, consumed by his own guilt? But, it only made sense if Peter actually did kill Colleen. I might have enough speculation to go to Brandt. It would be risky. Brandt, prior to this, trusted my instinct, at least a little.

Where is Dylan? Perhaps the most perplexing question of them all, at least the most urgently pressing. I can't shake the sensation that I'm missing something, just out of reach. If someone is targeting me, is Dylan in danger for his connection to Lilith, too? Why hadn't I thought of that before? My mouth tastes dry and fibrous at the thought, a sticky clicking in my throat. My whole life, it's been Dylan and me against the world. I've never entertained the idea that one day he might not be here. I've shunned friendships and relationships, mostly thinking that no one else could ever truly get what went on in the inside. Also, because I'm not that great of a liar. If I let someone in, I'd have to tell them who I was, who my mother was. Who would stay after that?

Dylan let Camille in and she stayed. He's argued this to me. I'm different. I'm a woman. I'd be a mother. Men marry to have children—it's Darwinian, evolutionary. My own mother had been a certain kind of poison and she'd passed that on. I was as deficient as her, just ask Mrs. Reston or Hazel.

I don't want to be a mother. I don't want to be a wife. I don't want to spend my days watching my own behavior—making sure I'm attentive but not too much, wondering if I'm going to devolve into some kind of motherly madness postpartum. It's far too risky. By the time I know if I've caught any of Lilith's genetics—they say thirty to thirty-five—I'll be too old to start the arduous process of marrying. Having babies. Despite what people say, I'm not self-centered.

I'm deliberately isolated to protect everyone around me.

But Dylan. He's reached out. Fallen in love. Led a normal life. And now he could be anywhere.

For the first time, it occurs to me to hack my brother. It's easy enough to pinpoint someone's location. If it wasn't easy, I wouldn't have bought and thrown away four cell phones over the last two weeks.

I take a deep breath and think. I need my computer and the internet, I can't do this from a phone. There are twenty-four-hour coffee shops scattered all over the city. After I look around—I'm on an abandoned block, surrounded by half-abandoned buildings, the weeds grown up over the wire fence—I pull up a list of them from my phone and find the closest one. As soon as I've got it, I turn off my GPS and location services. Three blocks away. I hustle, head down.

In the coffee shop, there is a barista behind the counter, reading. Despite it being the middle of the night, there are two patrons typing on computers. There's soft jazz playing in the background; the light is low and warm but the air is cool. If I could, I would move in here. I order a coffee, black, and open my laptop and hop on the public Wi-Fi.

I navigate to Google and pause. In the search bar, I type *Find my phone.*

I can't believe I haven't thought to do this before. I blame it on my focus on exonerating myself. On hiding. I had been chasing the truth and mistakenly believed Dylan could wait.

He'd never go anywhere without his phone. It's a living extension of his hand, always dinging and blinking. He claims the emails are potential employers. I've long since suspected he's exaggerating but I've never tried to prove it. I've never even asked him about it, what would be the point?

Google asks me for a name and password. Easily I type in DBeckett82@gmail.com. Password? I hesitate. No one knows Dylan better than I do, but I have a limited number of times I can attempt to log in before I'm locked. Maybe three, maybe five, maybe ten, depending on Dylan's security. And if he has two-point authentication, I'm basically screwed. I'm not overly worried. My brother is lazy. And trusting.

First, I try the easiest: *Matthew1024*. Baby Matty and his birthday, of course. *Wrong password. Try again.*

I try *Camille61807*, their anniversary. I try *Lilith* and *LilithWade*.

Wrong password. Try again.

Then I try, finally, *EdieB111487*. Edie-Bee. What he's called me since we were kids. EdieB. November 14, 1986, is my birthday. It works. The page opens and there it is: a blinking phone right over the map.

Dylan is at my apartment.

CHAPTER 23

Day 10: Sunday, August 14, 2016

There is a white city cab outside of the cafe with its four-ways flashing and I throw five dollars on the table. The barista yells that I forgot my change as I run out the door. I sling my messenger bag over my shoulder and bang on the driver's-side window.

"Hi. Can you take me to Kensington? East York Street?" I fish around in my pocket and hand him forty bucks. He doesn't look impressed. "I have more," I say. He motions to the back, *Get in.*

The car speeds down Germantown Avenue, hitting the greens. In the daytime, this street can be bumper to bumper. It's the longest, highest-traffic route between Peter's apartment and mine. Not that I've ever taken it directly.

Dylan, call me. I know where you are, I text him.

I wait but get no response. I text Tim. *Have you seen a man at my apartment? It's my brother.* Nothing makes sense.

The cab pulls up to my building and I throw two twenties and a ten through the plexiglass. There are no lights on; all the apartments inside are dark. I fish my lock-pick kit out of my bag and key into the building. I still can't believe the code hasn't been changed. Unless Brandt told them not to, waiting for me to come back. I use my house key and unlock my apartment door.

It's how I left it less than a week ago.

"Dylan?" I stage whisper into the darkness of the hallway, the bathroom, the living room.

My whole apartment feels foreign, like I've been absent for years. I can hardly remember living there. The way I'd kept it as mine and mine alone. The way no other person, besides a repairman or delivery man, had ever visited.

Tim.

Dylan is not in my apartment. The pieces start clicking together now. Dylan's relentless calling, his night wandering, his sleeplessness. The day he stood outside the CJC, waiting. The way Camille immediately, intensely distrusted me. His obsessiveness. His inability to keep a job. I'd been so worried about myself, the blood coursing through my own veins. The sickness in my own brain. I'd hardly given a thought to him.

Later I'd think about how you can know something on instinct. How the feeling so often comes before the words.

I sprint for the door and head straight across the hall to Tim's. I contemplate banging on the door, yelling. Instead I nudge it open with my toe. It's not even fully shut. The lights are off and I slide into the living room. Our apartments are set up identically: living room in the front, kitchen in the back, a small hallway from the living room to the two bedrooms, at the end of which sits a small, old bathroom. Mine smells like bleach, Tim's always smells like mildewed towels.

A soft nightlight glow emanates from the bathroom and I feel along the wall for Tim's bedroom door. I push it open and peer into the darkness. I let my eyes adjust to Tim's form on the bed, the steady rise and fall of the blankets. I feel a swoop of relief, unsure what I was expecting. He is fine. He was ignoring my texts because he was sleeping. His phone was on mute. Still, something feels off.

I sense a shift in the apartment. Maybe the soft opening and closing of the front door. The displacement of the air, the shape of another person.

"Oh, good. You're just in time," he says behind me. His voice is quiet but not whispering, conversational. Even, if I know him as I thought I did, a little bit excited.

Dylan.

· · ·

"Dylan. What are you doing here?" I cock my head, feigning surprise.

He laughs. "Don't be coy. I'm not stupid." He pauses and flashes me a smile. "I'm not as smart as you. But I'm far from stupid."

"I don't think you are, Dyl. What are you actually doing here?" I ask, suddenly overwhelmingly tired.

He pads softly back toward Tim's bedroom and I follow him, my heart thrumming erratically, my pulse in my throat. He flips on the light and Tim sits bolt upright in bed.

"What the fuck?" he asks. He sees me. "Edie?" His eyes dart from Dylan to me and back.

Dylan motions to me with his hand—and for the first time I realize he's holding a gun.

"Jesus Christ, Dylan, where did you get a gun?"

"Remember when you told me to get a hobby?" He smiles blandly. "I actually have quite the gun collection now."

I sit on the desk chair, facing the bed. Tim's face has gone ashen, he won't meet my eyes. He must regret the day he knocked on my apartment door.

"How did you know I was coming here?" I ask, realizing how stupid the question is only seconds after I ask it.

"I didn't know, I lured you here." He points the gun at Tim, but talks to me.

"Lured me?"

"Yes." His voice is frustrated. "Lured. You took the bait. You're easy to predict."

"How?"

He wiggles his phone. "Do you think you're the only one who knows how to find someone?" I see the app, a little blue dot. I assume me.

"How? I'm not using my phone."

He sighs, impatient. "You really think I'm dumb. It's so insulting. You always have." His tone switches, quickly, without warning. "You're the dumb one. You've called my house, twice, and emailed me from the same phone. Tracing software isn't that hard to buy, you know? You are even using the same Wi-Fi signal. Then it talks to an app. Easy, right? I just hang out in your apartment and watch you hang out in Peter's. Then I realized, you won't come here for me. But you'll come for *him.*" Dylan jabs the air in Tim's direction. "That's pretty sick, you know that? Whatever, I wanted you both here anyway."

"But I did come here for you." I shake my head, confused. "What do you want from me, Dyl?"

"Edie, do you remember when Lilith took us to that state park? We stayed there for days, no one knew where she was? She covered the tent with sticks, like it could hide us? We'd hiked up to this spot, miles from anywhere. Remember this?" He moves next to me, the gun still trained toward the bed but his eyes search mine, pleading. His head cocks slightly to the left, to the nightstand. There's a gun in the top drawer, of course there is. Tim is a corrections officer.

"Yes. I remember. Pop had her committed after that. She seemed to get better, for a while. You saved me. How could I forget?" I reach out, I want to smooth his hair away from his eyes. I want to touch him, my brother. To feel the warmth of his cheek against my palm.

"I don't know, Edie. I ask myself every single day. You did forget, don't you see? You've completely forgotten."

"I don't know what that means." I search his eyes, wide, red-rimmed and panicky.

"It used to be me and you against the world, right?" He leans closer, his gaze intense, the hand with the gun dropping, ever so slightly. I don't dare look at Tim. "Something has happened to you. You don't care about us. You care about everyone else, all these other people. Other people's families. Not your own. You're obsessed."

Was. I was obsessed. But I haven't thought about any of them in weeks, except Peter. And even then, my thoughts were about how to find his killer. How to preserve myself. How little thought I'd given to Dylan, besides how to shake him off so I could continue whatever I was doing—finding information on the internet, watching the Dresdens through their front window, following Lindy Cook. We used to meet for dinner. I used to visit him. I've blamed our distance on Camille. The baby. How much of it was my fault?

It didn't matter.

"Dylan, whatever this is, it's not the answer. We've grown apart, fine. We can fix that. But this?" I point to the gun, to Tim, to Dylan. "This is not how to go about it, do you get that?"

"That's not what this is about. This is about me. *Me*. I saw you leave that morning. You *stayed* with him."

"Are you talking about Peter?" I ask, then I feel the bottom fall out, a dizzying swoop of clarity. "Oh my God. You killed Peter."

"No. *No*. See?" He jabs the gun in Tim's direction and I take the opportunity to look, finally, at Tim. His face is white, but his eyes are alert, calculating. He's ever calm. "*He* killed Peter. Out of a jealous rage. Then, you killed him in self-defense."

"Why? Why, Dylan?" There is a sharp pain across my stomach. My brother.

His eyes flip from Tim back to me, and I see there what I've been too busy—too *self-centered*—to see, yet again. I missed it again. How could I miss it again? At least the first time, I was a child. All the time I've spent worrying about myself. My own mental and emotional failings. It's suddenly so clear to me.

Dylan is the one who isn't fine.

I've known this and yet, I did what Pop did with Lilith. I ignored it. I made excuses. I justified it. I didn't see what was so plain in front of my face.

Everyone ignores what they know to be true, when the truth is inconvenient.

I see the flash of rage, the wildness behind the mask. The spinning, out-of-control thoughts. Lilith was shaped by paranoia, jealousy, and intense, all-consuming rage. Dylan has taken those seeds and amplified them with obsession.

Yes. I've been obsessed. Watching. Recording them. Needing to be on the inside of their lives. But it's never been violent. I've even helped them.

We've both been given Lilith's compulsions. I see, in Dylan, that while Camille worked and took care of Baby Matty and I found ways to dodge him, he felt neglected, and something in him broke. He's hardly recognizable.

Or more accurately, he's *too* recognizable.

Years ago, a therapist assured me that I was not destined to a life of Lilith's rage. Her obsessions. Her afflictions. Her delusions, and yes, her compulsion to kill. *Of course, some mental illness is genetic, but some things are unknown: a combination of nature and nurture.* Is there a murder gene? What in Dylan's childhood could have gone so wrong, so awful, so differently from mine?

Dylan swings the gun from Tim to me and back.

"You *lied* to me. You've never done that before. You are obsessed with these people you don't know. They are not your family, *I am*. You said you had to work late, you went to the Dresdens'. You said you were tired; you'd cancel our plans *all the time*. I didn't matter to you anymore and I haven't for months. *Months!*" He spits the word out. "You are sick, Edie, and you don't even know it. You're obsessed and sick. She left us. Left me. And now you're leaving me. It used to be us against them. And now I'll have no one."

"That's not true. You have Camille," I say, knowing at once it's the wrong thing to say. He takes a step, stops, puts his head between his knees, and lets out an angry yowl, the sound of an injured cat. Tim takes the moment to lunge across the bed, his arm out to swipe Dylan, knock him off his feet. But Dylan is fast and the gun comes up, goes off, I can hardly take it all in, it happens too quickly. Tim seems to sit stock-still, his bulk absorbing the bullet like a pillow might, and then he falls backward before I see the blood bloom from the wound in his chest. On the right side, between his lung and shoulder.

I scream and run to him, forgetting that Dylan could kill me. Tim's breathing is labored and shallow and though his eyes are open, blinking, I don't think he's seeing anything. I pull the sheet from the bed and press it against his chest.

"Edie, sit back down or I'll kill you, too." The edge of wildness has seeped out of Dylan's voice. "You will listen to me. Tim killed Peter in a jealous rage. He saw you leave Peter's apartment. Tonight, he confronted you, and you killed him in self-defense. Do you understand?"

"Why? Why would I do that for you? No. Goddamnit, Dylan." I feel the tears pricking my eyes.

He places the gun against the small of my back and says softly, "Sit in the chair now. He will bleed out and you will let him."

"Dylan, do you want to be like her? They're going to put you away for a long time. Let me call 911. Let me save Tim's life. Maybe they'll spare yours."

"He has to die, Edie." Then he quiets. "This is the only way it works. Then we'll go back to how it used to be. You can come over again for dinner. We were so happy then. Even Camille was happy."

"Camille hates me," I plead. I watch Tim, who hasn't moved in over two minutes. Dylan is delusional. "I've only come for dinner one time. Let me just call an ambulance, please?"

My messenger bag still hangs across my shoulders. For the first time since I've gotten here, I remember it. I snake my hand inside my pocket and pull out my phone. My old phone. Before I had throwaways and burners, when I lived in this apartment building, before my own obsessions veered wildly out of control. I hold it up for Dylan to see. It's been powered off for a week. It was fairly new when I bought it. The battery should be still kicking.

It is. Barely. I turn on my GPS.

"Put it away, Edie."

"Please, think of what they'll do to you if you kill two men. You'll join Lilith, is that what you want?" I kneel on the floor, my hand covering his hand holding the gun, and speak softly. "Do you want to be like Lilith?"

His voice breaks. "I'm already like Lilith, Edie. This was inevitable. Do you see that now?" The gun is pointed directly at my heart, closer than point blank range. Contact distance. If he pulls the trigger now, I will die. The bullet will explode into my chest, ricochet off my bones, turn my heart to pulp.

"Dylan, what did she do to you?" I ask, feeling the answer somewhere in my gut, long buried. She did to Dylan what was done to her. He had both her nature and her nurture. I somehow didn't have either.

"She loved me." He says it so pitifully, so completely, without sadness or remorse. Like that, by itself, was enough.

I never saw anything, not directly.

I have flashes of memory: things I didn't know I knew. The summer he didn't come back and Lilith flew into a rage. The way he tried, that one and only time, to announce his independence and she wouldn't allow it. Nature vs. nurture. The way I was ignored, sometimes for hours, outside, running a Matchbox car up and down the dirt driveway, the dust kicking up in the hot July heat. Left wandering the streets of the trailer park. Chad. Where was Dylan while I ran wild? Inside with Lilith.

Incest and abuse were both cornerstones of Lilith's childhood—a fact I hadn't known until I read the book.

I breathe shallowly, the metal warming in my hand. I work my fingers under Dylan's, and pull the gun from his grasp. I do it so quickly, I'm not sure he realizes what I'm doing until I turn it around on him. Trained at *his* chest. My hands shake, just a little, but I'm steady. Pointing this gun at my brother.

"Dylan," I say softly. I feel my throat closing. My brother. "I'm calling the police now."

But I don't have to, they're already here. Through the window, I see the red and blue, the swirling lights and the far-off siren of an ambulance. A neighbor called in a gunshot.

If he was paying attention, Brandt would be right behind them.

CHAPTER 24

After

Psychosis can be brought on by trauma. Or drugs. Of course, people experience all kinds of trauma, do all kinds of drugs, and never turn into murderers. It's just in our blood: this thing that can turn us. A sleeping tiger, awakened with slight provocation.

Brandt came in close behind the district cops. They'd had something called a stingop on me. When I activated my phone at my apartment a powerful software notified Brandt's team that I was active again and pinged my location. It's a very expensive and controversial location method. It rarely holds up in court, but in my case, Brandt covered his bases and got a warrant.

He took no chances with me. He doesn't trust me any more than I trust myself. That's the thing that gets me the most. The whole time I was under, living in the shithole, hiding out at Peter's apartment in the dark, Brandt kept saying, *Trust me.* It was all a lie. I was right after all.

In Dylan's office, they found maps, notes, journals. An obsessive tracking of my daily activities. Even my journals paled in comparison. Brandt told me later that Camille wouldn't let them in. They had to get a warrant to search his office. They took everything: the computer, both laptops, the entire contents of Dylan's desk.

They won't let me see him. I am a prosecutorial witness. I can't explain why I want to when I've never had any urge to visit Lilith.

Except lately, I've thought so much about her. I can't explain that.

Was it jealousy? Dylan was possessive of my time. But what if I'd gotten a boyfriend, found a real career, anything else that would have kept me busy, canceling our dinner dates? I think back to all the excuses. None of it made sense.

Dylan was, simply put, psychotic. I was his fixation. When he couldn't control me, he spiraled out. I think he latched on to the idea that I cared more about Lilith than him. Or more accurately, the damage that Lilith had incurred. That I could seemingly care, so deeply, for strangers—enough to disrupt our status quo. Or that I could work toward a life in which my brother held appropriate space in it.

I've been thinking about appropriate space. Dylan and I spoke every day, multiple times a day. My therapist insists that this is not normal. When I pressed him about what is— how would I know?—he simply said we'd work on defining boundaries at a later time. I have no idea what this means, and I think I need a new therapist.

Oh, yes. I see a therapist now. Multiple times a week. At least for now.

But you know what the cops *didn't* find in Dylan's office, or on his and Camille's shared laptop? Any evidence of the book.

• • •

I am home. Finally.

I've spent the last two nights in Tim's hospital room. He

has been in and out of consciousness, woozy from pain medication and surgery. The bullet entered between Tim's ribs and exited under his shoulder blade, nicking his right lung and causing a partial collapse. That was the worst of his injuries. Many people take a .22 to the chest and live. This is what the ICU doc has told me, almost cheerfully, like a bit of trivia he trots out at parties.

Tim has a chest tube to drain the blood and a laparoscopic surgical repair to the site of the wound. His biggest medical trauma was something called pneumothorax, which is the act of breathing out of the hole in your chest as opposed to your lungs. Had he not gotten to the hospital in time, he would have died of oxygen deprivation. Eventually.

Today Tim will get the ventilator and chest tube removed and I want to get back to see him, so I move quickly around my bedroom, throwing clothes into a duffel bag. I shower and put on something besides jeans or khaki pants: a sundress that I haven't worn since Pop was alive. My apartment remains as I've seen it last, only three days ago: dirty, upended, tainted. I call Molly Maid and pay a nice chunk of cash to get it set right. Cash I shouldn't spend because technically, I don't have a job.

In my bedroom, I stare at the bare desk. Everything is gone. All my files, my notebooks. My drawers are emptied. I already decide that I will not ask for any of it back. My childhood journals sit stacked haphazardly in the corner. I leave them be, for now.

There's a knock on my apartment door. Someone who has gotten past the key code in the lobby. I expect a reporter; the whole story is sensational and I'm hurled back to those early days after Lilith's arrest when even going to the market or the corner store was an ordeal. When nice people were only nice until they realized who you were and their eyes would harden and mouths would twist and all you wanted to do was buy the gallon of milk and go home.

Through the peephole, I see that it's not a reporter. It's Brandt.

I let him in, apologetic for the condition of the apartment, as if he isn't the cause of it. Silly for so many reasons, but it's something to fill the silence.

"You look good with short hair," he finally says. I remember a day when Brandt telling me I looked good would send my heart reeling, my stomach knotting. Leave me analyzing his meaning for days. I poke at the feeling. I could say the same for him: his hair, graying at the temples, is still wet from a shower. He's wearing it a bit longer on top. He's shaved.

"Brandt," I say. "You're wearing a tie."

He holds it out, studies it, solemn and serious, a line forming between his brows, the slip of feeling there before it's replaced with his Brandt mask, smooth and unetched, emotionless, an occupational necessity, a personal hazard.

He opens his mouth to speak and I cut him off. "Let me ask you something. The knife. Peter's knife. It didn't match the other entry wounds. Why was Colleen put on Lilith?"

At the police station, that first night, I gave him my childhood journal. The dates lining up with Colleen's killing. I gave him Julie Kniper's recording. Neither are legally admissible, but it was enough for him to reopen Colleen's case. It would be a long road to Lilith's exoneration, and likely have no impact on her sentencing. Like Julie said, it was a lot of work for very little benefit.

He stares at me. Finally he says, "I think it was assumed that it was a shallow wound that nicked the right artery. The end of Lilith's knife was a smooth blade." He's quiet about it.

"That seems like a cop-out," I say, and he smiles. Just a little.

"Well, there are fewer fatal stabbings than shootings. We're always under pressure to increase our closure rates. Mistakes happen." Brandt slides the tie between his fingers. It is yellow and gray and his collar is frayed at the edges, pushing into his neck. "Of the, say, 275 murders in Philadelphia in a year, 230 of them are caused by guns and only, say, 40 of them are women. So women that are stabbed? That's like 25 people. Almost all of those are due to drugs or domestic abuse in poverty-stricken neighborhoods. We find a nice, married lady in a nice neighborhood stabbed and there's a rash of homicides that are even remotely similar? Yeah, we gotta pursue that. It's just numbers at that point."

I stand there dumbly, listening to him spout math, my mind blank, his voice thick like he's underwater. I still have so many questions. What does he make of Lindy, who lied over and over—why do that? I ask him and he sighs again. Looks around my apartment, almost fervently, I think, for an exit.

"Lindy was never part of any of this. She's young. Lost, troubled, she found Peter and clung to him. They shared a bond, she'd told me that. No one else understood her like Peter." Brandt is uncomfortable talking about emotions, always has been. "It's not uncommon. Victims of violent crimes often marry each other. She had a fantasy in her head and when it fell apart, she . . . well, she fell apart." I start to object, but he holds up his hand. "Leave her be, Beckett. She's been through enough."

She's been through enough? He's admonishing me? I'm suddenly, instantly, bone tired. Brandt is still sliding his tie between his fingers, the soft *whip, whip* is all I can hear.

Finally, "Edie," he says. "I have to tell you something." *Edie.* Not *Beckett.* His voice is different. Softer. He steps toward me, palms his hand back over the slick of his hair, his eyes searching upward, and it's then that I understand that something is wrong. His face changes and I realize that I've misread the whole visit. All my investigation questions, of course he didn't come here for them.

I grip the edge of the kitchen table. He reaches for me and

stops, either because of my face or because of our history, I can't tell. I must drop the mug I'm holding—I had offered him coffee and forgotten to make it—because I hear it clatter to the floor, but it doesn't break. Brandt continues talking, but I can't hear him over the *whoosh* in my ears so I ask him to repeat it.

"It's Dylan," he says again. "He hanged himself in his cell last night. I'm so sorry, Edie."

And I can't deny that for one fleeting millisecond, I'm relieved. I thought Brandt was going to tell me he loved me.

* * *

"How are you?" I ask dumbly, standing at the edge of the bed, my fingertips resting on Tim's blanketed feet. They've removed the chest tube, the ventilator. He's taken a walk today already. His color is coming back. He pats the bed next to him for me to sit. I do.

"I'm sorry for everything," I say. I've probably said it fifty times in the past two days.

"Edie, stop." He closes his eyes as he says it, shakes his head. He reaches out, taps my hand, his fingers drumming against knuckles. When he opens his eyes, he tugs on my hand. His face rearranges into something inscrutable. "Dylan," is all he says.

"He's dead," I say, willing a feeling to surface. A sadness. A certain flare of rage. All I can think about is that night, when the EMTs rolled Tim over and the paramedic took his finger and plunged it directly into the wound in Tim's chest. I must have made a noise, a throttling sound, it was so shocking. The cop next to me told me, *They pull the muscle back against the wound so it stops sucking air.* So the air would go into his lungs again, so his organs could breathe. *Good thing he's knocked out,* the cop had said to another uniform, forgetting I was there. *That hurts worse than the bullet.*

"I'm sorry," Tim says, and he looks like he means it, which is both incredible and ridiculous.

"Oh God, Tim," is all I can say back. I stand up, busy myself with getting him water. Ice. I ask the nurse for an ice pack and then later, a warm compress because he has a headache. While he drifts back to sleep, I ask the desk when his meds are due. I fill the room with quiet busyness when he sleeps and clatter when he wakes up. I change his socks. We converse about the weather. Baseball. He doesn't rush to fill the silence. There's nothing of importance to say. Or rather, there's too much.

Getting close to me isn't simple. There's always a cost. There's no comfort in being right all these years.

CHAPTER 25

Six Months Later

I see Dr. Doyle once a week now. He is kind and wears Pepto-pink golf shirts and rimless glasses and when I tell him a particularly harrowing piece of the Lilith puzzle—sometimes the memories come together furiously, things I'd long forgotten about—he clicks his tongue in a way that is supposed to convey sympathy, I guess. It grates on my nerves, but I still tell him things I've never told anyone.

I've read up on incest. People do what is done to them: it's all they know.

Mainly, I tell him little things I've been remembering, things I hadn't known I'd forgotten. Lilith sleeping in Dylan's room, long past an appropriate age. Her listlessness and vague surprise, always looking slightly startled when she saw me, like she'd forgotten who I was. Her attachment to Dylan, which had never seemed odd until I said it out loud, as an adult, with years of distance. His on-again-off-again visitation in the summer. It was his way of getting away from her. But he'd always come back.

There's no way to know for sure, of course. Dylan is dead

and Lilith no longer sees or talks to anyone. Brandt told me she screamed when they told her.

Sometimes the things I remember, even the horrific things, feel pleasant.

Faithful in the summer: the year Lilith didn't pay the electric bill and not only was there no air-conditioning (we'd only had the one window rattler anyway), but there were no lights. No stove. Lilith was in her room for twenty-seven days in a row and Dylan had boiled water over the burn barrel out back, and we ate gluey macaroni and cheese out of the pot. Dirty-water dogs. Soft-boiled eggs, their insides gummy and slick. Anything we could buy from the three-aisle corner store and cook in hot water. The neighbor invited us in for cookies and cold milk with flakes of ice floating in it, her double-wide kept frigid, the sweat drying in a salty chill on my spine. Eventually, Pop got wind of it, either from Dylan or the neighbor, and came to pick us up, banging on Lilith's bedroom door with a heavy fist so hard the front window popped out. He left it like that and we drove away.

We registered for camp the following week, and I remember going to the zoo, watching two tigers fight behind the glass, the smaller one pinning the larger one down, a bloody sheath torn from its neck, the skin flapping as he writhed. When he went still, his eyes looking out into nothingness, I remember crying into Dylan's chest, his heavy arm wrapped around my shoulder. *He's not dead*, the counselor told us later, *it's a defense mechanism.*

We never believed him. He seemed dead to me.

• • •

Dr. Doyle insists that I must have unprocessed feelings about Dylan. He talks around it during sessions and I avoid it. We dance like this for a while.

He tells me to try to come up with a feeling.

"Relief. Fear," I say, and pause.

"Why fear?" he asks.

I don't answer him and instead pick at a mosquito bite on my ankle until it bleeds. He passes me a tissue and I dab at the bubble. I'm acting childish. I can't seem to stop.

"You won't catch it. There's no magic number of years. Dylan was not bipolar like Lilith. He had some measure of depression. He likely had an undiagnosed personality disorder; most people who kill have an ability to dissociate from reality. Morality. Personality disorders aren't typically solely genetic. They're genetic and environmental."

"I've heard all this before," I tell him. I don't tell him that it does nothing to assuage my fear.

"Many sociopaths are made, not born. Generally speaking. There's contradictory research and debate, to be sure, and genetic predisposition exists. But Edie, you are not a sociopath."

"How do you know?"

"Because if you were, you wouldn't be this fearful of it. You'd be hiding your real feelings from me, because you would know—and would have known your whole life—that you are not like other people. By thirty years old, you would be practiced in how to behave. You wouldn't be sitting here, asking me if you're a sociopath. You'd be too busy pretending that you aren't."

"Okay," I say. I do feel marginally better about it, although not entirely.

"Can you tell me another feeling you have about Dylan?" he asks again.

"Emptiness," I tell him.

"Emptiness isn't a feeling," he says.

* * *

The state cremated Dylan and gave me his ashes in a cardboard box. I take half the box to Faithful one day and follow the dusty road to the creek bed where we used to play. I sit on the bank, with my feet on the rocks, the water lapping up over my ankles, spring-fed and so cold my bones ache. Minnows nibble at my toes and crayfish scrabble under rocks.

I don't pray, because it seems pointless. Murderers go to hell no matter what is said to them, about them, posthumously. Also because, well, I'm not a praying kind of person.

I do, however, think of him. He wasn't wrong about much of it. He did save me, on more than one occasion. The time in the woods with Lilith and the gun wasn't the only one. There was a stupid night out on Chad Fink's front porch, feet dangled over an old, torn plush sofa, nipping off a vodka bottle and washing it down with cream soda. I was still young—twelve. The summer after Hazel. I remember just going right back to my life, back to the trailer, to the things that mattered to me at the time, never seeing Hazel or Mrs. Reston again.

That night, the sky spun into the ground and I lay down on the sofa to set it right, Chad's friends—two, maybe three of them—slapping at me, horsing around until it got serious, turned into tittie-twisters, and I hardly had any fight at all, pulling at my jeans as I swatted at his hands. Dylan came from nowhere, suddenly just there, pushed one of them to the ground and gave him a bloody lip and took me home. Held my hair while I puked in the toilet. God knows where Lilith was.

I look out over the water, the bank of rocks on the other side, the swimming hole, eight feet deep. Another memory: the last summer we stayed at Faithful, the summer of the woods and the gun, but in June, maybe July. Swimming with a girl from the neighborhood, drunk. Skinny-dipping, the ice-cold water between my legs. Jumping in the dark from the cliffside into the deep part of the pool. I remember feeling disoriented, swallowing water, the dark so black you couldn't spot your fingers in front of your face. Lungs bursting, stars in my eyes blurring with the night sky, not knowing what was real. Being so tired. Dylan dragging me up, onto the rocks, his heavy fist on my back as he whacked out the water. His whispered *Hush, Edie-bee, you're okay. I'm here.*

I never questioned how he knew I needed him, I was always just grateful he was there. It didn't occur to me to wonder, even years later, how much of his childhood he'd spent following me. Like I followed the remainders. Obsessive. Tracking. Saving me from myself. The parity is as startling as it is unnerving.

We're a jumble of Lilith's proclivities.

* * *

I don't sprinkle his ashes in the water, he never liked to swim. I open the box and instead hold the dust in my cupped palm, spreading it out among the rocks and dirt.

Brandt came by again a week or so after the day he'd told me about Dylan. He took me to lunch and told me what they'd found out about Peter.

On October 15, 1999, Peter had gone to an insurance conference in New York City. He drove into the city, parked his car. He checked into his hotel and went to a late-afternoon reception. Sometime around 6 p.m., he called Colleen and their conversation lasted seven minutes, according to the archived phone records.

Brandt and his team believe that Peter took a train back to Philadelphia that night, not to kill his wife but to catch her. To figure out what, if anything, she was hiding. An affair, most likely. If Julie is to be trusted, Brandt believes that she and Colleen kissed passionately in full view of the kitchen window before they fought. Their fight was a short burst of anger; Julie was already planning to come back later that night. Colleen expected her to come back. Later, when the police processed the scene, the taper candles were burned down to the holder, suggesting Colleen hadn't blown them out after the fight.

The kitchen was processed and blood was found on the floor. It was determined that she was killed in the kitchen and moved or carried outside behind the Dumpster. While this wasn't exactly in line with Lilith's other killings, it wasn't far enough afield to discount it as Lilith's crime.

At the time, Julie told the police that they'd fought and she left the house. She walked around for a while, maybe an hour. Then she went back to Colleen's. She stood on the opposite side of the street and saw Peter leave the apartment, jog out to Julie's car, retrieve something, and go back inside. When he reemerged, he was covered in blood. But then they checked out his alibi and it seemed solid. Insurance conference. Car. People who saw him earlier that night. Someone who even thought they saw him at the cocktail hour later, but everyone was drinking, so the eyewitness accounts are hazy.

Julie was largely disbelieved. It was dark, who would know if it was blood? On a man that they couldn't corroborate as Peter?

She'd gone to the police countless times in the last fifteen years but they never took her seriously.

She'd also been afraid, she said. That he'd kill her, too, eventually.

I think of Julie's accusation: *He was an abuser.* I think of the Peter I'd met. The even-keeled insurance claims adjuster, with the genuine, quiet smile and clean bathroom. I'd always prided myself on my ability to judge people. I'd never gotten any kind of vibe from him. He'd always just seemed kind to me. Predictable. Even now, sometimes, I dream about him.

Dylan was a psychopath. Peter was in love, then, maybe, enraged enough to accidentally kill—by not only an affair, but a lesbian one. Did that play into it? It filled him with guilt for fifteen years. Because of me, their paths crossed and ended in something disastrous. Peter killed Colleen. Dylan killed Peter.

I wonder who Peter was, before he'd killed Colleen. How had the murder changed him? Had learning that his anger held no limits—that he'd kill if provoked—molded him into the cautious introvert I'd met? Or perhaps it was all an act, and in another life, if we'd been permitted to carry a relationship to fruition, maybe I, too, would have been abused. Controlled.

I remember the endless posts on the Healing Hope forum. The grief he'd felt was real. Coupled and magnified by guilt. And something else. Self-loathing? Fear of his own capabilities, previously unknown? You don't have to be psychopathic to kill someone. If Peter had lived long enough, would he have eventually killed again?

Brandt says that most killings are disorganized, idiotic accidents. That murder is a mostly stupid act committed by mostly stupid people in their most desperate moment.

I cannot for the life of me picture the Peter I know carrying his wife's lifeless body and leaving it behind a Dumpster, then returning to an insurance conference on a midnight train.

I say this to Brandt, who says, "Beckett, you might have known a lot about him, but you didn't actually know him."

* * *

"I've submitted my application to the Department of State Corrections," I tell Dr. Doyle, and he coughs and crosses his legs, picks at some lint on his knee.

"What does this mean?" He knows what it means but he wants me to spell it out. Tell him, in five easy words.

"I want to visit Lilith."

I can say this without hesitation. This surprises him, and I find that more and more, I enjoy doing that. I like the gentle lift of an eyebrow, or the slight turn of a chin. I like doing *more* than what is expected of me.

"What do you think this will gain you?" He writes something down on his legal pad.

"Closure."

He glances up, still. "You think that seeing Lilith Wade will bring you a sense of closure?"

"Why, you don't think so?" I don't really wait for him. "I do. I've never once visited her. I couldn't do it. But Dylan did. Every month. Ma, he called her. I've never been able to call her anything but Lilith."

"I think if you expect a visit to propel you forward in leaps and bounds and heal you somehow, you'll be disappointed. If you see this as a necessary rung on a ladder to some kind of future ability to put the past where it belongs, then I think you'll be fine." He smiles. "Maybe not fine, but we'll get through it."

"There's something else," I say, and this part I know he won't like. I rush on before he has a chance to interrupt. "I'm going to find out who wrote *The Serrated Edge.*"

"Why?" he says.

"I don't know. Call it curiosity. Is it unhealthy? It seems unhealthy." I am agreeing on the outside. Is it another way to channel my obsessive tendencies? Maybe. I say this hoping he sees me as improving. I can acknowledge my deficiencies now. I want him to write it down. *Improvement!*

"Someone hated me—hated all of us—enough to write it. Who? Why? Never mind, I know why people would hate us."

"No one has to hate you. Maybe someone just found it to be a good story and a way to make some money? People write books all the time, not out of hate."

"Okay, fine, then maybe they didn't hate us, but you'd have to dedicate *your life* to that kind of research. Who would do that without emotional attachment? None of the victims' family members wrote that book," I say, picking a ball of fuzz from my pant leg.

"Oh? How do you know?" he asks.

I stare at him. For a doctor, he can be incredibly dumb. "Because I know them all. They are all either too busy, too disorganized, too stupid, or too sad to do all that. I would have seen something while I watched them, don't you think?" Strictly speaking, I didn't know them all. I couldn't even *find* Quentin. And I looked.

"You don't know them, Edie," he says quietly. "Knowing *about* someone is not the same as knowing them." He sounds just like Brandt.

"You know what I mean, though," I insist, and he sighs again, all the gentle surprise of earlier leaked away.

Finally he asks, "How will you do it?"

I almost laugh. It's like he doesn't even know me. "How else?" I smile. "Follow the money."

CHAPTER 26

It was easier than I thought it would be.

The Serrated Edge still hangs at the top of the *New York Times* bestseller list and is translated into, at last check, over twenty-five languages.

I started with Brandt, of course. *Murder is a mostly stupid act committed by mostly stupid people in their most desperate moment.*

"Edie, she didn't tell me her real name. I talked to her on the phone, gave her one quote, a fairly meaningless one." I can hear his impatience.

"Did you get her number?" I ask, pressing him. He says no.

"It was a late-in-the-day phone call. Honestly, I forgot about it ten minutes after I hung up." Another sigh.

My obsessiveness has always been an inconvenience to him. It was almost a letdown, it was so easy. Once, of course, I channeled my penchant for searching and digging and prying my fingers into a particular fissure—I think, then, of Tim's wound and the paramedic, the faint sucking sound as the air went in and out with his breath, like a wet gurgle—I worked it open like the rip in a pair of pantyhose.

The first time I'd read *The Serrated Edge*, I'd done so with one eye closed, a reverent schedule of a chapter a day. Now, on second read, I rip through it. *It's just a fucking book about a bad person and a shitty life.* I repeat this until I mean it, until I *feel* it. Eventually, I read the whole thing, until I am hollowed out. The same way I felt when I talked about my brother, the word thick and meaningless in my mouth. What's a brother anyhow? Someone who once slept in the same womb as you, though not at the same time. Practically nothing at all—a wispy helix of DNA, possibly a shared eye color, the same flat thumb. The joint propensity to blink when we were nervous.

Either way, I read the book—*It's just a fucking book about a bad person and a shitty life*—and take detailed notes.

I find it in chapter two.

James Richard Beckett Jr., or "Pop," was born in 1956 in the city of Philadelphia to Constance and James Beckett Sr. He grew up in North Philly in a Jewish neighborhood, one of a handful of Protestants. He met Lilith Wade at a wedding of a mutual friend. They were married less than a year later, at the court-house, in 1985. Pop is likely the most interesting subject of the entire Lilith Wade investigation. He is staunchly blue-collar. The kind of man who worked at the wastewater treatment plant for twenty-five years before he retired, only accumulating a handful of promotions, and by all accounts a "content and satisfied employee." He donated to charity weekly—paper towels, boxes of spaghetti, jars of peanut butter. The kind of man with a closet full of plaid button-down short-sleeved shirts and jeans. The kind of man with two pair of shoes—dress and everyday. The kind of man who liked to sit on the porch and watch the neighborhood. The kind of man who sat his digital HD wide-screen on a 1970s console television that no longer worked but still functioned as perfectly fine furniture. He had few close friends, and an only slightly larger ring of acquaintances.

It was slipped in so innocuously, you'd hardly notice it if

you hadn't been looking: *The kind of man who sat his digital HD wide-screen on a 1970s console television.*

Whoever had authored the book had been in our house.

Pop's house. You could find out about his wardrobe by talking to his friends. You could drive by and see him sitting on the porch every day. God, everybody knew he had two pairs of shoes. But the television? That wasn't a neighborhood joke or even a conversation piece. That had just been our furniture, so normal and everyday I hardly saw it anymore. In *our* living room.

Everything else could be gleaned from public records and phone conversations, but not that.

It's easy enough to make a list. The author said himself: Pop had only a few friends. I think of every repairman—not as hard as you'd think, Pop had a furnace guy (Al), a plumber (Freddie Ray), an electrician (Pinky, because of his missing pinky finger). Every other repair in that three-bedroom row home had been Pop's. Every broken hinge, every wobbly door handle, every rain gutter.

I write down every neighbor, every friend of Dylan's and mine—there weren't many, Mia and Rachel, that's about it. Al, Freddie Ray, and Pinky. A childhood friend of Pop's. A few buddies from the plant. When I'm done, there are forty-seven people on the list. Al and Freddie Ray had both died and Pinky was in a retirement home.

Everyone else gets a column in the spreadsheet: name, address, occupation, married, children. I think about how my life would look stupid and pedestrian on my own list: an apartment in the city, no job to speak of, no husband, no children.

Here's what I know for sure: someone who authors a book anonymously doesn't do it for the fame or the love of writing. They do it possibly for revenge, but mainly for money. They don't sit on their earnings and wait to see how their work will perform in the market. They have no intention of writing another book. They take their advances and spend them. Before the ink on the check is fully dry, before anyone can change their minds, they sink it into what is still the safest investment, despite the market crash. They spend it.

On a nice big house.

Bingo.

•   •   •

When she opens the door, she looks the same. The same shoulder-length blond hair. The same pert smile, a lone dimple too low on her cheek to be cute. She has a stud in her nose, a tiny sapphire, the blue glinting in the sun.

"E. Green," I say.

"Holy shit, is that you, Edie?" Her voice hitches up an octave, echoes in the foyer. I can see her calculating how to play this, her eyes darting past me into the driveway where Tim's Honda sits. I've borrowed it. He wanted to come, but I waved him away.

The house is in a Main Line suburb, bought for a smidge under a million bucks, about the size of her advance. How else would she afford it? The front is lined with arborvitae, an ugly, functional, phallic tree. Piles of leftover gray snow clump and dot the lawn.

She wears skinny jeans and ankle boots and a gauzy teal top, a gold braid around her neck. She smells like expensive perfume, rich and layered. She presses her lips together and throws her arms around my shoulders.

"I'm so happy to see you!" she exclaims, her voice bright and burbling, but she blinks too hard, too fast.

"Are you?" I back up, my hands slick and shaking, and pretend to dig around in my purse to hide it. "It's clever, you know? E. Green? East Greenville, right?"

East Greenville was the other charter school in our district. It went under while I was still in school, the students filtering into Redwood Academy, and after a while, everyone forgot it ever existed. Almost everyone.

No one plucks a name out of thin air.

"Edie, I can't believe you're here!" She throws her head back, the raw white of her throat exposed as she laughs. "Oh, it's been years. You, me, Rachel. God, how's your pop, is he still alive—?"

I find my voice. "Just stop it." I know that I'm right because I'm still standing on the porch. If she hadn't written the book, if me standing on this stoop wasn't a perceived warning of some kind, I would already be standing inside her house. It's cold outside. I can feel the warm air seeping out from the cavernous space beyond the door.

She turns her head to the left, just a little. In that slight movement, I see Mia from Redwood. Mia, whose hair I dyed and cut right before the Christmas dance and made her mother cry, all those golden waves turned mud-water brown and shaggy with my inexpert snipping. I see Mia, across from me over a Ouija board, summoning someone, anyone, the planchette sliding across the gilded letters while Rachel screamed and Mia's mouth, etched in red—we'd just started wearing lipstick—curved into a smirk. Mia was smart, cunning, sometimes with a razor-sharp cruel streak.

"Why?" It's all I can think of to say.

She places her hands on her stomach, pushing in, her gaze at the floor, and for a moment I think she's crying, but when she looks up finally, she's clear-eyed. "I don't know what you're talking about," she says, blinking, looking at me with feigned incomprehension, almost hostility.

"Sure you do. Why'd you do it? Money? Couldn't have been fame, you wrote it under a pseudonym." I remember her stalker. Samuel Park. I guess she's still trying to stay hidden. "Did you remember that weird girl you went to high school with, the one with the crazy mother, and think, *Oh, well now, there's a paycheck?*"

She steps back, and her fingers tighten around the door handle. "Edie, please. If you came to chat about Redwood and reminisce, then let's. I can do lunch." She looks at her watch, an oversized gold face, crystals throwing sunlight around the porch. "But not today, unfortunately. I have an appointment. We can find another time."

"I'm just curious. How did you do it? Without anyone finding out who you were?" I ask her. It never made sense; how did she talk to everyone: neighbors and Lilith's family and social workers, teachers, Pop's old classmates and buddies from the plant, teachers at Redwood, my old middle school teachers at the public school? She'd talked to everyone. How?

"Edie, I feel like you're not okay. Are you okay? Do you want me to call someone for you?" That fake concern on her face, her lip caught between her veneered front teeth, the lipstick not smudging or staining. She reaches over, behind the half-open door, to a hall table that I can't see and brings her purse over her shoulder. She steps out onto the porch, shutting the door behind her.

"I'm fine." I have an urge to push her. I want to see her tumble off her small stoop, see her legs fly up when she lands in the topiary.

"I want to know why. Your actions hurt people. You need to know that." I block her path, standing firm on the step. I see her tense.

"My actions? What about your mother's actions? Your father's *inactions*? You hurt people, too." Her face goes hard, her voice low. There it was: her admission. Her anger was her guilt.

"Why do you care? You had to have devoted years of your life to this book. To research. Why?" I realize then that this is why I've come. To write a book of this magnitude, for it to take this much space in her life, it had to be personal. I think of the things she's sidelined: marriage, children. I wonder how many nights she'd left her fiancé alone, running off to talk to a source. *But why?* "You didn't write the book to avenge victims' families." I laugh then. The Dresdens were looking at two college tuitions and a wedding in the next decade. Lindy Cook was living in that shithole apartment, dancing for fewer than twenty thousand dollars a year. "You might tell yourself that. But if you did, you would have given them money! Instead you're here. In this enormous house, in this wealthy neighborhood, with good schools and probably a nice car or four. Engaged to a drug sales rep."

Her eye twitches. "How do you know that?"

"Know what?" I ask.

"What my fiancé does? You're psychotic, just like her."

For a second, it works. I falter, my footing slightly off, the heat of the sun suddenly warm against my forehead, a hapless, misting sweat. Then I right myself. I'm not, of course I'm not. I almost laugh, but at the last second, I swallow it instead.

"What I don't understand is, why write it under a pseudonym? If you're a journalist, wouldn't a book of this magnitude help your career?" It's cruel, I know this, but I keep going anyway. "Because of Samuel Park? What did he do to you, Mia?"

"Fuck you," she hisses.

"If I found you, then he can, too. It's hard to hide, you know?" I step back, off the porch, away from her. "It just makes no sense. Why do all this *work*? And not even get the credit for it?"

"You really have no idea, do you?" Her mouth opens, and her fingertips brush along her brow line. Her voice drops to a whisper. "Margaret Mayweather?"

Lilith's last victim. Right before she was arrested, mere weeks, in fact.

"God, you're so helplessly selfish. It's pathological." Mia's eyes narrow. "Margaret. Molly. Margaret Mayweather was Molly."

Molly.

No. I would have known that. Somehow. How didn't I know? Did I know Molly's last name? I must have. She was just a woman I saw sometimes at Mia's house. I'd hardly even spoken to her. I'd been taken with her, the idea of her, the intimacy of her and Mrs. Packer's friendship. How easily they laughed, touched, their hands patting each other's shoulders, backs, hair. I thought she was glamorous. Beautiful, even. But no, I search my memory. I didn't know her name.

"How?" I whisper, a thundering in my ears. "That makes no sense. I would have heard about that. We didn't know Molly died."

I try to remember, those few weeks before Lilith was arrested, the subtle shifting of alliances. I hadn't slept at Mia's in months. I'd had the distinct sensation of being a hanger-on, a barnacle. Mia and Rachel were the first friends, the original friends, and I had co-opted, but it was over. The sun was setting on the friendship long before Lilith's arrest.

"Of course we didn't know. They'd had a fight. Mom knew Molly's husband had been fooling around. She hadn't wanted to hear about it. They hadn't talked for weeks. Then they'd never talk again." Mia's mouth curved into a smile. "Because of your psycho bitch mother, who was apparently fucking Troy."

Troy Mayweather. Molly's husband. I feel sick, like I might vomit right there on her front step. Of course, now it makes so much sense.

Mia wrote the book because she is a remainder.

"My mother was never the same. There's a ripple effect to violence, you know." She spits this out, venomous, like this is news to me. "Your family hurt people, Edie. The world deserves to know that."

CHAPTER 27

December

They call me on a Tuesday and ask if I can come on Friday.

"Does she know I'm coming?" I ask.

"Inmates have to approve all visitors," says the nasal twang on the phone.

"So she said yes?" I ask again, pressing the phone against my cheek.

"Ms. Wade has approved you, yes. You'll have one hour. Friday, 9 a.m." She doesn't ask if that works for me.

"Okay," I say slowly, my mind racing. "Yes. I can be there." But she's already hung up.

•   •   •

State Correctional Institution—Muncy (SCI—Muncy, or just Muncy) reminds me of every movie I've ever seen with a 1960s college campus. The main administration building is brick, with pointed turrets and a clock tower. The walk is new concrete, the lawn is clipped and still green. There is a twenty-foot flagpole in a landscaped circular garden ten feet from the front door.

I am wanded and sent through metal detectors. The main

lobby is shining; the floors squeak under my shoes. There is a wide front desk, staffed with two efficient administrators. The phone rings nonstop and they are logging in visitors, recording information, passing out forms. Someone instructs me to take a seat and says I'll be called in a moment, like I'm at the DMV. I sit next to a wide glass case filled with brass trophies won by various prison athletic teams.

An ornate Christmas tree perches in the corner, bursting with paper tags with the names of inmates' children, candy canes, glittery bows, and tinsel, topped with a white, blinking angel. A sign on a bulletin board across from me shouts, SANTA VISIT DECEMBER 10 FROM 1–4 PM!, with jaunty holiday clip art underneath.

"Well, this is unexpected," Tim whispers.

When they call my name, they tell me that Tim must wait in the main lobby and I will be escorted to the death row and maximum security visiting unit, Building C. A kind uniformed guard suggests that I leave my purse, my cell phone, my belt, and a hair barrette with him. I fumble with the barrette, and he smiles apologetically at me. "The metal detectors in Building C are more sensitive." When I hand it all to Tim my hands shake, and he gives them a squeeze. "Good luck. You'll be fine," he says. Then, "I'll be here."

I'm led into Building C, and down a long corridor, past several general visitation lounges, equipped with tables and chairs. It never occurred to me what it would feel like to touch Lilith, to hug her. From everything I've read, that choice isn't mine to make, but I see inmates in gray prison uniforms embracing with men holding toddlers and babies, kissing their cheeks. I see mothers hugging sons and daughters. I see the tears in their eyes, the tracks down their faces. And I have to wonder how that would feel. To touch my mother.

I don't remember the last time I hugged her. Surely, if

I had known it would be the last time I'd ever touch my mother, I would have imprinted it more in my memory. But, like so many other things, you just don't know it's the last time until it's long over.

I do remember one of the last times I saw her. It was winter, the year she was arrested. She'd come to Pop's at his invitation. It was warm, sixty degrees in February. She brought Ritz crackers and slabs of cheddar, wrapped in cellophane. Since you never knew what actually made it into the fridge with Lilith, Pop had regarded it with skepticism.

He drank beer on the porch. Lilith sat on the rocker next to him. I sat on the steps. Lilith tapped the arm of the rocker, over and over, a skipping step pattern, until Pop put his hand over hers and held it there. She stayed for a beat and yanked it away.

She didn't say much, sometimes she didn't. Pop didn't talk because Pop wasn't a talker.

Dylan was away, off at a friend's house, or playing basketball at the park down the street.

Pop asked Lilith if she was taking her medication. She'd said yes and he'd nodded once, to himself.

That was it. That was the whole memory. I don't remember how she left or when. Later, at the trial, we'd find out that Lilith stabbed Margaret Mayweather—Molly—wife of Troy Mayweather, twelve times in the abdomen only four days earlier. All the information took weeks to assemble and come out in the press. By then, I'd left school, huddled in the house with Pop, reporters firing questions at us whenever we left. I'd never tried to call them, Mia and Rachel, and they'd never called me. Our lives—and our friendship—had been divided: before Lilith and after.

Wouldn't I have seen a picture of her? Recognized her? I think of the one grainy black-and-white photo that ran in the paper, her hair longer. Darker. The photo was only two-by-two. I quickly stopped reading articles at the time, for Pop's sake more than my own.

When I started researching the remainders, following them online, I'd given precious little thought to the victims themselves. I'd looked up Troy, found his current address. He lived in New Jersey, too far away to really pay much attention to. I might have eventually figured it out. If I hadn't found Peter first. I'd simply been derailed.

Later, when I read the book, it seemed impossible that nothing led me to Molly. I tried to recall what I'd known about her: Mrs. Packer's beautiful, but enigmatic, best friend. They had worked together, both nurses. But where? Which hospital? The city had several. When we sat under the kitchen table, listening to them gossip about coworkers, I was enamored with her *voice*, not her words. I'd hardly listened to what she was saying, just intent on hearing their laughter. Still. I'd known she was married. Now, in hindsight, of course I'd known her husband's name was Troy. I can even remember her saying it, the city accent heavy in her red-rimmed mouth. It was a detail that rang familiar only once I'd already heard it.

But the thing that has preoccupied me for years—before the remainders became my project, and still today, now that I'm done with them—is lining up events in my life with the timeline of the murders. Wondering at what point she'd thought of us: me, Dylan, Pop. Wanting to know, exactly, when Pop called to invite her down for a "porch sit," as he called it. Was it before or after? When did she call him back to say yes—before or after?

I can always ask her.

They lead me into the booths, high-sided with clunky black receivers on either side of shatterproof glass. They instruct me to sit and wait. I'm the only visitor today, the guard tells me, and I say, "I'm so sorry," but I have no idea why.

I sit. The chair is plastic with metal legs, like in high school. I wait.

I had a list of questions, topics to discuss, in my mind, but the closer I get to her, the more scrambled I feel, and I have a pulsing, panicky feeling that I won't say anything. That I'll sit across from my mother, silent, just like her, picking at the pinked skin around my fingernails, chewing on my lip, the skin raw and bruised. I have the suffocating sensation that we'll waste the whole hour, me a scrum of nerves, she dazed with medication.

Brandt told me that the solitary life of death row has done a number on her.

The door buzzes and a guard comes out, buzzes through the air lock and onto my side of the partition. He confers quietly with the guard who has been my escort and they nod in my direction.

When he approaches me, I really see him for the first time. He's tall, black, somber. He has straight, nice teeth and long eyelashes. He's handsome. He pulls a chair up next to me and leans forward.

"She's not coming down," he says. He doesn't mince words. He doesn't apologize. He knows Lilith, he knows what she did. He knows I'm her daughter and I've never visited. The weight of any of this isn't lost on him. He lets me have the moment.

I close my eyes, breathe in and out, and then, let out a small laugh. My breath feels sour. "I knew she wouldn't."

I didn't know I knew until I said it. The guard's badge, I realize for the first time, says OMAR.

"You can put money on a card for her," he says, finally. I nod, surprised that I'd want to, even more surprised that he'd know it. "There's a form at the Building C desk. There's a commissary. The DRs don't get to buy that much, but there's some. She likes to chew gum."

"What else?" I ask urgently.

He thinks for a moment. "She likes playing cards. She's allowed to have them in her cell. She's invented a few different variations of solitaire. She never cheats, not at least when I've seen her play in the lounge."

"The lounge?" I ask.

"They're all allowed out about two hours a day. She doesn't go outside much. She prefers the lounge, where she can play her cards."

I think of UNO in the dark. I think of the smell of bleach, the slick of it straight from the bottle against my skin, and the sting. I think of the feel of Lilith's cheek under my palm in the dark, the bend of her small, bony body around mine. I think of her lipstick, fanned into the creases in her mouth. I think of her hair, shining and clean when she was well, wet-looking with grease and grayish-brown when she wasn't.

We stand and he leads me back to Tim, back through the maze of hallways, Building C, outside, and back to the administration building.

"You can try again in a few months," Omar says.

"I won't come back," I say, and he nods. I pull on the door, seeing Tim in the lobby, where I left him next to the trophies. I turn back to Omar and ask, "How is she? Is she okay here?"

He pauses before he says it. "She never gives anyone trouble. She follows the rules. She takes her medication and visits her doctors. She doesn't talk much. If I had to say"—he licks his lips, a nervous twitch—"I'd say she's content."

Content. My whole life, I'd never known what that felt like.

• • •

Tim taps his hand on his knee as he drives. Every few minutes he turns to look at me, like I might suddenly break apart unless he keeps watch. It's unnerving.

"This is not the worst thing she's ever done to me," I tell

him, almost mildly. He turns on the radio and we ride in comfortable silence. I have a lightness in my chest, a buoyed sense of elation. I find myself wanting to make big plans: I'll go back to college, be the girl in the PINK sweatpants, the JUICY sweatshirt. Run a marathon. We could do it, Tim and I, train for months, buy matching wicking tank tops and get bib numbers one digit apart. I could write a book of my own. Get twice the advance Mia got, tell my own story, my way. Get a job in IT. Get out from under Brandt's thumb, start my own damn career without help. Stop drinking. For good.

I take his hand in both of mine, feel the warmth of his palm against my own. The twitchy pulse under my thumb. I could be in love. Tim is a good person, a good man.

There are a lot of possibilities.

My thoughts zing around, crashing into my skull. I can't focus on any of them.

Muncy recedes in the rearview mirror, the barbed wire and clock tower growing smaller. My mood switches without warning, suddenly somber.

What was the draw, exactly? How did I let it all go, so quickly and wildly out of my control? All those months ago, was it the idea that Lilith had severed us—all of us: the Dresdens, the Hoffmans, the Mayweathers, Lindy Cook, Walden Holmes, Peter—from the rest of the world? We were what she'd managed to lop off: the briny, dirty, unspoken underbelly of her crimes. Not just the killings, but the aftershocks, felt for years after. We were all, somehow, *other*.

Maybe we'd all felt as though none of us deserved to move past the horror that had been inflicted on us, simply because we could have stopped it from happening in the first place. It started with Mitchell Cook, who had held up his marriage to Penelope as a fractured, broken thing and had been seduced, however briefly, by the idea of Lilith: a pretty, lonely woman in a bar. We all had our own forms of proof—we deserved what she had done. If we had been better children, better citizens, better husbands, better sisters, better daughters, we would have been able to prevent it.

I'd been holding up Lilith as a portent. *See: I cannot be a normal person. See: I cannot be a mother.* Even blaming Lilith for Hazel. *I am defective.* Lacking. Less than. But it's all bullshit.

Lilith was a terrible person who did terrible things. I was a child who deserved a better mother. I was not responsible, at twelve or even fourteen, for suspecting Lilith of criminal acts and notifying the proper authorities. I was not responsible for the lives of Renee Hoffman, Melinda Holmes, Penelope Cook, Annora Quinlan, Margaret Mayweather.

I left Hazel in the car, not because of Lilith but because I was eleven. Because I'd been left in the car my whole life. Because I'd never babysat before. Because no one ever told me not to. Because I'd never known how to care for another person or be cared for. Sure, arguably, this all comes back to Lilith, but it's not something *inside me* that's broken. If I choose to, and I'm quite certain I never will, I could have children. There is no terrible mother gene, so I could not inherit it.

I could, starting now, leave the past here, Lilith here. It could, I imagine, be that simple.

At that moment, Tim looks over, across the seat, and gives me a smile. The radio is playing a song I don't recognize. I realize then that this feeling in my chest isn't elation. Or anxiety. Or anything I've grown accustomed to: it's not dread or fear or nervousness. Instead, it is soft and insistent, so benign that I could almost ignore it. It's a muted, cautious peace. Contentment.

The tentative wingbeats of freedom.

EPILOGUE

Gil Brandt, Philadelphia Police Department, Homicide Division, July 2018

Gil was in line for coffee when he saw her. Her light hair had been cut short; she wore a jacket and a pair of jeans, despite the heat. He used to do this on purpose: take the same train, get in the same coffee line, drop by her desk. This time, it was an accident. He wanted to get away before she saw him, he probably could have, ducked off to the right, his head bent low, rushing against the morning grain.

She didn't work for the city anymore.

She turned and saw him, doing a double take, and she smiled.

He'd forgotten that she was beautiful. He'd almost forgotten her, period. He went long stretches of time now barely thinking about her at all. His girlfriend, Sara, would appreciate it—if she'd known anything about her.

She hugged him. She'd gotten older, aged a decade in only a year. She wore lipstick and laughed. She'd been standing in front of him for thirty seconds and hadn't said *fuck* yet.

"I'm a journalist now. Working on it, anyway. Have a few

years left for the degree. I went back to school! I write some freelance for the *Inquirer*." She was breathless with the effort of getting her whole life into this conversation, of catching him up. She socked him lightly on the arm. "Seen my byline? I go by Jill Brand."

"Resurrecting your old PI name, eh?" He didn't know what to do with this woman, who was sleek and content and exuberant. He felt old, ancient. Creaky and cranky. He was coming off a double, a gang fight in an alley. The bodies were stacked up at the morgue, waiting on him and Merket. He smelled like a three-day-old suit and hand sanitizer.

"Yeah, well, I grew kind of attached to her." She smiled sideways, a lock of hair falling down in front of her eyes.

He'd forgotten this feeling: a mixed-up kind of longing, combined with the rush to save her. It was a quiet, soul-killing desperation to realize she no longer needed him. Hadn't for some time.

"We could get lunch," he offered lamely. "Not today, but someday?"

"Maybe?" Her tongue stuck in the side of her cheek and she narrowed her eyes. "The thing is, Brandt, I'm fine now. I mean, as fine as anyone else, probably, which is to say an average level of fucked up." She laughed then. "You haven't done this in a while." She gestured to the line.

"It was an accident," he said. "This time." Then, "I know you're fine. Lunch was just . . . lunch."

"I know. I know!" She hugged him again. "I still have your number. I'll call you, okay? I will." When she pulled back, she put her hands on his shoulders, really looked at his face.

He didn't know her anymore. He felt a pang, like he'd missed something great. He'd missed it when she put herself back together.

He'd stayed away, moved on, gotten promoted to lieutenant, started dating again—at his age, for fuck's sake, it was a constant exercise in humility. Somehow, in his absence, she'd become this whole other person: the kind of woman who shopped at Ann Taylor and Williams-Sonoma and bought lattes instead of black coffee. Who got professional haircuts and—he checked her hands—thankfully did not get manicures. It's shocking to go through hell with someone, only to see them come away transformed, in what felt to him like the magic wave of a hand. Like coming out of a tunnel into the bright daylight and realizing maybe you didn't have to take the tunnel after all. You could have been in the sunshine the whole time. She leaned in and kissed his cheek, her lips sticky against his skin. She held it there for a beat before turning to go. A few feet away stood a guy: tall with dark hair. His face lit up when he saw her. Brandt realized it was the guy from a year ago. She handed him one of the coffees in her hand. But nothing else about her was the same: School. Job. What looked to be a serious relationship. She pointed to Brandt, who gave a half wave, and the guy waved back. Brandt ran his hand across his jaw, trying to make sense of this new reality. He didn't know why he assumed she wouldn't change, except that she never had before.

They were only about twenty feet away when she stopped, turned, and called, "Hey, Brandt!" His heart hammered at an embarrassing clip. Her cheeks flushed, and her eyes squinted. "You should shave. You look like shit."

ACKNOWLEDGMENTS

Thank you to Sarah Cantin, who worked tirelessly to help me get down to the question of why. I have been grateful for your guidance and expertise before, but never quite this much. Thank you to the whole Atria team, but especially Stephanie Mendoza and Haley Weaver (who offered wonderful feedback!). And, of course, thanks to Mark Gottlieb, agent extraordinaire, tireless cheerleader, astonishing deal-maker, biggest retweeter.

I am so incredibly grateful for the writing community. You are my colleagues, my friends, my ardent supporters, and I wouldn't love this job half as much as I do without you. To my Tall Poppy Writers, you are my go-to girls. I'm so proud to be part of a community that lifts up and supports women. To my first readers with keen observations and kind delivery: Karen Katchur, Kimberly Giarratano, Elizabeth Buhmann, Ann Garvin, Sonja Yoerg. Writer pals and Calamity Dames: Emily and Kim, who talk me off ledges daily, bless them (but not bless their hearts). To my family and friends who come to my events, even now, five years later (it might be for the drinks after, though): Mom and Dad and Meg and the Peanuts Gang, Aunt Mary Jo and Uncle Jeff, Becky and Molly, Dottie, Chuck and Lauren. To BethAnn and Sarah (Reindeer Fur!), Sharon, Betsy, Kelly G., my A-Phi sisters who shout to the rooftops and are supportive in surprising and delightful ways. Finally, to the bloggers, Instagramming community, the reader groups (Hi, Bloomies!), the reviewers, and, of course, the readers. I'm so incredibly grateful for your support, kindness, and love of books. I could not begin to thank you each individually; I'd leave someone out and never sleep again. And of course, endless gratitude to all librarians and booksellers, particularly Moravian and Clinton Book Shops, who have always welcomed me with open arms.

I would also like to acknowledge Steve Rush, who gave me insight into all the psychiatry mentioned in this book. And Joe Murray at the PPD, who sat with Karen and me for hours at a diner in Center City and answered all my procedural and Philadelphia-related questions. My mistakes and liberties are my own.

Finally, I have my biggest thanks to my family. It's because of you that I actually leave the house. I appreciate your patience when I'm in writer la-la land, which is only about 95 percent of the time. To Lily and Abby, I hope I'm teaching you how to chase your dreams. To Chip, words cannot express my appreciation, ever. You take care of everything while I tap away. As usual, I'm so sorry I write about such shitty marriages.

IN
HER
BONES

KATE MORETTI

A Reader's Club Guide

This reading group guide for In Her Bones *includes discussion questions and ideas for enhancing your book club. The suggested questions are intended to help your reading group find new and interesting angles and topics for your discussion. We hope that these ideas will enrich your conversation and increase your enjoyment of the book.*

TOPICS & QUESTIONS FOR DISCUSSION

1. While few of us fear, like Edie, that we are doomed to become unhinged or murderous, many people worry about becoming like their parents. Are there traits or habits of one or both of your parents that you dread potentially inheriting?

2. Even years after her conviction, Lilith Wade and the murders she committed are able to garner media attention. What do you think it is about serial killers in general, or her story specifically, that captures the public's attention?

3. It's not uncommon to refer to researching someone online as social media "stalking" them, looking into their background, old photos, etc. to gather information about a new acquaintance or a potential romantic partner. Edie also uses the wealth of information readily available in the digital era to her advantage, but takes it to a level that can more seriously be considered stalking. Where is the line between everyday online "stalking" and inappropriately prying into someone's life?

4. During the course of her investigation, Edie receives a lot of contradictory information. Without an obvious, corroborated truth, how do you tell if someone is lying? On what do you think Edie based her judgments of who was being honest with her?

5. Why do you think Kate Moretti included excerpts from *The Serrated Edge* interspersed among the chapters of *In Her Bones*? What did it add to the story as you read?

6. Both Edie and her brother, Dylan, have obsessive tendencies and a disregard for healthy boundaries. Edie finds the impact of "nurture" reassuring, suggesting her mother's psychosis isn't "in her bones"—do you agree? Why, or why not? To what extent do you think Edie and Dylan have inherited some of their mother's unbalanced nature as a result of the trauma they suffered at her hands, as opposed to genetic predisposition?

7. If Edie's father had been the murderer instead of her mother, do you think her reaction would have been different at all? Why, or why not? And if so, in what ways would that have affected her? Would it have affected the way other people saw Edie or her parent's crimes?

8. The author of *The Serrated Edge* blames Lilith's family for not preventing her crimes. After hearing the author's motivation for writing the book, do you think this perspective was understandable? Do you think more could have, or should have, been done to preempt the murders or bring Lilith to justice earlier?

9. Gil Brandt and Dr. Doyle both assert that "Knowing *about* someone is not the same as knowing them." (p. 281) What do you think it means to truly know someone?

10. Were you surprised by the transformation Edie has undergone by the epilogue? What do you think the future holds for her and Tim?

ENHANCE YOUR BOOK CLUB

1. There are many true crime biographies of serial killers, in the vein of *The Serrated Edge: The Story of Lilith Wade, Serial Killer*. Consider reading one with your book group, such as *Manson: The Life and Times of Charles Manson* by Jeff Guin or *Unholy Messenger: The Life and Crimes of the BTK Serial Killer* by Stephen Singular. Discuss in conjunction with *In Her Bones*: Did reading Edie's story affect how you read the true crime biography at all? Did they raise any similar questions about the nature of serial killers, or what allows them to commit so many murders before being apprehended?

2. Edie repeatedly remarks on how easy it is to "research" people given our lax attention to privacy in the digital era. As an experiment, consider assigning everyone in your book group another member's name. How much information can you find out about that person (without actually hacking each other's accounts)? What inferences might you make about who they are and how they live based on what is publicly available online (profile pictures, public social media accounts,

professional information, etc.)? Share your findings with the group (and perhaps upgrade your privacy settings together!).

3. Ali Land's novel *Good Me Bad Me* also centers on the daughter of a female serial killer. Consider reading it with your book club, and comparing it with *In Her Bones*. What themes appear in both novels, and in what ways do they diverge?

4. Check out more of Kate Moretti's books, such as *The Blackbird Season* and *The Vanishing Year*. To find out more about Kate, visit KateMoretti.com, or follow her on Twitter @KateMoretti1 or Facebook.com/kate morettiwriter.